'If poetry was the supreme literary form of the First World War then, as if in riposte, in the Second World War, the English novel came of age. This wonderful series is an exemplary reminder of that fact. Great novels were written about the Second World War and we should not forget them.'

WILLIAM BOYD

'It's wonderful to see these books given a new lease of life [...] classic novels from the Second World War written by those who were there, experienced the fear, anguish, pain and excitement first-hand and whose writings really do shine an incredibly vivid light onto what it was like to live and fight through that terrible conflict.'

JAMES HOLLAND, Historian, author and TV presenter

'The Imperial War Museum has performed a valuable public service by reissuing these absolutely superb novels'

ANDREW ROBERTS, author of *Churchill: Walking with Destiny*

'A highly unusual war novel with several confluent narratives; moving, interesting and of great literary value.'

LOUIS de BERNIÈRES

PATHFINDERS

Cecil Lewis

IMPERIAL WAR MUSEUMS

First published in Great Britain in 1944

First published in this format in 2021
by IWM, Lambeth Road, London SE1 6HZ
iwm.org.uk

ISBN 978-1-912423-37-8

A catalogue record for this book is available from
the British Library.

Printed and bound in Great Britain by
CPI Group (UK) Ltd, Croydon

Every effort has been made to contact all copyright holders.
The publishers will be glad to make good in future editions any
error or omissions brought to their attention.

Cover illustration by Bill Bragg
Design by Clare Skeats
Series Editor Madeleine James

FSC
www.fsc.org
MIX
Paper from
responsible sources
FSC® C020471

About the Author

Cecil Lewis (1898 – 1997)

CECIL LEWIS (1898 – 1997) was a British fighter ace in the First World War and spent time as a flying instructor for the RAF (Royal Air Force) during the Second World War, as well as in active service in that conflict. One of the founding executives of the BBC, he enjoyed friendships with many of the creative figures of the day including George Bernard Shaw, winning an Academy Award for the 1938 film adaptation of Shaw's *Pygmalion*. Lewis was a prolific writer and his autobiographical account *Sagittarius Rising* became a classic of First World War literature, considered by many as the definitive work on aerial combat. He retained a passion for adventure throughout his life, and was the last surviving British fighter ace of the First World War.

Introduction

One of the legacies of the First World War was the proliferation of war novels that were published in the late 1920s and 1930s. Erich Maria Remarque's *All Quiet on the Western Front* was a bestseller and made into a Hollywood film in 1930. In the same year, Siegfried Sassoon's *Memoirs of an Infantry Officer* sold 24,000 copies. Generations of school children have grown up on a diet of the novels and memoirs published during the interwar period. Indeed, the author of this novel, Cecil Lewis, wrote a bestselling memoir of his time as a pilot in the Royal Flying Corps (which became the Royal Air Force in April 1918) entitled *Sagittarius Rising* (1936). George Bernard Shaw described it as 'a book which everybody should read. It is the autobiography of an ace, and no common ace either... This prince of pilots has had a charmed life in every sense of the word. He is a thinker, a master of words, and a bit of a poet'. These attributes Lewis also brings to his little-known novel about the Second World War in the skies – *Pathfinders*.

Cecil Lewis enjoyed an exciting and varied career, ranging from First World War pilot (and fighter ace), to teaching pilots in China during the 1920s, to becoming one of the founding directors of the fledgling BBC. He won a fourth share of an Oscar for the screen adaptation of George Bernard Shaw's *Pygmalion* in 1938. Contrasting the two world wars, Lewis sagely commented in one of his autobiographical volumes, 'in 1914 everybody wanted to fight: in 1939 nobody wanted to. It was a very different situation'. He continued, 'I remember feeling sick in the stomach at the prospect of fighting another war and particularly one where the odds seemed loaded against us to the point where we could not possibly win'. He re-joined the Royal Air Force Reserve and was initially a controller on Thorney Island, but was moved to the Air Ministry to join the publicity staff where he remained during the Battle of Britain. Lewis was later involved in ways of detecting enemy bombing attacks. He then, however, took a demotion from wing commander to flying officer in order to fly again, becoming a flight lieutenant having undertaken the elementary training instructor's course. He taught hundreds of pilots to fly at an Elementary Flying Training School, including his own son. In *All My Yesterdays* (his 1993 autobiography) he wrote: 'Pupils were graded by the time it took them to go solo. Any who managed this with nine hours' instruction were destined for fighters, nine to twelve went to bombers, twelve to fourteen to transport aircraft. Those who could not make it by fourteen hours would have to be content with other jobs in aircrew'. It was whilst training these potential pilots that Lewis wrote *Pathfinders*, set in 1942 and originally published in 1944.

The situation in early 1942 was extremely serious. The Japanese attack on Pearl Harbor and across South East Asia had turned the conflict into a world war. In the west, the situation was no better, which is made very clear early on in the novel:

> *It was the spring of 1942. The news was bad. The Russians were falling back under the hammer blows of the Hun. The Ukraine was gone. The Donetz basin was going. There was a threat to the Caucasus, to the Volga, to Stalingrad. No man could see the end, and though the Russians were putting up magnificent and heroic rear-guard actions, they were being slowly and inexorably forced back. In Egypt things were no better. Rommel was striking at the gates of Cairo. The British were in retreat. Tobruk had fallen.*

British Empire and Commonwealth armed forces were at a nadir, but with the promise of future Allied operations in the wider context of the war. The RAF's Bomber Command was the only branch of the armed forces that could take direct action against Germany:

> *There was nothing left to do but bomb. In spite of the calls made on her for aircraft to be sent to all parts of the world, the home bomber force was growing. It could and must be used in an all-out offensive on German industry. In no other way could England carry the war to the enemy. True,*

the darkest days when she stood alone against the powers of anarchy were over. 'The waves,' the Prime Minister had said that year, 'may be against us; but the tide is for us.' But the tide was still at ebb and the transformation that was to take place before the end of the year had not begun.

The strategic air offensive against Germany changed from precision to area bombing before Air Chief Marshal Arthur Harris (nicknamed 'Bomber' Harris) took over Bomber Command in February 1942, largely as precision bombing had proved inaccurate. With area bombing, whole cities were targeted in order to destroy factories as well as the morale of those who worked in them. One of the first thousand bomber raids was on Cologne in May 1942. The city was bombed for nearly two hours, destroying 3,300 houses, killing 486 people and making 59,100 people temporarily homeless. The bomber aircrews were well aware of the military necessity of what they were undertaking; the killing of civilians was not their primary objective but rather the military-industrial targets, in order to help end the war. Destroying cities began unintentionally, but became the eventual object of the bombing campaign.

The 'success' of Bomber Command has been contentious ever since, with 'Bomber' Harris remaining a controversial figure. Even at the time, the author and novelist Vera Brittain, who had been a nurse near the front during the First World War, was an active campaigner for the abolition of area bombing. As a result, there were calls for her internment and she was often ostracised by a British society that predominantly supported the raids. Unsurprisingly, *Pathfinders* stays away from moral judgement of area bombing itself, focusing more on the sacrifice made by the Allied airmen it depicts.

The novel also makes some interesting comments on the Prime Minister and his wartime coalition government, which, under the guise of fiction, could garner greater clarity to the wartime situation. For instance, when Thornly's father-in-law comments that 'Churchill's saved the country,' Thornly replies 'Yes... he has. And we're supporting his dictatorship today, in a way that would have seemed intolerable in, say, 1938. We're as much regimented and taxed as the enemy – more, in fact'.

The story centres around the crew of a Wellington bomber that acted as a pathfinder. Pathfinders were needed because often the bombers could not find the towns and cities they were designated to attack at night, let alone the industrial centres within them. The Pathfinder Force was established on 11 August 1942 under the command of Air Commodore Donald Bennett, but bomber crews were carrying out a pathfinder role earlier in 1942, as in this novel, by using coloured marker flares to guide the bombers to their targets. Bennett later wrote: 'Cecil Lewis's novel reminds us of the hopes and fears and the sacrifices, and of our ultimate success'. The crews selected were the best night flying crews who were able to find the target unaided. The crew in the novel comprises of six men: the pilot, Hugh Thornly, who is also the Squadron Commander; co-pilot Peter Morelli; the navigator Tom Cookson; wireless operator Benji Lukin; and the front and rear gunners Sam Dollar and Nobby Bligh respectively. Thornly believes 'with a crew like his, a man could do anything. They were absolutely first class. He couldn't do enough for them. They reciprocated by giving him their best all the time, in every emergency and when there was no emergency'. The real heart of the novel lies in the back stories of all these men, who originate from Britain, the USA, Canada and New Zealand. Indeed, by 1945 some 45 per cent of Bomber Command pilots were Canadians, Australians or New Zealanders. Many trained as pilots or aircrew through the British Empire Air Training Scheme at specially opened airbases in Australia, Canada, New Zealand, South Africa and Southern Rhodesia. Peter Morelli's training is described as part of his story (no doubt drawing on Lewis' own time as an instructor): 'Pilots were scarce then, and all were welcome. It took a year to get through it all. He had thought he could fly before: the standard was very high. Night bomber crews were the most technically proficient men of any air force in the world'.

After his time as an instructor, Lewis was in command of an air transport post at Catania in Sicily. From there he went to Baria, and then on to Athens where his unit became embroiled in the Greek civil war. After the war, he set up a failed farming community in

South Africa, was a radio producer for the United Nations and then worked for the *Daily Mail*, principally as the organiser of the Ideal Home Exhibition. In 1969 he sailed a boat to Corfu where he spent the remainder of his life. He died in 1997, two months short of his ninety-ninth birthday.

This wide-ranging novel, with back stories from across the globe, is heavily influenced by the author's wide variety of interests and jobs. The success of the work lies not so much in the combat scenes but in sketching out the inner life of each member of the crew:

> *There were hundreds of those worlds aloft... each with its complement of men, each dedicated to a single task, each trained and disciplined, each nothing but a name and number while the job was on, yet each one a Life! A life, precious to some, or one, for little things, the way the hair grew or a tone of voice or tender hands or body's strength, precious because of memories; mothers, of travail and the long hard years bringing them up to this; wives, of their husbands, clasped and torn apart, dearer than life and gone; lovers, of promises, the future in a kiss, the hope, the dream stretched out to; brothers and friends, of sport and work and the old coat of friendship: precious and separate, more than the jobs they gave their skill to, more than the messengers of death, more than their country's sons. More than all that... these men with dreams and hopes and plans of things to come, each with his past, the sheaf of personality, the soul.*

Casualty rates for Bomber Command were the highest across the armed forces – an estimated 135,000 men flew in combat in Bomber Command, of whom 47,268 died in action. Lewis' evocative novel, depicting the lives and fates of just six of these men, is here reprinted for a new generation of readers, showing the significance of the individual life stories of a Second World War aircrew.

Alan Jeffreys
2021

Out of my weakness, to her strength.
Out of my fear, to her courage.
Out of my doubt, to her faith.

'WE'RE FOUL OF SOMETHING.'

It was Sam, down in the engine room who noticed it first. He shouted up through the hatchway to the Skipper. The wheezy little engine had started to grunt and labour, straining and complaining at the sudden heavy load. The steam sizzled and whistled through the leaky pipe joints, while the whole squalid, smelly engine room with its pools of oil and coal dust began a crazy rolling, that swung the hurricane lantern back and forth on its nail as if it had gone mad, sent a shovel slithering across the floor and set the coal rattling against the sides of the bunkers. 'Another Goddam wreck,' thought Sam. 'Who'd be a fisherman in wartime? Mines and Heinkels and no lights and worst of all, no goddam fish.' This was their fourth trawl today and they hadn't boxed the price of a pint. He wiped his hands on a lump of waste and poked his head up through the hatch.

The Skipper was leaning out of the wheelhouse window, his eyes fixed on a pool of yellowish foam under the counter. They were foul of something all right. The *Daffodil* had no way on her and the propeller was simply churning up the sandy waters of the shallow sea. In the short steep swell that was tossing the trawler about like a bit of old cork, the warp kept snubbing and jerking as it flicked up out of the troughs, flinging the spray from it, vibrating like a banjo string, and then sinking back as the stern dropped. The towing post creaked and grunted. They were foul of something all right.

'Take up the bridle a turn or two, John,' the Skipper shouted to a deck hand who was gutting fish and packing it amidships. The man nodded, stuck his knife in his belt and lurched forward along the plunging deck. When he reached the capstan, where the bridle of the trawl was made fast, he opened the steam valve, unrove the tail of the bridle from its cleat and seized it firmly in his hands. The steam wheezed into the cylinder, and the drum, complaining and rattling, started to turn. He hauled on the tail of the rope till he heard the Skipper's voice, 'That'll do, John.' Then he closed the valve, made

1

fast the bridle and came aft.

Shortening up the bridle canted the trawler's head to port. She began to bear off in a wide circle, tethered like a nanny-goat to the trawl which was in turn anchored firmly to the sea bed. She made heavy weather of it, wallowed and shook herself as the beam seas came crashing against her rusty sides; but slowly, persistently and reluctantly round she went.

The Skipper was watching that length of dripping rope astern. It swung outwards in a long crescent behind the *Daffodil*. He was hoping to see the crescent straighten up. Pulling in a circle round the obstruction should free the beam from whatever was foul of it. Then he would be able to continue on his way. But no, there it stayed, that maddening crescent, 'til the *Daffodil* had plunged and lurched her way round a full circle and was heading back on her first course.

The watch below were fast asleep. The lurching and rolling of the ship didn't disturb their slumber; but when the motion changed, then they knew, even in their sleep, that something was wrong. One by one they woke, tumbled out yawning and swearing, pulled on their oilskins and came on deck. Now there were seven men, besides the Skipper, anxiously watching that straining warp.

Anxiously, because the whole gear was new, and it was new because a week ago they had fouled something and when at last they had got the trawl in, there bobbing and swaying under the water, right against the ship's side, was the huge rusty globe of a mine. It was big enough to blow up a battleship and firmly entangled in the trawl. When they saw it, leaning over the side, straining on the meshes of the net, they didn't like what they saw. They didn't like it at all. They were fishermen, not minesweepers, and this catch was no good on their market. There was only one thing to do and they did it quite quickly, though reluctantly and angrily, namely to slash the fastenings of the net clear of the beam and let it all go, mine, fish, net and all, back to the muddy bottom. Now they were foul of something again.

''Nother bloody mine, I bet,' said Fred Whiting, the mate.

'Might be a couple of mermaids,' suggested little Percy Condon, the humourist of the crew. 'Might be a couple of mermaids, waiting to kiss the end of your ruddy nose, young Fred.'

'Mermaids, my — ' growled Fred. He was cold and hadn't had enough sleep, and the thought of another mine didn't fascinate him. He remembered a couple of months back how they had been fishing, when suddenly, off to starboard, they had heard an explosion. When they got over to the place, the trawler that had been there was nothing but wreckage and floating fish and a cloud of seagulls. The sea was fuller of mines than fish, these days. Ten to one there was another bobbing in the poke of the trawl right now, pretty well underneath them.

The Skipper, seeing the trawl hadn't cleared, shouted down to the Engineer. 'I'm going to run back over her, Sam. Give me all you can.' He swung the wheel to port and the *Daffodil* turned on her heel and went about, bucking into the tide, squirming her way through the quarter sea. The bridle of the trawl went straight down under the counter. There was some danger of it fouling the propeller; but the Skipper knew his business. One hand on the wheel, leaning out of the window he watched the lie of the rope, watched the bight of it looping out on the quarter, keeping the *Daffodil* clear. When they had gone about, he spun the wheel central, and the trawler, gathering way now that she had no load, forged ahead. There were ninety fathoms of warp between the ship and her trawl, so she had quite a good run. The Skipper hoped her speed would jerk the beam clear. He watched the warp anxiously as it streamed out astern. Suddenly it tightened, flicked up clear of the sea. The strain, coming hard on the mooring post and the capstan, started both of them grunting and straining as if they would be yanked out of the ship. The warp itself stretched, fibre against fibre, the water ran from it, and the *Daffodil*, brought up all standing, squatted by the stern and bucked and plunged, while the old two-cylinder engine, forced to work against a sudden overwhelming load, snorted itself to a standstill. Another pool of yellowish frothy foam appeared under the counter.

'Bloody well anchored we are, and that's a fact,' commented young Percy; but the others took no notice. They knew what this meant. It meant another wasted trawl, a short haul of fish, less money for the wife and a good chance of being blown into Kingdom

Come. They looked at the sky. It was well on into the afternoon. The wind was freshening. They had to get back to port before nightfall. There was no time to lose. Some of them went below to get their aprons. Others went forward ready to cast off the bridle from the capstan. *Daffodil* wallowed in the trough of the sea.

'Will have to get her in,' the Skipper called to Sam and left the wheelhouse for the deck. 'If we can,' thought Sam, 'if we can.' He fancied they might have fouled on a wreck and that meant the whole gear would be lost again. He came on deck, donned his oilskins and boots, his sou'wester and apron, and went out to join the others.

The bridle had been cast off and the warp led forward and taken round the capstan. Now the steam valve was opened and the drum revolved slowly, bringing in the heavy rope. *Daffodil*, broadside on to the sea, rolled and lurched. Seas sluiced across her iron decks. A cloud of seagulls, appeared from nowhere and circled round, screeching and tumbling, while the men not employed on stowing the warp, stood at the leeward bulwarks, leaning over the side, anxiously watching it as it came slowly up out of the muddy sea.

When the slack had all been hauled in and the weight of the beam and trawl came on the warp, the capstan grunted and slowed up, but the line still came in. Those watching over the side saw the big swivel at the fork of the bridle and the two ropes running out to the ends of the beam. Then the beam itself appeared out of a trough of the sea.

'That'll do,' called the Skipper. The capstan stopped and the warp was made fast. The crew peered down into the muddy water, but the net held its secret and they could not see what was in the poke, for this was still dangling some twenty feet below. They did not like it. The trawl was not foul of the bottom, as they had thought. It had come up without a murmur. There must be something in the net, and that something was more likely to be a mine than anything else. Some were for casting the gear adrift at once and taking no chances; but the Skipper shook his head. He was not losing a second lot without making sure. He ordered tackles to be secured to the ends of the beam to draw it up. After about an hour's heavy labour they had it lashed securely to the bulwarks.

The next thing was to get in the net. It hung down from the beam, appearing and disappearing as *Daffodil* rolled. The men, spread out along the bulwarks, all leaned out together, seizing the meshes in their red, horny hands. As the ship rolled down, they hauled the net up over the rail, hung on as she rose and, as she dipped again, hauled a second time, taking the slack of the net down under the gunwale and holding it there with their knees. Between every haul they peered downwards, while the seagulls swooped past, screeching for scraps.

They had got in a few feet when young Percy suddenly yelled: 'I can see something!'

He pointed down under water, and all the men, holding fast to the net, leaned over to look where his arm stretched out. 'Something round, it is.'

'It's a mine for sure,' said Fred, and the thought of it there, just under the surface, kept them all transfixed, motionless.

But the Skipper was unperturbed. 'We'll just have a look. Haul away there. Steady. Easy does it.'

Again they reached out, seizing the meshes of the net and hauling as the *Daffodil* lurched over. When she rose again, there, in the meshes, a queer object broke water. It was a long black triangle with what looked like torn paper flapping from it. At one end was a sort of globe, choked with seaweed, silted with mud and out of it two spikes stuck up with little funnels at the end.

'It's a mine! There! Look at the horns!' shouted Fred.

'That's no mine,' said Jack. 'Them's machine gun muzzles. And the round thing's a turret, that's what it is. It's a bit of a ruddy acrioplane, that's what it is!'

'It's a bit of a Heinkel! Haul away!' and together they pulled their catch higher out of the water.

'That's no Heinkel,' said Percy. 'Jerry don't have turrets like that. It's one of our own. Look, I can see the red white and blue, there, on the fin!'

When at last they got it aboard, this, the strangest catch that ever men took from the sea, they all clustered round it on the deck. There was part of the fin and twisted rudder, the turret, eaten away with the sea water and clogged with sand and a long piece of fabric that had torn off. It had been painted black, but now, covered with mud and seaweed and barnacles, it was dirty brown. When they cleaned it up, sluicing it with buckets of sea water, they could just make out something. It was the aircraft letter, the letter P, painted in red on the black side of what once had been the fuselage of a Wellington bomber. Percy scratched his head, spat reflectively over the side.

'Poor sods!' he said. 'Wonder if any of them got away with it?'

***

A feeling of presentiment hung round Station HQ. The Group Captain had been to a conference at Command some days before. He returned in good spirits, but he didn't give anyone the 'gen', not even his two Wing Commanders, and this set the whole station agog. The feeling communicated itself without words, by a sort of telepathy, and ran through the camp. 'There's a big show on', 'It's Berlin this time', 'Or Hamburg, Cologne, Düsseldorf, Munich'. So went the thoughts and whispers. The station was on its toes. They were proud of their pilots and crews, proud that they had been chosen as a Pathfinder Squadron. They were picked men every one, picked for the efficiency and skill of their work, picked to be the spearhead of the Bomber Offensive, and their morale was on the top line.

Then the weather had gone dud for three days and the whole place grew restless. Only the ground crews welcomed the chance to get the kites perfect, to bring the serviceability up to 100 per cent. No leave was granted (Oh, there's a show on, all right!), nobody could leave camp, and the Met. Officer was the focus of everybody's interest and attention.

All day long he was closeted with his assistants, poring over his charts. Yards and yards of teleprinter stuff was always coming in and, when decoded, gave the pressures and temperatures and wind strengths and cloud formations from a hundred places. From America, from Iceland, from Africa, from Russia, from a hundred stations and observation posts the figures came in. 'Here,' said the messages, 'the weather is – ' and by piecing all these signals together a picture of the weather began to appear; a series of queer lines on the chart, bulging out here, running close together there, and moving, always moving, over the face of the earth. The forecasters ornamented them with little arrows and dots and hieroglyphs, the symbols of their own private magic. To the laymen the finished article meant nothing; but to the forecaster these contours, called isobars, meant a lot. Moreover by comparing the latest picture with those that had come in before, the tendency of the whole weather system could be observed. If each map had been transferred to film, the sequence, when run off, would have brought the maps to life and the depressions would have been seen, surging back and forth like the shadows of waves on the floor of a sunlit sea. But the film always stopped dead in the present. It could not look into the future, and it was with the future that the aircraft crews were concerned. They wanted to know the weather over the target in three hours' time, they wanted the weather when they got back to base in six hours' time, and this is where the genius of the forecaster came in. This was why a good forecaster was as valuable to air operations as any member of the organisation. For he had to guess and guess right. There was art in it: the art of the diagnostician, weather-sense, and, above all, clinical experience. If he made a mistake, the raid might be a failure; if he miscalculated the time that fog would set in by an hour or two, there might be dozens of aircraft lost, wandering about the country blind, staggering down on strange aerodromes, crashing, baling out; loss of life, loss of hundreds of thousands of pounds worth of war equipment... Small wonder the forecaster was a cautious and harassed man.

For the truth was that the weather was the Commanding Officer of all air operations in Northern Europe. Ministers and Air Marshals might trumpet announcements of what they were going to do to the enemy, but the weather had a knack of disregarding these outbursts and deciding, as it did in the winter of '40–'41, to keep the whole bomber force grounded for weeks at a time.

So when, on the fourth morning the Squadron was warned for Ops that night, there was considerable relief. 'Must be a decent forecast at last,' said the crews and dispersed to check up their aircraft.

On the perimeter track the lorry dropped the Wing Commander's crew near their aircraft. The men strolled over towards the machine. There were five of them, three officers and two sergeants; but the difference of rank would never have been noticed from their conversation. They didn't think of themselves as 'officers and other ranks', they thought of themselves as a unit, the crew of the aircraft, P for Pathfinder, the Wing Commander's crew, the veterans, who had done twenty-seven operational trips together. It was Nobby Bligh the rear-gunner, a pert little Cockney from the Edgware Road, who had got the sign-writer to put up on the side of the Wimpey: 'I go. I cum back.' And under it to paint one little bomb for each raid. The number had grown steadily, ten, fifteen, twenty, twenty-five... Now they would soon have to start a third row. Nobby was the tail-gunner, 'arse-end Charlie', and besides his pert cockney humour and good spirits, he could perform on the mouth-organ like a professional. Sometimes, after the show was over and they were well on the way home, the Wing Commander would ask him for a tune, and he would open his mask and play into the mike, while the others listened on the intercomm and sometimes joined in the chorus. It was strictly against regulations, so they kept quiet about it; but it helped to pass the time.

Next to him walked Sam Dollar, the Canadian front-gunner. While Nobby was spare and wiry, Sam was slow and heavy and thick-set. He said little, but was forever chewing mint gum, which gave him a powerful and pungent odour. But as Nobby said, 'Better to stink like roast mutton than like a drain, which you would otherwise, Sam.' While Sam's reply, admirably terse, is quite unprintable. These two were the fire-power of the Wellington and they knew their stuff. Nobby had already collected a DFM for getting a couple of Ju. 88s on one raid a month back, and Sam cursed his luck at having the front turret, since no Hun ever attacked head-on, and declared that they ought to change turrets every trip. 'God dammit, Nobby, give me a break, can't you? I'll sit in that goddam icebox till the end of the war, freezing my — off, and never fire a shot.'

'I'd swop with you, Sam, honest I would; but, you see, the crew needs an ace in the dustbin, and...' but usually at this point, he had to get out of range of Sam's right, which swung out and carried quite a lot of weight. But, if the men were not close friends, they got on together all right. Nobby got on with everybody, and Sam, who was slow on everything, except the trigger, grew used to the little Cockney's humour, and secretly admired in him the qualities he lacked in himself.

Next to Sam walked Peter Morelli, Flying Officer, the second pilot of the aircraft. He posed as a Canadian, but was really an American, and the way he came to England and enlisted would make a book in itself. He had a pleasant draw, a winning smile, and some intangible and irresistible charm that drew both men and women to him. 'He's a wizard bloke,' was the verdict of the Mess. He was only twenty-three, but had packed a lot into the years, and those who had been on a binge in town with him told how he knew everybody, how he remembered people's faces and their names, how he would laughingly push the pianists out of their seats in jazz bands and beat them at their own game. If it was a question of a party or a dance or any entertainment, Peter was always called in. 'An officer with exceptional social gifts,' the CO had written in his half-yearly confidential report, and it was no more than the truth.

A little behind these three walked Cookson, the navigator, and Lukin the wireless operator, his thin stalky figure stooping slightly as he walked. Lukin was a man of few words. Some thought a man with an inferiority complex. 'Perhaps it's because he's a Jew,' said the Mess, after a complete failure to draw him. But it wasn't that. He was a preoccupied man inside whose head a lot of things were going on. 'It's like a canful of maggots,' he confided once to his favourite brother before the war. The only person who could get him to open up was Peter, for Benjy Lukin had been a film critic on a London paper, and Peter knew all about shows; but even then he didn't expand much. 'Gee, but isn't he a dry guy though?' said Peter. And the Mess nodded and agreed; but, after all, he was harmless enough and carried out his work methodically and well, so they let him alone.

Both Lukin and Cookson were officers. Lukin had been

commissioned on the completion of his training. He wore the thin blue stripe of the Pilot Officer, which would get fatter when he automatically became a Flying Officer six months later; but Cookson had worn the broad single stripe for almost a year, and the general opinion was that he would be singled out to go on one of the advanced navigational courses and get his second ring, before it was due. He had become one of the finest navigators in Bomber Command by dint of a fanatical zeal for his job. He lived and dreamed navigation. Nothing else, except perhaps his little cutter, the *Dolphin*, now laid up in a yard far away in Fiji, was at all important to him. Or perhaps other things were, but he never spoke of them, and only his relations, back in Auckland, getting his rare letters every six months or so, knew anything of his philosophy of life. He had quite unusual powers of concentration. In fact this was the noticeable thing about him; he became absolutely absorbed in what he was doing. He was strongly made, fresh complexioned, and under his square forehead two blue eyes looked out that were so clear, candid and resolute that you did not forget that face once the eyes had been turned on you. You felt he knew exactly where he stood and exactly what he was going to do, why he was going to do it and where he would stand when he had done it. This self-confidence, backed as it was by high professional skill, was extraordinarily reassuring. The man seemed solid as a rock, absolutely dependable in all circumstances. The impression was heightened by his deliberate speech and his friendly smile. Yet, curiously, he was not a man you could get to know. He was strangely unapproachable. Men felt that he might be straitlaced or look with disapproval on some of the more bawdy spirits in the Mess; but if he was, he never showed it. He just didn't join in. He wasn't interested. It was preoccupation: he lived for the job.

The difference between competence and excellence in any profession is difficult to define. It is largely a matter of flair. Given the technical knowledge, given the ability, of two men the one who will stand out must have something akin to the artist, who in some mysterious way is able to synthesise out of dull facts a new situation, an unexpected deduction, always clear enough when it is stated, but to a lesser man fogged by other considerations, the pros and cons, from which he is unable to extricate the matrix: therefore this must be so, or therefore I must do so and so, therefore the result is... Cookson, as has been said, was a fanatic for detail. He checked and double-checked all his data, his courses, his wind speeds, his drifts. He politely but firmly insisted on accurate flying from his pilot, insisted on being informed of any deviation from course, the least change of airspeed, the least variation of height. 'By Jove,' said one pilot, after having been on a show with him, 'I felt like a bloody pupil back at an EFTS! Never had to fly so accurately in my life! Fagged out I was when we got back. But we came out plum over the target, in filthy weather too, got rid of the stuff and were off home before Jerry could do anything about it. He's a kingpin navigator all right.'

But this careful plodding, this infinite capacity for taking pains, was not the whole story. Cookson added to it night vision of an unusually high order and a photographic eye for country. Show him a landfall, the lie of a town, the shape of a target once and he never forgot it. If he returned to the same place at a different height on a different course in different weather, he always knew. Crossing and re-crossing the enemy coast on raid after raid, he stored away in his head every detail of the country. Then on a thick night, through a momentary gap in a cloud, he would spot a patch of country and know, without a shadow of doubt, exactly where he was. Many a pilot, flying over the same area day after day, absorbs the shape of it almost subconsciously, knows, almost without knowing why he knows, every road and field. All this is lumped together and called 'Air-sense'. Cookson had developed it to a degree that his assurance was almost uncanny. 'He doesn't navigate; he smells his way there. I believe he'd teach the pigeons how to navigate. Now then, Pidgy, he'd say, fly at 800 feet on a course of 274.5 True and allow 16 degrees of starboard drift. Wouldn't be a bad idea if he could. The bloody birds might get home then.' So said the Mess in Cookson's hearing, and he just smiled and went on reading.

Now as they walked over to the aircraft, he was thinking of Lukin. The man was new to the crew. Cookson hadn't flown with him before. Getting wireless bearings and fixes is the Wireless

Operator's job. Cookson used them, chiefly as checks on his own work and he liked to have them accurate. Therefore, for the success of the show, he wanted Lukin to feel at ease, wanted to gauge his ability, to form some sort of contact with him.

'Ever flown with the Wing Commander before?' he enquired.

'Not on a show.'

'He's first class. Wonderful on instruments. Steady as a rock. Makes my job far easier.'

'Anything particular you want from me?' Lukin inquired.

'No, I don't think so. I'll try to get a drift as we leave the coast. But if you can give me a bearing or two when we get up, it may help.'

I suppose he's all right, he was thinking. Supposed to be quite sound; but I wish we had Ginger, all the same. He was used to the man, had done upwards of twenty trips with him. He liked working with men he knew. Lukin seemed to read his thoughts.

'I expect you'll miss Ginger; but I'll...' He was going to say 'do my best', but altered it and the words came out, 'try to fit in.'

'Of course you will.' Cookson's tone was absolutely genuine. He meant it. 'Glad you're coming along. It's a swell crew to be with.'

P for Pathfinder stood in the edge of a wood. Trees had been cleared to pass her in and camouflage nets lay over her wings. You might have passed the aerodrome and never seen her, snugged down into the greenery. Her nose just protruded and her low cumbersome body lay close to the ground. She seemed heavy, ungainly, and her matt black paint detracted further from any grace she might have had. But she looked solid and reliable, very much made for the job, and the fact that Wellingtons had been in service ever since the outbreak of war, proved beyond any doubt the value of the type. The men who flew in them swore by them. They would stand up to any amount of punishment. 'By God, I believe if a Wimpey was shot in half, both halves would get home.' This was the pilot's verdict and, when you saw photos of the state in which some of them had got home, it was quite possible to believe it.

Sam and Nobby were already by the machine. Below the nose a thin ladder reached down to the ground. Sam's legs were disappearing up this. He drew himself in and clambered, doubled up, past the bomb-aimer's place up into the front turret, where the two Browning guns pointed forward and up into the sky. Nobby had walked under the wing to the entrance half-way down the belly. He clambered in and felt his way down to the tail. There he pulled back the two spring loaded doors and wormed himself through into the tail turret. Through these little doors he would have to leave the aircraft if ordered to bale out. He would spin the turret broadside on and then just fall over backwards through the doors. It was the best exit of the lot, provided the turret didn't jam, no chance of hitting the tail as there was when you had to bale out from the escape hatches forward.

Now he settled into the seat and began his inspection of the guns. He examined the breechblocks, the feeds, the ejector chutes. He tested the mechanisms with dummy-rounds, checked the reflector sight, saw that he had spare bulbs and then started giving the perspex a clean-over. He felt snug and at home in there, though there was hardly room to move. His two guns were mounted one each side of his knees. His controls to swing the turret, to raise and lower the elevation of the guns, lay on a sort of handlebar before him. These operated on hydraulic power derived from the starboard engine. He would test this as they taxied round to take off. Now he carefully reloaded the guns and placed the firing button on safe. Then he sat back.

He was quite alone down in the tail turret when they were airborne, and although he could speak to the others over the intercomm, he felt separate and was glad of his loneliness, looking back out over the empty sky. There he could relax, not from the job, for he never thought of letting up on that; but from the smoke-screen of good spirits that he put up all day and every day, to cover his grief. For Nobby's wife was dying, dying quite slowly and inexorably, and nothing could be done about it. But there, alone in the turret, he could think about her, send out his thoughts to cheer and strengthen her. Sometimes, under the majesty of the starlit sky, with the world so far below, he felt curiously remote and powerful, like a god. He knew then that his thoughts did do her good. His will would triumph over the hand of death. She would recover: he would make her.

Sometimes again he felt so very small, such an atom in the terrible void of night, that he despaired. Then he would pray. It came easy to do it up there in the dark, though he never could do it below: 'O God, spare my Sally and leave her with me for a bit longer, because I love her so.' That was all he could manage, not being a religious man in the usual way. But he was proud that none of his mates, nor relations, nor friends, knew. Only he and his mother. He could trust her. Nobody else. And Sally, of course, last of all. She would never know. There was some comfort in that. Not much; but anyway it was better for him to carry it for both of them. It was about all he could do for her.

His reverie was interrupted by a voice coming through on the earphones in the helmet that hung nearby. 'Hullo, Tail-Gunner. This is Wireless Operator. Can you hear me?' Nobby switched on the mike and answered. 'Yes, getting you okay. Guns tested and found correct. Are you receiving me?' 'Receiving you loud and clear,' came the answer. Nobby hung up the mask and helmet again and clambered out of the turret up the fuselage to join the rest of the crew forward of the bomb bay.

The aircraft would be bombed up later in the day and everything checked by the Armament Officer. The load was almost entirely incendiaries, slim cases of magnesium and phosphorus, that would burn and burn and burst and burn again. For wholesale arson they were about as effective a weapon as anyone had yet devised, and P for Pathfinder carried dozens of them, neatly tucked away in their racks and canisters like so many viper's eggs. These small inert objects, hidden inside the black fuselage of a bomber in a corner of the English countryside, were destined that night to be carried several hundred miles and to be dropped whistling down on the roofs of houses and warehouses, to start vast raging conflagrations, in which whole areas of a city would be laid waste and hundreds of human beings would be burned, crushed, suffocated or mutilated for life... It didn't bear examination, of course; and none of the crew ever dreamed of examining it. They were entirely devoid of conscience, all of them. Their only thoughts on the matter were technical: how to get there, how to get a direct hit on the target, and how to get back. It was as if a man conceiving a murder had become so entirely absorbed in the technique of carrying it out, in its ingenuity and success, that he entirely lost sight of the fact that it was murder. The crime became quite incidental, unimportant. The interest and satisfaction lay in the technique. No man could have carried on with a bomber's job if he looked at it otherwise.

As Nobby passed the bomb bay he heard voices from forward, Lukin's voice testing his transmitter: 'Hullo Columbine, Hullo Columbine, this is P for Pathfinder calling, this is P for Pathfinder calling. Are you receiving me? Are you receiving me? Over.' Switches clicked and the voice of base was heard coming back so loud that Nobby could hear it standing by Lukin's headphones: 'Hullo P for Pathfinder, Hullo P for Pathfinder, receiving you loud and clear, receiving you loud and clear. Over.' The switches clicked again and Lukin continued his tests, closed down, switched on his loop receiver, tested that, tested his morse key, saw to his spare coils and batteries and bulbs. He went through it all slowly, methodically, while the wireless mechanic stood watching him.

At this moment the starboard engine started up with a roar and a minute later the port engine joined in. Morelli was at the controls and sat there doing a general check while the motors warmed up. Meanwhile Cookson was lying flat on his stomach in the bomb aimer's position, testing the selector gear, looking over the sight, and testing the bomb doors. Morelli checked the hydraulics, fuel gauges, flaps and all the rest of the pilot's controls. He ran up the engines one after the other, looked out of the port side window to the Flight Mechanic on the ground below and gave him the okay, then called up the rest of the crew on the intercomm. A few seconds later P for Pathfinder crept slowly out on to the perimeter track and turned towards the runway to carry out her NFT.

All crews were summoned to the Ops room for briefing at 6 o'clock (eighteen hundred hours). They crowded into the bare room with the maps and charts on the walls, and waited for Wingco Ops and the station Navigator. When they arrived, with the Group Captain himself, the whole room stood to its feet. He acknowledged with a salute. 'Carry on. Smoke if you like,' he said, took off his hat and laid it on the table. Then he turned to the crews as they sat down and lit up.

'There's a big show on for tonight and I have a message from the AO C-in-C, to read to you.' He took the paper from a folder and paused before reading it... 'The more heavily we can bomb the enemy the sooner the war will be over. His heavy industry, his shipyards, his centres of communications must be smashed. The people who work at those industries must be bombed out, evacuated, and their work disrupted. We have now a big enough bomber force to do this, and we are going to do it. Town by town, city by city, German industrial life is going to be annihilated. I therefore call on all of you for a maximum effort tonight and in our future raids. Leave nothing undone. Let nothing stand in your way. Get there. Send your load down on the target. Every bomb is a nail in Germany's coffin. Make sure you drive it right home. Good luck to you.'

He put the paper away and a murmur ran round the room. The faces became more expectant. 'The target tonight is Kiel,' he went on. 'Some of you have been there before and given it a pasting; but tonight we intend to flatten it out. Now there's a difference between this raid and others we have made before. We're going to use a new technique, which we think will not only be more effective against the enemy, but will also reduce our losses. So,' – and he smiled – 'I expect you'll all want to know what it is. Well, it's quite simple. We're going to send everyone in at once. There will be several hundred aircraft on the target and the whole raid will be over within half an hour. You can see what this will mean. The ground defences will be swamped, the fire-fighting services will be swamped, the whole organisation that the enemy has built to deal with raids will be inadequate. With so many aircraft over the target at one time he'll be paralysed, the anti-aircraft won't know what to shoot at. His radio location will go haywire, and altogether it ought to be a piece of cake...' he paused '...for the main body of the force, that is. Our job is the same as ever, to light up that target, to make it a beacon that the other boys can see thirty miles away. But what applies to all the others in the C-in-C's message, applies particularly to us. We've got to get there, to make sure of getting there and nowhere else. The whole success of the raid depends on us. It also depends, of course, on the most accurate timing. Nobody must be late. The times of departure must be those arranged, to the second. The courses must be accurately steered and adhered to. They've given us five minutes grace to check up, make the final approach as we like, find the best height and so on. All that's up to you. But you must be off target at the time specified. Don't hang about. Kiel's going to be like Piccadilly at the rush hour, so, when you've done your job, get out as quickly as you can.' He paused again and looked round. 'I know you'll all put up a good show. That's all I have to say. Will you carry on, Hobbs?'

Then the routine of the briefing was carried out. The best height, having regard to the forecast, the time of the run out, given the Met wind, the best approach to avoid concentrations of flak and Night Fighter areas, prominent landfalls and landmarks, the bomb load to be carried... so it went on. To a stranger much of it would have seemed jargon, almost a shorthand speech, for it assumed a background of common knowledge so thoroughly understood that it never needed to be referred to.

At last the meeting broke up. The men dispersed. There was a meal to be got in and, for some, a brief rest to be fresher for the job. But for the Navigators there would be no rest. They still had a lot to do. They went into a huddle round the table, discussing the gen., consulting the forecast; working carefully on courses and drifts and times. It was fascinating and important work, for a duff navigator who miscalculates can ruin a show. Most of the calculations were preliminary, subject to alteration in the air; but the basis of a good show is laid in the Ops Room. These men were leaving nothing to chance.

'Let's see,' said the Group Captain, 'you're taking Lukin in place of Ginger, are you, Hugh?' Hugh Thornly, who had been following all Cookson's calculations, straightened up when the Group Captain spoke. Below his Wings a DSO and a DFC, besides two other service medals, decorated his battledress, making a dirty coloured line on that well-worn garment. The three full rings of Wing Commander rank were stitched on his shoulder straps. He was the Pathfinder

Squadron Commander and the leader of the night's operation.

'Yes, sir,' he said. 'Nicolls' a bit fed up at having to put in a stooge; but I think it's best if I borrow Lukin, in view of the importance of the show.'

The Group Captain nodded. 'Got a moment?' he asked.

'Of course, sir,' Hugh rejoined. 'Nothing more you want of me, is there, Cookson?'

Cookson shook his head. 'No thanks, sir. I think I've got it all buttoned up.'

The CO closed the door of his office and strolled over to his desk.

'I was talking to Group today on the phone. It seems they may want you to take over a Station pretty soon.'

'Where?' Hugh's face didn't seem particularly pleased.

'One of the new ones down South. It's not settled yet. I said I couldn't spare you; but of course it is time you got your other ring.'

'I don't want to go – much, I shouldn't like to be off flying. I sometimes wonder how you stick it, Steve. All the bumpf, all the kicks, all the stooging around between here and Group and Command – and none of the fun.'

Stephen Burleigh smiled up at the younger man. He had always liked Hugh Thornly, and now, after seeing him on the job for three months or more, he admired him. But, as he looked at the quick intelligent head and the sure expression of the eyes, Burleigh detected a slight tendency to nervousness, a touch of strain. It was the merest trace, nothing the casual observer would notice; but Burleigh had done a lot of Ops himself. He knew how it took you, and he was used to detecting it in his men. He could tell, sometimes before they could, when it was getting too much for them. He was a good CO and he positively pampered his crews – if the men were good; if anyone tried to swing the lead or wavered, he was as hard as nails. But the good ones, and that went for most, when they were getting near the end of their tour of Ops – you could always tell. They didn't say anything. They wouldn't admit it, even to themselves, most of them; but he knew, and he could see it now in Hugh. The way he moved about, sat first on the edge of the desk and then on the edge of the chair, the way he shook the coppers in his pocket; yes, it was time he had a rest. He had had a long talk up at Group with the Air Vice Marshal and succeeded in getting Hugh the Station. He deserved it, if ever a man did. And his eyes looked decidedly tired. The face was somehow drawn, older. Yes, it was time he had a rest.

'Oh, I don't know. You get used to it. It's interesting, looking at the thing more broadly, getting an idea of the general plan. Some of these conferences are damned instructive...' He got up. 'Well, I expect you want to get along. How's Nobby?'

'Wonderful! He makes the trip for me. Some of his comments over the target ought to be collected. They're wizard.'

Hugh strolled over to the door and paused with his hand on the knob. 'Dollar's a curious bloke, you know; a real backwoodsman. There's something secretive about him. I never have been able to size him up. The others I know pretty well. You do after a bit; but Dollar... He's queer...'

'But tough.'

'Tough as they make 'em.'

'You've got a swell crew, Hugh.'

'The best ever.'

'Always seems a pity the way crews break up at the end of a tour.'

'We've got it all fixed up to keep in touch, after the war.'

Burleigh smiled and nodded. 'Yes, I know. One does. Oh, by the way, Hugh, any news from the home front?'

'Any minute now!' He turned laughing and blushing slightly. 'I rang last night.'

'How's Helen?'

'Well, it can't be much fun for a woman really; but she sounded frightfully cheery.'

'You know, Hugh,' Steve Burleigh leaned against the wall, looking at him, 'I admire you for the way you've managed the wife business. There's no getting round it, they're a damned nuisance when chaps are on Ops. It's only natural, of course, but they do undermine men. What can you expect? They ought all to be sent to concentration camps that can't be reached except on long leave. I believe the men would be happier too. I don't like them hanging around, or being within range even.'

Hugh nodded. 'Yes. I quite agree. Helen and I talked it out long ago. We decided she oughtn't to be around while the party was on. I couldn't stand it, and she couldn't either... I'm glad she's had the kid to think about. That's helped a lot. And Squirrels isn't quite a concentration camp, either.'

'How old's Pam now?'

'Rising three and much too all there. That young woman will be a menace when she grows up.'

'What's the betting this time?'

'It's ten to one on a son. Will you take me?'

Steve shook his head. 'No; but I'll stand godfather, if you like. That'll cost me a packet.'

'It's a deal.' Hugh turned to go again. 'I must be off, sir. See you at supper?'

'Yes, I'll be around. It ought to be quite a show tonight.' Hugh nodded. 'If only the weather doesn't clamp. Well, so long, sir.' He went out and closed the door.

A tender dropped the Flying Control Officer at his post on the leeward end of the runway. He tried out his signalling lamps and the Chance light, tested his field telephone, saw that the Blood Waggon and Fire Tender were present with their crews, and then strolled over to his position near the runway and lit a cigarette.

Night had fallen. The big wind had blown up some cloud, but there were clear patches through which he could see the stars. The vast flat expanse of the aerodrome seemed to stretch to the very confines of the night. Two rows of lights, tiny bright hooded pinpoints, marked the edges of the runway, a long smooth concrete track, wider than an arterial road. This was the gateway through which the bombers had to pass up into the night. This was the gateway through which some of them would return. Not all, he supposed, not all. Must expect some losses, and he began to wonder who – but checked himself with a guilty feeling. He was superstitious, like many who live close to danger. Perhaps a man's thought might somehow influence the course of destiny. It was probably rot; but there, alone on the runway, near to the men who were to go, messmates with them, a man gets curious twinges of foreboding, curious throw-backs into his own prehistoric past. He lives, through them on the edge of a precipice, never knowing the hour. 'So we fly up and down the valley of the shadow of death, till one by one we fall into it.' So a close friend, a scholar, one of the bravest and cheerfullest, had written some time before he never came back.

Most of them didn't see themselves from the outside like that, couldn't or wouldn't face it, believed that, whatever happened to the others, they would come through. A good thing, he reflected, a good thing. Better so. He stamped up and down to keep warm, flicked his torch on to his wristwatch – ten minutes to go – then stamped up and down again. It was a bad time, the time just before the take-off. Everybody hated it. The crews said it was the worst of the lot. The tension affected him and keyed him up. He who had nothing to do but flash a Green at them, he who ran no risk and would sleep sound that night in a warm bed, he felt one of their company and, perhaps just because of his impotence, every bit as strung up as they.

Out of the darkness from all points of the compass he could hear engines running. At each dispersal point crews were assembling, piling in their parachutes, handing up their pigeons, their sandwich boxes and thermos flasks, squeezing up the narrow companionways, taking their places. Little flickers of blue flame sputtered out of exhaust manifolds, torches flashed here and there, from within the cockpits came the dull glow of instrument lights. There was activity everywhere, silent activity of men who were used to a job and didn't need to speak about it. It wasn't a time when anyone had much to say, and anyway it would have been drowned by the motors. To the silent listener out there on the flare path, the roar of the distant engines rose and fell as they were run up, a curious deep angry roar of power, thousands and thousands of horsepower, unleashed at a touch, controlled by a finger, flying out in a whirl of fury, dying back to a sullen whisper. There was something compelling and inspiring about it. It throbbed through the very core of you.

The Fitter was leaning over Hugh Thornly's shoulder as he ran up his engines. He ran them up carefully, first the starboard, then

21

the port, testing the magnetos, the mixture controls, checking the oil pressures and the boost, the variable pitch airscrew control, and going through the whole of that complicated routine, the ritual of the cockpit check. He did it methodically and unperturbably, while the Fitter, watching over his shoulder, followed his eyes from dial to dial. Satisfied, he put his thumb up and the Fitter handed him Form 700, that form without signing which no RAF pilot goes into the air, the form which certifies that the pilot is satisfied with the state of the aircraft. Thornly signed, handed back the greasy stub of pencil with the form. 'Good luck, sir!' the Fitter shouted in his ear. Hugh smiled and turned to Peter Morelli who was settling into his seat beside him. 'All set?' Peter nodded. Thornly slipped his mask in front of his face, flipped over the microphone switch with his finger and called up the rest of the crew. One by one they answered with a brief 'All set' or 'Okay'. Then he released his brakes, opened his throttles slightly and began to taxi out on to the perimeter track.

The big bomber crept forward slowly. Thornly followed the directions of an Airman who was walking backwards ahead of the machine, signalling him how to steer by means of two torches. Once out on to the perimeter track, he swung the aircraft right, and still very slowly crept round the airfield to the leeward end of the take-off runway.

'Front gunner to Captain,' came the voice on the intercomm. 'Permission to test my guns, sir?'

'Okay.' A burst of fire from the two front guns blazed out past the starboard wingtip into the gunpit beside the perimeter track. For a split second the spinning disc of the airscrew and the underside of the wing were lit by the tracer flashes. Then darkness again. The bomber crept on. 'Guns okay,' came Sam Dollar's voice, and he swung his turret back to bear straight ahead. A moment later came Nobby's voice from the tail, making a similar request, and again the guns stuttered out in rods of fire and the darkness came back. Nobby swung his turret to bear dead astern.

Behind the Wing Commander other bombers had crept out from their hiding places and now there was a queue of them all moving slowly, steadily round the perimeter to get into position to take off. The Flying Control Officer watched them as they came round, counting. All he could see was their navigation lights, the port light glowing red on the wingtip nearest him, the white light at the tail making a little patch of silver on the concrete, and all of them sliding forward, slowly forward.

P for Pathfinder stopped at the end of the runway at right angles to it. As he looked up Thornly could see the double line of the flarepath stretching away into the distance, the night sky beyond. A few stars came through the patches of cloud. He only glanced up and then began his final check – his Vital Actions. He set his trimming tabs, tightened his throttle box nut, pushed his mixture controls into Rich, set his airscrew pitch to Fully Fine, looked over his fuel gauges and fuel taps, tested and set his flaps, checked the hydraulic system, set his gyro compass, his gills and had a good look round...

The front and rear gunners had left their flight positions. Both stood just behind him, over the centre of gravity. When the aircraft was airborne, they would go back to their stations and the Captain would re-trim the aircraft. Now they hung on to anything within reach to steady themselves. Their helmets were strapped under their chins, oxygen mask and microphone dangling at one side, their thick flying suits, gloves, boots and parachute harness made them slow moving and clumsy. The black intercomm plug dangled at their knees.

It was a bad moment, this moment. The second before the start of the race. They felt low, with a curious tight burning spot in the pit of the stomach. Lukin had a feeling of nausea, and Peter Morelli wished he'd taken a leak, though he had taken one not ten minutes before. There was a green glow on the perspex by the pilot's seat. Flying Control had given them the Green. Thornly looked at his watch, and Cookson did the same. They were dead on time. P for Pathfinder swung round and pointed up the runway.

Thornly released the brakes, set the gyro once more, looked round, smiled cheerfully, then turned to look ahead, slowly pushing open the throttles. The bomber gathered way, her tail lifted, she shot past the runway lights, and lurched uncertainly once or twice under her heavy load. At last she lifted clear. Thornly switched his gaze from the flare path to the instrument panel before him. He settled down into the climb, retracted his undercarriage and, as the speed rose, reduced his boost and coarsened the pitch a little. The gunners went back to their places, while Thornly, still climbing in a wide circle, trimmed the aircraft again for cruising revs and did an all-round check. Below them now the perimeter lights of the aerodrome could be seen. Another aircraft had moved on to the runway and was starting her take-off run. Thornly continued climbing and switched off his navigation lights.

'Zero three four, you said, didn't you, Cooky?' Hugh was calling his navigator. He knew the course, but checked to make sure.

'Zero three four. Yes, sir. I make it Twenty-two twenty-four hours exactly, sir, so we're on time.'

They were crossing the aerodrome on course for the target at precisely the time ordered. 'Fine!' thought Hugh and settled down to fly on instruments for the next couple of hours.

P for Pathfinder climbed steadily eastwards. It was dark, but as their eyes got accustomed to it, they could just make out the earth. It was more a blacker blackness than anything else, with a faint difference between earth and sky at the horizon. At three thousand they were approaching cloud base.

'No good getting a drift below this, is it, Cooky?' the Captain's voice came over the intercomm.

'No, sir,' came the reply. 'I think we shall be out of it in half an hour and I can drop a float.'

'Okay.' Thornly continued to climb straight into the cloud.

They came out at four thousand, came out into a wonderful fairy landscape of a million stars. Below to the west was a plain of silver, the top of the cloud layer, stretching as far as the horizon; to the east this silvery disc broke off, crumbled away to darkness. Beyond to the east there was nothing between the stars and the earth. With any luck it would be clear over the target.

The Wellington continued to climb steadily. The crew settled down to their vigil. The front and tail-gunners began their systematic sky search, down across up across, peering into the immense emptiness of the night sky. They knew that, were they to see anything, it would not be when they were looking at it, but when they were just not looking at it. For the eye is a curious organ and one of its properties is that (at night) it perceives things best when they lie just out of the focus of vision. To see something 'out of the corner of your eye' is not the lucky chance it used to be thought, but an especial quality of the human lens and retina. Hence the eye must always be kept moving in order to pick up the enemy just off centre. After a time this search becomes automatic. One part of the mind attends to it, while another is free to think of something else. Just as an actor gives his best performance when it is entirely unconscious, dissolving an audience in tears while he feels nothing at all himself, while the active part of his mind is engaged in considering some domestic worry or planning his evening supper, so men engaged on long monotonous tasks learn to do them with one part of their being only. When they give them their whole attention, as they do at the outset, great fatigue results and, in the case of the gunner, may sometimes be followed by sleep – the greatest danger to be guarded against.

'Hullo, tail-gunner,' called the Captain, 'asleep yet?'

'Not yet, sir,' Nobby's voice came back cheerfully.

'Oxygen working?'

'Nicely, thank you, sir,' came Nobby's voice again.

Thornly called up the crew in turn, making sure they were warm and comfortable.

Meanwhile Lukin had tested all his sets again, picked up base and tuned in accurately. Now there was nothing for him to do but listen out. He reached into his flying coat for the book he always carried, opened it under the dim pool of light on his little table and began to read, his finger resting lightly on the knob of his condenser dial, which he swung slowly back and forth, back and forth, over his listening wavelength. The volume was a pocket Shakespeare.

Lukin knew all the plays, had seen most of them acted, but Shakespeare had, among other things, the wonderful quality of being always new, like a clear bubbling spring forever recreating itself. The plays were better to read, once you had seen them acted, for then you could imagine the scene, and concentrate on the magnificence, the aptitude of the words, the beauty of image and phrase. Best of all you could go back and read a speech a second time. It did not fly past you as it did on the stage, dying on the actor's lips at its very moment of creation. It was there, captive on the page, and you could savour it again and again. He opened the book at random.

Fear no more the heat of the sun
Nor the furious winter rages.
Thou thy earthly task hast done
Home art gone, and ta'en thy wages...

He read on. The thing was a masterpiece, down to the very last couplet...

Quiet consummation have
And renowned be thy grave.

It was a lyric of mature years, occurring in an obscure play. It was melancholy, a dirge; wherein then lay its healing power, its astonishing gift of consolation...?

'Hullo, Lukin,' came Hugh Thornly's voice. 'Are you okay? All the gadgets working?'

Lukin quickly put his microphone to his face and flipped over the switch. 'All sets tested, sir, and all in order. I'm listening out.'

'Good. If you get any news, pass it along.'

'I will, sir. By the way, sir, do you object to my reading?'

'Not a bit – as long as you keep your ears open. Young Peter here's reading. Wait till I tell you what it is...' There was a pause. 'It's *The Poisoned Orchid*.' You could hear a titter coming through the intercomm from all over the aircraft. 'Can you beat that?'

'I'm afraid not, sir,' Lukin answered. 'Mine's Shakespeare.'

'Is it, indeed!' the Captain's voice came back, and he quoted:
'He that outlives this day and comes safe home
Shall stand a tiptoe when the day is named
And rouse him at the name of Crispian...
And gentlemen of England now a-bed
Shall think themselves accursed they were not here...
I've missed out a bit, haven't I?'

'Nearly the whole lot, sir!'

'Navigator to Captain,' Cookson broke in. 'We're clear of the coast now. Have I permission to drop a float?'

'Go ahead. I'm still on zero three four.'

Cookson took the flame float, a long cylindrical tin, slipped it into the chute, released it and then went forward to the drift sight.

'Navigator to Tail-Gunner. Stand by to take a bearing.'

'All set,' came Nobby's voice.

Some seconds later a tiny point of light appeared far off below, about a mile behind the aircraft. The float had struck the sea and was burning. Cookson took his bearing, got a confirmation from the tail-gunner, noted the time, came back to his chart table, calculated the drift, the wind direction and strength, and the new course to steer, to make good the track they had chosen.

'Navigator to Captain,' he called when he had completed his calculations. 'The wind's from 352 at this height, sir. I make its strength 46 miles, so if you alter course to Zero three one, that should keep us on track, sir.'

'Zero three one. Right. Altering now.' Thornly applied a little bank and the aircraft swung slowly to port on to its new course and steadied there. 'On course,' he called back to Cookson.

'Okay, sir.' Cookson noted the time, the height, the indicated airspeed, and made the entry in his log.

'You might see if Lukin can get you a bearing to check,' Thornly's voice came again.

'I'm taking a bearing, now, sir,' Lukin interposed. He had snapped over a switch and was carefully turning the remote control of the loop above his head, listening intently all the while. Then his hand steadied and he jotted down a number and handed it behind him to Cookson, who took it, noting the time again.

P for Pathfinder rushed on through the night. She was well out into the North Sea now and behind her a stream of others followed. Lancasters, Halifaxes, Stirlings, Wellingtons swarmed up in her wake. Whitleys and Blenheims on diversionary attacks. Bostons and Hurricanes on Intruder operations. From a hundred aerodromes they rose up into the night and spread out on their allotted tasks. All over the East and South-East counties the darkness was filled with the heavy drone of engines. On the ground below an army of men and women were following their tracks, listening to them, plotting them. A vast and complex signals organisation was at work, passing the intelligence of their movements back to the nerve centres of the Commands. Flying Control was ready, waiting to guide them home if they got lost. Air-Sea Rescue was standing by, ready at a moment's notice to rush out to pick up crews forced down into the sea. Tens of thousands of men and women were alert, backing up the lonely men aloft there in the recesses of the night.

At the head of this great Armada, the very spearhead of it, P for Pathfinder droned on under the stars.

It was the spring of 1942. The news was bad. The Russians were falling back under the hammer blows of the Hun. The Ukraine was gone. The Donetz basin was going. There was a threat to the Caucasus, to the Volga, to Stalingrad. No man could see the end, and though the Russians were putting up magnificent and heroic rearguard actions, they were being slowly and inexorably forced back. In Egypt things were no better. Rommel was striking at the gates of Cairo. The British were in retreat. Tobruk had fallen. In the Far East it was catastrophic. The Japanese had overrun the whole of the South West Pacific. Burma had gone. The enemy was at the gates of India. They had overrun Malaya, taken Singapore, Sumatra, Java and the Philippines. There seemed little to stop them landing in Australia. Everywhere the initiative lay with the aggressor powers and the magnitude of the task of containing them seemed superhuman. Russia was feeling the strain and calling on her Allies to open a second front; but England could not do it. She could not risk making a premature blow which, if it failed, would leave her open to the heart, defenceless.

There was nothing left to do but bomb. In spite of the calls made on her for aircraft to be sent to all parts of the world, the home bomber force was growing. It could and must be used in an all-out offensive on German industry. In no other way could England carry the war to the enemy. True, the darkest days when she stood alone against the powers of anarchy were over. 'The waves,' the Prime Minister had said that year, 'may be against us; but the tide is for us.' But the tide was still at ebb and the transformation that was to take place before the end of the year had not begun. The English felt impotent. They had carried the burden of the war for three years, suffered defeat after defeat, and rallied from each of them, with that fortitude and invincible faith in victory which to the cynical neutrals seemed absurd, however heroic. But England had been in plights as desperate before. She had seen these tides of human fanaticism sweep to her shores when a bestial French Republic overran Europe as Hitler was doing now. She had seen the stricken refugees, the persecuted minorities, the corruption, the sadism, seen an almost exact parallel to current events – and had been every bit as unready to meet it. But she had come through in the end. 'I will die,' said Dr Johnson, on his deathbed, 'but I will not capitulate.' England held on. For the moment there was little she could do. She had to pile up reserves. Her industry was still not at peak. She had to answer calls from every quarter of the globe. In the West she was not yet ready; but she could bomb. And bomb she would, by God.

The crews of the bomber force did not see themselves in this great perspective. They did not think of themselves as the sword-point of England, as the dauntless men they were, flying hundreds of miles through ice and thunderstorms, pushing on through screens of flak, running the gauntlet of night fighters, bombing the enemy and then returning, sometimes crippled and wounded, to their own shores. To shoot a line about their work would have been the height of bad form. They were mostly young men, unreflective, concerned only with the day-to-day doings, with the technique of their job, with their simple relaxations, beer, darts, shove-ha'penny, and the girlfriend on leave. Had they not been so, the job could not have been done, for the strain of these operations was too much for all but the most phlegmatic natures. The long hours of inactivity, sitting in the same cramped positions, the cold, the danger, not sharp or sudden, but long-drawn-out over hours of suspense. Nothing in all modern warfare could exceed the stoic heroism of the night bomber crews, nothing also could exceed the technical skill they brought to it. To the layman it was little short of a miracle, and even members of the RAF, pilots themselves, flying on other jobs, would shake their heads, honouring the men who nightly seemed to accomplish the impossible.

Hugh Thornly certainly never thought of himself in any heroic light. True he had twice been decorated for gallantry; but in both cases he considered that the award should not have been given. What was heroism? The job and self-preservation, in nine cases out of ten. He had only done his duty, after all, and what about all the other blokes who did theirs and were not singled out for a gong? He never thought of himself as the fine leader he was, nor saw in his mind's eye all the hundreds of bombers coming in behind him. He knew that they were there, of course. Therefore it was essential he should get to the target and set it well alight. That was the job. He also knew that the first aircraft would draw all the flak and that there was a good chance he might intercept some. But that didn't worry him unduly. He had done it before and got away with it. He could do it again.

With a crew like his, a man could do anything. They were absolutely first class. He couldn't do enough for them. They reciprocated by giving him their best all the time, in every emergency and when there was no emergency. They did more, they idolised him and would gratify, if they could, his slightest whim. He often thought about them. Indeed, when he was not thinking of Helen and Pam, and wasn't immersed in the Squadron bumf, he thought of nothing much else but his crew.

But he often reflected that although he seemed to be intimate with them and share their daily life, he really knew nothing about them at all. It was one of the things that puzzled and worried him most in life – the way human beings are divided from one another. He believed that if we could only overcome these barriers, we should gain greater understanding each of the other, and that many personal and social misfortunes would disappear. But how reticent men were, when it came to the point! How security-minded we all were about our souls! Even the most intimate friends kept something back, kept their deepest secrets inviolate. Nobby, now, never talked about his wife. And Morelli with his charm, what secrets he must have! And Cookson with his candid simplicity that was nevertheless quite self-contained, quite apart. He felt he could understand anything they had done, could pardon or console, help or advise, and yet, there it was, they were practically strangers to each other.

Only the job kept them together. It had brought them together. When it was over, they would go their own ways, back to the life they had known before. It was grand the way war mixed people up, threw them in contact with all manner of people they would never have otherwise met, broadened their horizons, made them clarify their ideas and their ideals, forced them to face the issue of what was worthwhile and who was worthwhile. There was much to be put on the credit side in war, apart from courage and testing your character under strain. But all the same there was really no contact... With Helen he felt he really did know everything, that there was no barrier, nothing to cloud their perfect understanding. It was the result of love. Love made it possible to know what people would do and say almost before they said it. It made possible the communion of the spirit in the bond of peace, as the Book put it. But these men. It wasn't the love you felt for your wife, but it was love of a sort, responsibility, affection, and a readiness, after all, to go through with them to death.

Yet there they were, all six of them, roaring along through the night at 12,000 feet, strangers to him and to each other. It was a great mystery. It was the damnedest thing.

Take young Morelli. Thornly glanced sideways at him sitting there at his side. Their arms were touching. What was going on inside that head? He had put down his thriller. It lay on his knee. His face, hidden up to the eyes in his oxygen mask, was averted. His eyes were looking out through the perspex of the cockpit. But there was nothing to see out there: nothing but the monstrous blackout of the universe. His eyes were staring, quite unseeing. His whole body was still, thinking. He was miles away. Hugh smiled. He was fond of Peter. There was something likeable and eager about the boy. 'Some young woman, I bet,' he said to himself and turned back to the Blind Flying Panel. 'Some young woman.'

PETER MORELLI

PETER MORELLI WAS not, at that moment, thinking about a young woman, though Estha was always intermingled with his thoughts. It was like one of those double exposures in a film, where you saw one scene clearly and another was there coming through it, mixed with it. The foreground of his mind, the focus of his conscious thought, was worrying at a peculiar problem – considering the circumstances – what was a ghetto like? One of these modern ghettos, a Himmler-designed ghetto.

He remembered seeing one in some film, years ago. But that was in a mediaeval city. It was a tangle of twisted narrow streets and alleys, the houses almost meeting overhead. There were dark latticed windows and people moving silently, secretly, always in shadow. The atmosphere was one of grief and persecution, but it was tempered, as he remembered it, with dignity and nobility. The Rabbis had calm faces, long cloaks and silky beards. The women with their tragic eyes were hooded like madonnas, lovely serene, long-suffering. The whole thing was opulent, picturesque. There was no squalor, no poverty, only patience in adversity, and in this film, as far as he could remember, the patience was rewarded. Quite obviously these German hells could be nothing like that.

Were they just dreary acres of draughty huts, surrounded by high fences of barbed wire, with guards and machine guns, like prison camps, where thousands and thousands of luckless human beings in conditions of filth and misery were being systematically done to death? Or were they streets of hovels, tenements, or whole towns? Peter couldn't focus it at all. It didn't do any good to focus it. It was better not to, being so impotent; but he couldn't help it. Estha was part of his life. He couldn't accept her as a transient vision, which had suddenly appeared and as suddenly vanished, like a ghost. He couldn't only remember her there, in the little boat with the fireflies behind her head. It was necessary for him to think of her in the present, somewhere, living and breathing. If indeed she was still living and breathing... He cut off the thought.

The truth was that this persecution was too vast for the mind to grasp. Thousands, hundreds of thousands of people, all with their lives, their families, their properties, their businesses; all with their hopes and plans, had been brutally ripped out of the fabric of society. The people were innocent. Quite innocent. How could they help their blood? What had they done? No, the imagination gaped at it. The mind froze with horror, turned aside, gave up.

Yet Estha remained there shining in his mind. She grew there like a tree, spread out and graced his life more and more as the days went by. He hadn't fully realised it at the time. If only he had done so, he might have saved her; but it was no good; he hadn't. He'd let the moment slip...

It was a strange chain of events. His life really had been quite unusual, if you looked at it objectively. The plain facts were that Peter Morelli, on his way over to Germany in a British bomber, was an American subject, with an Italian father, a half-French half-Spanish mother, and Estha, to whom his heart was given, was an Austrian Jewess with Polish, Greek and German blood in her veins. Genealogically there was something farcical about it; something tragic too; but Peter did not see that. It was all quite natural, because it had happened to him.

His grandfather, the old Giuseppe, now hobbling about bent double with his rheumatism on the piazza of Tremezzo, had gone off to England in the eighties to find his fortune. He had found it, first in the kitchens of the Café Royal, and then in those of the Ritz. It was not a big fortune; but big enough to bring him his life's ambition, a small albergo in some pleasant corner of Italy, where he could spend the afternoon and evening of his life in modest comfort. It took him twenty years of hard work to achieve this, and when he came back to his beloved Italy at the turn of the century he brought with him his wife, Emma, and his two sons, Carlo and Pietro. Emma had been in the Gaiety chorus, but was glad enough to leave it for a comfortable little home off Great Portland Street, and the tempestuous adoration, jealousy and tenderness of her Giuseppe. They had been, for their honeymoon, to Tremezzo. Emma had never been out of England before. She fell in love with the tender beauty of the Italian skies. There and then they made their plan: to return 'some day' and set up their albergo at Tremezzo. When, at last they achieved that plan, and the big gold letters RITZ were put up across the stucco front of the modest inn they managed to acquire, they were the proudest people in the world.

Emma's sensible management and Giuseppe's excellent cooking soon gained the place a reputation. Its terrace overlooked the lake. A guitarist sang sentimental songs during the summer evenings. Visitors voted the place 'quaint' and 'so cheap', and Giuseppe was able to put up his prices. Meanwhile his boys were growing up. Carlo, the elder, would inherit the hotel one day. Pietro would have to fend for himself. Giuseppe trained the boys thoroughly as he had been trained. At the age of sixteen he had them helping in the kitchens. At eighteen he sent them off to Paris to learn the mysteries of waiting, of service and a foreign language. Carlo was a born cook and found Paris exactly to his taste, but Pietro was more ambitious. He was a good-looking youth with a charming smile and the suave manners of a successful waiter. Serving the élite in a Paris restaurant gave him a peculiar satisfaction. It also gave him a chance to observe them. He moulded himself on these people. Soon he could recognise the authentic touch of style, knew almost subconsciously their means and their tastes, never forgot a name or a face, and in fact developed all the traits of a successful maître d'hôtel.

After a year he went on to London, where Giuseppe's old crony, Rudolfo, took him under his wing at the Ritz. It was now 1910 and Pietro was 22. Again he learned the language and pursued his career assiduously. London had not the elegance and chic of Paris; but it had enormous wealth. Pietro was immensely impressed by these English milords who knew nothing about wine or food, but attacked both with extravagant gusto. From time to time even more extravagant clients appeared. They had loud uncouth voices and clothes, queer accents and strange manners. These were Americans. To Pietro American millionaires were fairy tales; but when one genial old man gave him a £10 tip with 'Say, buddy, have this, will you,' he knew they must be true. From that moment to get to America was his one ambition.

One day a stoutish middle-aged man came in to lunch, accompanied by a dark sprightly woman somewhat younger than himself. Pietro knew at once they were not of the wealthy class, but there was a quiet assurance about the man which puzzled him. He couldn't place it. He seemed to notice everything, scanned the menu carefully, made one or two enquiries about the dishes and ordered very precisely, making a particular point of the sauces. Pietro saw at once that he knew what he was talking about and, as it was a pleasure to serve those who really appreciated their food, he gave special attention to the order. He was interested. He noticed the man had chosen two fine and delicate wines, the best of their kind in the Ritz cellars, and, as the meal progressed, made one or two very discreet attempts to try to draw him. But it was no good. He was pleasant, rather unbending, and had a trace of accent, not American, not French. Pietro was hanged if he could place him.

At the end of lunch, as Pietro was bowing them out, the gentleman proffered his card. 'I have a suite here. Perhaps you could spare a moment to come up and see me. Any time after four.' Pietro bowed, said he would be delighted and could hardly wait to get out of sight to read the name on the card. When he did so, he whistled. It read: 'Simon Grosjean. Continental. New York.'

By such casual encounters is the course of a life decided. Grosjean turned out to be the manager of the Continental, one of New York's biggest hotels. They were opening a new Grill the next season. He wanted competent staff with European experience. The wages were fabulous, the contract definite. Pietro, if he accepted, could sail in a month's time. That was the gist of the interview. Pietro went out wildly elated and gave in his notice.

To a young man of twenty-two, New York was thrilling. Pietro was captivated by the tremendous vigour and drive of the place. America was still the land of infinite opportunity, where plain men could and did acquire fortunes, where there were no social distinctions, where you went to the top through ability and not through birth or cast. It was strange and rough, of course; it lacked any semblance of style; but when you got the hang of it, there was a wonderful sense of elbowroom. You could kick up your heels. You could try things. People seemed to want you to try them. They welcomed initiative. In Europe they said 'Why?' to a new idea; in America they said 'Why not?' After a year, with things going well for him, Pietro took out his naturalisation papers and became an American subject.

A week before the Grill was due to open, the head waiter resigned. Pietro saw his chance, persuaded Grosjean to let him take over and carried the thing through. Like most young men, he was far better than the circumstances of life had hitherto allowed him to be. The climate, he found, was so invigorating he could do with four hours' sleep. The rest of the time he spent in the hotel, seeing to everything personally, taking an increasing load off Grosjean's shoulders. The Grill was jammed for lunch, dinner and supper. The money rolled in. Pietro was on the crest of the wave.

Away in Tremezzo his parents were inordinately proud of him. His letters told of a life they had never known. Prices and wages seemed unbelievable to their thrifty ears. Pietro, at twenty-three, head waiter of a grill seating four hundred, earning more in a couple of months than the old couple did in a year! It seemed fantastic and they wrote begging him to put by his money, to save, to invest, for it seemed impossible that such things could last.

But they did. In three years Grosjean and Pietro had become close friends. The Frenchman looked upon the boy almost as his son. They decided to go into business together and jointly opened a restaurant downtown. The first European war was on. America was bubbling with excitement and in the middle of a great boom. Money flowed like water. The Paradiso, as they called it, was a gold mine. It seemed impossible to go wrong.

Then there was Netta. She was only a child when Pietro first saw her at Grosjean's apartment. A dark spindly creature with long black plaits and enormous blue eyes. Simon Grosjean and his wife, Carmen, adored their only daughter. She could do as she liked. Wayward and imperious in her teens, she matured early and acquired something of her mother's Spanish docility and domesticity. Yet Carmen was always anxious about the child. She knew the warmth of her own blood, the temptations and curiosities of youth. Both parents were still very European in their outlook, so that when a young Lieutenant in the Army Air Corps came along and started dating their daughter up for lunch, tea and supper, they grew anxious. They hardly knew the boy, Denis, who had brought an introduction from a friend in Philadelphia; but Netta was evidently infatuated. She moped and dreamed all day. She would hardly speak to Pietro. She was rude to her father, ignored her mother, lost her temper at the slightest interference.

Pietro was beside himself with jealousy. He had long thought of Netta as his own. They got on together like brother and sister. He was only waiting for her to grow up. After all she was only seventeen. He had hardly realised how much he was in love. He had taken it all for granted. Too much. And now this.

'Take her away! Per l'amor di Dio! Take her away!'

Carmen thought so too. But when their decision was hinted at, Netta screamed, refused to go in a torrent of incoherent words and relapsed into hysterical sobbing that went on most of the night. It was more than her father could bear. He loved his daughter. Something must be done. Next morning he got up early, and went to call on the young man. He had come to ask him, he said, to leave their daughter alone. The young man was easy and candid. 'Why, certainly, Mr Grosjean. Just as you say. Netta's very young and sweet. I'm kinda fond of the kid. But I've got a wife in Atlanta and I'm leaving for France in a couple of days.' Grosjean restrained his satisfaction as much as he could. He even made some sort of excuse for coming, explained how anxious he was for his daughter's happiness, and hurried out, leaving the young man smiling with a maddeningly superior air.

He got back to the flat and went straight to his daughter's bedroom. This would soon bring her to her senses. He found her reading, told her of his visit and the young man's marriage.

Netta burst into tears again. 'But I know that, damn you, I know that! Leave me alone; can't you?' And she buried her head in the pillow, convulsed.

At last they got her away. Carmen took her down to Florida for a change. But she was in love as only the very young can be, and with the young man gone, her sensitive passionate nature relapsed into a wild despondency. Two months later came a letter from Atlanta. It was from Denis's wife. He had been killed on active service.

It took all that winter to nurse her over it. But, with the spring, she recovered. She had grown up. Pietro married her and just as the war ended their son, Peter, was born.

The years after the First World War were free from anxiety. America, sick of the complexities of European politics, withdrew into herself, and settled down to develop her own prosperity. Pietro, after two years, gave up his place at the Continental. With Grosjean he floated a company for hotel management. They did very well. In a very few years he was on the way to becoming a rich man.

Every two years he took a trip back to Europe to see his parents. Netta came with him and, when Peter was old enough, he came too. The old people still had the Ritz at Tremezzo; but times were changing. Competition was keener. Tourists were of a different class. Como had been the mecca of the painter and artistic dilettante: it was becoming a playground for the young people who wanted to dance, sunbathe and swim. Pietro saw this. He bought up the albergo next door, ran the two places into one, modernised the kitchens, laid a dance floor, put running water and bathrooms to every room, enlivened the lake front with gardens, swimming floats and diving-boards, engaged a dance band and doubled the prices. The English and Germans flocked to the place and the Italians (though they hated the water) took to running out there in their cars at weekends, to sit under the gay umbrella and listen to the bands and motor horns. They enjoyed the noise and bustle, paraded their women, and talked at the tops of their voices. It cost Pietro a lot of money; but he was glad to do it for the old people, and the place was packed.

It was not until 1937 that young Peter made his first trip to Europe alone. After the slump things had never quite recovered in America, and his father was kept at home. He had lost heavily, but not ruinously during those years. Europe was drifting helplessly towards war and America was determined to keep out of it. In Italy the hotel business was ruined. Giuseppe, now an old man, wrote that Tremezzo was getting more and more deserted every year. The ominous signs were growing. Europe's economic structure was rotten and the threat of a world catastrophe loomed like a thunderhead on the horizon. Old Giuseppe worried about the money that Pietro had put into the Ritz, worried about the terrible losses, worried about shortage of staff, couldn't decide whether to close the place down or keep it going for 'prestige'. Pietro, training his son as his father had trained him, decided to send the boy over to discuss things with his grandfather.

Peter had grown up into an attractive young man. He was finely set up, tall, straight and manly. There was the warmth and charm of his southern blood, natural good manners, and with it all, the vigour of an American outlook and an American upbringing. He was spoiled, of course. He was a rich man's son, petted by adoring parents, given all the freedom to which young America is accustomed. But the happy home atmosphere, Peter's admiration for his 'old man' and his affectionate nature prevented this youthful liberty from becoming headstrong. True to the decade in which he grew up, he was pleasure-seeking and idle. But Pietro, when he looked back on his own youth, realised that there had been no years of freedom and irresponsibility in his own life. From the age of sixteen, he had been at work. He wanted his son to enjoy the things he had not known. Moreover he was inordinately proud of the boy, more particularly of his natural talent at the piano. Nobody knew quite how Peter had picked this up. It began when he was quite a kid, but he was never taught. He just had a wonderful ear and a fine sense of rhythm. His father had bought up a controlling interest in a music publishing business and this gave Peter opportunities to develop his bent. Though nothing had been definitely decided, Pietro thought it would be a good thing to let the boy take it over. England, Italy and Spain occasionally turned out 'smash hits', and Peter would be well equipped to run a London office.

So in 1937 and again in '38 and '39, Peter visited Europe. He stopped off in London, took a trip over to Paris, went on to Milan, ran out to Tremezzo, and then on down to Rome and Naples. He had a wonderful time, made friends wherever he went, and managed at the same time to bring quite a lot of useful information back to his father. War clouds were gathering. Looked at dispassionately, the thing was inevitable. But people obstinately, blindly, hoped against hope. Italy, although she was politically ranged alongside Hitler, hated the Germans. 'She'll never fight against England or risk fighting America, Pop. Carlo says there'll never be any peace in Europe till every German has been strung up – and most people seem to think that way.'

As for Tremezzo the boy was quite definite. 'There's no future in it, Pop, honest there isn't. Grandpa's worried about the losses and they certainly are making 'em alright. The place is like a morgue. Why don't you sell out to the syndicate that wanted to buy last year? Honest, Grandpa and Grandma will worry themselves to death if you don't.'

Pietro decided to take his son's advice and this, chiefly, was the reason for Peter's visit in 1939. His parents were anxious about his going. The news was growing more ominous day by day. But, promising he would return at the least sign of trouble, Peter left. Pietro was obsessed with the idea that the old people would be trapped in Italy. He wanted to get them out of harm's way, and gave Peter strict instructions to bring them back with him to the States.

So Peter sailed on the *Rex* for Genoa. He called in at Milan and went straight out to Tremezzo. The old people were evidently relieved that the Ritz was to be sold, but try as he would Peter could not get them to think of leaving Italy. They had lived there for forty years. There wouldn't be a war. They would take their chance. Peter tried all his powers of persuasion, but it was no good. He believed the old man would have come, but Emma dug her toes in. 'Hitler can go to hell,' she said, in her downright way, 'I'm staying put'. Peter laughed and left them for a week in Paris, where he had been offered some new tunes. It was while he was there he got a note from his cousin, Rico, with whom he had spent one or two hectic evenings in Milan. 'Caro,' ran the note, 'I missed you in Milan and now must go to the campagna to make mock battles. Let me know when you shall return. Do you remember the Signorina Morgen? She was meeting you at Bobby's last year. Now she is back in Milan and ask me to say her address is 73e Via Firenze, Telefono 34736. She has songs you will buy, she says. In a month I come back. There is a swell band at the Caserne. We shall hit it together and you will play. Thy affectionate cousin, Rico.'

Peter stuffed the letter in his pocket and thought no more about it. But when he got back to Milan, en route for Como, he was held up for a day or two, waiting for the Rome representative of the syndicate buying the hotel. It was July. The summer had been atrocious; but now it had suddenly turned hot and Milan was stifling. Peter chafed at having to stay in the city when he might be swimming at Tremezzo; but he had promised to wait. In the meantime he had nothing to do. Milan was deserted by all the people he knew. They had gone to the seaside or to their country villas. Turning out his pockets he came upon Rico's letter which he had quite forgotten. He read it again. Signorina Morgen. He hadn't the slightest idea who she was. He vaguely remembered an evening with Rico at Bobby's the year before; but there had been quite a crowd and they had got him to the piano. However... He had no date for lunch, nothing to do and the girl might have something. You never knew when you would pick up a good tune. He took up the telephone.

An Italian voice answered. Peter asked to speak with 'Signorina Morgen' and there was a pause while she came. Peter wondered vaguely what he was letting himself in for when a very soft and deliberate voice spoke: 'Hier, Estha Morgen.' Peter explained who he was.

'Peter Morelli! I am so glad. I was just going out. How fortunate that you rang up.'

She spoke carefully, as if she were choosing her words. The tone of her voice was warm and friendly and there was hardly a trace of accent. Peter explained about the letter, asked about her songs, told her he was staying in Milan over the weekend and – would she care to lunch? It was agreed they would meet at the Biffi at one o'clock. Peter rang off.

He strolled into the Galleria, a high arcade flanked with shops and restaurants, saw the head waiter at the Biffi, ordered a table for two and a couple of martinis, and sat down to watch the crowd passing. It was only then he realised he had no idea what this Signorina Morgen was like! How would they recognise each other? Stupid. He should have told her what coloured suit he was wearing, should have asked about her hat or something. His heart gave a thump or two. After all, it was something of an adventure to be lunching with a completely strange girl. He hoped she would recognise him. Otherwise they might wait for each other indefinitely. Time went by. The hour of their appointment had passed already. He crossed and uncrossed his legs nervously. Then he began to scrutinise the passers-by. Hundreds of people hurried through the Galleria in the luncheon hour. He saw girls coming, far down the arcade, and wondered to himself, 'Is this her?' or 'Not this one let's hope!' and eyed them surreptitiously as they went by. Then two girls came and sat at a table near to him. Perhaps she is shy, thought Peter, and has brought a friend with her. He watched the two girls carefully. One of them saw him and smiled. Then the other got up and went inside. Peter was on the point of going over to introduce himself when two elderly people joined her. He gave a sigh of relief, drank up the other martini and ordered two more. The tables were filling up now. The place was a chatter of conversation. The waiters hurried to and fro. Peter felt somehow conspicuous, sitting there alone, with so many parties round him.

'I am so sorry to be late...' He heard the low voice behind him, whipped round, stood up, and there she was.

'It doesn't matter.' They were shaking hands. Her grip was firm, gentle. She was smiling up at him.

'Do you remember me?' He was stammering something, for he didn't remember; yet he couldn't have met anyone like her and not remember. 'You do not remember at all, do you?'

'But I'll never forget.' He was blushing absurdly, ashamed of having forgotten, of not knowing what to say next, of being somehow caught off his guard, of showing that he was only a boy and not a man of the world quite accustomed to inviting strange ladies to lunch and, damn it, he was still holding her outstretched hand and she was letting it lie there. This would never do. He let her hand drop, turned, pulling back a chair for her.

'Won't you sit down?'

She moved past him to the chair. Small. Neat. Dark. Lissom. White dress, white shoes, white bag and such brown arms and legs. In that moment of time he took it all in. They were seated facing each other.

'My, but that's a cute hat!'

'It is a turban.'

'It sort of matches your dress.'

'And my teeth also!' She was laughing at him, showing such an arch of white small teeth.

'This is your martini.' He held it out to her. 'I'm two up on you. I ordered them while I was waiting.'

'So I am to be blamed if you are – high, yes?'

'Sure. But everything's under control.'

'I am glad to hear that.' She lifted her drink. 'Cheerio!'

'Here we go.'

They drank. Peter noticed her hand. It was tiny and yet somehow strong, not dimpled and podgy like the hands of Italian girls, but neat and capable. It seemed to blossom up through the slender wrist and have a life of its own. 'Like a flower on a stem.' That was how Peter thought of it afterwards, that was how he remembered it when he looked back, when every moment was lived over again in his memory, when he strove to get every gesture, every intonation by heart. At the time he could only say:

'That's a pretty cute little hand too.'

She held out the other. 'I have another one like it.' She was laughing at him again, laughing softly as if she understood quite well why he went on making inane remarks, understood and forgave and even liked him for it. 'Well, they're both cute.' Peter was getting back his self-control, getting over his nervousness. 'Say, you know we started all wrong. I ought to have introduced myself. My name's…'

'Peter Morelli. I know.' She was laughing again, a sort of low laugh that was half giggle half gurgle. 'And mine is Estha Morgen. So now we are introduced, yes?'

43

'Estha Morgen! Say, that's a cute name, isn't it?'

She was laughing again. 'But do you know no other word but "cute"? Really...' and she was laughing all through and over the words, '... but it is too silly, too sweet... Look, you may say that my hat is smart, that my hands are – nice, that my name is... whatever you like... pleasant pretty... I don't know, but they cannot all be just "cute".'

'I guess they are, all the same.' Peter stood his ground. 'I guess they're all cute, and that goes for you too.'

Then the waiter appeared and they ordered lunch. Peter could never remember afterwards what they ate or what they talked about. All he could remember was a sort of floating feeling of gaiety and lightness, of laughter woven through words that were meaningless, of glances, of sudden silences, a tissue of gossamer in a mist of sunlight. His memory held her face like a lens that holds a focus sharp and throws all else into a blur of shadows. For this was afterwards. Afterwards, and he could never see it clearly, never believe that it hadn't happened at once. Yet, truthfully, it had not. The moment of revelation had not yet come to him. He was still trying his best to be the worldly young man of twenty, alone on a trip to Europe, preoccupied with his father's affairs, bored in Milan with nothing to do, inviting a stray girl to lunch in case she might have the odd tune he could pick up cheap. He thought he was still doing this. This was the part he imagined himself to be playing. Rather worldly and cynical, that was him, a young man old for his years who knew all about life with a capital L. How else could you account for the way you behaved, how else could you explain that you ever dreamed of asking her...?

'My, but it's hot in town. Wouldn't it be fine to be out on the lakes and go in swimming?'

'It would be lovely.' She answered so directly, so easily that he was taken aback for a second. He covered it, or hoped he did and went on talking. But his mind was working quickly behind his words. After all, he knew nothing about her. They were absolute strangers. She might just be a pushover. But somehow that didn't seem to fit. She was not at all sophisticated. She must be awfully young. There

44

was something which made him reject the idea… and yet it would be fun to take her out away from the city… He talked on about other things. Then he returned to it again.

'Say, look at that sky – Doesn't it seem sort of indecent to see over the top of that garage or whatever it is?' She answered something and he went on: 'What do you say we make a weekend of it and go out to the lakes, some place?'

'Yes. If you like.'

The answer came quite simply and directly again. It wasn't charged with meaning glances or with any kind of implication. It was just an agreement to his proposal. The simplicity was too much for him. He couldn't quite believe it. Again he sheered off and went on talking. But his heart was pounding so loudly that he thought she must hear it. After all he was only twenty. He'd never taken a girl away for the weekend, gone to an hotel, registered with her as man and wife or whatever you had to do, for a double room, and all the rest of it. But he kept on telling himself, there's nothing to this – really. She's a decent kid. She just wants to get out of town and have a swim. I don't expect any more, so there's no need to get so hot about it. But the heart went on pumping just the same.

Lunch came to an end. Coffee had been cleared, the bill paid. They still sat there, talking, loath for it to end. But Peter wanted to know.

'So we really are going away for the weekend?'

'Why not? Do you want to?' He brushed the question aside, for he was not quite sure at that moment whether he wanted to go away with her, or just wanted the adventure of it all.

'Where shall we go?' he asked.

'I don't mind. You see I do not know the country very well. You must decide.' She was still perfectly naïve and frank.

'I know plenty of places.'

'Then I will leave it to you. I should like to go far, far into the country.'

Peter escorted her to his car and drove her towards her apartment. Before they got there she stopped him. 'Please. I shall get out here.' He did not question her, but it seemed curious not to take her right to the door.

'Where shall we meet?'

'I will come to the Biffi at 5.30. Will you wait for me there?'

'Sure, but won't you let me come and pick you up? You'll have a grip and...'

'No. Please. It is simpler if you wait for me.' She held out her hand. 'Auf wiedersehen, Mister Peter.'

'So long, little Estha. Five-thirty at the Biffi. Be good till then.'

She smiled and walked off briskly down the street. Peter watched her till she turned the corner. 'Well! If that isn't the damnedest thing,' he said to himself. Then he turned the car and drove back to his hotel.

It was very hot. He flung off his clothes and took a shower. Then he lay down on his bed to think about it all. The thing was outside his experience, for truthfully he had little or no experience. He'd had his share of necking parties back home, moonlight swimming parties, barbecue parties, and all the rest of it. There was plenty of adolescent love-making, wandering off in couples, kissing, holding hands and generally imitating the close-ups of the movies. Boys and girls got their first sensual experiences this way, tried their first incompetent fumblings. It made them feel frightfully grown-up, quite little Don Juans in fact; but it was all vicarious and led nowhere. Most of the girls didn't 'go the limit'. Peter truthfully found it rather boring. His southern blood made him warm and romantic. He couldn't turn this feeling on with just any girl. Some instinct kept him clear of most of it. But, of course, there had been girls... That kid last year up in Montmartre, and Pauline back home. He'd stayed all night with her and felt awful when he saw her next morning, sort of ashamed and cheap, though God knows why. But it had all been casual, almost offhand, something that was expected of a young man.

But, damn it, this was casual too. You couldn't call it anything else. And yet, somehow, it was different. There was something romantic about it. It was Italy and that was romantic in itself. And then there was Estha... Her face, her expression, something young and yet ripe, something naïve and yet frank, and the warm tone of her voice. That deliberate and very correct English, with sometimes a pause for the right word, and the beautiful articulation in which the only trace of an accent lay not in the way she pronounced, but in the intonation, the lift to the end of the sentence. With it all a sense of gentle mockery, of laughter and somehow, for all her youth, an implication of maturity. How different from an American girl of her own age! They would none of them have that poise, that intuitive wisdom. It was in the blood finally. It was in the root of an old culture. Peter's own blood answered it. They understood each other.

But that made it all the more curious. She was no push-over. He was willing to bet on that. Yet if she wasn't, this was fast work. It certainly was fast work. And then, suddenly, he remembered young Sam Shultz back home telling a story of his summer vacation in Germany. He'd met up with some girl and asked her to go for a trip with him. And she'd gone and they'd had a fine time; but there was absolutely nothing doing. She was a grand companion and when he got the idea, it kind of simplified things. But that was the way they grew 'em in Germany nowadays, self-reliant, companionable. 'She was a fine husky kid, hiked over the mountains like a goat. Yes, sir. At the end of a couple of weeks, boy, did I feel fit!' Peter had laughed at the time; but now it all fitted in. Not that there was anything of the mountain goat about Estha; but the frankness, the directness with which she had agreed to go with him, all that fitted perfectly. Yes, that was the answer. Peter found it a bit disappointing, perhaps; but that was it. It would be swell out on the lake... cool on the water... they'd go for a row after dinner...

He dozed off, in a wonderful contentment.

It was five when he awoke with a start. Gee, it would be just like him to sleep right through till dinner and ball the whole thing up. He leapt up, took another shower, packed his grip, went down to the cashier and drew some money, filled up the car, drove to the cathedral square and parked it, and just made the Biffi by half-past five. She was not there. He sat down, ordered an ice squash and waited. It was baking hot. His clothes stuck to him. Gee, it would be good to get out of all this. But she didn't come. He grew impatient.

Suppose he'd been fooled! Suppose it was that. Suppose she just said she'd come without the least intention of... Well, the hell with it. He would go by himself. He would go to Tremezzo. But that must be it. After all, he'd asked for it. He'd had a nerve, asking a complete stranger to go off with him, and she'd got out of it very neatly, very tactfully...

'Had you given me up, Mister Peter?'

'Hullo there!' He was not going to show his nervousness this time. 'I certainly had. I was just going to walk out on you. Give me your grip. The car's over there. Gee, isn't it hot, though.'

They went off together. She had put on a long white dust coat over her dress, her head was bare and in her hand she swung a white linen helmet. As they settled into the Packard, she put it on, strapping it under her chin, looking so small and neat in the big two-seater. Peter glanced sideways at her as they slipped away out of the city. 'I certainly am the luckiest guy,' he thought to himself, and again his heart started thumping at the adventure, the promise of it all.

She did not ask where he was taking her. In fact she did not speak at all. Just sat there smiling as he threaded his way along the narrow streets, past the noisy trams and out on to the autostrada. He stepped on the gas and the car jumped forward. It was cool with the wind on their faces. The countryside, rich with its crops, was almost ready for harvest. Pollarded mulberrys flanked the fields, the maize stood six feet high, huge hoardings, advertised hotels, Cinzano, Fiat cars; but as they left the city behind, these got fewer, and soon, far to the north-west, they could just see the line of the Alps, misty crenellated ranges of rock, lifting their snowcovered peaks over the horizon.

The autostrada forked. 'Como' said one fork, 'Varese' said the other. Peter pulled up. 'Where would you like to go?'

She was laughing at him again. 'Really, Mister Peter! You do not know where you are taking me?'

'Well, you see, I...' He almost said, 'I've never done anything like this before.' But he managed to cover it and went on: 'I... thought you'd like to choose. We could head for Como and then out along the lake to Menaggio or someplace like that, or we could take the road for Varese and through to Maggiore. Como's sort of crowded and hot this time of year. Maggiore will be cooler; but I don't know much about the place. Only been there once; but there are one or two cute villages... I guess I could find my way there; but it'll be kind of primitive, no hot and cold water or anything like that...'

'But, for heaven's sake, we do not need hot water in this weather! Let us go to the real country, where we can do what we like and wear what we like without everyone staring at us.'

'Sure,' said Peter, and his tone sounded a bit hurt. 'We'll go anywhere you say.'

'Oh, Peter,' she leaned forward quickly and laid her hand on his arm, 'please do not be offended. It is only that I...' and she paused and said in such a low quiet voice he could hardly hear it, '...that I should like to be alone... far away from everybody... with you.'

His heart was thumping again and he couldn't think of anything to say, and after a pause, looking down at her head, which she had laid sideways against the cushion, not looking at him, sort of still and wounded, showing him her love for the first time (though he didn't see, didn't understand), he slid in a gear and the car rolled away up the road.

The evening had come down before they arrived. They had left the wide straight fascist roads and threaded their way through a maze of lanes winding up and down sharp slopes, seeing from their summits the campaniles of the village churches and the rolling lake-studded countryside. There were oleanders and hibiscus in the gardens, and the standing crops in the setting sun made that scene the most tender, the most pastoral, the most holy in the world. The great mountains stood sentinel over it the sky banded with pink clouds arched over it, the warm evening light breathed over it. Time stood still, as if it wished to hold fast to its perfection, never to let it go...

They didn't speak much for the rest of the drive. Only from time to time, Estha would ejaculate a quiet 'Look! Look!' at some new view the twisting lane revealed. For the rest of the time she simply sat, lost in a maze of wonder. Peter had to give a lot of attention to the road, which was just wide enough for a car to pass, and to be on the alert for the bullock carts and to think up some way to get round this damned hotel problem. It preoccupied him. He didn't want to look a fool in front of the reception clerk...

'Listen, honey, it'll look kind of funny you and me arriving to stop the weekend, unless...' He tailed off, not knowing how to phrase it.

She looked at him, concentrating on the turns in the road and an almost motherly expression came into her eyes. 'You mean that I should register in your name?'

He was frightfully grateful to her for helping him out and glanced quickly at her, smiling. 'I guess it would make things a whole lot simpler.'

'But that is quite easy for me. I know how to spell it.'

He laughed involuntarily, for that was the last thing he had been worrying about. But there was another... Yes, there was another. It took him another five miles of silence to make up his mind to say it.

He was not conceited. It never occurred to him that he was in the flower of his youth, that he had more than his share of good looks, that he was someone a girl might fall in love with. An older man would have grasped the situation at once and would have carried it off with hardly a thought. But Peter was out of his depth. A few hours ago he had never seen this girl who now sat so quiet and composed at his side. So lovely, so simple, so – well, pure was a strange kind of a word to use; but that was it, pure, innocent; and here he was taking her to an hotel, getting her to sign as his wife, and...

He was blushing and stammering and so obviously concentrating on his driving. 'Listen, honey, don't get me wrong, I don't want to offend you, but... should I book two rooms or one?'

There. He had said it. After all, he told himself with a kind of bravado, she can only give me the air. I'm giving her the option, I'm treating her right, I mean to treat her right... There was no answer from beside him and he glanced quickly at her to see her face averted, looking out over the wide stretches of the lake which now lay below them. At last she spoke, simply and quietly, but in a small constrained voice, as if something within were using her lips and she no party to it.

'One would be nicer.'

When Spring comes to the Italian lakes the snow upon the mountain ranges melts and swells the tiny streams that run down their flanks. During the winter the lake is at its lowest, for all the rainfall (to be Irish) is snow and is held in white suspension upon the peaks. But if the temperature rises suddenly, the snow melts almost overnight, and then the whole countryside is a roar of falling torrents and dashing spouting waterfalls. The lakes, some of them sixty or more miles long, gorge themselves with this glacier water and their level may rise ten to fifteen feet in a couple of days. These beautiful spring floods give quite another aspect to the lake shores. They swell up against piers and steps, cover the stony beaches and fill out over the meadows. They carry away all the debris of the winter and make the whole place new. Hundreds of millions of tons of ice green, ice cold water take some time to escape; but slowly the level sinks again, down, down, to a midsummer low, till the autumn rains begin to raise it a little before it sinks at last to the full ebb of winter. Then in the spring, the cycle repeats itself.

All this podgy little Signor Maschetti, the proprietor of the Bella Vista Albergo, explained to the young couple as he served them with dinner on his terrace. 'But this year the *stagione* (season) has been 'orrible, 'orrible. Only now, in July, has the snow melted. *Per la Madonna*, it was about time!'

The jovial little man had welcomed them warmly. He was impressed by the big Packard, but hardly less so by the youth and good looks of the couple that got out of it. He took them along the dim tiled passage, opened a door, and threw open the shutters, letting in a flood of evening light. It disclosed a tall bare apartment with dark chestnut settle, chests of drawers and two marble-topped wash-hand stands. Against one wall stood a huge *letto matrimoniale* covered with a white cotton counterpane. The walls were distempered pale blue and were quite bare, save for a bedraggled family wedding group now discoloured with damp and bulging in its frame, and a green frieze stencilled round the room at shoulder height. The floor was polished wood. There were no curtains. A single electric light in a crinkly porcelain shade hung over the bed.

'*Ecco!*' said the Padrone. Then, after they had complimented him on the beauty of the room, he made discreet inquiries as to where they had come from, how long they would be staying, what they would like for dinner, and explained where the bathroom and lavatory were. Then he took his leave.

Not married, he thought to himself, as he went downstairs; but the girl! What looks! What clothes! What charm! He kissed his hand to the ceiling; he had been a connoisseur in his time.

Peter stood with Estha on the little balcony, looking down on the gravelled terrace below. Big spreading nespoli trees gave shade to it. There were red oleanders in tubs, climbing roses against the walls, some geraniums round a little fountain, and the whole simple tidy little place was edged with a balustrade against which the lake lapped gently. It was a sheet of dull gold in the glow of the sunset. On the further shore the mountains rose high and higher into the evening. Far away a tiny white sail lay becalmed. A snatch of song came from a garden nearby, and then the Angelus, mellowed by distance, came stealing over the water, giving its benediction to the day.

They stood for a moment, surrendered to the magic of it, and then went in. It was the first time they had been quite alone together. Peter felt too shy to stay in the room with her. 'You'll be wanting to change and powder your nose and all that. I'll go see it I can shake up a cocktail. Will you come down, or shall I…?'

'I will not be long. Wait for me downstairs, yes?'

The little boat moved slowly away from the shore. The night was windless and the lake utterly still. Not a ripple moved on the surface of the water. Only the summer mist rose like a bloom over it, softening the globe of the rising moon. Peter dropped his oars in quietly, rowed a stroke or two and then lay on them, watching the drops from the blade-tips forge a growing chain of rings on the water. The creamy radiance of the moonlight laid, as it were, a luxurious mantle of repose over everything. After the heat of the day, it seemed as if the whole earth had stretched and relaxed and fallen into a dreamless sleep. It was this that gave the night its mystery. It was the mystery of sleep, the daily resurrection from death to life, to the joy of waking, to the innocence of dawn. So powerful was the illusion that those who went by night, moved stealthily and silently, spoke in whispers, as if they were afraid to wake the world.

A trance of wonder descended on the two children in the little boat. To Estha it was the consummation of a dream. And now the reality was more dreamlike than the dream itself. Even Peter was a little awed. The thing had taken on quite a different complexion from the casual luncheon he had planned. It was as if something bigger than himself had got hold of it, had lifted the ordinary into the extraordinary. In the space of a few hours too. He was no mooning dreamer lying in wait for romance. He was fresh, eager and vigorous. The situation had crept up on him quite unawares. There she sat, only a foot or two away from him, this stranger who had promised herself to him, a girl he did not know, had never touched and did not desire. Desire, as he knew it, seemed utterly out of place, sacrilegious. But he had begun to worship without knowing it, had taken one leap, like an Indian fakir, straight from the humdrum daylight down, down, down into the bottomless well of love.

Then out of the mist the pollarded head of a willow loomed up in the water. The floods had hidden the trunk and now the crown lay on the surface like some huge floating thistle-down. The boat had floated in over the submerged meadows. They were drifting over a bed of summer flowers that, in the daylight, would have lain there, daisy, clover, buttercup, imprisoned under a sheet of crystal. The stern of the boat touched one of these thistledown trees and from it a cloud of fireflies darted out, tiny pulsing sparks of fire that floated in the air, paused, alighted, went out, rekindled themselves again. He saw them there behind her head. He would always see them so.

'Alles ist so schön bei dir.'

It came from her in a whisper. It seemed hours since either of them had said a word. Yet it made him feel quite ridiculously and unreasonably proud, as if somehow all this magical beauty were of his making, as if he was responsible for creating it. Absurd, of course; but none the less it seems there is some plot, which on occasion conspires to perfect a moment in the little life of man, as if Nature paused for a second on her uncaring way to lift the trivial into eternity.

'Could we not swim, Peter?' They were out on the lake again, far from the shore. The mist shrouded everything. The moon shone, whiter now, on a disc of mercury. It seemed as if they were quite alone in the world.

'Sure. It'll be cold though!'

'But the night is so warm.'

She stood up, kicked off her shoes, loosed her belt and in one movement lifted her dress up over her head and dropped it in a heap on the seat. For a second Peter saw her moonlit nakedness standing erect on the stern of the boat, then her body arched in the air, and, as the boat, relieved of her weight, suddenly heaved and swung upwards, there was a splash, shattering the stillness of the night.

'Come! Come, Peter! It is marvellous!'

He stripped and put his things and hers up in the bows and then leapt himself over the stern, leaving the little boat bobbing there like a huge beetle with two black oars for legs sprawled on the water. He gasped as he came up, for the water was icy cold, and swam after her. For a moment they splashed and gambolled together, but it was too cold. Peter regained the boat, heaved himself up over the stern and stood there gasping, rubbing the water from his arms and thighs. When Estha came, carefully balancing himself at the stern, he reached down, lifted her under the shoulders and brought her up, like a mermaid, out of the water till she could swing aboard.

'Here, take my shirt for a towel.'

They were both standing in the rocking boat and Peter found himself quite unashamed of his own nakedness and incurious about hers. It all seemed utterly natural. He somehow took it for granted that she would have the perfect immaculate figure of girlhood, and tossed her the shirt.

'Here! Catch!'

She caught it, laughing. They were both panting a little, exhilarated with the cold water and their own exertions. Then she paused in her vigorous rubbing and stopped to look at him as he shook the water from his hair and hands. He stopped also and so they surveyed each other.

'Adam and Eve,' she said.

'And not an apple for miles!'

It set them off laughing, as silly remarks will, and they almost upset the boat, shattering the silent mystery of the night with little shouts and cries.

'Oh, my poor hair!' She shook her head from side to side.

'Mind! You'll have us over.'

'Catch!' She tossed him back the sodden ball of his shirt, slipped on her dress and found her shoes. He was wringing out the shirt.

'My poor Peter! You can't wear that.'

'I've got my coat.'

He had pulled on his trousers, slipped on his coat and sat down to row back to the shore.

But, back in the dim bedroom, with the long patch of moonlight creeping over the floor, it all seemed quite different again. Peter found himself overwhelmed with shyness. How on earth was he going to get undressed? There was a horrible and vulgar finality and blatancy about it. It seemed to announce: this is what I came for, this is all I'm interested in and it's time to get down to it. And he didn't feel like that, didn't want to drag this wonderful sudden thing down to any lower level. So he sat there on the edge of the bed, staring out into the moonlight. All the time he was aware of her there in the shadows. She had slipped into a wrap, she was brushing her hair, she was moving deftly and quietly in the gloom. There was a tinkle of bottles and glasses, drawers opened and closed the big door of the settle creaked and snapped to. And then she was beside him, lightly touching his hair.

'Sad, little Peter?'

He managed with a great effort to turn and look at her. 'No... no... I'm fine. I'm... happy.'

'I am happy... so happy. I think I shall never be sad again.'

And then somehow he was holding her, touching her hair, smoothing her cheek, and the contact that he had dreaded as a degradation was transformed into a new and exquisite intimacy and the barriers were down between them.

He was lying there curled over her, kissing her neck, her cheeks, her eyes, holding her to him, tight in his arms, pouring out his new-found adoration in a torrent of tenderness and wonder.

'Peter, little Peter...' He paused.

'What is it?'

It was a moment before she spoke again and when she did it was in a whisper. 'Be gentle with me. You see, I... You are the only man I love... You are the first...'

It was like a stab. 'Estha!' He turned from her, moved away not touching her, lay there on his back staring up at the darkness. The mystery was complete now, complete and wholly inexplicable. Such things didn't happen, couldn't happen. There was no rhyme or reason in them. It had been curious enough to begin with. He had rationalised it as best he could, thinking of young Sam Schultz and his mountain goat, but that had broken down, and then when she had promised herself to him, that only made him feel humble as if he were taking her on false pretences... It was just something unbelievable and wonderful that had happened to him. He supposed girls did sometimes throw themselves at a man, though what there was about him... But she hadn't thrown herself at him. She had made it all inevitable, natural, easy... but this...

She had raised herself on an elbow and was leaning over him. 'You are not angry with me?'

'Angry!' It was almost a snort. He could not begin to explain the thoughts that were whirling in his head. He was positively irritable at her lack of understanding. Could she not realise that girls couldn't do this sort of thing, that it was impossible, impossible...

'Have I spoiled it all for you?' There was so much sadness in her voice.

'No, no... but can't you see, honey... I can't... a man can't...'

'Listen to me, little Peter, please listen. When I saw you last year, I knew that this was bound to happen. I cannot explain why, to you, to myself... I knew you had not noticed me; but I thought... I hoped... that if we could meet again; if God, in His goodness, would help me to meet you again, that... somehow... oh, I don't know... I could show you... that you would see and feel for me... oh, not so much I know... but that perhaps you would love me... a little.'

There was nothing to say, nothing to answer, only a sense of unworthiness, of utter humility... but she was going on:

'Then today the miracle happened. I had been waiting such a time, such a long time in the dusty city, hoping that somehow it would happen, and I had almost given up hope... But, you see, God had not forgotten and brought you to me... Oh, I know, you thought it just fun to be going off with me; but I did not care what you felt, if only I could be with you, could... give myself to you. That is all I asked. But you have given me more, so much more...'

'But, Estha, if we knew each other better, perhaps you would change your mind, would regret...'

'People do not know each other better, Peter. Perhaps they learn more about each other, but if they feel, as I feel, all that... if it comes, it comes; but it does not matter...'

She was silent, but he did not answer and after a moment she went on again:

'My darling, you come from a great country that is far far away from all the troubles of poor Europe. There will be war this year...'

Peter protested. There wouldn't be a war, the thing would be tided over. Politicians weren't so damn silly. Even Hitler. He'd cool down when his bluff had been called.

'No, no... everybody says so. Once the harvest is in. Then who knows what will happen to all of us? You see, my mother is Jewish... there is no future for us... Once this war starts, life will be over for me.'

And then the shadow of death fell over them, there in the moonlit room, and the thought that it might be true, that he would never see her again, that any harm might come to her, swept over him in such a wave that it choked him, and suddenly he had her in his arms again.

'Darling, don't say such things.'

'Then kiss me, my darling. Kiss me, make me yours. Oh, Peter, my little Peter...'

When they returned to Milan the world, which for a brief space had been so completely shut out, took its revenge. Peter found himself involved in a series of duties and responsibilities. He had dropped Estha and arranged to pick her up for dinner that evening; but, on his return to the hotel he found his grandparents and his uncle Carlo, together with representatives of the syndicate that was buying the hotel, all collected, all waiting for him. For weeks the final signatures had been held up. Now, as it always happens, having at last got the contract agreed, they were anxious to complete immediately. Peter's signature, on behalf of his father, was necessary. But there were clauses that his father had insisted on having incorporated. All this had to be attended to. He could not leave the old people for dinner. They were already clamouring to know where he had been, why he had left without giving an address. Only Emma, still spry, caught his eye and winked. She had not forgotten her young days and the blades that hung round the Gaiety stage door. You've been off on the loose the wink said, and Peter smiled and made evasive answers.

The Hall Porter too had contributed to the mess by presenting Peter with a cable. He opened it and read:

'Your Mother and I think European situation extremely grave stop please return at once wiring time of arrival New York stop love to all at Tremezzo Pop.'

All this threw Peter into a state of uncontrollable irritation. Why did his grandparents have to turn up like this without warning? Why did his father send gratuitous cables calling him home, as if he were a child? How could they possibly judge the European situation back in America? And anyhow America was not involved in all this. How could it possibly affect him, as a neutral, whether war were declared or not? All this, and much more, Peter poured out to Estha on the phone. He had slipped away to ring her and explain why it would be impossible for him to get away to dine with her. She listened, and when he had finished his outpourings she said quietly, 'But I understand, Peter. I understand very well. You must do these things. It is part of your life. It is the world which must come between us. It cannot be helped. It is our fate.'

To Peter it seemed as if a cloud had come between them, as if the sun which had warmed them through had suddenly gone out. And why grow so portentous over little things? After all, it was only one evening. There was tomorrow and the next day and the next. There were all the days. He begged her not to be upset, he was mad as she was; but it was just one of those things...

'Look,' he said, 'I guess I can get quit of them by about ten. What do you say I come round and pick you up and we go and have a drink together at Bobby's or some place?'

'But I do not want to be among all those noisy drunken people.'

'Then we'll go for a run in the car somewhere, out into the country. We'll do anything you say.' There was no answer. He fancied he could hear a faint sound of sobbing at the other end of the line.

'Estha! Darling, you're not crying? There's nothing to cry about. Listen, I'll be around for you at ten.' There was another pause. Then her voice came, very quiet and sad.

'Good-bye, then, my little Peter... till we meet again.'

The receiver clicked as she hung up and Peter waited a second before replacing his. There was something terribly final in her last words. He could not understand what had happened, why this short delay of an hour or two should have upset her so. It was unreasonable. He went down to join the others in a mood of violent irritation and frustration.

Somehow or other he got through the evening. He could never remember what he said, what was discussed. It was a trance, a sort of nightmare. At ten he excused himself and abruptly left.

He had some difficulty in finding the address, for the little street in which the apartment house stood was dark. He rang the bell. It was a long time before anyone answered. Then a man without a collar put his head round the door. Peter asked for the Signorina.

'There's no signorina here.'

'But there must be. Signorina Morgen.'

'There's nobody here.'

'But isn't your telephone number...'

'There's no telephone here. We're not on the telephone.'

The door slammed in Peter's face, leaving him baffled. He pulled the letter out of his pocket, read the phone number again, crossed to a wine shop nearby and asked if he might use the phone. When he was connected, he asked for Estha.

'The signorina has just left.'

'Left! Where for?'

'How should I know, signor? She packed her suitcase, paid her bill and left.'

'What is your address?'

The woman gave it him. Ricco had put 73 in his letter. The number was 78. When he got to the place, a drab apartment house, the woman opened the door. But she could add nothing to what she had said on the phone. The signorina seemed upset. She had been staying for a month. It was sudden, yes; but the news was bad. Perhaps she had to get home. No, she had left no address. Peter was speechless. But he had to say something... They were friends. She had agreed to meet him at ten. It was quite impossible that she should...

The woman shrugged her shoulders. She was sorry; but there it was. If the signore would care to come and see for himself. Her room was empty. Yes, it was very sudden, and the signorina was so sweet, so kind. She too was upset at her sudden departure; but it was none of her business... She had begged her to stay till the morning; '*Ma!*' and she threw up her hands with an expressive gesture, '*e andato deciso, proprio deciso.*' Peter stood for a moment, dumbfounded. Then he managed to apologise for having troubled the woman, and left.

Looking back on it afterwards, he could never remember how he had spent that last week in Europe. Like his mother in her teens, he had been in a daze of grief. He railed against his relations who had, all unwittingly, been the cause of Estha's departure. He blamed himself for not having placed her first, absolutely first; but it had seemed such a little thing. He could have had her to dinner with all of them. Why not? Why had he not thought of it? Simply because he wanted her alone, not in the world of other people. Surely she must have understood that? He blamed himself for not having found out all about her. He should have asked her where she came from, taken her address so that he could write to her... But those two days had been so idyllic, so perfect... They had lived in the moment. He did not remember thinking about anything but her. The future, the past, it was all cut off, non-existent. Everyday things had simply not entered his head. Or hers. She had asked nothing about him, about his life or his country. It was fantastic. He milled around in a maze of thoughts that led him nowhere. He left letters at the apartment house, in case she should write, left instructions at his own hotel to forward any inquiries, any letters, anything that might come for him. Then he remembered Rico. Perhaps he would know something. He had written about her. He must know. But Rico was away on his manoeuvres. Apparently they were secret. All Peter's attempts to communicate with Rico were politely but quite firmly refused. The authorities evidently suspected him. He left messages, letters at Rico's address. He would get them, when he came back. But as to when that would be, the authorities shrugged their shoulders, 'Who knows?' It was maddening. He seemed to be surrounded with a sort of fog, as if everything was conspiring to make it impossible for him ever to find her. He could not sleep, could not eat, he went through the days, waiting, hoping that something would come from her, some letter, a wire, something... But nothing came except two more cables from home, each more insistent than the last that he should leave Europe. At last he came to himself. There was nothing to wait for. The frustration was driving him mad. The thing had started in mystery; it had been wonderful, exquisite beyond hope or imagination; mystery had pervaded it all along, and now it had ended as mysteriously as it had begun.

His parents had found him very changed. He had left a boy, but he returned, in some indefinite way, quite different, quite old. They tried to question him; but he was evasive, unapproachable. He spent all his time alone, most of it flying. Somehow the action, the thrill of the air, was the only thing that relieved his obsession.

Then war was declared. The annihilation of Poland made the world gasp. Stories of the persecution of the Jews began to appear in the American press. A sudden wave of hate swept through him.

All this was directed against her. He felt Hitler as a personal enemy, a maniac bent on her rape and torture. Sometimes, afterwards, looking back on it all, he wondered if, during these months, he had been quite sane.

At any rate when he happened to see a paragraph in the paper saying that the French would accept American pilots and were forming a new Lafayette squadron, something clicked inside him, and he announced to his astonished parents that he was going to France to fight. They forbade, they remonstrated, they argued. Netta had hysterics and grew ill; but nothing made any difference. He was sorry, of course, sorry they were upset; but... he must go.

The way he was smuggled out of America would, in any other circumstances, have seemed a fantastic farce. America disowned her volunteers in order to retain her strict neutrality. French consuls made the arrangements. Ridiculous subterfuges, that would not have done duty in a third-rate detective story, were employed. He changed his name, was given a bogus passport, waited on railway stations for mysterious guides who sidled up and led him off to secret conferences. This in America!

At last he was smuggled on board a liner, steerage, and arrived in France to find that nobody knew about him or wanted him. Again there were interminable delays. Arrangements that were never implemented were made out in interviews of extraordinary secrecy. The thing was a huge and preposterous joke, only made sinister by the crass incompetence of the authorities. Meanwhile Paris was gayer than ever. The war hung fire and was not to be taken seriously. Hitler was not ready. The thing would fizzle out and come to nothing. Instead came the blitzkrieg and the panic.

In desperation, Peter had joined an American ambulance unit. He was out of Paris only just in time, and joined the wretched miles of lost souls who flooded south over the packed roads. In Bordeaux he managed to get on a ship that was evacuating the army and the refugees. It was bombed and sunk, Peter's leg was shattered by a flying piece of railing; he was knocked unconscious and remembered nothing till he awoke in hospital in England. As soon as he was well enough he asked the matron to wire his people in America telling them where he was.

He did not make a quick recovery. His leg healed as good as new; but there was shock and he could not make headway. A heavy lassitude seemed to hang over him and nothing would rouse him from it. But slowly, very slowly, he did improve, until one day letters arrived from America.

They were from his parents, asking the usual solicitous questions, begging him to write, giving him news. They enclosed a letter forwarded from Italy, from Rico. Inside it was another note in a writing he did not know.

'My little Peter,' it ran, and he knew then, at once, and his heart bounded. He read on. 'Do not think I went away because I was angry. I could never be angry with you. But all was so perfect between us. I was frightened that it could not last. I wished everything between us perfect as it first had been. I went before it could change. It was the beautifullest thing that ever happened to me in my short life. Now the days are dark and the end of my world is near. But I shall not worry. The little light you lit in me will never go out. Think sometimes of your Estha.'

Again there was no address. Rico's letter told him nothing. A note, he said, had come from her, asking him to forward this letter which he did. Peter read the letter over and over again. It worked him up into a fever. Again he was baffled, could not reply, could not reach her, could do nothing to save her. He knew now that all the threats and blusters of the Nazis were true and that all those with Jewish blood were doomed to starvation, extermination and every sort of cruelty that fanatic sadism and bestiality could devise. The thought of anyone touching her, humiliating or degrading her, drove him mad. For weeks he was light-headed. The letter put back his recovery by months.

But at last, as the winter drew in and the long ordeal of London started, he was well enough to move about. He went to the Embassy, told his story, said he wanted to volunteer to join the RAF. Officially they could know nothing about it. Privately sent him along to see the right department at the Ministry. He gave his qualifications, was accepted as a pilot and sent off to undergo training. Pilots were scarce then, and all were welcome. It took a year to get through it all. He had thought he could fly before; but the standard required was very high. Night bomber crews were the most technically proficient men of any air force in the world. So he went back through his elementary training, on to his advance training, then to a pool to wait for a posting, and then after a maddening three months on again for a further training at an OTU, and at last was posted to the Wellington Squadron of Pathfinders.

Outwardly, he was now quite recovered. The discipline, the effort, requiring all his powers of concentration, steadied him, while the good fellowship of the Mess restored him to something approaching his old carefree self. His hatred for the enemy, his immense regard for Thornly and his natural good spirits made him an invaluable member of the crew.

But in periods of suspense, when he was alone, as everyone was during the long run out to the targets, rushing madly through the black vacuum of night, he dreamed again of the moon over the summer lake, of the fireflies in the willows and heard that voice whispering in their quiet room. Those days seemed the only ones in all his life during which he had really been alive. All the excitement, all the danger, all the risks were not so real as that had been. After the war, he told himself, after the war, I will search. I will find her… But that seemed infinitely remote, too vague a hope even to be satisfying. Meanwhile… he glanced down at the time, the height, the airspeed, the course. Everything jake. He took up *The Poisoned Orchid* and read on.

'Front-gunner to Captain,' came Sam Dollar's voice on the intercomm. 'Flak away on our starboard beam, Sir.'

'Somebody must be going in over the Dutch Coast,' Thornly was answering.

'Just about Terchelling I should say, sir,' Cookson chipped in.

'Sure it isn't the Northern Lights, Sam?' Nobby's voice, perky and sarcastic, piped up from the tail.

It was a standing joke how Sam, on one occasion, mistaking his left for his right, had reported the fires they had left burning over the target for the Northern Lights. Nobody, especially Nobby, ever missed the chance of pulling Sam's leg about it.

'Gee, won't I ever live that down,' he was heard to say, almost to himself.

'I suppose you often see the Northern Lights in your part of the world?' Thornly questioned him.

'Sure we see 'em, sir, two nights out of three in winter.'

'Must be a wonderful sight.'

'Sure is, sir.'

'I expect you're looking forward to getting back home.'

'You bet, sir.'

'What are you going to go in for?'

'Trapping, sir.'

'Can't you stop him sir?' came Nobby's voice again. 'I was reading an article in one of them American magazines. Trappers go balmy after a bit, it said, just through being alone. But as Sam's balmy already, why bother about trapping...?'

'Just wait till we get back, young Nobby.' Sam's voice sounded angry. Without knowing it he had almost hit the nail on the head. For the truth was that Sam had really come to the brink of madness, once, back home...

SAM DOLLAR

WHEN THE TRAPDOOR is lifted and the bull bolts out into the arena, he charges wildly around, rushes the swinging cloak of the matador, and after a little, baffled in all his attacks, takes up his position in one particular place. After every encounter, in each of which he is progressively weakened, he always returns to this same spot. It is no different from any other; but it has become a sort of home to him. It is called his terrain. He fights from it and, usually, dies in it.

This curious predilection for a bit of earth, in itself little different from any other bit, is not confined to bulls. Human beings have it too. Often the reason for their preference is every bit as obscure as the bull's choice of terrain; but be it the Mile End Road, the Island of Capri, the wastes of Greenland or the Gobi Desert, you will find human beings who regard each locality as essentially theirs. Take them away and they long to return to it; only then do they feel complete.

Sometimes, when others share their enthusiasm, they speak loudly of their affection for the chosen spot; at others, when they feel this would be misunderstood, they are silent. Sometimes, its hold on them is so great that it becomes almost holy, a wonderful secret, too perfect to share with the herd. Sometimes there is a feeling of jealousy: the place is theirs – they will share it with none. Yet all of them, if taxed, would be hard put to define what it is that beckons them from across the world, urging them imperiously and everlastingly to return. In other places, they know, they might be more comfortable, make money or a place in the world. But no, they must go back. And when the insistent logician demands his everlasting 'why?', they can only stammer, vaguely wave a hand: 'Oh, I don't know. You wouldn't understand: there's something about it.'

Sam Dollar had his terrain. To him it was so perfect that, being inarticulate anyway, he never spoke of it. It was a primeval stretch of forest and muskeg, of river, lake and swamp with no beginning and no end. Geographically it was situated towards the north-western border of Alberta, Canada; but Sam never thought of it as a place on the map. He could not have defined its limits or its size. He knew where you went in, and when you were in you just went on and on. When you came out, it was like leaving the world behind. In it he had known his only happiness. In it, too, he had known abject terror. In the end he had fled it, perhaps for ever. Yet in it he had lived, he had been free. Now exiled from it, he felt a lodger in the world, and waited and longed for the day when he could go back.

Ned Collins and his wife Molly, Sam's mother and father, had emigrated to Canada in the spring of 1914. Theirs was a runaway marriage, for Ned was a farmer's son and Molly had been brought up as a 'lady'. But as her father had worked his way up from clogs in the mills of Sheffield and as she was as determined as he was, she refused to allow his money and ambition to stop her marrying the man she wanted.

Besides Ned was no farm lout with fewer ideas in his head than the pigs he tended. There was something of the old yeoman stock of England in him, the freedom-loving tolerance and self-reliance of the eighteenth century. He knew what he wanted. It wasn't much. It was just Molly; just a comfortable home with some kids and comfort – and Molly; enough land to make a farm self-supporting, enough room to turn round, enough leisure to enjoy it – and Molly. It was a simple decent ambition; but he could never have realised it in England. So, one winter's night the two eloped, got married in London and took the first boat to Canada.

In those days, Edmonton, the capital of Alberta, was little more than a straggling makeshift of wooden shacks and barns, primitive lodgings, stores and drinking saloons, such as figure in Wild West pictures. In winter the sleds ran over the frozen roads, in spring the tracks were deep in mud, in summer the wagons sank up to their axles in fine dust that settled (like the flies) in clouds over everything. But, winter and summer, the town was a-bustle with life. The Grand Trunk Railway ran through it on its way West. Every train was packed with goods which were snatched up as soon as they were displayed in the stores. Ploughs, saws, axes, stoves, saucepans, rope, seeds, buckets, blankets, bright coloured shirts and corduroy breeches, whips, harness, shawls, guns, traps and boots – all that a thriving community of farming folk would buy. Wheelwrights, wagoners and blacksmiths plied their trades. There were markets for cattle, oxen, horses and pigs. Timber merchants were felling and dragging spruce to the mills and freighting it East in trainloads. There was work, work and still more work from dawn till dusk, work for all who came. The populace, rough, hearty and friendly thrived as the town expanded. The settlers, from England, Scotland, Germany, Sweden, Poland and the Ukraine, multiplied year by year. The lure of the good land brought them from the ends of the earth. The tracks grew into roads, the trails into tracks, and the surveyors out ahead, mapped the contours of the undeveloped land. They told tales of the fabulous riches of the north-west; of the endless miles of spruce forests; of trappers coming in with fortunes in pelts: mink, muskrat, beaver, ermine; of coal lying on the surface of the earth to be had for the trouble of shovelling it; of rivers stocked with trout and salmon; of land, land, and still more land, stretching away and away, unknown, unsurveyed...

'All ya gotta do is to get out, pick yer spot, settle and stake yer claim. Nobody'll ask questions. Take all ya want and when the government men come, show 'em what's yours. That's the way folk start in over here...'

The heavy wagon behind its team of four oxen jolted on slowly down the trail. The huge patient beasts had great pulling power but no speed. Ned and Molly walked beside the wagon or rode as they chose. Round the growing town the country was parkland. Farms stood in the clearings. Much of the earth was under plough and fresh with green corn. It was spring. Birches and poplars had burst into leaf. In the warm sunshine the odour of the good earth was heavy and sweet and sent the promise of life surging and tingling through the blood. Ned laughed and cracked his long whip. Molly, at his side, petted the oxen as they strained under the yokes and looked up at her with limpid eyes, fringed with lashes as long and curled as any chorus girl.

The trail first followed the railway, then headed out north-west. Some thirty miles on it came to an end. After that the country was wild, unexplored, unsurveyed. They would just go on until they found a spot that suited them. A high sense of adventure and promise filled both their hearts. They had broken away from the world they knew, they had taken the great gamble of life together, they were young and the unknown called to them. It was good to have life before you. It was good to be in love. It was good to be alive.

Once they left the railway, farmers, just settling in themselves, gave them hospitality and they talked after supper over the stove. It was farming talk, of crops to set, of ways to fell timber, to build cabins. It was talk of other men's success, the reward of labour, of hope in the riches of the earth. 'It's all good land, there's no two ways about it. Grub out the underbrush and fell the trees. Once you've got it under plough, goodbye to worry. You'll be set for life.'

One morning, waving their hosts of the night goodbye, Ned and Molly left the last farm behind them. Now none but trappers and wandering Indian tribes knew the country ahead. The world was theirs.

Ned usually went on ahead with a chopper to blaze the trail, while Molly followed with the team. The stillness of the morning was broken by their calls to each other, he bidding her hurry to view the next prospect, she chiding the oxen, summoning him to come back to help her with the wagon; but slowly, very slowly, they made their way deeper into the unknown. The country was more densely wooded now. Pine forests had taken the place of parklands, though there were still clearings where wild lilies raised scarlet heads or golden drifts of dandelions spangled the grass. It grew more hilly also, for they were approaching a divide and above they could see the crests of the hills. Now the timber was almost continuous; but here and there lakes shone in the sun, fringed with a sombre mantle of spruce, and streams chattered in the gulleys. The country had a wild grandeur, sharpened for them by the feeling that it was new, that no other eyes had ever beheld it, that, in a sense, it was theirs. It was peaceful too, with the peace of lonely places, and sometimes in the dusk, when they had made camp for the night, it seemed to

Molly that life was so rich and strange and different, it could not possibly be true. She reached for Ned's hand to be sure of the reality.

Once over the divide the going was easier. The prospect of forests stretched away below. Lakes could be seen in the folds of the woods. Far ahead was a wide valley that invited them. They trekked towards it but it took three days to reach the place. It was the bed of what once had been a huge glacial river. The greedy water had eaten down two hundred feet into the earth. Now at the bottom was a plain, miles across, and through this, curling among the woods that covered the valley floor, ran a stream. Traversing the steep slopes carefully, sometimes felling trees to make a trail over which the wagon could pass, they descended bit by bit and at last came down. The stream that they had seen from above was in fact a broad river (so deceptive was the scale of this great country), flowing steady and still between banks fringed with willow and poplar and backed by dark forests of pine. In a loop of the river they made camp that night. It was a perfect spot, sheltered from the winds, utterly secluded and peaceful, lost to the world. They stood together that evening in the twilight, looking down through a clearing over the water. A gaggle of geese came down. A fish jumped. A bird called. Ned and Molly looked at each other: they had reached journey's end.

For a year they did little or nothing towards developing the land. They were young. They had enough to go on with, so they spent the days exploring all the country round about, mapping out their claim and planning its development. 'Lonely River', as they called the place, grew in their minds. Meanwhile they lived on the game and fish with which the country abounded. They built a simple log cabin, a stable for the oxen and cleared enough land to plant vegetables. It was a spartan life, muscled with health and hope, immeasurably finer than anything they could have known back home. They no longer thought of it as exile. Ned was so happy that sometimes in the middle of digging in the clearing or felling a tree, he would pause and look up. Here all around him was a land richer than anything he had dreamed of, a prospect magnificent and simple and secure; here, only a few yards away, was Molly, whose love and courage had made it all possible. A feeling of elation, almost religious in its intensity, would flow through him, and he would throw down his axe, run back to the cabin, gather Molly into his arms and hold her to him as if she were life itself.

But once Ned did start in on the farm, the thing went ahead surprisingly quickly. The surveyors had been round and granted their claim; a 'section' as it was called, six hundred and forty acres, a square mile. It included all the low-lying ground in the bend of the river, together with some on the plateau above. They had already planned it all: now it was a question of opening it up, piece by piece. Indians, wandering through the country as they had done since time immemorial, helped in the clearing of the timber. They usually worked through the summer months and then moved on again in the autumn. For years the sound of axes rang through the woods. The straight trunks of spruce fell with a melancholy crash. Their heads were lopped off and their trunks stacked against the time when Ned would settle down to the building of the home he had promised himself.

Meanwhile he used to walk twenty-five miles every week to get mail and supplies. For long months in the winter, when the snow lay deep and the treacherous blizzards blew in a temperature of twenty below, the little cabin was completely isolated. Ned and Molly hibernated almost like animals, snug beneath a coverlet of snow. Then when the spring came back, the work would be renewed. Fields of grain appeared where the woods had been, orchards and meadows, barns and outhouses. To the clearing of the place, Ned brought English eyes, eyes attuned to quiet vistas, to memories of copse, thicket and lane. He refused to massacre the ground as other settlers had done, burning the forests wholesale to get the maximum acreage under plough. Lonely River must yield something more than a livelihood; it must yield beauty, seclusion and peace. Years later, when it was all developed, the visiting stranger would sense, almost without knowing how, the spirit of the Old Country in the warmth and welcome of the place. Ned and Molly, by labour and love, had made it so.

In six years the greater part of their dream had been realised. The fruit trees were coming into bearing, the meadows were maturing, the grain yielded, the homestead had been built. It stood on a rise looking down over the river from the spot where Ned and Molly had first seen it. The woods still stood round about, but beyond stretched the fresh pastures. It had been five years of tremendous labour. Labour carried through under difficulty owing to the Great War which was raging in Europe, but of which only rumours reached them from time to time when Ned trekked into Wabanum or Edmonton for stores and mail. Yet, during these years, the country went on being opened up. Soon there was a gravel track as far as Lake St Anne. The Catholic Mission started a hospital at Onoway. It was here that Molly was confined the year after they had settled and their first son, Michael, was born. Two years later Betty came. Molly always said that the worst part of the confinement was the trek back to the farm in the ox wagon. Three years later when she bore Sam, it proved only too true. It was spring and she was in a hurry to get home. She left the hospital too soon, the wagon got bogged on the trail and, in an effort to help Ned with the team, Molly overstrained herself, had a sudden haemorrhage and died.

This stark tragedy coming at a moment when they stood on the very threshold of accomplishment was a blow from which Ned never really recovered. He was tempted to sell out and go home, but Lonely River had been developed out of Molly's money and he felt, in a sense, that it was not his to sell. He was by nature punctilious and tenacious. As a boy he had lived a hard life, driven by his father, who for as long as he could remember had scraped and struggled to wrest a living from the reluctant earth. In these years of hope and dawning prosperity he had almost forgotten all that. Molly had freed him from the spectre of poverty. But now, in his extremity, this bitter schooling came back to him. By growing silent and bitter he sought to revenge himself on his fate. Life, which for a moment had been happy and carefree, reverted to its old pattern. There was no release, no ease. Even the children…

Michael and Betty were only five and three, Michael a sturdy youngster and Betty quite self-possessed and able to take care of herself; but Ned had no idea of how to look after them. Of course the neighbours rallied round, but they (Ned thought) were a damned nuisance. They patched and mended and made do, found fault, upset the routine of the house, fussed and worried, and did their best to marry him off again to cousins and daughters. After a year he could stand it no longer. When the Indians came by the next summer, he managed to get a couple to stay. The neighbours retired in disgust. 'Ned Collins has gone to live with Indians' went the gossip. But Ned was free again, free to get back to his old groove, free from having busybodies under his feet, free to call his home his own.

But, of course, he could do nothing about Sam. He handed the baby over to the Nuns and left him entirely in their hands. He was glad to do this because, beyond all reason, he could not escape the emotion that possessed him whenever he thought of the boy. Sam was responsible for Molly's death: that was the kernel of his thought. If Molly had not had him, she would never have gone to Onoway, never have come back in the wagon, never have strained herself, never have died... She would be alive, and the thought of her living again there, in the home they had built together, that was now so empty without her, drove Ned almost mad with grief. All this, in a way that was utterly unjust, utterly illogical, he transferred into a deep-seated antipathy for Sam, who was as innocent of it as any new-born babe could be. Nevertheless the feeling remained and festered as the years went by...

When, at the age of ten, Sam came home to Lonely River to live under his father's roof, he found himself, if not an outcast, at least not one of the family in the sense that Mike and Betty were. Though his father had visited him at the convent from time to time and had received good reports on his progress, Sam did not really know his father at all. In a way children do, he sensed that these visits were made from a sense of duty, not from affection, and he feared the big stern man.

'Now, son,' said his father, on his last visit before Sam came home, 'when you get back to the farm, you'll find plenty of work to do. We all do a job. Your brother Mike looks after all the machinery, the tractors the sawmill and the old gas engine and the car. Your sister milks and makes butter, what would you like to do?'

'Don't know,' said Sam, looking at the floor.

'Well, think. Would you like to learn to plough, or mind the cattle or look after the garden? You must do your share, son, like all of us.'

'Like to go hunting with the Indians,' ventured Sam, greatly daring.

His father laughed. 'Hunting!' he said scornfully. 'That's not work, my boy; that's play. That's what I do, what we all do, when we can get a day or two free. That's a holiday.'

'Sister's got a brother who comes to see her. He traps animals. Said I could go along with him sometime. He's got a rifle and a hunting knife. Sister says he's a bad man.'

'Why?'

'He drinks,' answered Sam.

His father laughed again. 'They all do, son. They all do.' His contempt for trappers was rooted in his farmer's upbringing. They were all poachers, living off the land and putting nothing back into it. He'd sooner the boy went to town and worked in a store. He looked at him, fidgeting there unhappily. If only Molly were with him. She would have known what to do. It was a long time since...

'How old are you now, son?'

'I'll be ten next April.'

Ten years. Ten years since she went. He never passed the spot on the trail without a tightening of the lips. Hell Corner, he called it. Ten years... He sighed and got up.

'Well, we shall have to see when you come home,' he said.

To bring up a brood of young children is never an easy business. Ned did his best; but all his hardness, his drive, his choler, things which had disappeared when he fell in love with Molly and had, he thought, been ironed out of his system for ever, now flared up with renewed fire. It is not good for a man to live alone. Ned's obstinate refusal to marry again, though it may have shown devotion to his dead wife, did not result in a happy household. True, his outbursts were not frequent. He was not an unjust man. It was more that he magnified small faults and failed to make due allowance for the high spirits and natural devilry of boys living a healthy, wild life, subject to none of the usual softening influences of the home.

Sam lived in perpetual disgrace, for he not only felt an interloper in the house, but he had no interest nor aptitude for a farmer's life. While he was still hardly big enough to hold a gun, he formed the habit of sneaking away to the Indians and it was they who taught him his first steps in hunting. In that part of the world settlers used firearms and traps as a matter of course, for the country was full of game. It was as natural to go out with a rifle and bag a partridge or prairie chicken for supper as it would be in England to go round to the shop and buy one. But Sam showed exceptional talent as a hunter. He was a clean shot, had a keen pair of eyes and the patience of a cat in stalking his quarry. Also he soon began to acquire, partly from the Indians and partly by observation, a wide knowledge of the haunts and habits of wild things. He knew the nesting-places of the duck; the trails of the coyote and the thickets where the moose came to grub roots in the winter time. He knew where the salmon fed and the beavers built their dams. He learned how to trap muskrat, patting down a little step of mud just below the surface of the water on the river's bank, setting the trap on it and hanging an inviting turnip on a twig above. The muskrat would come swimming by, smell the turnip and come up on to the step to nibble at it. Then, Wham!, the jaws of the trap snapped and you found it there next time you came round. But sometimes you did not, the rat having bitten through its own leg to get free...

All this Sam learned at the price of many hidings. When hunting he lost all idea of time. He would miss meals altogether, leave jobs unfinished, and forget to do things he had been told to do. Ned was a thorough and orderly-minded man. He did not like unpunctuality and could not brook disobedience. When he found that repeated thrashings had no effect, he tried reason. He explained that life was a serious business, that young men when they grew up had to have a job or a career, had to make money to live, had to leave home and start in on their own. But it was no good. As well explain to a born painter the virtue and necessity of becoming a shop-walker. Sam was contrite, promised obedience and did try to do what his father wanted, but then a fish would jump or a pheasant call and all his resolutions were forgotten.

Sometimes when he wrestled with the problem of what to do with the boy, Ned blamed himself, for when Sam had first come home he was really too young to work. He had let him run wild then, glad to have him off his hands. Sam had gravitated to the Indians, and once he had tasted the freedom of that life, it was too late to corral him again. Of course the situation did not grow impossible all at once. As a boy Sam was biddable enough; but as he grew into a youth, he became steadily more obstinate. When Ned forbade him to use his guns, he borrowed from the Indians; when he locked up his traps, Sam contrived them out of string or wire. He had learned to skin, slitting the pelt round the ankles and up the inside of the thighs and then drawing the whole up over the neck, like a glove, and stretching it on an outhouse wall with drawing-pins to dry – and smell. When his father tore the stinking things off the side of the house and flung them away, Sam picked them up and fastened them to the trunks of trees. The truth was that Ned had come up against a will just as strong as his own and it was therefore the more maddening to have people encourage him in it. When one day a fur buyer, travelling round the outlying districts, stopped off at Lonely River for a night's hospitality, made straight for Sam's skins, and, to make matters worse, actually bought a few from him, the fat was in the fire. Sam was enormously excited. 'There's a dollar bill waiting for every one you ketch, pal, so go to work!' Here was a man who understood him, who encouraged him, who didn't treat him as an outcast, half hobo, half poacher. He took the crinkly dollar bills to his father to keep for him. Ned looked at them.

'Where did you get that?'

Sam hesitated. He was proud of having 'earned' the money. This would show his father that it wasn't a waste of time going after animals. His father often talked about being hard up. Perhaps, he thought, this would help. He pointed outdoors to where the buyer was talking with Betty.

'That man gave it me.'

'What for?'

'F'r muskrat skins.'

'Damnation!'

Ned pushed past Sam, taking no notice of the bills in his hand, and strode outside.

'Don't you encourage my boy in bad habits by giving him money for worthless skins, d'ye hear?'

This sudden descent knocked the man back on his heels.

'Why, Mister Collins, I...'

Ned's face was red and the veins swelled in his neck. 'I won't have it, understand? You can ply your damned trade where you please; but not in my house.'

But the buyer was not to be intimidated. 'My trade's as honest as yours or anyone else's, Mister Collins. Skins have a market value. Why shouldn't the kid have the money? He's earned it.'

'I won't have it, that's all... and you'd better keep away from here.'

'Suits me, pal. Plenty of room without coming to your dump.' And he strolled over to his car and got in. 'Must be fine being one of your kids!' And with this parting shot, he pressed the starter and swung off down the trail. Ned glared after him and went into the house.

As the years went by the situation deteriorated, as such things will. Sam had built himself a log hut down by the river, out of sight of the house. He kept all his gear there, rods, rifle, traps and nets. He had acquired them all himself in the course of time. Traps and snares and fishing tackle he had bartered for skins. His dog Jumbo, a black retriever, was a gift from an Indian whose daughter he had saved from drowning. His rifle Betty had given him for a birthday present. She was fond of her brother and pitied him. When he had been younger, it was she who had brought food to his room when all the house was asleep, long after he had been sent to bed supper-less and in disgrace.

Sam was only happy among all these things, happiest of all with Jumbo, the only living creature that really understood and loved him. He had trained the dog himself, trained him to retrieve until he could bring back an egg in his jaws without breaking it. The two were inseparable. Both were fanatical hunters and when they were out

77

together after game, seemed almost to know each other's thoughts and to work together in perfect harmony by a kind of telepathy which won the respect of those born hunters, the Indians themselves. Jumbo allowed nobody to come near his master. At night he slept at the foot of his bed and by day never left his heels.

By the time he was eighteen, Sam and his father hardly spoke. Then, in that year – it was 1938 – several things happened. One day, enraged over some small thing, Ned called Sam and told him that he'd kept him long enough, that he was useless and worthless and that he had better get out into the world and fend for himself. Next, Betty announced her intention of getting married. Her boy was the son of a prosperous store owner in Edmonton. Evidently Ned approved of the match for he took his daughter into Edmonton quite a lot and left the management of the Lonely River to Mike. It was unlike him to be away from home. Besides he was unusually even-tempered, and that was unlike him too. Sam gave little thought to it at the time. He was no happier round the farm when his father was away, for Mike and he did not get on.

Ned's eldest son had inherited his father's farming instincts. He was quiet and regular and law-abiding. Secretly he rather admired Sam's independence, but he knew he was not cut out for that kind of life. Ned had promised to build him a house on Lonely River when he got married. Someday he would inherit the farm. The prospect pleased him. But he was in no hurry. He was patronising and condescending to Sam, the bad lot, the useless mouth to feed; but he was frightened of him too, frightened of his silences and his temper; he would be quite glad to see him out of the way. Both boys went in dread of their father, but while Mike respected him, Sam, lonely and bitter through all his childhood, because of the grudge his father bore him (the reason for which he never knew), simply hated him. He felt that, if the chance came, his father would give him no pity, no pardon. But, though Sam's will was hard, he was still young and he feared the blackness of his father's anger. Now that he knew he must leave home, he was glad. It had never occurred to him to go before. But now it seemed the obvious thing. But what was he to do?

His instinct was always towards the unexplored regions in the north-west, so, one summer morning, leaving Jumbo in Betty's care, he hit the trail, jumped a freight train and rode out like a hobo to the end of the 'steel' at Whitecourt. This little settlement was in much the same state, on a smaller scale, as Edmonton had been when Ned and Molly arrived there twenty years before. It was the end of civilisation. Beyond it the country was unsurveyed. It stretched away north and west to the boundaries of British Columbia and beyond. Whitecourt was just a cluster of log cabins and saw mills and stores and saloons; but, like Edmonton in the old days, there was work for all who wanted it. Arrived there Sam wandered around, and, attracted by the sound of a saw, walked over to watch it at work. There was something grand about the bite of the teeth on the huge trunk as it moved along on its cradles, something clean and wholesome about the smell of the resinous wood, something triumphant about the fountain of sawdust that rose in the air. Sam watched it, fascinated.

'Lookin' for work, kid?' said a voice at his side. He turned to look into the red face of a man in a check shirt and a battered hat, covered all over with sawdust, as if it had snowed on him.

'Sure,' said Sam.

'Got a raft of logs up river. Want a man to pole it down. Pay ya three bucks a day. Take ya three days. How's about it?'

'Suits me,' said Sam.

'Fine! Ed'll run ya up in the canoe. All ya gotta do is cast her off and ride the raft downstream. Easy! A kid could do it – only I ain't got no kids, see.' He laughed and started to turn away. 'Okay, kid. Be here six o'clock tomorrer morning.'

'Okay,' said Sam and moved on.

Whitecourt lies on the great Athabaska river and back beyond it many tributaries flow into the main stream. The country is thick with standing timber. When this has been felled on the hillsides, the logs are rolled into big water-filled gutters, carefully engineered and graded and, slithering downhill, at last shoot out, like torpedoes, into a pool by the river's edge. Sam watched them, as the canoe slid upstream under its little outboard motor, watched them elbowing their way down with a swift silent motion which increased as the log gathered speed for its final run, watched the glorious leap as it left the trough, the huge fan of foam as it struck the water.

'Sho' wouldn't stop to argify with one of them debbils on de way down. No, sir,' volunteered Ed, as he sat with the tiller of the motor under his arm. He grinned and showed white teeth in a chocolate face.

'Sure is a fine sight though, isn't it?' said Sam.

He loved the river and the wildness of the country and would have been happy to go purring up along it all day. But just then, Ed cut the motor and turned the canoe into a backwater. Here lay the raft, a frame of trunks fastened end to end with chains and spikes, and within this pen, hundreds of logs packed tight together so you could walk on them.

'Here she is, kid. Yo jest casts her adrift, poles her out into de stream and sets down to smoke yo pipe till you reach de mill. Den you whistles for me, ah throws out de line, we hauls her in and dat's anudder good job done.'

Sam jumped ashore with a bag of food and a blanket. Ed, without more ado, pushed off. 'S'long, sunshine,' he grinned, spun the little motor and slid off downstream.

Sam dumped his gear in a shed nearby, examined the raft and its moorings and then looked out over the river. It was broad and stately, moving like music between the pine-covered hills. At intervals where smaller streams flowed in were secondary valleys, clearings with clumps of birch or poplar and stretches of meadow grass. He sniffed the air. It looked good country. It was too late to start back that day. Why not explore?

He set off along the river's edge. After a couple of miles he came to a stream which slid away to one side through an inviting valley. The forests stood back a little, as if to give it sun. Grass sloped gently up from the water's edge. There were big clumps of kingcups in the swampy patches, clumps of underbrush, of willow and briar. Some distance along it, a solitary pine, whose roots had been half torn out in a winter gale, leant over the water. The afternoon sunlight poured into the place, butterflies hovered over the grass. There was a continuous murmur of insects on the wing. A wild pigeon went clapping over the tree-tops.

'Gee, what a peach of a place!' thought Sam.

He followed on up the valley in the shade of the timber. It was very hot. Soon the trees crowded up to the water. There was a deep shadowy pool. At its far end the sound of a waterfall. When he came to it, he found a narrow gulley between rocks, overhung with trees, where the falling water boiled between boulders and mushroomed out over their tops. He waded in, clambered and struggled up these rapids to see sunlight through the trunks beyond. At last he emerged, his breeches soaking and his boots squelching at every step, to find himself on the shore of a reed-fringed lake. The blue water stretched away for a mile, framed in golden sedge. A breeze rippled the surface. From the reeds came cries of wildfowl. When Sam fired a shot at random, clouds of mallard rose, calling, and circled up and away on their scimitar wings. Then, gradually they settled again in bays out of sight. To one side this lake seemed to reach away to low ground where willows fringed its shores, but to the other the hills rose sharply and the dark drooping pines, rank on rank, stood like a million barbed arrows against the sky. Sam, always drawn to the uplands, skirted the lake, turned up into the dim woods and began to climb. Soon he could see the water below between the trunks, like a shining blue eye. Swamp and muskeg lay beyond it, then in the far distance the purple hills began. Above him the wind sighed in the pine tops. The going was cool in the shade. After he had climbed for some distance the trees thinned and he came out into a magnificent natural amphitheatre, where four valleys met. When the snow melted in the spring, there would be a fierce torrent here. Now all was dry, bedded in tall grasses and wildflowers.

Sam stood marvelling at this place he had found. Above him, high and higher, rose the pine-clad hills, fold upon fold woven in upon each other by light and shade in blues and greens. Nearer and below were the valley fingers, which he could trace by the run of the trees, curving away to right and left, holding their silent secrets. Nearer and lower still were their mouths, with jagged granite teeth and a spew of boulders tumbling down over grey scree. Here, in the centre of it all he stood on a rock, the only man perhaps who had ever looked on all this, the discoverer, the emperor of it all!

There in the timber above, the wolves would run in the wintertime. Moose and deer would come into this hollow for shelter. There would be marten and ermine too, muskrat in the river below and beaver...

Already he was planning where he would run a line of traps, where he would build a cabin, what he would need, how he could porter the stuff up river and bring a light sled in the boat, or maybe if the river was frozen, get almost up to the waterfall by car over the ice... He sat there in the sun, drying his moccasins, leaning on his gun, feasting his eyes on the wonderful secret place he had found. It was his. He was part of it. Like a lover he had fallen in love with it at first sight. He had found his terrain.

It would be easy to represent Sam simply as a boy who, through no fault of his own, had been given a raw deal; to draw him as a misunderstood and unhappy child, forced into solitude and misery through the cruelty of his father. In fairy tales things are as simple as this. But in life action and reaction are equal and opposite, though usually different in kind. To his father, Sam was a living reminder of his wife's death, an unwanted burden, to be got rid of and forgotten as soon as possible. Sam's answer was an obstinate independence, a feeling that the whole world was against him. He would have to fend for himself and, since he had been treated badly, he was at liberty to treat others badly. All that his father had acquired to make life secure was denied him. Very well, he would make himself secure, and since he was young and alone, he could not be particular as to methods. He had been shut out of the society of the family, therefore he was himself against all society. He feared it, but he would outwit it if he could. A boy turned loose on the world had to think of number one... He did not use these arguments, nor indeed reason about it at all. It had become second nature, the working of the subconscious, and was now character, which could only be changed by some fortunate influence in life, and then it would be a tedious business.

Sam wanted (as he had never wanted anything), to set up as

a trapper in this corner of the backwoods he had found. But that meant money. Not much money, but enough to buy necessities: food, a stove, an axe and suchlike things. But where was this money to come from? From his father; but, of course, his father would not give it him. Very well then, he would take it. He did not look on it as stealing. His father had promised to look after Mike, to give him a house, to leave him all his property; why should it all go to his brother? Why should he not have his share? If his father would not do him justice, he would be himself the instrument of justice. He would pay it all back, someday... So his mind worked, tentatively at first, then quickly and urgently. He would return to Lonely River and, somehow or other, get hold of the bundle of notes his father always kept in a cupboard ready for incidental expenses or emergencies. The loss would probably never be noticed. If it was, well he would be away by then, and anyone who came after him would have to search pretty well before they found his hideout...

He had no exact plan as to how he would go about it. The house was often empty. There would be plenty of opportunities. He could return, as indeed he must, to get his gear. Then he would take what he wanted and disappear. It was really quite simple. It was typical that it never occurred to him to wait, to work steadily for a year or two and save the money he wanted. That was the social way, the honest plodding way, the way of fools. None of that for him. He would be revenged on his own father, take a penny from the pound that should have been his. Like all selfish people, he had a highly developed sense of justice when he felt life was unjust to him.

He arrived at Lonely River late one afternoon. The house seemed deserted. He whistled and called Jumbo, expecting to see the dog come bounding down the trail. But there was no sign of him. When he reached the house, he saw Mike in his shirt sleeves coming from the byre. 'Hullo, Mike!' he called.

Mike stopped and looked at him as if he were a stranger. Sam came up.

'You sure look pleased to see me, Mike.'

'I'm not,' Mike said shortly. 'What have you come back for?'

'To get my stuff. I shan't be staying long. Cheer up, fellah. This is the last you'll see of me.' His tone was ironic.

'Got a job, have you?'

'Sure I've got a job. Damn sight better than any I ever had round here. Where Sis?'

'Gone to town.'

'And father?'

'Gone with her. He'll be back for supper.'

'I'll be gone long before then. Be too bad if I met my own father wouldn't it?' He laughed shortly. 'Where's Jumbo? I'll be taking him off your hands too.'

'You don't need to worry about him.'

'Why not? Have you adopted him, or somethin'?' The idea of Jumbo changing masters made Sam smile.

'No. I haven't adopted him. I've shot him.'

For a moment Sam couldn't believe his ears. He felt the blood rush hot to his throat. 'You've – what?' he managed to say.

'Shot him. Lousy cur killed three chicken, started worrying the calves, so I –'

He never finished the sentence for Sam hit him with all the force and fury that years of jealousy could muster. Mike recoiled under the blow which had caught him off guard and Sam came at him like the embodiment of rage. He was shouting at him, shouting all the filthy words that came to his tongue; but he did not know what he said. He was mad, possessed. He leapt at Mike as his brother stumbled backwards, got his hands round his throat and bore him to the ground. Mike struggled and tried to fight back, but Sam was above him, beating his head on the ground, beating the life out of him, beating him silly, beating him dead… Suddenly his brother's struggles stopped. After kneeling on him, still mad, hating him for giving up so soon, before he, Sam, could beat him to pulp, he let go, got up and looked at him on the ground, lying there stupid and senseless as he was, dusted his hands, shook back his hair and went into the house.

'Wonder if I've killed him,' he thought. 'So what?' another part of his brain answered. He would be out of the way before anyone came back. Anyway it was revenge on the world that was always against him. He went to the place where his father's money was kept, opened it, found a bundle of notes and stuffed it in his pocket. There! That was all he wanted. They were cheaply rid of him.

When he came out of the house, Mike hadn't moved. Sam looked at him casually, feeling nothing, then hurried away down to his hut. Quickly he collected traps, nets, a blanket, his winter mitts, cap and other necessary gear. Then he set off again. Before dark he was riding the steel back to Whitecourt.

All through the rest of that summer and the autumn, Sam worked up in his secret valley above Blue Eye (as he called his lake) preparing for the winter. He cut timber sufficient to make him a small cabin at either end of the line of traps he had planned. These cabins were little more than huts, six feet wide and ten feet long with a roof of saplings covered with earth and pine bough thatch; but there was a deal of work in the making of them. The logs had to be cut, dressed and squared at the ends, the chinks had to be plugged against draughts, there had to be a shelf for stores, a hole for the stove pipe, a rough table, stool and some sort of a bunk. Before winter set in they were both done. Sam was very proud of them. They were artfully placed out of the wind and in the sun. They were snug. They were lonely. They were home.

During those months he made several trips to Whitecourt for supplies. He managed to get a lift downstream with the lumberjacks and returned with them, loading the canoes with as much gear as they had room for. All this he stored in a cache at the mouth of the valley where 'his' country began, and then, trip by trip, he portered it all up through the rapids, past the lake, high into the secret valley. Before the first cold snap and the first light fall of snow, everything was jake.

With the coming of winter the whole character of the country changed. Browns, greys and greens disappeared. It was all black and white, burnished with sunlight and backed by a flawless panel of blue. Clumps of underbrush, boulders and all the smaller configurations of the place were hidden or smoothed out. Snow drifts gave every turn in the trail a new aspect, strange, silent and serene.

Sam was out all day, surveying the territory over which he would work. Now, in the snow, it was far easier to find the game trails. The wild did not wander haphazard over the country, they had their highways and byways as we had paths and roads, leading from feeding ground to nest or burrow; they had, like birds, their territories, worked within them, owned them and defended them against intruders. All this, for a hunter, was written in the snow, and Sam, with his quick eye, noted where the deer had been feeding, where the coyotes had passed, where the partridge had been after berries and the marten had come galloping by.

With all this in his mind he began to lay his trap-line. About eight miles separated the two cabins. Sam planned to cover the distance once each day, sleeping a night at each hut alternately. Eight miles, over hilly country, carrying traps and sometimes game, was a day's march, when the day was short and the temperature below zero. But the place was a trapper's paradise. It was unspoiled. It had never been hunted over. Sam was kept busy all day and well into the night, skinning, cleaning and drying his pelts, mending and patching his clothes, cooking and cutting firewood for the stoves. It was a grand life.

He was seldom lonely. True he had formed a habit of talking to trees and hills and wild creatures as if they understood. Indeed in some queer way he could hardly define, they did seem to respond. The forests had their spirits of good and evil. Trees were alive, some friendly and benign, others sinister and evil. So Sam peopled his solitude. As the months went by his moments of longing after his fellow men, to see a face or hear a voice, grew less and less. Before the turn of the year the very idea of going back to civilised life repelled him. Men spread over the world like scum, soiling its perfection. His world was hard and cruel; but a man could respect its truth. Not like that lying human world which clung together like cattle and had always been against him...

Nevertheless after three months he had to make a trip back to Whitecourt. His axe had split, he was out of matches and candles – and he had two big bales of pelts to sell. So, piling these on to his sled, he set off down to the frozen river. Two days later he trudged into Whitecourt after dark.

'Hiya, Sam!' called Ed, when he came into the Saloon. The place was hot and crowded. Sam saw Ed's raised hand and grinning teeth across the room and went over to his corner.

'How do, Ed,' he said. 'How's things?'

'Fine. How's things with you?'

'Fine.'

Ed turned to a man sitting opposite him whose back was towards Sam.

'Didn't Ah prognosticate dat ole Sam'd blow in bye an bye?'

Sam turned to find Mike looking up at him.

'Hallo, Sam,' he said, in a quiet even voice. 'I'm not dead like you hoped.'

Sam felt the anger mounting in him again. 'Ain't nuthin' to me if you're live or dead. I'd bait traps with your carcase soon as look at you, see?'

Ed was enjoying the situation. 'Sounds like yo' bes' friend, Sam,' he laughed.

'It's my bloody brother, Ed – and I'm 'shamed to have him sitting here.'

'Well! what do you know?' exclaimed Ed, softly. 'What do you know?'

'You'd best get out of here, before I throw you out.' Sam was glaring down at him.

Mike smiled at his brother and slowly shook his head. 'Sit down, Sam. Things have happened. I've got things to tell you.'

'You can't tell me nuthin' I want to hear.'

'I gotta message from father for you. He's in trouble.'

'So what? He's made trouble for me often enough.'

'This is different trouble – he's getting married.'

Ed, who had been standing by, popeyed, guffawed with sudden laughter.

'Scram outa here, Ed.' Sam turned on him. 'Leave me to fix this bastard.'

'Okay. Okay.' Ed was apologetic. He went over to the bar.

Sam slid into the seat opposite his brother.

A slow sarcastic smile got no further than his eyes. He was looking at Mike for the first time without anger. 'Getting married, is he? That's swell!'

'It sure is, Sam. He's kinda younger – and different. Guess it ain't good for a man to live alone. Makes him kinda sore. He feels bad about you, kid.'

'You don't say!'

'That's why I came along.'

'Thanks for nuthin'. Who told you I was up this way?'

'Nobody. Betty told me when you first went off you aimed to head for Whitecourt, so when Dad began to worry and wanted to do the right thing by you, I just came along on the off chance. I figured somebody'd know you round this way.'

'I don't need nobody to do the right thing by me. I do the right thing by myself, see?'

'I know that, kid. I know you've had all the tough breaks and I don't blame you. I only came to tell you the old man feels bad about you. He gave me this to give you, in case you was – stuck.' Mike handed over a fat envelope. Sam took it. 'Five hundred bucks,' he said. He looked at the roll of notes and smiled.

'Thanks, Mike. I'll take it. It's my money. See?'

'Sure I see.'

'Okay. Now take it back. It's just about what I stole from the house that day. I reckoned it'd take me a coupla years to square it. Now it's fixed.'

Sam flung the envelope on the table. Mike shrugged, picked it up and put it back in his pocket. Sam got up. 'Now I'm square, see? I don't owe nobody nuthin' – and you can all go to hell.'

Mike got up too and faced him. 'You always were a mean little runt, Sam. You never did a hand's turn for the home you lived in and the grub you ate. I don't wonder father thrashed hell outa you. But he let you go your own way, didn't he? You never did anything but please your damn self. You're selfish as hell.'

Sam stood there, taken aback, glaring at him. Mike went on: 'Course I know it's been tough. Well, it's been tough for the old man too. He told me why you and he got off on the wrong foot. It was his fault – and he owns it. I reckon that's pretty swell of him. Now he wants to let bygones be bygones. He's in trouble about you, kid. He feels bad about you, like I said. I told him I was going to come out and get you. Know what he said? "You haven't got a hope, son. He'll bump you off and then we'll have to hang him." He was laughing, of course. He don't expect you to come back. He don't think you've got it in you. But I do. That's why I came. So quit talking like a small town big shot and be yourself.'

Sam was looking at the floor. 'Why did father say we got off on the wrong foot?' he said at last.

'Sit down, kid, and I'll tell you. What about us having a drink?'

Pride and obstinacy usually go hand in hand. It was a mixture of the two that made Sam take his brother with him next day back along the trail up country. It was pride that had made him agree to go back to Lonely River. He was not going to be meaner than his father and his brother. If they were going to be big, well, he could be big too. Moreover, since he had been up alone in the forests, he had grown up. He had proved he could live his own life and earn his own keep. The fat roll of bills he had got by the sale of his pelts, showed it. He could stand on his own feet. It was pride too that brought him round to the idea of forgiving his own father. It didn't occur to him that his father had much to forgive. Mike had told him the story of his mother's death and the way his father had felt. That clinched it for Sam. He was not to blame, never had been to blame. Now, he would be magnanimous, he would forgive the old man. He saw himself waving away his father's apologies, telling him to forget it. It made him feel good.

It was pride too that made him take Mike along with him. He had worried a bit about the way he had left him that day when he had stolen the money. He was mad at him, of course; but the idea of having actually killed his own brother had preyed on his mind. Of course if it had happened, he was not to blame. He had been provoked. His dog had been shot. All the same, he was glad Mike had been no more than stunned. But he certainly wasn't going to let Mike patronise him. No, Sir. Now he would show him, show him the way he worked, Show him the country he had found, initiate him into this trapping that, following his father's lead, Mike had always despised. He would respect him then.

So his mind worked as they trudged through the snow. He would do what they wanted, but he would do it in his own time in his own way. That was where the obstinacy came in. He could just as well have gone straight back with Mike; but no. He had left a line of traps up there. He must go through the line, put everything shipshape, get all his gear back into the huts, tidy up, before he left it to go back home.

Mike had fallen in with the idea willingly enough. He was pleasant and easy-going by nature. When Sam agreed to come home, his heart warmed towards his brother. He was all right, after all. Besides he liked to hunt now and then. It was good fun, for a bit. They would only be up there a couple of days. He took off his cap and jacket: it was hot in the sun. There had been a cold snap, but now the temperature had risen. He could hardly believe it was mid-winter.

By the waterfall that ran out of Blue Eye, Sam had built himself a cache. It was a sort of half-way house. Sometimes when Ed brought him up stores in the canoe, he left them there in the cache, so that Sam need not come right down to the river for them. Here the boys stopped at midday for a cup of tea and some biscuits. To lighten the sled before starting the climb, Sam unloaded a few stores, tins of meat and cocoa and other things and left them in the cache. When he came back he could take them on up and make two journeys with half the load.

'You know what we'll do,' he said to his brother as they boiled up the melted snow to make tea. 'Tomorrow we'll go over the line. You can come half-way and then go back with the traps and anything we get. If you follow our own trail you won't be lost. I'll go on and pick up the rest and park it in the other cabin. It'll take us pretty near all day to do that, so you can sleep this end and I'll stay at the other. You'll be okay on your own?'

'Sure,' said Mike. 'Got any blankets?'

'Yep. Blankets on the bunk. It'll be better to do it that way, so we can each have a bunk. Isn't room for two bunks in one cabin. I don't figure to have visitors in the usual way.' He smiled and brewed the tea in the cups, then he went on: 'Yep. That's the way. Then next morning, I'll come back over and pick you up and we'll start down together.'

'Swell,' said Mike. He sipped the hot tea and looked down the little valley the way they had come. 'Certainly is swell country up here.'

'This is nuthin'. Sam was proud. 'Wait till we get on above Blue Eye.'

It was about a couple of hours after the boys had separated half-way along the trap-line that the snow began to fall. Clouds had come up during the night and the weather was warm, as it often is before snow. It didn't look bad and there wasn't much wind. Mike had loaded up the sled and started back, and Sam, moving off along the trail, had turned and waved to his brother as he went round the bend of the valley. 'See you tomorrow,' he called. Mike had waved his hand in reply and Sam had turned to carry on. He wanted to get all the traps up before the snow buried them.

But when it started to snow steadily and the wind rose, Sam didn't like the look of it. The great blizzards that sweep down from Alaska are not things to get caught in. Every year people do get caught and those that lose their way or fail to find shelter are buried and not found till next spring. The driving snow quickly obliterates all landmarks. Men can and do get lost a hundred yards from their own back yards.

So Sam gave up the idea of getting in the rest of his traps and hurried on to the hut. Luckily it lay in the shelter of the woods and, knowing every inch of the country, he managed to fight his way along, leaning against the wind, almost bent double. At last, sweating with the effort, he got to the door of the hut, and slammed it behind him. It was a relief to be in. He shook the snow from his clothes, stamped his feet and started the stove going. He listened to the wind outside, It was howling now. The snow flew past in white whip lashes. The temperature dropped. Night was coming down.

The gale increased.

Sam, safe in the little hut, cooking his supper over the roaring stove, wondered how Mike was getting on his end. He hoped he would be all right. He knew they were in for at least three days of this. He liked it, liked the feeling of snug security, alone in there, with plenty to eat and keep warm with and nothing to do. To pass the time, he mended some traps, darned some stockings and made himself a fur cap. The blizzard howled outside. He knew that the cabin would be buried by now. The snow melted on the chimney and fell sizzling on to the stove top. He made up the fire, wrapped himself in his blankets and slept. He woke, made up the fire, ate and slept again. So the days passed. On the fourth morning, the blizzard blew itself out. The wind dropped to a dead calm. Sunlight flooded the earth. Sam came out of the hut into an enchanted world.

Nothing looks so pure and lovely as a wooded landscape after snow. Sam stood at the door and gazed. After the roar of the storm, the stillness left his ears staring. As a man might stare into darkness, so his ears now strained to hear something, anything, that would make the exquisite picture real. But he heard only a low singing in his own ears, then the sound of his breathing, as if he were the only living thing in a new world. He leaned against the door and the sudden creak of the hinge seemed as if it could have been heard miles away. The curve of the valley receded through the pines. All the trees seemed to be listening, like him, to the magical silence. Nothing moved. The landscape seemed arrested, eternal.

It was some time before he awoke out of his trance to the mundane things that must be done. He cut steps up on to the snow level which was higher than his waist. He got the fire going, brewed some tea and fried some venison. Then, having cleared everything up, pulled on his mitts, his jacket and cap, he wedged the door to, put on his snowshoes and set out along the trail to meet Mike, who would probably have started out from the other end to meet him. The snow was deep and soft and the going heavy. New drifts had quite altered the contours of the valley. In certain places it was hard to find the trail. At each turn he expected to see Mike in the distance coming towards him. He stopped and let out a piercing yell to let him know he was on his way. It echoed away over the treetops. He waited for an answer. None came. He called again. His voice sounded tremendous in the stillness. He went on, then stopped and shouted again. It was a sort of bravado to wake the sleeping spirits of the place. His voice was, after all, so small against the vast silence that came lapping back over the echoes as if crushing the sound into silence. He set off again labouring in the hot sun, screwing up his eyes against the glare of the snow. At last he came in sight of the hut and stopped.

It was sunk almost up to the eaves in a snowdrift and looked somehow lost there in the shadow of the pines. No curl of blue smoke came from the stove-pipe. The door was shut. No tracks led away from it. Curious. Perhaps Mike was still asleep. But surely he would have the stove going? It was too cold to be without a fire. He shouted loudly: 'Mike!' But there was no answer. Anxious suddenly, he quickened his pace and came running, sliding down the slope towards the hut.

Outside the door he called again: 'Mike!' But there was something about the silence that followed. It was the dead silence of a deserted place. Sam, working frenziedly now, dug away the snow before the door with his hands and at last got it open. He looked inside, knowing he would see what he did see. The hut was empty.

He stood there, looking round the little place, breathing heavily from his exertions. There was a pile of wood by the stove. Untouched. A blanket lay half off the bed, stiff and frozen. Snow had silted through the chinks of the logs and lay in a crystalline dust over everything. The remains of their last meal four days ago still stood on the table.

The inescapable truth was there. Mike had never returned to the hut. Inevitably he must have missed the trail, been caught in the blizzard and now be lying somewhere under that dazzling white carpet outside. Dead. Frozen. Sam knew all this with one part of his mind; but he could not realise it. There had been plenty of time to get back, plenty of time. He had made the other hut with much further to go. True the timber was thicker here, but the trail was plain. He couldn't have lost his way. Yet he must have. Must have.

So Sam stood there in the doorway, numbed by his thoughts. He remembered how a few winters before he had been out hunting with the Indians in the woods quite near home and got lost as dusk fell. It was queer how quickly you could lose your bearings in the timber. He had called and called. Nobody had answered. He fired off his gun and went on firing it at intervals, and walked and walked and called and called; but it wasn't for two hours, after night had fallen and he was getting desperate, that the others found him. Mike must have got lost like that, wandered, got in a panic just as he had done, fired his gun, and then been overtaken by the blizzard and fallen exhausted to freeze to death there in the snow.

Still he couldn't believe it. He looked round over the slopes behind him. They were smooth and even and perfect. There was no hump, no small mound which might have made the outline of Mike's huddled body. He was dead. There was no escaping that. And, in a sense, he, Sam, had killed him. That was a ridiculous way to look at it and yet... Suddenly he remembered how Mike had told him of his father's joke: 'He'll probably bump you off and then we'll have to hang him.' Who could prove that he hadn't? Who could prove what happened up here in the silence of the forests? Ed had heard their quarrel, heard how he had spoken to Mike. He could swear that when they last met it was not as friends...

Those who live alone in the desolate wastes of timber and snow, cut off from the world and the ways of men, grow very queer in their minds. You see them sometimes when they come into the settlements with their furs, strange men with a glint in the eye, a half-crazy laugh, almost subhuman and yet somehow pathetic in the courage with which they wrest a living from the jaws of winter. They are 'touched' men; men gone mad with loneliness, dazed by the beckoning spirit of the snows and the timber. Yet they cannot live again the life of mankind. They are set apart, not of the herd, and must return in spite of themselves to the life that will destroy them. Most of them die at last, in some mishap or other, as Mike had died. Nobody mourns them. But their spirits haunt the wild, haunt the deserted cabins, haunt the sombre turns in the trail as if waiting for the others to join their scrawny company...

Sam, as he stood there in the doorway, his mind working fast, playing with the thought of the murder that could be charged against him, was suddenly aware of them. He could feel them, these glitter-eyed zanies, watching him and waiting. A prickle of terror ran down his spine. He turned and ran out from the shadow into the sun.

There he stopped again, looked all round, quickly, furtively. Thoughts bulged and burst in his mind. He must escape, he must get away. 'They' would be after him. But he would elude them, defeat them, go where they could not follow, trick them. He had his gun. He had money. He would go. Now. At once. Not to Whitecourt, not anywhere he was known. No, he would cross the hills, make a detour, jump a freighter, go with it to Edmonton, then on East, right out of the country, where 'they' would not follow, where 'they' could not get him, where he would be safe.

There in the sun, in the ineffable silence and serenity of the snow-draped forests, he felt icy hands stretching out to him, closing round him, crouched and stealthy as a snow leopard crouches to spring. He heard imaginary laughter behind him, he saw things moving between the trees. The very silence was ominous. Things were creeping up on him, netting him round with invisible cords, hypnotising him. He would be caught, petrified, entombed. No! No! Suddenly, he started to run.

He ran, stumbling with haste, back along his own tracks, turned off to make a detour, to go by no way he had ever been, over the hills, down to the river. There he would wait till night came. He would bypass Whitecourt. Mustn't be seen – mustn't be seen. Then jump a freighter. Yes, that was it. His mind worked as he ran. He looked furtively to right and left. He ran, in a sweat of horror, to escape the icy hands that stretched out after him, that were going to get him, there, even in the sunlight, in the full light of day. Men went mad in the forests. Oh, yes, they went mad from the faces in the tree trunks, from the clawing fingers of the pine twigs that scratched at his face as he ran ducking under the boughs, from the sudden chutes of snow that fell, sliding, silent, swooping down from the branches just behind him. They went mad from the sudden cracks of snapped branches, from the silence, the awful pouncing silence that you must not stop and listen to, because if you did they would get you, as they had got poor Mike. Mike was now one of them! Mike was after him too! Sam ran, on and on, a crazy figure in the grip of terror...

It was true that Mike was after him; but he was far from dead. He had reached the cabin well before the blizzard started, chucked the traps against the wall (where the snow had buried them later), and set off with the pelts down to the cache by the waterfall. By doing this they would have less load when they made their trip down together next morning. Also he could bring up the rest of Sam's stores. There was plenty of time before nightfall. But when the snowfall began and the wind rose, he gave up the idea at once. He knew the danger of the blizzards too well and returned to the cache, snugged down with the little stove and managed to make himself quite comfortable till the storm went by. Then he turned out and began his climb back up to meet Sam.

When he got to the hut and found no trace of him beyond the tracks that came in, went back on themselves and then doubled away over the hills, he could not understand it. He went back into the hut, looked to see if Sam had left any sign. But the place was untouched. Sam had never set foot across the threshold.

He called once or twice; but there was no answer, so he returned to the hut, got the stove going, unpacked the stores, and prepared to cook a meal for both of them. Sam must have gone out on another line; he would be back later. But when night fell and he had not returned, Mike grew anxious. He went out into the night and called again. There was no answer. He left a lantern burning outside the door and, after waiting till it was late, dozed off to sleep. Next morning he started out to follow Sam's trail. He followed it all day and the next till it dropped down towards Whitecourt. But when he got there and enquired there was no sign of Sam. Nobody had set eyes on him. Nobody around those parts ever set eyes on him again.

At last Mike returned to Lonely River and told his story. It was a mystery. Ned shook his head when he had heard him out. 'The boy was a bit touched, if you ask me, son. We'd best forget it.'

Afterwards Sam could never clearly remember what he had done. It wasn't till he reached Edmonton and took a ticket East that he came to himself. He was still haunted by the idea that the police would be after him, that he would find a notice in the paper that a man answering to his description was 'wanted'. He bought the papers on the train next morning and went through them carefully. There was nothing about him. The headlines blazed with the declaration of war. A stranger leant over to him. 'Travellin' in to join up, pal?' he asked. Sam thought quickly. That was as good excuse as any other.

'Yep,' he said.

'Shake,' said the stranger. 'So 'm I.'

There were others on the train doing the same thing. They were all young men. Soon they got together and started drinking and singing. They seemed the focus of everybody's attention. Sam, lifted unwittingly into the middle of all this, found himself accepted as a man among men, a patriot, a fine fellow. He liked the sensation. He liked the idea of pulling out, over the sea, far away. Nobody would get him there. But he was not used to whisky. His memory of the rest of the journey was a blank. Then he was in Ottawa. He remembered getting off the train. Then the thing went all misty again till he was awakened by a barman in an empty saloon.

'C'm on, buddy, time to move on.'

Sam stumbled to his feet, felt himself all over. He was stiff. His head throbbed. He put his hand in his hip pocket. His roll of bills was gone. He felt in all his pockets. There was only one dollar left, in small change.

'I've been robbed. My money's gone,' said Sam, but he was still dazed with the drink.

'C'm on, buddy. Outside!' Before he knew how, Sam was pitched on to the street.

When he found his way to the recruiting centre, the big sergeant shouted at him: 'Name?'

'Sam,' he answered, still fuddled.

'Sam! That's no name, son. Sam what?'

'Sam...' his hands were in his pockets, fingering his last quarters and dimes... 'Sam... Dollar,' he managed to say.

'That's a helluva name, son. C'm on then, sign here.'

Sam signed. It wasn't till next day he realised that he had joined up.

'Wireless Operator to Captain,' came Benjy's voice on the intercomm. 'Base have just come through with a gale warning.'

'It was blowing up before we took off.'

'Anything about cloud conditions or icing?' Cookson chipped in.

'No. Only the direction. Three twenty degrees.'

'Well, we can't do anything about it.' Thornly was speaking. 'I expect they'll let us have some more dope later. Let me know, will you?'

'Yes, sir. I'm listening out.'

Benjy switched off his microphone, tore the message off the pad, when he felt a tap on his shoulder. It was Cookson reaching forward from behind him with his hand outstretched for the message. Lukin handed it to him. Both men made a note of it in their logs.

Lukin laid down his pencil, started swinging his dial again and went back to his Shakespeare. He was reading Julius Caesar. *Not the earlier hackneyed scenes which are the play's main claim to popularity; but the later ones where the stature of the work seems to dwindle into intrigues, conspiracies, marches and counter marches. Nobody but Shakespeare could have survived the anti-climax, for the play is really over after Antony's speech. But it meanders on. It comes to no end: it just stops... Still there were wonderful scenes... Benjy, lost again in his reading, was translated out of the present, back two thousand years to the fatal plains of Philippi...*

BENJY LUKIN

There is a tide in the affairs of men,
Which, taken at the flood, leads on to fortune;
Omitted, all the voyage of their life
Is bound in shallows and in miseries.

BENJY STOPPED READING, halted by the edge of the words which cut into his mind. It was extraordinarily true. He was one of those men who, in those days before the war, had been obsessed by a feeling of having missed his way. Now, of course, the personal career had ceased to be important. That was quite a relief... But there had been this tide. He could recognise it clearly now. A surge that had carried him along, directed his thoughts, his instincts even. Partly it had been youth. The élan vital of Bergson. Youth rides this flood of vitality, almost without recognising it. Between twenty and thirty half a man's success lies in his enthusiasm.

Of course the time at which Benjy began to have this feeling was one in which most people shared it with him. 1935 and 1936 were not years in which the western world looked to the future with much confidence. Benjy shared the general frustration; but, all the same, he felt that, had he taken the right road, he would have been able to face the broader disaster with greater assurance. The outward frustration exacerbated the inner one, but the root of his trouble was inward. It was he who had gone wrong, aided and abetted by the general set-up, no doubt; but still, he put the blame on himself in those moments of introspection when he tried desperately to get back on to the track he had missed.

Life had never been hard for him. His father was a prosperous divorce lawyer, and the family had been settled in the big house off Frognal for many years. There were four sons, all doing well in their various fields, Jake on the Stock Exchange, Jo in the civil service, and young Ronny in medicine; but Benjy, was, in the family circle, considered the most successful of all... At any rate he had made his success more quickly.

They were a united family, devoted to their mother, who lived for them, and immensely affectionate to their father, an able and cultivated man. The boys were free to do whatever they liked; but it was typical of their Jewish blood that they all continued at home in the bosom of the family at an age when most young men would have found such ties irksome and set up on their own. It was also typical of their blood that, at a time when young people's conversation ran on nothing but sport, jazz, and the movies – distractions with which the world was then preoccupied – the general tenor of the conversation round the supper table at Frognal was on a different level. It was not exactly more serious, for the whole family had a good sense of humour; but it was more balanced, better informed and more intellectual.

Partly this was education. Benjy had taken a scholarship at his public school and a degree in English Literature at Oxford. All of them had done well; but whereas many men forget their schooling as soon as they have passed their exams, the Lukins did no such thing. They knew their European history and their classics. They were interested in the Arts. They knew why they preferred Tiepolo to Tintoretto, and Beethoven to Brahms. They kept themselves mentally alert by arguing and disagreeing violently on almost every subject. They accepted no point of view until they had hammered it out, with the result that they acquired positive qualities, character and personality, and had little time for the reach-me-down morons who lived by clichés and catchwords. To all these family discussions, their father brought an unfailing sympathy and judicial point of view. He was proud of his sons, and had no pleasure in life so great as sharing with them the adventures of the mind and spirit which, in his own youth, had been so absorbing. Looking around on a chaotic world, with its irresponsibility and lack of values, he never ceased to be grateful that, here, by his own fireside, some semblance of charity, reason and objectivity remained. That his sons should be sound men and good citizens seemed to him his prime responsibility, and he was happy that he had been fortunate enough to discharge it with some success.

He worried about Benjy more than about the others because he saw that the boy might fall a victim to his own brilliance. He saw that he felt things more deeply, would be more profoundly affected by his emotions than his other sons. He wanted to save him, or rather, he wanted so to direct him that he might save himself. The boy was too introspective, too divided within himself, to be happy. It would take him longer than the others to integrate his experiences, to find a way on which to tread surely and steadily. Without this, his father knew there could be no inner peace. The very nature of the career he had chosen tended to disrupt him.

John Lukin felt deeply responsible here, because it was he who had obtained for Benjy an introduction which, when he came down from Oxford, landed him straight into the job of dramatic critic to a highbrow weekly paper. It was only a temporary job, ghosting for the regular man while he took a three-months vacation; but Benjy's incisive style, his wit and acumen, would have turned the job into a permanent one had he not been invited before the summer was out to join the staff of a Liberal London daily. The rumour that he was a 'coming man' had got about Fleet Street, and the Editor, who never missed a trick, took a chance and put him in as assistant to the regular film critic. For a year or more Benjy spent his time covering all the less important stuff, the special newsreels, the cartoons, the nature films, the classic revivals at places like the Curzon and Studio One. Besides this he interviewed stars and directors, did stories from the studios and generally helped to fill the page that the paper devoted three times a week to the films. He soon developed a good newspaper style, curt, factual, arresting and easy to read. When the regular film critic collapsed with a duodenal, the usual result of ten years on Fleet Street, the Editor put Benjy in. So, at the age of twenty-three, he found himself in a position of considerable importance, with an audience of a million readers, a chance to do something both to educate public taste and influence the 'trade'. It was then that the germs of the inner trouble began.

Up to then it had been a meteoric career, a Success Story with a capital S. It had been exciting to read himself in print, to see his name at the head of a newspaper column, to find that men deferred to his opinion and courted his praise. He had done it all himself. It was essentially a personal success.

But this was only the beginning, he told himself. He looked further ahead. He had a real interest in the film medium. He saw it as a new art-form, the drama of the future, and he aspired to be far more intimately connected with it than as a mere commentator. To be Scenario Editor or Managing Director of a film corporation, that was the goal he set himself. He was ideally placed to make the change-over. He was constantly meeting the heads of the film industry, lunching with them, talking with them. The opportunity was bound to arise. One of them would make him an offer and this would take him on the next stage of his career. After that it should be easy…

So, without realising it, he had sold his critical faculty down the river. He was now using it, not as an end in itself, as an honourable and detached spectator; but as an interested party. He began to allow his ambition to colour his work. He was not as scrupulously fair as he had been. He knew it himself and excused the pricks of conscience by the belief that it was more important for the future of the film that he should be an active participant than a mere looker on. It was getting dangerous.

'I wish the boy was not so successful, Nellie,' said John Lukin to his wife, one night before they went to sleep. 'It's not doing him any good.'

'But it's wonderful, John. You ought, we ought both to be proud of him.'

'Mm… I shan't be proud of any of the boys unless they're happy. Happiness, or content rather, is the only basis for a good life.'

'What makes you think he's discontented?'

'Can't you see it? It's the most artificial thing to be connected with, and we haven't brought him up on artificialities. I wish I had never got him that introduction. I never dreamed it would lead to this.'

'I really can't see what you're worrying about, John. He's doing so well. Everybody thinks the world of him.'

'Mm… It's very difficult to be successful when you're young.

That's the value of joining a profession with some tradition, where an apprenticeship of about ten years is necessary before you're allowed to stand on your own feet – like medicine or the law. When success comes too early there's often an element of luck in it – and often a certain amount of fake too.'

'Fake! How do you mean, dear?'

'Well, Benjy hasn't the experience to run such a big job. He's too young to be certain what he wants to make of it. After the first flush of excitement, if he finds his heart's not in the work, he's bound to fake. It's all because his success has come too quickly. Had it been slower he would have had time to find out about himself, to save himself from getting involved.'

'Involved in what?'

'In the worship of money, of position, of power and so on. He's got all three now. They're great temptations – and not easy things to give up.'

'But why on earth should he give them up?'

'He should give them up at once if they're undermining his integrity, if they're making him do and say things he doesn't believe in. It's fatal. It's a sure road to misery and frustration. I don't want to see Benjy join the ruck whose only standards are expediency.'

'I think you're worrying yourself unnecessarily, John.'

'I hope so.'

His father's worries were well founded; but the thing went even deeper than he surmised. A young man, setting out on the course of life, is full of dreams and ideals, none the less vivid and important to him because they are 'half baked' and have not been sufficiently cooked in the oven of experience. Contact with the adult world soon puts a crust over these nebulous hopes and sometimes hardens the man into a lump of cynicism and materialism. At other times the inner core of his being remains fresh and soft and sensitive to the spiritual prompting of the heart. Such men are continually bruised and wounded by what appears to them to be the cruelty and hypocrisy of their fellow men. But by then it is too late. They are launched on some career or other. Economic considerations force them to continue it. It needs great courage and resolution to fight a way out of the groove and re-orientate the life on a genuine path, genuine in the sense that in it a man feels at one with himself. Benjy was a case in point. Because he had ability to the point of brilliance, he had shot off along the first path that offered and the momentum had carried him well off his true track. Indeed, paradoxically, he did not know what his true track should have been until he was off it. A year as critic and reporter had left him no illusions as to the motives of the film industry. He saw that were he to follow up the idea of getting into the executive side, the prospects of its being aesthetically satisfying were exceedingly slim…

It was on one of those rare evenings when he was at home for supper that father and son sat down together, after the meal, in front of the fire. Benjy admitted to some worry about his job. There was no future in it. He broached the idea of a change-over to the production side, first as a writer, then perhaps as a scenario editor… Such a lot could be done once films were less commercial, once they could be induced to seek artistic integrity and take themselves seriously.

'Art for Art's sake,' said his father, knocking out the ashes of his pipe on the side of the grate, 'means life in a garret, means years of poverty and struggle until the genius of the artist is recognised. Money may appear a sordid standard, but it is quite a fair way to measure public interest. No money in the box-office means no interest in the play.'

'Nonsense, Dad. It only means the public hasn't been educated up to the level of the artist. Look at Shaw's plays: There was nothing wrong with them, but it took him a generation to educate the public up to his standard. Look at Somerset Maugham's *Our Betters*. Nobody would touch it for nine years, and then it became a smash hit.'

'Oh, yes, I know all that; but during those nine years you have to live. Life in a garret seems romantic to suburbia; but all the same it's no joke, particularly to someone brought up to comfort as you have been.'

'I didn't say I wanted to live in a garret. I'm not certain I have talent as a writer; but I should like to write free from the mercenary considerations that govern my work at present. I object to being given the hint to praise a picture because the firm that made it has just signed a handsome advertisement contract with the paper.'

'I can well understand that. But if you were free to write what would you write about?'

It was a poser. Benjy blushed. 'Oh, I don't know. About Life, about People, about the World-As-I-See-It.'

'I think you ought to try to get it clear. You often hear people say they would love to "write" – as if it was something you could do in a vacuum like crystal gazing. But to write with any success you have to have something to say. Shaw's plays are founded in an acute social conscience. Maugham's play, that you just referred to, arises from an ability to pillory the manners of his time. Of course there are other things besides; but these men – and indeed all successful artists – have been successful because they had something to say and said it with fire and conviction. They were also, don't forget, a good deal older than you!'

'I know. But suppose I have something to say – and perhaps I have, Dad – I shan't find out what it is until I begin to write about it. Somehow I can't think clearly until I set things down. People say that when you begin to write, the work grows as you go, characters come to life, situations develop and so on. I'm sure it's true. I've got lots of ideas, but I shan't know all that's in them till I start in.'

'Well, what do you want to do?'

'I wish I was more certain.' Benjy sat gazing into the fire, abstracted and depressed. His father relit his pipe and went on:

'I know you won't be happy unless you can find something which really satisfies you. This sort of frustration is one of the things that is at the root of the breakdown in our social system. Ninety per cent of the world is doing a job it doesn't care for. How would you like to chuck yours and take a year or two off? Come home here, and see if at the end of it you know a bit more clearly where you want to go?'

Such a course had never occurred to Benjy. 'It's awfully good of you, Dad.'

'My dear boy, I've tried to do my best for you all. I want nothing so much as to see you contented in life. The top room next to the box-room isn't exactly a garret, but it's the best we can do in Hampstead.

Your mother can put up a few cobwebs and rickety chairs to give it atmosphere! It'll be reasonably quiet up there.'

'It's a marvellous idea, Dad. But I feel I ought to be out in the world earning my keep. I've been on your hands quite long enough.'

'I can afford it. I'd sooner pay as I go than have to admit you to a mental home in five years' time!'

They both laughed and Benjy got up. 'I'll sleep on it, Dad. And thanks again.' He crossed and kissed his father and went up to bed.

'What might have happened if,' is always an interesting speculation however abortive. Had Benjy really chucked his hand in with the paper, had he come back in home and started to write, would he have emerged a 'great' writer, or even a good one? Or was that final touchstone of the artist – the fiat to create – missing in him? Was he bound, by his own character, to be no more than a clever journalist? It is useless to speculate, for, of course he never put himself to the test – though he had every intention of so doing. The reason was Christina.

It happened the very next morning after he had talked things over with his father. Before going to sleep, he had fully decided to give the paper a month's notice. Next morning, as he drove down to Elstree, he found the prospect elating. The idea of getting out of the whole racket appealed to him. He was in high spirits. The job he had come down on – to see a big composite set and interview some of the players – seemed pleasantly unimportant. He could knock that off in half an hour. He showed his card at the gate, was met by the Director and went in on to the 'floor'.

It was the usual pandemonium of shouting electricians, frantic assistant directors, scurrying dressers. A dozen things were going on at once. Cameramen were focusing lights, microphones were being hung, prop men were nailing up curtains, moving furniture, extras chatted to each other in corners, principals ran over a sequence of dialogue in the centre of the set, quite absorbed, as if there were nobody there. The whole place was like a cartoon by Beuttler. If you were seeing it for the first time it was impossible to make head or tail of the thing, impossible to believe that, out of this chaos, could come the impeccable timing of a perfect 'take'; but Benjy of course, knew it of old. The Director took him round, briefly indicating his sequence of shots, where he tracked and where he panned, where he cut away, and how he came back...

'Oh, Harry,' called a charming voice, with a bogus American accent, 'will I do like this?'

Both men turned to see the owner of the voice, who stood, in considerable décolleté under the powerful lights. She was slim and rather tall, but you could go over her with an X-ray without finding a fault in the casting. Besides which she had the freshness of youth, a short tilted nose, a full spoiled mouth, a magnificent pair of legs – and one or two ideas as to how to get on.

'Swell!' the Director replied, looking at her carefully, as she turned round for him. 'You couldn't get it just a bit lower, could you, Tina?'

She came through the tripods off the set towards him. She was laughing, deliciously, provokingly. 'Well, I can, Harry; but it'll never stay up through the take.'

'And wouldn't that be wonderful?' Harry laughed back. 'All right, kid. Leave it as it is – and meet my friend, Benjy Lukin. Benjy, this is Christina Shy.'

Benjy took her hand and looked down into a pair of quite starry eyes which Christina between the split second of hearing his name and taking his hand, had managed to make moist with a sort of dumb, dreamy devotion. 'How wonderful!' she murmured and clung to his hand, limply, heavily, as if it were her one hold on life.

That was how it had begun. Benjy, for all his year about the studios, had remained curiously naïve in some respects. Christina Shy – her girlfriends said her name should have been Sly – was putting on an act, of course. The critic of a leading London paper was important to a girl who was going to get on. Christina, truthfully, had little or no acting talent; but she had audaciously attractive looks, and enough sex appeal to put a lens out of focus. When she looked in her mirror, quite deliberately assessing her value in the film market, she decided there was no reason why she should not get to the top.

It was just a matter of handling men. She knew all about that. You held off until the contract was signed, then you allowed them what they expected... It was easy.

Benjy Lukin meant publicity, and, if you could handle it right, good publicity. Good publicity meant bigger and better parts, and bigger and better parts meant, of course, still more publicity, and so, as Tina figured it, you could snowball yourself to the top. But over supper in the Café Royal that night Tina found this Benjy Lukin was different. Most of the 'boys' were easy. They talked stars and stories and clothes and Tina knew her way about. Clothes she really understood. But Benjy Lukin talked directors, camera angles, montage, rhythm, tempo. Most of it was well over her head and didn't interest her anyway, but she picked up a phrase here and there, to impress someone else later – and all the time she listened so rapt, so absorbed, so exquisite really... Benjy was properly caught.

'A nice boy,' Tina was thinking. There was something infectious about his enthusiasms. And he wasn't bad-looking in a quiet sort of way. Yid, of course; but he had 'class', and of course to get on you had to have class or give a good imitation of it, so she could pick up a thing or two... But when he stripped him (mentally), a thing she always did with men, she shook her head. Not enough insolence, not enough attack...

'You haven't heard a word I've been saying.' Benjy was staring at her, hypnotised. She blushed and kept her eyes averted. 'I was thinking what beautiful shoulders you must have,' and she looked up, shy and confiding. 'I'm sorry. Please go on.'

Benjy was staggered at her audacity.

'No fear. I've been talking for hours. Do forgive me. What would you like to do?'

'Go to bed.' She was stretching, adorably. Somehow even bad manners in a public restaurant became her.

'I'll get the bill and a cab.'

In the cab, she nestled up, took his arm and put it round her, then snuggled her head on his shoulder. 'Sleepy,' she murmured. Benjy just held on to her, as the taxi swung round the corners. He felt all drunk and fluttery, as if there were pigeons in his head; all the blood in his veins, in his wrists and temples, was throbbing; the perfume rising from her hair was intoxicating... The taxi stopped.

'We've arrived,' he said. There was no answer. 'Tina!' – it was the first time he had called her that – he gently lifted her away from him. 'We've arrived at your flat.'

'Come up and have a nightcap.' She spoke through a stretch and a yawn.

'No. You're tired. I'll see you to the door.'

'But, darling, it's right at the top of the house. Better pay off the cab.'

It was a large bed-sitting-room under the eaves, with a tiny kitchen and bathroom tucked away in one corner. There was a deep sofa and armchair, a large divan bed, thick rugs, low tables and flowers. The whole thing was done in quite good taste. 'It belonged to an artist,' said Tina, when Benjy remarked upon it, as if that explained everything. 'Help yourself to whisky. It's in the cupboard,' she said as she disappeared into the bathroom. 'I'm going to bed.'

Benjy poured himself a whisky, lit a cigarette and waited. When she came out a few minutes later it wasn't exactly a sedative. The night-dress was transparent, and the long negligée paid no more than lip-service to modesty; the hair, shaken free, fell both sides of the face in heavy abandon, the toenails were coral and the feet narrow and straight. The whole picture, rustle and froth and languor, was an invitation to break all the Commandments.

Benjy got up and she came straight towards him. He was quite dazzled. 'You're terrific, Tina. Nothing can stop you!'

'Mind you print it,' laughed Tina.

The marriage took place about two months later. There was a good deal about it in the papers – Tina saw to that. 'Film Critic marries rising Star,' ran the headlines. Benjy didn't realise what it was to have a 'public'. It was the first time he had been lionised. It was flattering of course, but at the same time rather uncalled-for, he thought. His marriage was something between himself and his wife: it wasn't public property. He didn't mind photos of the ceremony, but he objected to the way the phone was always going and reporters asking the most ridiculous questions. Did he believe in careers for women? Could a woman have a career and children? Did he intend to have children? What were his plans? It was an intolerable intrusion on his privacy, and he resented it. But Tina, of course, adored it. She said Yes to everything. Benjy very soon saw himself committed in print to Tina having a career, a large family, a honeymoon in Monte Carlo, a picture with Clark Gable, and a hundred and one other things. When it came to plans, Tina was quite definite. 'My plans? To get to the top and stay there! Couldn't be simpler, could it?' and she laughed at the 'boys', who plugged her as hard as they could. 'That kid certainly is going places,' was their opinion. But over the Fleet Street bars, they shook their heads. 'Poor old Lukin! It's marrying dynamite. I give him six months.'

The family behaved with admirable tact. They disapproved, of course. Not because they weren't broadminded; but simply because, after Tina had spent an hour in the house, it was quite clear that she would not make a wife for him, or indeed for anyone. This quiet solid home with its intimate family circle was something she had never experienced before. It seemed incredibly dull to her.

'Whatever do you *do* with yourselves in the evenings?' she asked Mrs Lukin. 'Don't you ever go out to a show? Benjy can get you tickets for anything in the West End. You ought to go out more.'

Mrs Lukin smiled, began to explain how they liked being together, and that they did go out, at least once a week. For instance, they had all been to see Pirandello at the Embassy the week before.

'What's Pirandello? A ballet? You know I think ballets are dull. Of course you've got to have them for production numbers to fill up and give a show style…' Tina babbled on, airing her opinions, while Mrs Lukin thought of Nijinski in *Spectre de la Rose*, thought of Karsarvina in *Légende de Joseph*, thought of Nina Theilade in the *Dream*…

'It's all a matter of taste, my dear,' she smiled when Tina had finished airing her opinions. 'Shall we go in and have supper?'

Benjy rather avoided his father. He had not forgotten their conversation. But all that was out of the question now. He had burned his boats. Clearly, with a wife, he was committed to carrying on with his film criticism. Indeed it was this, and the plan he put forward to Tina one night of going in on the Executive side of films, that had decided her to marry him. At first she saw him as a useful critic who, if she handled him properly, would always be good for a puff; but when he came out with his idea, she really sat up and took notice. She saw quite clearly that he had ability, and that if he wanted to do this, he could probably bring it off – then, if he could, why there was no end to it! She was made! He wouldn't just criticise her in her parts. He would choose the parts, get the scripts written for her, see that she was suited, build her up... There was no end to it. She saw ahead a long vista of part after part, each bigger and better than the last. Tina laughing, Tina amorous, Tina sad, Tina quarrelling, Tina making it up, Tina weeping, Tina triumphant. In bed in the mornings, she stretched her lovely young body and dreamed... Success! Success!

She rushed the marriage ahead as quickly as she dared. She was frightened of Benjy's family, jealous of the obvious hold it had over him, scared of the possibility of losing her chance through 'those old frumps up in Frognal', as she put it to herself. And when Benjy mildly suggested postponing the date for a month, till the season was over and his paper could spare him more easily, she dissolved into tears. Benjy couldn't face that: he gave in unconditionally.

Looking at the thing objectively – which he was not able to do till a couple of years later – Benjy wondered how on earth he had managed to make such a gross, such a monumental error. He very definitely kicked against the pricks then, for, he argued, how can a man be expected to make the most far-reaching and important decision in his life at an age when he has relatively no experience of the world? Unless he has luck and instinct, he cannot possibly know how he is going to develop and how his wife is going to develop. Why should he have to pay so heavily in bitterness and unhappiness, when he has done the best he knows at the time, when he has contracted himself in honesty and hope with the serious intention of making it a pattern for life? How could he have made such a mistake?

The answer was the old eternal answer: the most imperious summons in life, the blinding strength of desire. The folly from which no man, from Romeo to Faust, is exempt. Benjy had never had anything to do with women before. Up to the time of his marriage he was ignorant of all sexual experience. This was no prudery, it was just that he didn't happen to have been awakened, that his life had been too busy and too full of other things. But Tina had awakened him in no uncertain manner. She knew all about sex. She had taken to it at an early age as naturally as a duck to water. She knew, without knowing why or how, that she could provoke men, could play with them, hold them, use them, make fools of them, with a glance, a laugh, a half-promise, a sigh. It was really amazing how simple it was! Usually she didn't exert herself about it; but Benjy didn't react quite so greedily as most. Actually he was a little shy, a bit scared. He kept himself to himself, subconsciously scenting danger.

This excited Tina wildly. She couldn't make him lose his self-control, couldn't overwhelm him as she could every other man she had ever met. He would quietly put her away. 'Not until we're married, darling, please!'

'But why? We're going to be married. Oh, Benjy, I'm crazy about you,' and she almost fainted in his arms.

'So am I, darling. But we ought to have something to look forward to, don't you think?'

There is an old chestnut concerning a young couple on their honeymoon, in which the bride, the moment the hotel manager had bowed himself out of their room, began tearing off her clothes and flinging them out of the window. When her husband, somewhat amazed, began to expostulate, she replied, 'Before I want these again, they're going to be out of fashion.'

Tina didn't quite do that, but the effect was the same. For days after they arrived in Monte Carlo, they hardly left their room. For, to Tina, Benjy's eventual surrender was thrilling. She soon found she had made a mistake in thinking him cold. It was only his reserve, and it gave her a new sense of power to break it down. With her own exuberant vitality, she never tired of rousing him. She whetted his appetite, provoked him with whispers and kisses and touches, till he came at her and the first movement of his renewed desire set

112

her quivering in answer. He was in her power again; but she was in his, and she abandoned herself to him, letting the love ebb from her in tide after tide, panting in ecstasy till he lay inert, exhausted. She had taken him again, taken from him his strength, his essential power, his creative manhood! He lay like a child in her arms: she had enslaved him.

Subconsciously he knew this. Deep under the layers of civilisation, under the tenderness, under the chivalry, the essential male in him began to peep out, the essential antagonism between the sexes flared up in him. She was his thing, his chattel, he would do what he willed with her. He took her wildly, roughly, abruptly. Terrible instincts rose out of the depths of him, desires to hurt, to strike her, to kill her, so that he might be free of her in the very act of succumbing to her beauty. But to all this she answered every bit as violently. Their love-making became a wild primitive thing, as fiery as the rape of the mare by the plunging stallion, as terrible as the drone who falls dead from the clutches of the Queen. It was an orgy of lust, but at last Benjy drew back horrified at himself, at the abysses in his nature. 'The expense of spirit in a waste of shame is Lust in action' – so Shakespeare had written and, as usual, had incomparably summed up the matrix of the thoughts that writhed like snakes in his head.

Had it been just an affair, such an experience in the flood of youth would have been memorable for both of them. Complete sexual compatibility is rare. The breaking down of all barriers, the utter abandon, the freedom of another body has an unequalled intimacy. Yet, for all that, it remains finally unsatisfying. It is a battle which must be fought and refought to achieve a moment of victory. Lust, though fine when it is wild and unashamed, is not love. In its very abandon lies the key to its disintegration. People who know so much about their grosser natures, when the excitement and novelty have worn thin, tend to despise their partners for the very traits they adored.

Benjy had married Tina out of a violent infatuation, while she had accepted him as a useful hostage to success. Both had therefore deceived each other, Benjy unwittingly, Tina with purpose. When at last he climbed out of the mire of his sexual appetite, it was to find that whatever he felt, or had felt for Tina, it was not that quiet confidence and mutual trust which he recognised in the relationship of his father and mother as 'love'. He hoped that it might settle down into this, and, being naturally kindly and patient, waited for it to happen.

Tina returned from her honeymoon unwell. She suffered from morning sickness, and when Benjy, suspecting the truth, sent her to his doctor, the good man examined her carefully and took her hand. 'Mrs Lukin, I congratulate you,' he said.

'Whatever for?' asked Tina.

'You are going to have a child.'

'What!!' Tina was aghast. 'How revolting!'

It was the doctor's turn to be surprised. Tina was pacing up and down in a rage, against life, against marriage, against her husband. It was a trick to catch her, to get in the way of her 'career', of her success; but not likely, not much, none of that dreary domesticity for her.

'Now listen, doctor, I know you'll think me simply awful; but I really can't have a baby – just yet. I, my husband and I, we can't afford it, really. Besides I've got a big picture coming along and a great deal depends on it. I'm in films you know, and you can just imagine what my figure means to me. I simply daren't lose it. Later, of course, when I'm really established and can afford the time, then it'll be different. But now, it's out of the question.'

She came and laid a hand on his arm and looked up into his eyes with that warm soft appeal which was, she thought, irresistible. 'Now, you'll help me, won't you, Doctor, you see I… '

But the Doctor was past the age when this kind of appeal could touch him. 'Madam,' he said, freeing his arm from her hand, 'I do not practise abortion.'

Tina was not in the least abashed.

'Why not? Lots of doctors do. Good doctors too.' She softened her tone. 'Listen now, I'll pay you in cash. Nobody will know. I promise I'll keep it secret… '

'Mrs Lukin, I'm sorry, but I cannot help you – and that is an end of the matter.'

'But, for heaven's sake, why?' Tina was now openly furious. 'Very well then, if you're so squeamish, give me an address of someone to go to.' It was just like Benjy to send her to an old fool like this.

'I know no such addresses. And if I did, I should not give them to you. You seem to forget, young lady, that what you propose is against the law.'

'Damn the law! I've got to get rid of the thing.'

The doctor shrugged his shoulders. Tina flounced out of the room.

Benjy was delighted at the idea of her having a child. He thought it would help to settle her and quiet her highly-strung nature. Besides, again following his blood, he had a strong family instinct. A home is not really a home without children, and he hoped to repeat for them the happiness that he had known in his own childhood. So, naturally, he only smiled at Tina's appeals, gave her very good arguments as to why she would be well advised to have her first child now, and refused point blank to put up the money for her to have an illegal operation. Tina dissolved into tears. It was the first time in her life she had really failed to get her own way, without question and at once. She cried, not with sorrow, but with rage, impotent rage. But after a while she calmed down and appeared to accept the situation. Benjy hoped she was reconciled to it.

It was true that she had a film coming off. Her marriage had borne fruit. Harry, the Director who had introduced her to Benjy, cashed in on her marriage publicity, wires flew back and to between Monte Carlo and the studios, and before she returned, it had been arranged that Tina should play second lead in his new picture. It was by far the biggest part she had ever had and she was wildly happy. At last she had her foot on the ladder. She was on her way. It was quite natural therefore that she should go to Harry in her trouble. She told him the whole story. He was perfectly cynical about it. He thought she had been foolish to marry and told her so. A girl with a career to make had to put that first. However, the mischief was done. He wanted her for the picture. The money meant nothing to him. The address was easy. Tina returned to the flat a few days later, pale and unwell. She stayed in bed a couple of days and then confessed to Benjy, tearfully, that she had had a miscarriage.

'Just as I was getting used to the idea,' she sobbed to her husband. 'Isn't it terrible?... Poor little thing...'

Benjy was frightfully upset, but he put his arms round her and comforted her. 'Never mind, my darling. We'll just have to hope for better luck next time.'

Tina nodded her head sadly. (I'm getting quite an actress, she thought. It's wonderful practice. Perhaps I'll be able to use it on the screen some day.) But aloud she went on: 'I think, perhaps, I'm not meant to have children, darling... I can't think why this happened... Perhaps I'm not strong enough...'

'You're very highly strung, darling. After all you've had quite a hectic time. All the preparations for our marriage, then going abroad, then the picture offer and now this... It's been too much for you.' Tina nodded and went on sobbing quietly. 'Now you must take great care of yourself until you feel really strong again.'

'Of course I will, darling... Oh, Benjy,' – and she nestled up to him – 'you're so good and patient with me.'

But apart from this the marriage did not prosper. Tina was useless as a housekeeper. She would come home with a terrine of *foie gras* and forget the bread. She couldn't manage the maid. She was lazy. She was used to dining out and lunching out and being looked after. It was quite foreign to her to look after anyone else. Benjy had been spoiled of course. At home the household was beautifully run and he had looked forward to coming home in the evenings. Now there was nothing to come home to. The expense of always eating out was heavy and the absence of a quiet fireside upset Benjy, upset his stomach, and this in turn upset his work. He found he had less and less interest in it, and besides, he didn't get through so much. He travels fastest who travels alone. When she was not working herself, Tina insisted on going everywhere with him. Useful contacts were to be made and she didn't intend to miss them. She monopolised the conversation with the men Benjy had to meet, prevented him getting their stories and so his column, which used to lead the London press, sagged back and had somehow less drive, less wit, less attack. He couldn't quite realise himself what was happening, but things didn't seem to go with their old bang. Tina was always under his feet. He wasted hours waiting for her in London bars, waiting while she had her hair done, or was massaged, or fitted new dresses. She was late for everything as a matter of course and took it for granted he would wait. After all, she was worth waiting for. He ought to be proud to be seen about with me: that was her point of view. Her conversation was limited to clothes and food. 'I'm wearing a simply wonderful dress in the new sequence. It's a Hartnell. I look as if I'd been poured into it.' Such was the tenor of the conversation. Sole Veronique. Homard Cardinal. Points d'asperge and raspberries and cream. That was her idea of dinner. It was all right; but Benjy sometimes longed for roast beef and beer and a hunk of cheddar; but those were not to be had at the smart places that Tina insisted on frequenting.

'It's so important to me to be *seen*,' she would say, when Benjy suggested the Cheshire Cheese or Soho. 'You must understand that.'

So they were 'seen' together at smart places, dining together in lugubrious silence. Then Tina would suddenly brighten up and begin chattering gaily about something. 'Korda's just come in,' she would throw into the middle of it. 'I must make him notice me. Say something funny. Make me laugh.' And at this she would laugh herself, rather loudly, and look round in the great man's direction and strike a pose. It made Benjy writhe.

But why go on? The marriage smouldered on in growing hostility for a couple of years. Benjy took to coming home in the evenings. He would fry himself an egg and bacon and try to read. Tina would be out somewhere and would get back at all hours. Sometimes he noticed smears of lipstick on her cheek in the morning, but he wouldn't face how they got there. Things came to a head, as such situations usually do, by chance.

'I didn't see you down at Harry's last weekend,' said a friend while they were waiting to go into a Trade Show. 'Tina was looking lovelier than ever. You're a lucky man, Benjy.'

'I couldn't get down. I had to spend the weekend with the Editor,' Benjy lied; but he tackled Tina that evening.

'I thought you went to your Mother's for the weekend.'

'So I did.'

'Frank told me today that you were at Harry's. Why didn't you tell me you were going?'

'It's nothing to do with you.'

'Why did you lie to me?' Benjy was angry.

'Because I'm tired of these eternal arguments. You dislike Harry, I know. But I like him. Besides there were some important people there.'

'Do you never think of anything except getting on?'

'Well, I've got to get on – and you don't do much to help me.'

'I'm sorry I'm not satisfactory. But if you think that a second-rate director like Harry Peters will ever get you anywhere, you make a great mistake.'

'Harry's a good sort – and he's done more for me than you ever have.'

'What – particularly?'

'That's my business.'

Benjy looked at her, standing there defiant with the corners of her mouth pulled down.

'Tina, dear, I don't want to be cruel; but someone must tell you. You have wonderful looks and you wear clothes like an angel; but you haven't any talent for acting. Really, you haven't. That's my business and I know what I'm talking about. Why don't you chuck it all and be content to be my wife? You could do it so well, so graciously, if you chose.'

Tina clenched her fists and her long red nails sunk into her palms. All the venom of inferiority, of the inner conviction that what Benjy said was true, came out in a spiteful torrent of words.

'If we're telling each other home-truths, I may as well tell you some too. You're a bloody bore – and a rotten critic. Everybody says so. You're selfish. You never think of me. You'd have landed me with a kid, if I'd given you half a chance. And who got me out of that? Who helped me when you went on bleating about how lovely it would be to have children? I'll tell you. Harry. He did it because he understands what my career means to me. He found the money and the doctor and saved me from growing into an old frump like your mother, with no thought beyond her brats. That's why I like him and I'll spend as much time with him as I damn choose.'

A fishwife could have done no better. Benjy stood very still. He felt as if the inside of him was withering away. The lying, the insults, these were nothing; but the shame of it, the cheapness, the vulgarity... He looked at her steadily.

'I suppose you're his mistress?' One might as well know the whole of it.

'It wouldn't be much for him to ask after all he's done for me. Certainly, he can have me whenever he wants – and he wants pretty damned often, if you'd like to know.'

Benjy nodded his head slowly. Then he went to his dressing-room, packed a suitcase and left the flat.

In the days that followed he had plenty of time for introspection. He said little to his people. When he knocked at the door late that night, his father had welcomed him warmly, but scenting something was wrong, had wisely made no inquiries. His mother put clean sheets on his bed and turned on the fire. His room was just as he had left it. He undressed and tried to sleep, but the miserable scene he had just been through kept him lying there awake in the darkness. Had he deserved it all? His mind repudiated any responsibility. He had behaved throughout quietly, decently, and patiently. Tina had simply made use of him. He had long ago suspected it. Now it was clear. But why had she picked on him? Because she thought he would be in clover once he was on the executive of some film company. How often had she nagged at him to leave his job on the paper and start in. At the time he had thought she was ambitious for him; but it was because she was ambitious for herself. Why had he ever suggested that he might do such a thing? He remembered the evening well. They had had a bottle of wine and he had put it forward, just as an idea, just to dazzle her, to show off. Of course she had been impressed. He remembered now how there had been no talk of marriage till after that evening. Yet, all the time, inside himself, he knew that was not what he wanted to do. Weeks before he had told his father so.

So, to that extent, he had cheated her. For, once having made the boast, he hadn't the courage to withdraw it, to say it was nothing but swank and that he didn't mean it. From that all the rest had followed. And after all, why had he married her? How does a man know when he is in love? Benjy had never known such feelings as he had for Tina. Indeed he had never been aroused before. How was he to know that the exquisite spider's web of lust was not the right thing? He dreamed of her day and night, of the warm pressure of her thighs against him, the curve of her proud breasts, the languor, the abandon, the desire to be possessed. All this must be love. It was marvellous enough. Yet now, when he thought of it, there was no real contact, no sympathy, no common bond of interest. Everything had been coloured by the promise in her.

He did not face up to all this immediately. At first he had too much sense of being deceived, insulted and wronged. The image of Tina's lovely body lying under that obese, half-bald Harry Peters, blinded him with jealousy and anger. It was so dirty, so vulgar, so aesthetically disgusting – apart from the deception, the dishonour to him. But all this took him nowhere. He shut it out of his mind. Finally it was the deception he had practised upon her, from which all else followed. 'To thine own self be true...' as that old bore Polonius had said. Well, he hadn't been. And now he had paid for it. Had paid, was paying and would pay. For how was he to climb out of this mess? His life had been snapped right in two. To a less sensitive, less idealistic man it would have mattered less. To Benjy, because he had aimed high, because he had set some store by self-respect, it was ruin.

When he had got the whole thing straight in his mind, he went with it to his father, as a man might go to confession, to rid his bosom of the perilous stuff, to be absolved, to receive counsel so that he could look life in the face again. His father heard him out, patiently, quietly, puffing at his pipe, saying nothing till his son had talked himself clean. Then:

'My boy, I'm proud of you and not at all sorry for you. You made a big mistake, as of course we all knew at the time. Now you're well out of it – and cheaply out of it, in my opinion. I spent a good many hours, I don't mind telling you, wondering whether to try to dissuade you from it or not. It isn't easy to stand aside when you see a man going wrong – particularly when that man is your son, of whom you happen to be rather fond...' and he turned to smile at Benjy. 'I worried a good deal, and so did your mother. But that's all over now, thank God. You've got rid of that girl, who never could have been anything but a drag and a burden to you. That's why I'm not sorry for you.' He paused. 'I'm proud of you because, instead of putting all the blame on her, as nine men out of ten would have done – and the courts would do too – you've seen deeper into it, and realised that, in the final analysis, it was you who were to blame. That not only requires a good deal of self-criticism, it needs a lot of guts. I'm not sure it's entirely true, but it's highly salutary that you should be decent enough to think so. So now the only thing to do is to cut your losses and start again. I always remember that remark of Shaw's: "You have learned something; that always feels at first as if you had lost something." You certainly have learned a lot, about yourself, about life, and about what is of value in it, and though you may feel you've lost something, you'll soon come to see you have gained much more. So, put it out of your mind and fix your eyes on the future. What are you going to do?'

It was a wonderful tonic to Benjy. He had expected to be pardoned, but he certainly had not expected praise. It had all loomed too big for him to put it into perspective and regard it only as an unfortunate episode that could be relegated to the past. But, once you had seen it in this light, it made everything much easier.

'Well, I've chucked my job, Dad. I couldn't go on with it, when I'd faced up to all this. If I'm going to begin again, I'd better not start by cheating my employer.'

'I shouldn't worry about that. I expect he's used to it,' laughed his father.

'I told him why I was going. I think he was a bit surprised. We had quite a heart-to-heart. He finished up by saying he wished he were young enough to chuck everything and start again. Made me feel quite a hero!'

Benjy's tone was already lighter. The life had begun to come back into his voice. His wonderful Dad! How simple and easy he had made everything! He jumped up like a boy, put his arm round his father's shoulders and kissed him. 'Bless you, Dad!' he said quietly. His father squeezed his arm.

'By the way, d'you see there's a music festival on at Venice, and an interesting Leonardo exhibition at Milan? Why don't you run over and have a look round. I'm sure something really highbrow would do you good – for a change...' He turned and smiled slyly at his son. 'It would be a change, wouldn't it?'

'You're a malicious old devil – but it would.' Benjy considered it. 'I wonder if I ought to?'

'Why on earth not? Do you good. Pack your bag and catch the train today. You need some action.'

'Porteur! Porteur! Deux cent quarante six. Deux piéces, B'en, M'sieu. A la Douane, M'sieu!' The besmocked porter hurried off in search of further custom, and Benjy walked down the gangplank, found his way to the Lötchberg Express and settled into his compartment. His spirits rose at the prospect of a complete change of scene. The train rolled out of the Gare Maritime. The sound of a tiny handbell crescendoed down the corridor, and the attendant passed, crying, 'Premier Service! Premier Service!' Benjy got up and elbowed his way along the rolling corridor to the Restaurant Car. The waiter put him at a table for two where a woman was already seated. She was absorbed in her book. As Benjy slid into his seat, he noticed the book's title on the spine: *The Lost Girl*, by D. H. Lawrence. He turned and sat looking out of the window. The train was running through the evening fields. Dirty white horses stood stock still watching. There were poplars and willows and watercress and garish cottages and hoardings shouting 'Pernod!' Then the waiter rushed in, flung a couple of cupfuls of soup at them. The woman put down her book. They looked at each other, Benjy smiled.

'I see you're reading Lawrence. A great writer.'

'Is he? He always upsets me, I know.' She answered thoughtfully and tentatively, quite at her ease. Her expression was alert, boyish, intelligent. There was a wedding-ring on her finger. She was simply but fastidiously dressed.

'That's because he's different. There's no one in English literature remotely like him. Have you read his Letters?'

'No.'

'There's a remarkable preface by Huxley in which he makes that point. His standards and values never correspond with the normal. It's as if he were a visitor from another planet and saw everything with quite a fresh eye. That's what gives him that curious X-ray effect when he probes into character and motives. But you're right, it is upsetting.'

She finished her soup, looked out of the window and sighed.

'What a relief to get abroad again!'

'Isn't it. Are you going to Italy?' he asked.

'Yes, to Venice for the Music.'

'So am I!'

'How curious! Are you a musician?' She was looking at the shape of his hands.

'No, just a concert-goer. A lot of the stuff will be over my head. But it doesn't matter, there are plenty of other things in Venice.'

'A lot of the modern stuff is quite meaningless to me.'

'Thank heaven you have the courage to say it!' Benjy liked her directness. 'One gets so used to people praising the latest thing up to the skies. It's just the same in painting.'

'But, on the whole, I think the painters are more fun, don't you?' She questioned him, smiling, and then before he could answer, went on, 'I know what you're going to say. "Should Art be fun?"'

'It was exactly what I was going to say.' Benjy grinned broadly. He was enjoying the conversation. It was the first intelligent talk he had had with a woman for years. He'd forgotten, with Tina's eternal clothes and food, that there were women who could take an interest in other things. He warmed to the subject. 'Of course it must be fun, in the sense that it must stimulate you, absorb you and give you a sense of well-being. Fun is rather a trivial word for so much, don't you think?'

'But I don't think a lot of it does that. I think fun's the right word, because it is trivial – like a cocktail. That's why I prefer the painters. They're not pretentious. The composers take themselves too seriously.'

'I can't think why you're going to Venice!' laughed Benjy.

'It's just an excuse. I'm running away.'

'From what?'

'From the world I knew.' She looked at him, seriously, questioningly, to see if he would understand.

Benjy looked back at her, nodded, smiled, and then the comedy of it struck him. It was too wonderful! Here, in the utter detachment of a train journey, right out of the blue, to meet someone who... He burst into laughter. It was the first really carefree laugh he had had for months.

'You must excuse me,' he got in between convulsive gurgles that grew somewhere near hysteria. 'You must excuse me... But you see... It's too farcical... I'm... I'm doing the same thing myself...' There were tears in his eyes, and the other diners were staring, but his companion evidently found something contagious in his abandon.

'Are you really? How frightfully funny!' She threw back her head and joined him. The waiter flung a couple of dollops of omelette on their plates. They were friends.

Venice, in that summer of 1939, seemed gayer than ever by day and more romantic than usual by night. Everyone who thronged the crowded Piazza San Marco, feeding the pigeons, staring at the Cathedral, or diving into the shops under the arcades, seemed to have the feeling that they might never be there again. There was a brittle gaiety in face of the steadily darkening news. Italian and German officers strutted about more arrogantly than usual. Destroyers were anchored off the Salute. Fast grey motor launches shot across the lagoon. But the tourists and holiday-makers conspired to pass over these ominous signs of preparation, and the shopkeepers repeated to their clients a hundred times a day, 'Ma, non che sera la guerra!' as if by ridiculing the idea of it, they could avert the disaster.

Benjy was staying at the Europa on the Grand Canal, while his train acquaintance had taken a room at a little Pension on the Giudecca. Before they parted at the station, she had written out her

address: Mrs Ruth Harper, Pensione Eden, Giudecca, and asked him
to call for her for lunch next day. Venice, in the summer, is sultry and
the motor-boats churn up the canals, making the city smellier than
usual; but the Churches and the Galleries are cool. After lunch under
a shady vine terrace overlooking the Giudecca, they walked through
the narrow streets to the Accademia to see the Bellinis, caught a
steamer up the Grand Canal and got off at the Piazza. After tea they
hired a gondola and told the man to take them out on to the lagoon.
It was cool on the water and the indolent motion of the boat was
almost a soporific after the tiring journey and the bustle of London
that had preceded it.

Benjy found his companion wonderfully restful. He had no sense
of effort. She talked or listened or was silent, so naturally and in
such perfect accord with his own mood that he felt at ease with her
as you only can with an old friend.

'I feel exactly as if I'd known you all my life,' he confessed, after
having stretched and yawned, lying there at her side on the cushions,
and, suddenly realising his breach of manners, excused himself
profusely.

'Don't mind me! I'll do the same when I feel like it,' she rejoined.
'I expect we both need to relax. I know I do.'

'I'm not living up to the traditions of the place,' smiled Benjy. 'I
hope you don't mind.'

'If you mean the romantic tradition, I'm delighted.'

'After all this is Casanova's hometown. A man feels he ought to
do something about it – or most men do.'

'In my experience it doesn't need Casanova or Venice to
make men feel that,' she laughed. Benjy looked at her. She wasn't
pretty, but definitely good-looking, he thought. She had style and
distinction and poise. Cool and intelligent, without being aggressive
or domineering, as so many modern women were. Very womanly,
but yet quite independent. Attractive without being alluring, without
always parading herself like Tina. Grown up, not a child always
satisfying her appetites and demanding attention. You could respect
her. That was it. That was the heart of it. You could respect her and
for that reason... But she interrupted his thoughts.

'Was it really Casanova's hometown? I didn't know.'

'He was born and bred in it – and at the time when it was at its height. You remember the Wordsworth Sonnet: "Once did she hold the gorgeous East in fee"? About then, or rather when the fees were beginning to slip through her fingers – the end of the eighteenth century, that is. I suppose it was the most corrupt and exciting place in Europe, in his day. He certainly lived up to that side of it.'

She was looking at him curiously. 'Do you know everything?'

He laughed. 'Almost nothing. But Dad has a copy of the Memoirs, the full version, in French. Twenty volumes. I've read some of it. It gets a bit boring in the long run.'

'Plus ça change…'

'Yes, but his escape from the prison over the Bridge of Sighs is fantastic. And the earthquake! When he couldn't get out and was up there under the leads and the terrified warder heard him shouting "Another! And a bigger one, please God!" He was an astonishing chap, a genius at mental arithmetic, a dabbler in black magic, a first class financier in his heyday – that's all thrown in, with the – rest.'

'It must have been awfully boring for him.'

'Being irresistible to women, you mean?'

'Yes.' She was dangling her hand in the water and looking away over the water.

'It doesn't appear to have been. But, of course, he had unusual vitality. He just couldn't help it.'

'Don't I know.' She spoke quietly; but with a sort of exasperated boredom.

'You speak with feeling.'

'Yes.' She watched the water dripping from her fingers. 'You see, I'm married to one.'

The days flew past. Their tentative first meetings seemed to develop naturally into a constant companionship. The music, as Benjy had forecast, was too highbrow. But they never tired of the churches, the little byways, the hidden romantic corners of the place. Both of them, as they soon admitted to each other, had come away intending to be quite alone, to try and sort their problems out undisturbed; both, as it turned out, found that the problems seemed less important after they had talked them over with each other. It seemed easier for them to do this, just because they had been strangers. Neither had any idea of the background of the other. They came to each other fresh, and felt that comment and advice and help must be more valid because it was quite uncoloured by the web of the past. And the conclusion, after all, when all the argument was concluded and the pros and cons discussed, was really very simple. 'We must start again.'

'Easier said than done,' was Ruth's comment.

'I don't see why. The first thing is to get free legally.'

'Wash our dirty linen in public.'

'It isn't as bad as it sounds, I think. In court it only takes about five minutes. What really stops people is the confession of their own failure, I believe. But once you've faced that, the rest is mere mechanics.'

'And then?'

They looked at each other. It was impossible that the thought should not have been in both their minds; but it remained there, half promise, half hope…

'I think that Life will sometimes give you a second chance, if you are worth it; but one ought to be careful about using it.'

Ruth nodded. 'Once bitten, ten times shy, as far as I'm concerned.'

It was their last day in Venice. They had been out to see the little church at Torcello, where the great blue Madonna stands framed in her mosaic of gold. The simplicity of this primitive masterpiece affected both of them. It was such a clear categorical credo, cut down to essentials, stark and profound. It was not Art at all, or perhaps it was the highest form of Art, the symbol through which men and women can grasp the final realities of Faith. Neither Ruth nor Benjy were religious in the accepted church-going sense; but the universal message of Belief and Hope shone from that towering figure, witness of the Eternal before the souls of men. For nine hundred years she had stood there in mute and gentle testimony. 'Blessed are the pure in heart for they shall see God.'

So they were silent as they sat together on the deck of the little steamer and came home over the still lagoons in the cool of the evening. Venice lay low on the water, the great Campanile pointed to the sky. The air had that clarity and softness that only breathes in Italy.

'I think it would be a good idea,' said Benjy, 'not to worry any more. If we leave it to Time – or to God, if you prefer – it will sort itself out. By nagging at it on the mental level, we only get in the way of the purpose of Life.'

'"Cast thy burden upon the Lord."'

'Yes. "And He shall sustain thee." Funny, isn't it, how, altho' the Church has completely failed to grasp its opportunities, as soon as you come to any problem, personal or social, and begin to probe it, you are forced back to motive and from motive to belief.'

They were silent again, watching the drowsy city creep nearer over the water. Then, without looking at him, Ruth laid her hand on his arm.

'Benjy, I want to say – how much you've helped me.'

'My dear.' He looked at her tenderly. 'I've quite decided in my own mind that you were "sent".'

'We were both sent, then.'

'If Life did that much for us, shouldn't we just wait – and hope?'

'Yes. Now… thanks to you… I can hope again.'

But in the winter of 1940 it wasn't easy to hope. The war had reached its ebb for England. Nightly London reeled under the blitz. The darkened city burned and crumbled. Londoners grimly emerged from the cellars and shelters, pale and sleepless, walked or hiked to their jobs when the transport broke down, got through the day and at night went to ground again. It became a routine, but where would it end? The thought was in many minds, but the perky humour and resilient temper of the population refused to admit it. They carried on.

The pre-war life seemed something that belonged to another planet. Steadily, as the situation worsened, the horizons had been narrowed down and down, till the country's whole aim was concentrated on victory. Restrictions and prohibitions, that grew heavier and heavier, were accepted cheerfully and inevitably. The latent character of England emerged from a morass of selfishness and leisurely optimism to a realisation of the meaning of the word duty, to a pride in responsibility, to a solid determination which rightly earned the admiration of the world. The war transformed England, and it must be put on the credit side of the disaster that the national character was much improved thereby. For years men and women had been running away from realities, drugging their consciences in a round of self-seeking and pleasure. For years they had taken refuge in fantastic optimism and inglorious 'ostrich-ism'. Not a few despised the lethargy and defeatism of their own land. But now, it was different. It was Old England again, the England of Agincourt, of the Armada, of Waterloo, the England that had built an Empire. The people rallied to its flag. They recanted, and demanded burdens and sacrifices. They stripped for labour and for battle. Personal and private life no longer had any place. It survived only under the veto of the general good. Family life had been broken up. Sons and daughters were serving and living strange monastic lives. Fathers and Mothers tried to hold the home together under difficulties and obstacles that were almost insurmountable. But through it all came a new hope, born in the fire, of a nobler and better world. England had regained her old place in the vanguard of civilisation. She had her duty to the future. She looked out of the valley of the shadow to horizons beyond the war and her ardent faith made the burden worthwhile.

Benjy had taken a job in the Ministry of Information shortly after the war broke out. Ruth joined the WVS. The two saw each other when they could and Benjy's family took Ruth to their hearts. She fitted perfectly into their little circle, and, now that three of her sons had joined up, Mrs Lukin sought her company and treated her like a daughter. Discreetly, neither Benjy's father nor Mother made any enquiry about their relationship. It was tacitly understood that they meant a lot to each other. Nobody enquired what they were going to do. The war suspended such decisions. But Benjy knew now with certainty that Ruth was woven deep into his life. She was bound up in all his hopes and plans for the future and, though nothing was avowed between them, he hoped and believed that she felt as he did.

It was just after the year had turned, that his phone rang one morning and he heard Ruth's voice saying that she must see him. Could they dine together that night?

'If you don't mind the blitz,' said Benjy. 'Why not come out to Frognal and stay the night? It's a bit quieter there usually.'

'No, I can't manage that. What about that little place in St Martin's Lane. It's open for dinner, isn't it?'

'Yes – or was two nights ago. But one never knows…'

'I'll meet you there at seven.'

'Right. We shall probably have the place to ourselves.'

'So much the better. Goodbye, dear.' Ruth rang off. Benjy paused for a moment before going on with his work. Ruth's voice sounded strained. He hoped nothing had happened. Well, he would have to wait till dinner to find out. He took up the article he was censoring and read on.

As he left the Ministry that evening the sirens went. The night was pitch black. A damp cold drizzle was falling. He felt his way along the deserted streets, crossing with the aid of his torch, colliding with other pedestrians hurrying by. An occasional taxi shot past. Tiny pinpoints of light showed the islands. London was like a tomb.

The distant drone of the bombers came as he turned off Charing Cross Road and hurried down through Seven Dials. The guns over in the East End started as he reached the door of the little restaurant, went in, closing it behind him, and then pushed his way through the heavy blackout curtains. It was strange inside to see the lights on the tables, the waiters standing about, the buffet loaded with hors d'oeuvres – and nobody there. He remembered in peace time how crowded and gay it had been. Now it was like a place set for ghosts. He took off his hat and handed it with his raincoat to the waiter. Then he saw Ruth, already seated over in one corner, behind a screen. He sat down beside her.

They talked desultorily as they ordered some food. Waiters with nothing to do hovered about, stopping to listen now and then, when the sound of the bombers passed close overhead. They all seemed to want to pass the time of day with the clients. One by one they came up, made some opening remark and then went on to tell about 'their' bomb, their casualties, what happened the night before last in their street. They vied with each other describing craters and damage and death. 'Just like fishing stories,' Benjy whispered: each felt he must cap the other. Their meal was almost over before they were left alone. Several times they heard the bombs that came close, and felt the building tremble with the shock of the explosion. There was a curious unreality about the whole scene. An intensely reasonable nightmare was going on. This street, that had been gay with theatres and hooting taxis and crowds of people, now utterly silent except for guns and bombs and the menace of the eternal droning overhead.

'Benjy,' said Ruth, as they drank their coffee, 'I've had terrible news.' Benjy looked at her quickly and saw how nervous she was. He forgot everything that was going on around them and waited for her to go on. 'I told you that Roger – my husband – was in the Auxiliary Air Force, didn't I?' Benjy nodded. 'I haven't heard a word from him for a year or more. As you know we're absolutely separated. Well, two days ago, I had a wire from his CO telling me he had had a bad crash and was in hospital. I got through on the phone and found out where he was and rang the hospital. They wouldn't tell me much, but they said he was asking for me. I felt I had to go – that was why I couldn't lunch with you on Tuesday. I didn't say anything at the time, because I didn't know how serious it would be, and I didn't want to worry you.' She paused, and was evidently in some difficulty about going on. The place shook as a bomb fell near. Neither of them paid the least attention.

'When I got there, they showed me in to see the Doctor. He was a very nice man. He told me that Roger's machine had been shot up, crashed on landing and caught fire. The rescue party apparently just managed to get him out, but the doctor warned me he was badly burned and in great pain. He said, was I used to things of this kind, had I ever been a nurse or anything? I told him I'd done my VAD course and First Aid and so on. It didn't seem to reassure him much. He told me that I must be prepared for it to be pretty bad. Ordinarily they wouldn't have let me in to see him, but his condition was critical and apparently he had been calling for me in his delirium.' Ruth paused again, then she said very low, 'It was horrible, Benjy. You see, besides the rest of his burns and a broken leg, he's been blinded...' Her voice trembled and she paused before going on. 'I'm afraid I didn't put up a very good show. I stood it long enough to speak to him, and promised to come back and see him again and so on; but then I had to go out. I was most frightfully sick... Afterwards I went in to see the Doctor again. I felt I had to know what would happen. It didn't seem possible he could live. Of course the Doctor hadn't any idea of what our relationship was, or had been, and he was at pains to reassure me. He told me that, of course, it would take a long time; but they would be able to give him a new face, lips, eyebrows, nose and so on. He went into a lot of details and showed me photographs of the wonders they had done for others who had been just as bad. Of course, he'll never see again, he said, but in every other way we'll patch him up and make him quite presentable. Try not to worry too much, he said, he's alive and that's the great thing; It's a miracle, if you want to know.'

Ruth stopped and Benjy pushed his brandy over to her. She took it and drank. Then she looked at him and looked away again and took his hand.

'Darling – I can say Darling to you now – I've had two days to think it all out. Or rather I took two days to reconcile myself to the inevitable and to make up my mind to see you... We've never said anything about what we feel for each other. But I know – and so do you. I suppose it needed something like this to make me face up to that too. I was too young to know anything when I married. I wasn't in love, though I thought I was. It was six years of... of misery... until I broke away. He treated me like – well, it's no good going into that... As a man I feel nothing but contempt for him; but it's not a case of that now...' She paused again. 'I'd hoped that someday, you and I, that we could be married... I love you, Benjy.'

He could not speak and just waited, feeling as if the end of the world had come, and hearing the whistle of a bomb falling, prayed earnestly that it would annihilate them both. But it fell with a crump a few streets away. Ruth took another drink of brandy and went on, jerkily:

'There it is... We're just unlucky, that's all... I've tried to argue with myself that it isn't my responsibility, that any of the women would do just as well; but he's given his sight... I happen to be his legally – and there it is... I must do my duty... So, my dear love,' – and she looked deep into his eyes – 'this is goodbye.'

'No, no!' Benjy was shocked, staggered at the awful finality in her voice. He felt numb with misery, with frustration. Why, why why did life come to shreds in his hands? He stammered on, knowing it was useless, hopeless.

'Be fair to me... Don't leave me... I need you... You'll need me... You'll never get through this...'

But she stopped him. 'I need you so much that, if I was to go on seeing you, I should never go through with it at all. Do you remember that evening coming back from Torcello when you talked about leaving things to God? We left them too long, my dear. We forget that He helps those who help themselves. Oh, I know I was as much to blame as you... Well, now Life has other plans for me, it seems. I wish I knew what I had done to deserve it...'

Benjy went on mechanically swinging his dial, lost in thought. 'In Shallows and in miseries...' There wasn't anything really worth living for without her. He had lost the way. In spite of the effort – and he had made the effort – in spite of the love, in spite of everything... Life was an inscrutable, damnable business; but it was no good thinking about it. No good. Nothing was any good. His eyes slowly focussed on Peter Morelli's back sitting there in the second pilot's seat and he remembered where he was. Going in to bomb Kiel! Of course! Going in to bomb Kiel... The heavy roar of the engines lapped the aircraft round. The motionless back of Peter, the motionless floor, the motionless seat on which he sat, were so unreal it seemed like a ghost aircraft, a droning spirit, condemned to wander for ever, lost, in the fathomless reaches of the night...

'Where are we now?' came Thornly's voice, 'Isn't it about time we altered course?'

'Not yet, sir.' Cookson was checking a list of figures on his pad.

'I've just got an astro fix. We're nicely on track, sir. Just passed the third meridian. I think we shall be over target a bit ahead of time.'

'Good! That'll give us a chance to have a look round. Let me know when you want me to alter course.'

'I will, sir.'

Cookson went back to his figures.

TOM COOKSON

'WHERE ARE WE now?'

Tom Cookson smiled to himself, as he bent over the chart table again. It reminded him of young Dick. Young Dick sitting there, stripped to the waist, laughing in the warm sun, sitting on the cabin top of the *Dolphin*, after they had weathered their first storm, laughing at him, as he tried to take a sight from the plunging deck. 'Where are we, Tom?' he laughed. 'Where are we now?'

Tom didn't know. That was the truth. The mystery of navigation, which still fascinated him was a far greater puzzle to him then. In theory he knew more or less what to do. But it is one thing to have the whole thing buttoned up in a solid room ashore, and another to concentrate on figures in a reeling cabin, and still another to bring the sun down on to the horizon of a sextant mirror from a small yacht's deck when the seas are running high. It was like snipe shooting, one instruction book had said. Tom had never done any snipe shooting; but he gathered that meant you had to be pretty quick on the trigger and pretty sharp in the eye. The book didn't exaggerate. Tom had been trying for half an hour to get a sight, and he'd failed miserably. Neither the sun nor the horizon would stay in the field of his sextant long enough. Dick had been watching his efforts sceptically, listening to Tom swearing under his breath and when at last he'd lowered the sextant – for it got pretty heavy to hold up after a bit – he'd laughed and jeered, 'Where are we, Tom? Where are we now?'

It was their first cruise; the first time they had ever been out of sight of land, the first time they had undertaken a deep-sea voyage in their own little ship, the ship they had planned and built together. They were three days out from Auckland. The gale had hit them the first evening and hadn't let up for two days and three nights. Now the wind had moderated and the sun had come out, though big seas were still running. They were alone in the magnificent desolation of the ocean. The long rollers towered up behind them, lifting the little *Dolphin's* counter, then, as the crest hissed under them in a smother of foam, she seemed to pause there on the summit of the world. They could see far out over the angry emptiness to the four horizons. Then, as the wave rushed off to leeward, the *Dolphin* would slide down into the trough and lie becalmed in a deep valley of water, till slowly she climbed the far slope, her sails filled and she poised herself again on the next wave-top. The rhythm repeated itself everlastingly.

Tom had been trying to use the sextant, wrapping a leg round the mainmast to steady himself; but it was no good. He couldn't catch that fleeting second on the crest when the horizon was visible. He came aft, placed the sextant back in its case.

'We'll have to wait a bit,' he told Dick, 'I can't get a sight yet. It needs practice – and I haven't had any practice. Meanwhile we may as well carry on. It's more or less the right direction.'

'It's a fine thing,' commented Dick, 'when the ship's captain gets lost in mid Pacific, five hundred miles from land. Where is the nearest land, anyway?'

'About four miles away,' said Tom.

'Four miles! You're crazy! Where?'

'Right under the keel,' laughed Tom. 'What about the Captain's dinner?'

The two were great friends. They had been brought up together and spent all their spare time mucking about in boats. They had raced the *Tikiteris* (fourteen footers) on the Waitemata. They had made short cruises up the Gulf with seasoned yachtsmen. They haunted the waterfront. Dick's father owned a ships chandler's. The boys had been brought up on the scents of paint and tarred rope, the cold bitter smell of anchors and the musty odour of size in unbleached canvas. The dark, cavern-like store where men could buy anything for a ship was the Aladdin's cave of their childhood. Every day their young ears were filled with the sweet-sounding names for the gear of ships. Lanyard, deadeye, tackle; the halliards, the runners and the falls; the jibboom, the mizzen and the spinnaker. They heard men using these words and the music they made in young heads conjured up the grace of sailing ships, large or small, under way or at anchor, made pictures in their minds of bellying sails and breaking seas, the surge of the bow wave, the glitter of the wake. Dick would never forget the first time he held the tiller in a stiff breeze and felt the thrilling tremble of it under his small hands, felt the yacht rushing and swooping along with her gunwale under, felt the power of the invisible air striking the up-curling wing of canvas above him. He started to laugh and his eyes sparkled and he hung on, guiding the ship, giving to the gusts, keeping her on course. 'She's alive, Dad! She's alive! he shouted. 'I can feel her tugging! Oo! How lovely!' And his father, smiling, looking down at him, ready to help if he got into trouble, thought to himself, 'Smart kid! Ought to make quite a helmsman one day!'

Five years later, when he was leading the fleet in his fourteen-footer *Marama*, with Tom hard after him in *Terito*, Dick sailed so hard that he sailed himself under, and Tom, when he saw Dick's dinghy capsize, luffed up and stood by to rescue him. 'Go on, go on, you fool,' shouted Dick from the water, 'you're throwing away the race!' But Tom had shaken his head and stood by, till the rescue launch came up and took Dick in tow. Then he quietly carried on to finish a half-mile behind the rest. Somehow that cemented their friendship. Dick crewed for Tom all the rest of the season and *Terito* was always in the first three.

It was not for another year, when Tom was twenty and Dick eighteen, that Tom voiced his great idea. They were standing together watching a big ketch anchor in the Waitemata channel. The idea had been lying about in his head, sub-conscious, unformed, for quite a time. 'Why don't we build our own boat, a decent seagoing boat, and do some deep-water sailing?'

'That's an idea, Tom. I'm game. But where's the money to come from?'

'I can find that. I've got some.'

'You never told me!'

It was a strange story; but Tom didn't choose to discuss it then. 'If we build her strong and weatherly, we could sail to Fiji, to Tahiti, to California even.'

'If we could find the way!' Dick laughed:

But Tom was taking it seriously. 'I can find my way all right. You leave that to me. There's no difficulty about that.'

'Who'll design her?'

'We will! We'll make a half model, like those in your father's office, and then take off the measurements from that. Let's see, she ought to be about thirty on the line, around eleven in beam and draw five feet.'

'More.'

'P'raps. We'll make the model half-inch to the foot, then we can see.'

'Cutter rigged?' asked Dick.

'You bet, with a nice short gaff and a boomed staysail.'

'But we'd better have the main loosefooted. It'll be safer if we jibe.'

'Mm...' Tom considered it. 'I was thinking of roller reefing. I don't fancy tying reefpoints at night in dirty weather.'

So they began to hammer it out. The dream ship began to take shape in their minds. They talked to their friends. The news got around, 'Bridgeman's boy and Tom Cookson are going to build a boat'. It was surprising what a lot of interest it aroused. Men would drop into the store and ask for details. Old sailors like Ned from South Carolina would call by and remark, apropos of nothing, 'Hear that son of yourn is goin' to built a boat, Mr Ben. Hope it ain't no fancy craft, like these here modern cockle-shells, cut away like a cucumber forrard. Wants to be good and sturdy with a snubby little forefoot and a nice hard turn to the bilge. What size would they be making her, now?'

And when Ben Bridgeman told him, Ned nodded his head slowly and thoughtfully. 'Sounds as though she might be a trim little craft; but, say, Mr Ben, you ain't goin' to let them kids go seafarin' in a ship with a stern cut off like a row-boat? That sartin murder! Ain't no surer way to be pooped in a followin' sea. No sir, must have a transon. Good ship, like a good woman, must have a nice ass.'

So it went on. There wasn't a man on the waterfront but had ideas to offer, opinions, prejudices, reasons why the ship should be built his way. Hardly one agreed with another, for there is nothing so personal as a sailor's dream of a perfect ship. They came to offer the boys advice; but what they really offered were their dreams. Dreams conjured out of the attic of reminiscence of bucking into heavy seas, of running before gales, dreams of squalls and hurricanes, of storm and calm. And always, when the story ended, came the advice, the moral: 'Well, son, that taught me a lesson. If only…' and then would come the solution to the danger or disaster.

Tom and Dick listened to it all as their model began to take shape under plane and spokeshave. Dick was the more easily impressed of the two and sometimes wondered if they were on the right lines; but Tom worked away quietly, unheeding.

'She's going to be okay, Dick,' he said, eyeing the sheer. 'We were right when we argued it out in the first place. I haven't heard much to make me change my mind. We want a boat that the two of us can handle easily in a tight corner and that one of us can sail single-handed most of the time. That limits the size, and we've taken the size to the limit. We want a ship that sails upright and not on her ear, we'll get that in a good firm midsection and not too much canvas – we aren't in a hurry and half a knot more or less won't worry us. We want something that'll go to sea and take what comes, so we must have a nice long keel for running and heaving to. We'll have plenty of beam and a bold sheer to keep her as dry as we can, a nice clean run and a good bit of ballast inside to keep her motion easy. Everything's got to be sturdy, hull, rigging, and canvas. She'll be all right, Dick, don't you worry. In fact she'll be more than all right, she'll be a peach.'

It was September and the summer was coming on. The boys decided to build in the open on the beach out beyond Cox's bay. Once the model was finished, all they had to do was to scale it up to full size and start in! Simple! But there was a lot of laborious calculation of sizes and measurements before they could get down to the actual building; lots of timber to be sawn and hauled to the beach; a hut to be run up for tools and drawings; a thousand and one details to plan. But at last they got to the point of making a start.

The first part nearly broke them, for it was the heaviest work of all. It took them over three months to set up the *Dolphin's* backbone.

The heavy timbers that formed the stem, keel and deadwood were cumbersome to handle and laborious to fit. Drilling holes two feet long through tough kauri pine is skilled and difficult work, and the boys were no shipwrights. They ruined a fortnight's labour by getting one hole out of truth, were forced to scrap the stern post and start again. But at last they got it together. All the bolts home. Sternpost and deadwood morticed and jogged into the keel, stem scarphed and rabbett cut. Then with the help of tackles, they lifted the whole thing into position on the 'ways' they had built to take it and thru' bolted it firmly to the iron keel.

Dick's father had had this cast in the foundry. It was the only job the boys had agreed they could not tackle. Four tons of iron take some moving. The day the keel came down to the beach on a lorry, it took six men with crowbars to unload it and level it on to its chocks. The backbone was now ready for the frames, but it still looked nothing like a boat. More like the skid of an enormous toboggan, standing there lonely on the sand pointing out over the sunny waters.

The next job was to set the 'formers' up on the keel. These formers, or ribs, were temporary frames, carefully scaled up from the model. When long battens were nailed around them from stem to stern, the ship, which up till then had only been a keel and a lot of lumber, was transformed into a boat. It was a sudden change, for the formers only took a day to get into position and when all ten were in place, they saw her shape for the first time. There she stood!

Tom and Dick spent the whole of the next day just standing round gazing with admiration at their own handiwork, examining the hull from every angle, and inviting all their friends to come and look. But then they started in again. All the frames had to be cut one by one, carefully bevelled and fitted to the keel between the formers, first tacked in place against the battens and finally bolted to the keel, the bilge stringers and the shelves. When they were all in place, the original formers were taken out, leaving the 'skeleton' of the hull complete.

Day after day the boys worked in the hot sun. They went brown and their forearms grew tough and muscled. It was fine work! Fine to breathe the sea air, the healthy smells of tar and paint, the fresh sweet odour of cut wood. Strength and patience and thought went into their ship, and bit by bit, as they slowly progressed, the boys began to get the fever of the shipwright, who thinks while he hews of the compound curves of the underbody, the swelling beauty of the topsides and the neat tucked hollow of the run. In their minds, as they fashioned the timbers piece by piece, they began to sense the way the wood should go, began to allow for bevelling and fairing and trimming down. They made blunders, of course, for there is no art so intricate as that of the boatbuilder, where no joint is square and the shape of the structure changes at every point from stem to stern. When they got stuck, they stood round scratching their heads trying to argue it out, and sometimes, in an emergency, went to the professional boatbuilders who sawed their lumber, to pick their brains.

The work went slowly, but once they could see the skeleton of the hull, the worst was over. They set about the planking which, altho' it looks so smooth and easy when complete, is in fact, the most tiresome and maddening job of all. At first it seemed they would never get the garboard strake in place. For days it defied all their efforts with clamps and chain tackles to bend it snug against the frames. But once they had got it on, the rest was easier and slowly the skin crept up. Then they started at the sheer and worked down and, at last, there remained only the 'shutter' strake to fit. When it was done, they stood on the beach, looking up at their creation, marvelling at the lovely lift of the stem, at the firm strength of the body and the long shadow that marked the run. It was their boat! They had made it, out of brains and brawn and baulks of straight timber! They were proud in a deep and satisfying way that only comes when artist and craftsman are merged in the act of creation. They knocked off, threw a party for all the unpaid hands who had come along and helped through those long months, and toasted the ship. Now for the last lap!

It was one day over a year before, while they were watching the band saw break up the huge kauri logs for their keel, that old Sid Bergman, the owner of the yard had said to the boys: 'If you ever get her afloat, boys, which I misdoubt you never will, you can bring her round here and the lads will give you a hand to fit out.' He had said it more or less as a joke, for he'd seen many an amateur start in to build his own boat and give up before the frames were on. The prospect of finishing seemed far away then, but the boys had nodded gratefully, watching the flying sawdust and Tom had shouted over the screeching saw: 'It's a bet, Sid. We'll hold you to that.'

But Sid was as good as his word, and when they had carefully caulked the seams and given the hull a rough coat of paint, the day came to launch her. 'Bring her round as soon as you can, boys. Don't start weighing her down with decks and ballast and bulkheads and such-like. You'll never get her off if you do – as it is, you'll have a job.'

He was right. Only a bit of beach separated her from her future home, and yet, now it came to getting her over that hundred yards, it seemed a hundred miles. Their plan was simple. They would build a cradle to hold her upright, place rollers underneath and, at low water, tow her down the beach, as far as they could. Then when the tide came up, she would float off her cradle. Easy! But they had reckoned without the weight. The sand was soft and the deadweight of the hull and cradle made the rollers sink in. After great efforts, with lorries towing and everyone hauling and pushing, to say nothing of shouting and swearing, they only succeeded in moving her thirty yards before the next tide. When it came in, she stood there knee-deep in the sea, and it looked as if nothing would ever get her into deep water.

When the tide went down again, they tried another plan. They laid a tramway of planks on end under the rollers, and again, towing hard with the lorry and levering under the cradle, she went forward slowly. But again before they could float her, the tide came in. This time it lapped the underbody and the bigger waves came perilously near lifting her off the cradle. It was an anxious time. If a storm got up and lifted her clear, she would ground in the next trough, fall on her beam ends and, having no deck, would fill and sink. Tom realised the danger. At all costs they must get her back on to the beach and put on a deck before she was moved; but when they tried to move her, she was stuck. Nothing would coax her back up the beach. Tom had noticed the glass that day. It was falling. A rough sea with big breakers would be the ruin of their eighteen months' work. He was desperate. There was only one thing to do. He went round to the harbour-master and told his story.

Two hours later a tug with a towing hawser heavy enough to take the *Empress of Britain* came nosing round from the docks. She edged into the beach as near as she dared and Tom rowed back with the hawser and made it fast to the cradle. A second lighter warp was run out and securely fastened to the hull. Then the tug headed seaward and took the strain on the rope. But the cradle would not budge and the tug, grunting and labouring, churned up the water under her counter. For an hour she strained there, swinging port and starboard in an effort to loosen the cradle. Nothing happened. But all the time the tide was rising. The wind rose with it, bringing the rollers high on the beach. Suddenly there was a shout from the little knot of people anxiously watching from the shore. A wave had lifted the boat, and the tug took her a few feet forward into the next trough. The next wave lifted her again. She seemed to bounce once or twice, and then at last slid free and floated. Tom, standing at the bow let out a yell. The *Dolphin* was launched!

It was another six months before she was 'ready for sea in all respects'. Tom and Dick never forgot the day when, at last, they cast off for their first trial trip. There was a fresh breeze, and when they hoisted the jib and sheeted it home, the *Dolphin* nodded once or twice as though she knew what was expected of her, and then payed off a little, answered her helm sweetly and began to move. The water lapped and splashed against her bows. There was no music like it in the world! They took her clear into deep water, rounded up into the wind and got up the mainsail. When the sails filled again, she began to foot it, clean and steady, heeling a little to the breeze. Nobody said anything at first. They stood, watching the set of the sails, feeling the motion, gauging the bow wave and glancing back at the wake.

Then Sid came aft to the cockpit where Tom was at the tiller. 'She'll do, Tom. Nice easy motion and plenty of power. Sheet the sails home and see how high she'll point.'

Tom hauled on the mainsheet and Dick hardened in the jib. The *Dolphin*, as if she knew it was up to her to show her paces, heeled to the freshening wind and got down to work. She pointed high and held her way into the short seas, brushing them aside smoothly and easily; then, when Tom put the helm hard down, she swung smartly over on to the other tack losing no way, and settled down again to thrash her way to windward.

'A good six knots, Tom. She's a real credit to you boys. Now all you want is a bit of dirty weather. You'll not know what she's worth till you've been reefed right down and hove to. But she shapes well. Now let her run.'

Tom brought the helm up, payed out the mainsheet, while Dick goose-winged the jib. The *Dolphin* slipped off downwind. She ran straight, leaving a clean glittering wake. Sid took the helm while Tom walked for'ard to Dick. The two boys stood by the mainmast. They were laughing, jubilant.

'She's a peach! Look at that bow wave!' Dick pointed.

'And the wake! Look at that wake! When we were beating just now I watched to see if she made any leeway; but she pointed clean as a whistle.' Tom was already thinking of his course.

'She's marvellous! We can go anywhere in her.'

'It was worth the eighteen months just for this, wasn't it, Dick?'

'You bet! I can't wait to get her into deep water.'

'Another month and then we'll be ready!' Tom was working it out. 'There are a lot of small jobs to finish off. Why don't you take the helm off Sid? I'm going below.'

The boys were well contrasted. Dick was gay, mettlesome and fiery, light-footed, nimble hearted. Dick was all that, had been all that... for he was dead now... His Flight Commander had written Tom how he had taken his Hurricane down on the circle of Messerschmitt 110's, finished one, broken up a second, caught the crossfire from a third and fourth and dived on down, burning, with a last 'I'm gone' on the intercomm and plunged into the sea. That was three years later. Into the sea! Tom was glad he was laid there. Dear Dick with his light quirky laughter: 'Where are we now, Tom? Where are we now?' And where are you, Dick? where are you now, under the summer waves that lap the coast of England...

Tom had loved all that in his friend, loved his dash and fire, for Tom had no dash, only a quiet determination that goes ahead, goes through obstacles not round them. Even in argument he advanced slowly, methodically, from premise to premise, marshalling fact upon fact, until the issue could never be gainsaid. Dick used to laugh at the slow Socratic way he would consider a problem and then begin, point by point, almost pedantically stating his argument, forcing agreement at each step and so driving his antagonist to concur in his own conclusion. But it was all done with such kindness and clarity, with such a fund of slow good-humour, so unruffled, so serene. You gave in, you followed, you were ready to follow because you admired and in the train of admiration came affection, came love – was it too big a word? No, it was not too big, Dick thought, for the way he felt...

'Who the hell was your father, Tom?' They were sitting in the *Dolphin's* cockpit running back to Auckland down the Hauraki Gulf. 'I bet he was a bloody lawyer, from the way you talk.'

'I often wonder!' laughed Tom. 'I may be the son of an Admiral or a King's Councillor – or a roadmender, for all I know.'

Dick was wide-eyed. 'I never knew you were an orphan, Tom.'

'No more did I till that legacy arrived a couple of years ago... There was a letter with it. I meant to tell you about it one day. The letter didn't say how my foster-parents got me, but I presume, if I wasn't just left on their doorstep, they must have acquired me from some charitable institution. If that is the case then the chances are I am illegitimate.' Tom paused and slacked the mainsheet.

'I can remember my "father" well. He was a clockmaker and jeweller. I believe he must have been quite a master of his craft. A strange little man with spectacles, his hobby was the collection of old typewriters. He had all sorts of typewriters. He kept them in his private workshop at the back of the shop. Queer people used to come to see them. There was a canary in the window, I remember, and the little room was full of the ticking of clocks… Yes, he was a weedy, meticulous little man. Funny to think of him as dead… Looking back on it now, I often wonder why on earth he adopted me. I suppose the truth is he didn't. He did whatever his wife wanted. She was big and florid and, as I remember it, frightfully untidy. There were always empty bottles of beer on the window-ledge and the place smelt of stale cigarette smoke. I remember unmade beds and dirty dressing-gowns and my mother tinting her hair with something out of a bottle. She used to shout when she got angry, which she did very often. "This is no place for you, Tommy," said my father, after one of her outbursts, when we were alone. "Nowhere to play and nothing much to do, How would you like to go away over the sea to a country with lots of green fields and mountains?" I'd never seen sea or mountains, so I said I should like to very much. "All right, Tommy, you shall. I'll send you to my sister. Now this is a secret between us two. Don't say anything to your mother. Promise!"

'I promised, and one day, about three months later, when my mother was out and I'd almost forgotten about it all, my father got a telegram. He hurriedly packed all my clothes into a suitcase and bundled me out into a taxi. It was a long ride. I suppose we must have been going to the London Docks, though I didn't know it then. My father didn't say much, except to tell me that I was going on my "journey to the sunshine", as he called it. I hadn't much idea of distance at that age – I was only seven – and I didn't realise, of course, that I was to leave England for ever. "No place for you," my father kept muttering to himself. "No place for you. No home for you. You're well out of it, Tommy, if you only knew. Well out of it! And shan't I catch it from your mother!" He chuckled, bought me some sweets and gave me some money in a little leather purse. I can't remember the ship's name, but I know she seemed enormous to me then. I looked up her tall black sides to the white paint of her upper works, as we went up the gangway.

'The Captain met us on deck. He was a bluff pink-faced man. "Well, sonny!" he greeted me, "coming on a trip with us down under?" I suppose I must have answered yes. Anyway we went below and I was shown into my bunk in one of the stewardess's cabins. She was to look after me. Then we came on deck again and my father took me all round the ship. There were crowds round the gangway, and when the All ashore! went, my father lifted me up in his arms and kissed me – a thing he had never done before. "Now be a good boy, Tommy. Don't get into mischief and mind you do whatever the Captain tells you." Then he gave me another hug and I remember my cheek was wet – the little man must have been crying! Funny how saying goodbye upsets people... He put me down and positively ran down the gangway, and disappeared along the wharf. That was the last I ever heard of him – till the letter from the lawyers turned up a couple of years ago and a cheque for £1,000. Apparently he left me all his money. When we docked at Auckland, your mother was waiting for me on the quay.'

Built with the idea of making ocean cruises, the *Dolphin* had plenty of stowage space. Built to sail in warm latitudes, she was open from end to end below, to allow the air to circulate and keep her cool. There were no frills or fancy fittings. All the forepart of the ship was given over to ship's stores – sails, spare anchors, warps, and the hundred and one things that may be needed for running repairs or emergencies on a long cruise. The main cabin was simple. Sofas either side served as bunks. There were big water tanks under them and room for blankets and bedding behind. Above were deep lockers. Between the sofas was a swing table with lead weights below which kept it level when the *Dolphin* rolled. Lights, a stove and the little motor for use in emergencies, all ran on paraffin. An Elsan and a bucket sink, completed the domestic arrangements. Crockery and cooking utensils were reduced to a minimum. Everything had its place and was securely fastened in it. The ship could roll her deck under, and loosen nothing. Perhaps she was too primitive for some; but for a couple of young men she was all that could be wished.

When you went below into the airy cabin, bare and clean, you felt that here was a ship built to go to sea. There was nothing that would suffer by contact with sea water, nothing that could not be scoured and scrubbed, nothing that would break if you were thrown against it when things got lively. There was plenty of headroom under the cabin top, plenty of light from portholes along it, and handholds everywhere. The only place where Tom had spread himself at all was on the chart table. It was large, with a deep drawer underneath for charts. A carefully fitted cupboard above it had divisions for sextant, chronometer, books and navigational tables. Opposite this was a place for oilskins and the tiny galley. Between, the companionway led up to the cockpit. It was roomy. There was plenty of length to lie out in the sun, and depth to afford shelter for night sailing. It was made to be 'self bailing', that is, the water, if you shipped any, ran out of two tubes in the floor of the cockpit, back into the sea. A compass was mounted at the fore end of the well, so that you could sit at the tiller and see it clearly. The tiller itself could be pegged in any position. Then she would steer herself with no attention from the crew. On deck everything was simple and seamanlike. The *Dolphin* could be sailed without leaving the cockpit, except when it came to reefing or handing the sails. The boys had a light genoa and spinnaker, and a strong storm jib and trysail, roped all round, for dirty weather. When they had all their gear aboard, they knew the ship lacked nothing – the rest was up to them.

The heights of the Great Barrier Island sank below the horizon and the *Dolphin* was alone in deep water. A fresh westerly was blowing and the little ship was moving fast on a broad reach, her bow wave talking. She was headed North East, bound for the Kermadec Group, some seven hundred miles away, and thence on to Tahiti, the mecca of the Pacific. The boys considered themselves seasoned sailors now. They had cruised to Norfolk Island and back without mishap. They had learned how to sail, how to cook in a rolling galley, how to take a sight in rough weather and how to sleep through a gale. They had learned also all the humours and qualities of their ship. She was able and sea-kindly and, beyond strengthening the main-shrouds and the horse for the mainsheet, there were only minor adjustments to be made before setting out on this, their second deep-sea cruise. The wireless had announced that the weather was likely to be settled and the wind gave them a good slant, so they had said goodbye to their friends, cast off, and set sail for 'ports beyond the seas'. They had five weeks' food and water on board and the greatest ocean in the world before them. As the sun went down they took a reef in the mainsail and set their watches, four hours on and four off. Dick turned in. Tom remained at the tiller.

The *Dolphin* was very small, a mere speck on the face of the waters, as small as a man in a desert, as small as the world in the sky. Yet she had her guiding hand, her course, her life, her destiny, under the will of God. When night came down, the wind freshened. Tom, alone in the cockpit, nursed the ship on her course. No man in the world that night was happier than he. This was Liberty! This was Freedom!

These beautiful words are the names men give to fond illusions; for they are inevitably bound to their fellow men, to those who depend on them and on whom they depend. Autocracies bind them by rules imposed from above, democracies and fraternities by rules imposed from within. By regulations or obligations, they are proscribed in all that they do. In spite of this inescapable truth, men cling so persistently to the desire for Freedom and the ideal of Liberty that they are prepared to kill their fellows sooner than submit to having it curtailed. This age-old longing is too deeply rooted and too tenaciously held to be no more than a catchword. Groping his way painfully down the centuries man has always striven to free himself of his shackles. Only those ignorant of the taboos of primitive tribes advocate a return to the simple life. Today men have more liberty than at any period of the world's history. And there is no reason why, in the future, this should not be enlarged. It depends upon men. In proportion to their tolerance and uprightness, the need to restrict them will diminish; in proportion to their goodness will they walk the garden of Peace.

Of all freedoms there is perhaps none so complete and satisfying as to set to sea in a small boat. The hazards are great, the struggle continual, the domain limitless. It is true that men who do such things prove themselves only to themselves, learn the limits of their courage and endurance, their patience and skill, exercise to the full their faculties of self-reliance and initiative, call on every reserve of determination and strength. But their reward is no less than the purest draught of the wellspring of Liberty. Man can never come closer to the heart of things, to the mystery of the Universe itself, than by communion with the moods of the unbridled ocean. Here, seeking freedom, he is at once at the mercy of wave and wind, while the headstrong seas themselves rise and fall at the bidding of the moon. So, reaching from liberty to liberty, the sailor learns the futility of seeking to escape the eternal rhythms of the Universe.

Tom did not think of sailing in these terms. He put it much more simply. 'I was happy,' he thought, 'I was free. I was my own master. I went where I wanted: I knew where I was going. I had responsibilities and anxieties, but they were of the kind I could discharge. I had a goal in view and I reached it; but the best part was getting there.'

Now as his watch wore on, he grew more and more occupied on the tiller. The breeze was increasing and backing towards the south, so that to maintain her course the *Dolphin* was soon running dead before the wind. It was anxious and thrilling work keeping her straight when she got up and began to plane down the face of the seas. As the big rollers lifted under her stern, they tilted her forward, and she would rush down towards the trough before the pursuing wave, her bow wave roaring. If he failed to keep her straight, the *Dolphin* would jibe all standing and that might wrench the mast out of her. At best she would broach to and lie on her beam-ends in the sea. The next wave would smother her, she would founder and that would be the end. But Tom was a good helmsman. He knew his ship and held on. After all the wind was a fair wind and was taking them in the direction in which they wished to go. It seemed a pity to waste it. But when it got quite dark and he could no longer watch the leach of the mainsail, the thing became too tricky even for his nerve. It is one of the most difficult things in seamanship to know when to give up running, and heave to. Difficult because with the wind abaft, its strength seems less than it is; difficult because if it is left too long, rounding up into the wind is extremely dangerous and requires great judgement and skill. After one terrific plunge at breakneck speed, in which Tom thought the *Dolphin* was really going to take a header into the next sea and go straight to the bottom, he decided that something must be done to ease her, and yelled for Dick.

'We've got to get the mainsail off her,' he shouted, when Dick's head appeared silhouetted in the companionway. 'She's steering pretty wild.'

'You're telling me!' Dick shouted back.

'Daren't heave to. Can't see what's coming,' Tom yelled again. 'Go for'ard and stand by on the main halyards. When you hear me yell, drop them.'

Dick nodded and disappeared along the deck, clinging to the handholds in the cabin top. Tom carried on at the tiller, while two more heavy seas took the *Dolphin* careering along with them. Then when they were in the next trough, he hauled for dear life on the main sheet, swinging the boom inward, yelled to Dick and gave a sigh of relief as he heard the halyards come down with a run. The main-sail was a jumble of canvas on deck.

But the effect on the *Dolphin* was remarkable. Instantly she ceased rushing headlong through the night. Her staysail was still set and this still gave her plenty of speed; but all the pressure was off her, she rode higher in the water and no longer plunged madly down the faces of the seas, Dick was working slowly, fighting to subdue the intractable mass of canvas and spars on deck. It took him an hour to get sail, boom and gaff firmly lashed down. Then he came back to the cockpit, exhausted.

'Good work, Dick,' Tom shouted. 'I can hold her now. We'd better not risk heaving to till daylight.'

Dick stayed crouching in the bottom of the cockpit for a minute or two. Fighting that thrashing mass of canvas on the slippery deck in the pitch dark had pretty well finished him. Then he revived, took over from Tom and carried on, nursing the *Dolphin* through the night. After four hours he banged on the cabin top and, a few moments later, Tom appeared.

'Okay, Dick. I can hold her till morning.'

'Call me if it gets worse.'

'I will.'

Dick disappeared down the companion way. Tom was left alone again with the tiller. The *Dolphin* was taking it easily now. The big seas came roaring up behind but they slid under the counter, and the *Dolphin* hung for a moment on their boiling crests and then sank back into the trough. Tom still had to steer carefully, keeping the wind on the back of his neck and his eye on the compass; but it was relatively easy. He relaxed, and began to enjoy himself. He loved to be alone on the tiller at night. It gave him a queer sensation of power, to be abroad in a nutshell in the wastes of a great ocean. So vast and majestic were the forces of nature! So small was the ship, and smaller still the man who sailed her. Yet he did sail her, did contrive to keep that tiny hull moving under his will over the turbulent waters, did meet the storm singlehanded and hold his own.

So when at last dawn came, he was stiff, cold, covered with salt and spray, utterly weary and completely happy. Almost imperceptibly the sky lightened. He could make out the mast now, could see the staysail, then the white of the bow wave, then the face of the wave ahead. The storm had not abated. If anything it was blowing harder, but everything seemed less overwhelming once you could see. He yelled for Dick, who shortly poked his head out of the companionway, still towsled and sleepy, Tom laughed at his expression when he saw the size of the seas.

'Gosh! Have we been running through this all night? Let's heave to, Tom. You must be dead.'

Looking aft they waited for a patch when the waves seemed less terrifying. Then, just as a crest passed, Tom put the helm down, while Dick hauled on the staysail sheet. The *Dolphin* swung round in the trough of the sea, and before she rose to the next crest, lay comfortably with the wind about six points off the bow. Dick went forward, backed the jib and made it fast, while Tom put down the helm and lashed it firmly. Now the wind howled in the rigging; but the ship rode buoyantly to the waves, breasting the great swells easily and confidently. The boys crouched together in the cockpit watching the *Dolphin* carry on her fight alone. It seemed impossible that she should not be overwhelmed, yet she rose to the great seas like a duck, and let them slide off to leeward beneath her.

'She's all right!' Tom shouted in Dick's ear. 'I vote we turn in.'

Below, in the cabin, it was warm and dry, difficult to believe that a storm was raging outside. Dick boiled up some cocoa, while Tom peeled off his sodden clothing. After a hot drink and a cigarette, both of them turned in and soon were sound asleep, while the *Dolphin* fought it out with the storm.

All day the wind continued to blow. Late in the afternoon Tom put his head out. The wind showed signs of moderating. There was a break in the clouds; but it was too soon to get under way again with night coming down, so they decided to remain hove-to till daybreak.

By the following morning the wind had veered back to the west, but it was dying out to a calm, and by midday everything was slatting. It was perhaps the most trying time at sea. The ocean still felt the after-effects of the storm, swells moved interminably over it, rolling the *Dolphin* gunwale under. The ship had no way, the booms swung, the blocks crashed about, the tiller snatched back and to in its pintles. Everything chafed, groaned and squeaked. The boys got the sails furled, put up chafing pads, lashed the dinghy securely, and sat about in the cockpit in the warm sun, thrown perpetually from side to side. There was nothing to do but have patience. Tom managed to get a sight, which put them about half-way to the Kermadecs, a bit to the south of their course. They dried out their clothing on the mainboom. They smoked and talked and cursed the rolling ship. By evening the sea had gone down to a flat calm. There wasn't a catspaw. The ocean was till as a dew pond.

Not a breath stirred. The wild expanse of threatening seas had changed to a placid disc of gold. The gentlest of swells, final aftermath of the storm, stirred the surface, like the slow breathing of a sleeper. The *Dolphin* nodded her head as if she too were dozing, and the boys talked fitfully, almost afraid to disturb the serenity of the evening.

One immense cloud spread out like a wing above the setting sun. The light was rich and clean after the storm, like a draught of well water. As he sank lower and lower, the sun gilded the spars and rigging. The *Dolphin* lay like a golden ship on a golden ocean. A fish jumped in the stillness, fell back, and the ripples spread like a burnished watch-spring, wide and wider, till all was still again. As the sun sank the clouds glowed copper, and the sea in its reflected light turned russet, faded with the sky to pink and mauve and grey. The stars came out and the night came down.

While the line of the horizon was still visible, Tom took two or three star sights, went below and worked them out.

'We're about 250 miles south-east of the Kermadecs,' he called to Dick. 'But we're dead on course for Tahiti. What do you say we carry straight on?'

'I thought we were going to get some of those famous oranges at Sunday Island.'

'If you like; but there isn't a decent anchorage. The Tahiti oranges are pretty good by all accounts.'

'I don't care. Let's leave it until we see what sort of a wind we get – if we ever get one. Looks as if we were stuck here for good.'

Tom came up the hatchway and looked round. 'There'll be a wind all right. Before morning anyway. Out of the south-east, I should say.'

He sat down by Dick. 'Did you know the wireless has packed up, by the way?'

'It was all right this morning.'

'I know. I've changed the battery and fiddled about with it. I can't get a sound out of it.'

'I'd just as soon not hear the news anyway. It seems to get worse every day.'

'I was thinking of the weather forecast. A calm like this is unusual.'

'I'll have a look at it in a minute, when I've finished this cigarette.' Dick took a long draw and looked round the sky.

'What a gorgeous night! Look at the Milky Way! It's like a waterfall.' He paused, then apropos of nothing:

'Tom, have you ever thought what you would do if there were a war?'

'Yes.'

'The news from Europe looks pretty bad.'

'If England fights, so shall we.'

'Of course.'

They were both silent, trying to visualise what it would mean. Then Tom spoke slowly. 'I believe it's inevitable, Dick.'

'Well if it comes, it comes. We should worry. Good God! Look at that!'

There was a luminous flash under the water not far from the starboard side. Then another. And another. The next second the *Dolphin* was surrounded by a school of porpoises, gambolling and jumping. Their movement stirred up the phosphorescence in the water and each fish as it sped along seemed clothed in a skin of bluish-green light. When they leapt in the air, the phosphorescence streamed from them in cascades of silver. As they plunged back again, there were pools and eddies of light in the water. All the time they grunted like pigs, a strange sound, ill-assorted with their exquisite luminous movements. They came right up under the *Dolphin's* quarter, leapt into the air higher than the deck, arched over in a wonderful curve of light down into the sea. They were big, and in the night looked bigger, and Dick found himself wondering what would happen if one misjudged his leap and came aboard. Then, just as suddenly as they came, they disappeared. For a time the sea continued to boil and eddy with light. Then it went dark again.

The boys were just getting over the excitement of all this, when a slight tremor ran through the whole ship as if the keel had grounded. Instinctively they clutched the side of the cockpit. It was impossible that there should be anything under their keel right in the middle of the ocean. Yet, unquestionably, there had been something... Before they had time even to speak, there was a vast commotion on the surface right alongside the boat, a tremendous snort followed and a column of water and spray rose high into the air. It fell on the deck of the *Dolphin* in a heavy cascade. The spray drenched them. A hot rancid smell turned their stomachs. Then an immense body broke water. It was boiling with phosphorescence. The whale must have been over sixty feet long, twice the length of the *Dolphin*. The boys remained clutching the cockpit coaming waiting for what would happen. But the great brute, instead of sounding, remained lying there on the surface not thirty yards away, partially submerged, for all the world like a submarine. Then, by some freak of gravitation, as two tea-leaves will drift together in a teacup, the whale and the *Dolphin* drifted closer and closer together, till, by reaching out, they could almost have touched the creature's back. The boys held their breath. One strike from the flukes of his tail would have staved in the side of their ship. The immense strength of the creature obsessed them although he was lying perfectly still and inert, like a monstrous log.

'Get the gun!' whispered Dick – as if afraid the whale would hear them.

'Gun. No fear. It'll only tickle him.'

'You could go for a half mile walk on his back. Gosh, this makes me religious. Let's get out of here.'

'Where to?' Tom had stolen to the side and was gazing at the whale curiously. You could see the enormous shape under the water outlined in phosphorescence. 'I can see his tail! It's as big as the *Dolphin*.'

Dick was still whispering. 'Don't I know it. Gosh, he's drifting nearer! When he touches us, he'll get a shock and lash out with that tail and then God help us.'

Nearer and nearer they drifted. Then with a slight jar the whale touched the side of the boat. The boys waited for a sudden heave that would capsize the ship. Nothing happened. The two bodies touched again, gently and quietly… It was uncanny.

'What the hell's the matter with him?' whispered Dick. 'He must be dead.'

'I think he's gone to sleep.'

'To sleep!' Dick was indignant. 'With the whole Pacific to sleep in he has to doss down just here!'

Tom was peering under the water, then he crept back. 'It's a mother whale, Dick. I can see her baby against her flank. That's sure to make her violent. Heaven knows what she might think we were. Start the motor. I'd better stay at the tiller.'

'The motor! Why on earth didn't I think of it before!' Dick rushed down the companionway. Tom heard the sound of the panel being removed and Dick grunting as he swung the engine. There was a pause. Then Dick's voice came up from below. 'Is he – or she still there? I can't start the damn thing.'

'Still here.' Tom was leaning over the side, fascinated. Then as he looked he saw, below the whale, slowly and stealthily moving up from the depths, outlined in the phosphorescence, something so grotesque and awful that it made his blood run cold. It was a sort of ball, like a mine, and trailing beneath it, working in and out in fantastic patterns under the water, like seaweed in a tide, were long tentacles, which slowly propelled the creature towards the baby whale nestling alongside its mother's flank. The huge devil fish, for it could have been no other, was stalking its prey. Tom wanted to shout, to warn the whale, to stop that horrible and sinister approach. Just then the motor started and the *Dolphin* moved forward. A moment later, there was a tremendous commotion on the surface of the sea. The water was churned into foam. Tom saw the whale's tail rise out of the water and come down on it with a crack like thunder. A long silver tentacle rose into the air, as if groping for its sucker hold and disappeared under the sea again. For a few seconds longer the struggle went on. Then the surface gradually subsided and the stillness came back. What had been the outcome of that weird and gruesome duel? They would never know. It was a glimpse of the eternal struggle for existence among the giants of the ocean, the sort of thing that no man might ever see again. Tom slid back into the cockpit and took the tiller. The *Dolphin* chugged steadily away over the still water along a gleaming furrow of silver.

At daybreak a light air came in from the south-east and the wind freshened with the day. It was a fair wind for the *Dolphin* and she was soon making six knots under whole mainsail, topsail and big genoa. They carried the wind throughout the day. It was perfect 'yachting' weather, a firm breeze, practically no sea, bright sunlight and a sky dappled with lines of cumulus, bunched thick on the horizon, spreading out thin overhead. The *Dolphin* knocked off almost 150 miles in the next twenty-four hours. The four days that followed were much the same. The glass was steady, with no more than the usual diurnal rise and fall; the wind slackened a little with the evening, blew quite hard through the night and the sea developed a long steady swell to which the *Dolphin* rose easily and smoothly hour after hour. With the tiller pegged, she sailed herself most of the time, and life aboard developed into a quiet routine of watches and meals, of sunbathing, of small repairs and much reading. It was the sort of weather that every yachtsman dreams of when planning a cruise, the sort of weather that earned the Pacific its title. Wind and sea seemed fixed in their motions, eternal. The ocean was without limit, the wind without end. Tom and Dick would have been happy for it to go on for ever. Their little world was so snug and orderly, so free from complication and care. They knew that, when they made port again, though it might be a relief to set foot on solid ground, there would be nothing finally to equal these days of perfection.

They were getting into warmer latitudes. Sweaters and wind jackets could be discarded. The first flying fish appeared. Portuguese 'men o' war' drifted by. Tom lay for hours up in the bows, watching the foam curling away from the *Dolphin's* forefoot, listening to the music of it, seeing the flying fish, scared by the ship's approach, flash up from the depths, to break water a few feet ahead and dart away in a long curve low over the water and plop in again on the breast of the next swell. Dick spent much of his time in the cockpit dismantling the wireless, tracing out the circuit. and trying to locate the fault. But all his efforts were fruitless. He couldn't get as much as a whine out of it. So they continued steadily across the ocean. Tom pin-pointed their position each day and the plot of their course inched itself slowly across the chart. They were approaching the Tropic of Capricorn. If the wind held they would sight Raratonga in two days' time.

Then, on the evening of the fifth day, there was a subtle change in the weather. The wind died out in the afternoon. The swell went down and the *Dolphin* lay becalmed. They were now in the area where the Trades should have been blowing without intermission, and the calm was ominous. Tom looked at the glass. It was falling rapidly. The sun shone clearly, but the air seemed torried, and towards evening a light haze, very high up, began to spread in from the east. It was followed at sunset by wisps of cirrus and scattered clouds below, getting more solid on the horizon where they lay in a sombre bank. The sunset was gorgeous, but frightening. To the west the sun sank in a cloudless sky; but to the east the sky glowed yellow, green and purple.

'Just like a bruise,' Dick put it.

There was clearly some dirty weather coming up. Tom and Dick got out the storm canvas and went over it carefully, strengthening the cringle in the jib and renewing some of the parrels on the hoist of the trysail. They put extra lashings on the dinghy and saw that everything was securely stowed below. It was always trying, waiting for a blow, the more so when it came after a dead calm. The stillness of the evening was uncanny. The glass continued to fall. The *Dolphin* rolled uneasily in an oily swell which gradually increased. Everything creaked and slatted. The boys hoisted the storm jib and sheeted it in flat, took down the mainsail and lashed it, gaff, boom and canvas, firmly to the rail. Then they hoisted the trysail and made sure the tack was well and truly bowsed down to the deck.

'I don't like sending up the trysail on the main halyard like this,' said Dick. 'Look at all that hoist above the head. If anything parts on the luff, the whole lot will go. We ought to have had a special halyard and sheave for the trysail at the proper height.'

Tom stood looking up at the sail. 'Yes,' he said, 'it would have been better.'

'It's too late now, anyway.'

'The gear's pretty heavy. I don't think we need to worry. Still it's wise to take "seamanlike precaution", as they call it.'

'You bet it is,' said Dick. 'After that sunset, caution's the word. What about getting outside a good meal? It's probably the last we shall eat for days.'

'Cheerful, aren't you?'

'Look at that sky!'

The high cloud that had been spreading in from the east was now coming up and covered half the sky. It was inky black and looked blacker because of the host of stars that still shone limpid in the west. It needed no weather forecast to foretell that something with a lot of weight in it was on the way. The wireless might have warned them earlier; but, had they been warned, there was nothing much they could do. When you go to sea you take what comes.

The laws of 'revolving storms', as hurricanes are technically called, are well known. Hot air at the equator rises and is given a spin by the turn of the earth. A spiral is formed, like a gigantic turbine, and this gathers momentum as it goes. It rapidly increases in size – hurricanes are often two hundred miles or more across – and whirling round, sets off moving bodily westwards at about ten miles an hour. As it moves west, the storm begins to slide down towards the Pole. After a bit, still dropping Pole-wards, it changes direction, and begins to move eastwards. At last when it reaches colder latitudes it disperses. Thus the path of the storm is a parabola, like the toe of a boot, and the most dangerous part of the path is when it reaches the toe, and goes about. This usually takes place in about 30 degrees of latitude. The *Dolphin* lay, that evening, in latitude 26° 31'.

Tom knew all this theory. It is the sort of thing that anyone taking a ship to sea, makes it his business to know. But knowing the theory doesn't save you from the storm, nor tell you where it is. However, there are certain rules you can follow to help you to get out of the way as quickly as possible. The great thing to know is where you are in relation to the oncoming storm. Are you on its left-hand side, or its right, or are you right in the centre of its advancing path?

As the first puffs of wind began to reach the *Dolphin*, Dick was at the tiller. Tom was below, hurriedly reading through the directions again. The wind rapidly increased in strength and soon the *Dolphin* was doing a good four knots under storm canvas. The wind was gusty and the swell had increased. This much Tom noted as soon as he came on deck. The first thing was to heave to on the port tack. This they did and the *Dolphin* lay uneasily, bucking into the increasing swells. Tom faced the wind. The bearing of the storm's centre would lie on his left, and as the glass had been falling rapidly it looked as if it would soon be off the bottom of the drum – he judged that the storm was approaching fast and was about at right angles to him. In other words, the *Dolphin* lay right in its path. He announced this news to Dick.

'Gosh, Tom, I don't like the look of it, nor the feel of it. Let's get going. The sooner we're out of this the better.'

The quickest way to clear the storm was to run for it, with the wind on the port quarter. Dick put the helm up and the *Dolphin* swang down wind. They gibed over the trysail and eased off the sheets. Soon the *Dolphin* was doing five knots, scudding along before the rising seas.

'I'll nip down below and we'll have that stew.' Tom started for the companionway.

'Good idea. We shall feel better with a meal inside us.'

They crouched in the cockpit eating the stew while the *Dolphin* ran. The wind was increasing in strength, but so far it was no more than a good blow. Without the ominous signs in the sky, they might still have been carrying their old course which would have taken them right into the centre of the storm. Now they were running practically north-west, roughly in the direction of Tonga and Fiji and, unless it was coming up too quickly, might hope to miss the worst of it. You could never tell. But anyway they had done all they could.

'There's one thing about it, we've got plenty of sea room,' said Tom.

'Thank God for that,' Dick answered. 'If we'd struck this anywhere among the islands, we shouldn't have had a chance.'

'It isn't where we want to go, of course.' Tom was vaguely upset at having his navigation interfered with. 'We're heading miles north of our agreed course.'

'Listen, Tom,' said Dick. 'Our agreed course is out of this. That's where we want to go and it can't be too quick for me.'

Tom took the empty bowls and looked back over the quarter. The seas were getting larger and the wind made a low moaning note in the rigging.

'It's going to be worse before it's better,' he said cheerfully. 'I think I'll turn in and get an hour or two's sleep. Call me if it gets dangerous.' He disappeared below and closed the hatchway.

Dick carried on at the tiller. The seas were beginning to break and the low rumble of their boiling crests had an ominous sound. But he had learned the first rule of the helmsman when running in a bad sea: never look behind. Many of the old sailing ships had sentry boxes built round the wheel so that the helmsman could not look back. Only by keeping the ship straight on her course is it possible to avert disaster when things get really bad. So Dick looked resolutely ahead, peering through the darkness, feeling the motion as the *Dolphin* corkscrewed over the seas. He kept the wind steadily behind his left ear. The *Dolphin* was a buoyant little ship. She rose like a duck to the crests and slid off manfully down into the troughs again. It would have been thrilling to steer her on a night like this; but all the time at the back of his mind was an ugly presentiment. He was scared, and admitted it to himself. Tonight there seemed to be a vindictive rage in the power of the ocean. The roar of the water and the note of the wind in the rigging was rising. It was a hurricane all right; but the *Dolphin* didn't seem to mind. She ran on, true and steady. But when Dick put his hand on the trysail sheets, they were taut like bars and vibrating under the strain.

Below in the cabin, Tom didn't sleep. The motion was not violent, but down there, out of the noise, it was possible to collect one's thoughts. Half the difficulty, thought Tom, is the din. One would be a better sailor for being deaf. He lay on his bunk and went over everything carefully again. Mentally, he remembered how he had stowed all the gear, tested the pump and put on the skylight covers. He went through it all, item by item, and came to the conclusion that they had done all they could. Unless something carried away, they would weather it all right. After all, as long as the ship was watertight, it couldn't sink. His thoughts were interrupted by a crash and a shout from outside. Quickly he slid back the hatch and clambered out.

The cockpit was half full of water. The *Dolphin* had barely cleared a big sea on her counter. They had almost been pooped. Dick was clinging grimly to the tiller. The contrast at being outside again, in the fury of the increasing storm, took away Tom's breath for a second. He tried to shout to Dick, but the wind was now blowing a full gale and his words were inaudible.

'Can't hold her,' yelled Dick. 'Nearly pooped then. Get the trysail off.'

Tom came close to Dick and shouted in his ear… 'Knife in case

162

anything parts.' Dick nodded and produced his knife. Tom got his own handy in his belt and started for'ard. He was not a man to be easily intimidated, but to go forward over that bare expanse of deck in the pitch dark made him pause. The *Dolphin* was making heavy weather of it now. It was clear she was being pressed. The deck plunged and reeled as she was flung over the seas. Not much solid water was coming aboard, but the spray whistled by with the sting of hail. To get that sail down was not going to be an easy matter. The mast seemed a mile off. He could not see it. It must be a mile off. Too far, too far to go... but still it had to come in...

He steadied himself and began crawling forward on hands and knees – it would have been quite impossible to stand. After what seemed an age he felt the pinrail by the mast, pulled himself along and clasped the mast firmly in both arms. There he rested. It had taken him ten minutes to do those twenty feet. He felt for the trysail halyard and began to uncoil it from its cleat. He planned to lower it a bit at a time, bunching the sail down as he did so. But the moment he slacked the rope, it took charge, the tail of halyard was jerked from his hands and the sail began to flog like a demon. In a second the parrels burst from the luff. The whole sail flew up into the night, with a clap like thunder. A second later it was gone. Dick had slashed the sheets clear. It was all over so quickly Tom could not remember exactly what had happened. But the ship was certainly easier. She did not bury her head so much and seemed more buoyant.

After a rest Tom crawled back to the cockpit again. He felt for Dick in the darkness, heard his voice weakly as if it were miles away. 'What happened?' Dick was yelling.

'Parrels parted... took charge.'

'One way... get sail off...' Dick was shouting. Then after a pause he heard another word, 'Warps'.

Tom went below and began bringing up the warps. He fastened the old mainsail to two of them, an oil drum to a third, some lengths of plank to a fourth, and slowly, with infinite difficulty, managed to get them up through the hatchway one by one and stream them over the stern. The braking effect on the *Dolphin* was noticeable. Trailing all that gear behind had the effect of making the seas break before they reached the *Dolphin*. There was less chance of being pooped. But still, they were rushing through the night at an alarming pace.

The wind had now reached whole gale force. It was blowing at something over sixty miles an hour. In comparison with the speeds attained by man-made inventions in modern days, it may not sound much. But nobody who has experienced the ferocity of a whole gale is likely to forget it. The wind shrieked in the rigging. Air and sea were inextricably mixed. The spray, whipped off the wave crests, was coming by continuously like a tropical downpour. The roar of the seas breaking all round filled the air with rolls of thunder. The scream of the wind sent a chill through the bones. Tom took the tiller from Dick and heard his voice in what sounded like a whisper, though he was bellowing at the full power of his lungs.

'Ought to... get jib... down.'

'Daylight,' Tom yelled back. Then he added, 'Glass... Try pumps.'

Dick disappeared in the darkness and a moment later a glow of light showed as he opened the companionway hatch to go below. It seemed impossible that in the fury of the storm there should still be a light burning below. It gave Tom great comfort, steadied him, to see it there. Then, as Dick closed the hatch, all was darkness again.

Below Dick tried the pump. He found they had made water and started swinging the arm to and fro. But after two minutes it ran free. The bilges were dry. 'Thank God for that,' he thought, 'she's not making any water. Good old ship! Tight as a bottle.' Then he looked at the glass. It was still falling: 29.3. 'It can't go much lower,' he thought to himself, and looked at the clock. It was 3am. Another three hours darkness! The night seemed interminable already. Endless. It was a nightmare. Down in the cabin it was comparatively quiet. The motion seemed less, too. The fact was that the force of the gale was now so great, as the centre of the storm approached, that the wind was actually levelling out the seas, blowing them flat. Dick had just realised how tired he was after that long spell at the tiller. He sat down on the couch and hung on to a handrail. A moment later he was fast asleep...

He was awakened by a heavy knocking. He opened his eyes. It was daylight, or what went for daylight. A weird twilight seeped through the portholes. He got up, feeling stiff all over, ashamed of having slept and left it all to Tom. He went up the companionway, slid back the hatch, to be confronted by a lurid world. Sky and sea seemed one. The air was full of water. The seas roared all round. Tom was sitting crouched there at the tiller, still looking ahead. His face was caked with salt. His eyes seemed to burn in his head. He grinned weakly when he saw Dick and beckoned him with a nod of the head. Then he pointed forward and motioned Dick to take the tiller. It was impossible to hear oneself speak now. The storm had reached its climax.

It seemed madness to attempt to go forward. The storm jib had been blown to ribbons. There was nothing but a shred of canvas and sheets, tugging and slashing wildly at the shrouds and forestay. But if the standing rigging went, then it would be all up. The remains of that jib must be cut away. Tom started to wriggle himself along the deck on his stomach, holding on tight to the handrail on the cabin top, hauling himself along, hand over hand, towards the mast, his knife in his teeth. Arrived there, he laboriously worked himself up into a sitting position and reached forward along the horse to cut the jib sheets. At that moment the *Dolphin* gave a violent lurch, Tom's other hand was wrenched free, he made a despairing clutch at the rail, missed it and disappeared overboard.

Dick cried out, seeing him go and remained staring transfixed at the rail. A second later he saw Tom sliding past the counter. There was nothing to throw to him. It was impossible to stop the *Dolphin*. She was careering along madly under the bare poles at a good eight knots. Then, to his amazement, he saw that Tom had managed to grab one of the ropes trailing over the stern. He had got it! He was holding on! Dick saw him, very slowly and with great difficulty, pulling himself back towards the ship, hand over hand. It was a great feat of strength for a man exhausted by hours at the helm through the height of a hurricane. And Dick was helpless. It was impossible for him to leave the tiller, impossible for him to do anything to help his friend. At last he saw Tom under the counter. He rested there for what seemed an hour. Then, with a final effort, he managed to pull himself aboard. Dick caught him by his belt and dragged him into the cockpit. He lay there, like a dead man.

Dick had lost all account of time. This world of terrifying chaos was eternal. Human endurance could not withstand it. In all storms, there is always the danger that the crew will give out long before the ship. Now they had reached their limit... Tom stirred and sat up in the bottom of the cockpit. He made a sign to Dick, crawled to the companionway, lowered himself below and shut the hatch behind him. Dick was left alone in the full fury of the storm.

A split second later there wasn't a breath of wind.

The roar stopped as if it had been cut off by the closing of some giant door. It was absolutely still. So still, Dick used to say afterwards, that he could have lit a match on deck without it going out. He swore it was true. To port was a torn mass of whirling cloud and above – blue sky. Blue sky! Sun! It was crazy, incredible! The world had gone mad.

But the sea had gone mad too. In the calm centre of the maelstrom, the seas, released from the pressure of the wind, were rushing together. Mighty pyramids of water rose on all sides and crashed against each other. The *Dolphin*, having lost all her way, was flung, literally flung, from wave to wave. Then two black monsters, towering over the *Dolphin's* masthead and rushing together, closed on her. Dick saw them coming, left the tiller and made a wild dash for the shrouds. In some way, as he explained afterwards, he thought his only chance of safety lay in hanging on to them. A cliff of raging water came down on him. The shrouds were torn from his hands. All was green. He was under water. Instinctively he struck upwards to the surface and looked round. There, a few yards away, lay the *Dolphin*, keel uppermost. It was all over. They were done for.

He would drown, of course, but meanwhile he struck out for the overturned ship and tried to clutch at her side. The keel, above his head, was almost within reach. It swung down. He was able to grasp it, actually, so it seemed to him, to draw it down towards him. He held on; but it did not occur to him till a second later, that the miracle was happening. The *Dolphin* was slowly righting herself! Her shrouds and mast came up out of the water, she swung upright again. Dick let out a yell! Brave Ship! Ship they had built! She was unsinkable! He reached for the rail and clambered on to the deck.

Tom was lying on his bunk when the ship capsized. He was flung across the cabin and up on to the roof. He remained sitting there, comparatively comfortable, thinking he was on his way to the bottom, for there was nothing but water to be seen through the portholes. Actually, he told Dick afterwards, he was not very perturbed. If there was air in the ship, she must float. Some rigmarole he had heard back in Auckland about stability factors flashed through his mind. A ship must right itself if… and at that moment, sure enough, she had begun to turn and then swung him back on to the floor again. Not much water had come through the hatch. The floorboards were awash, no more. But he imagined, of course, that Dick was gone. Well, there was nothing to be done… He was exhausted. He decided to stay where he was and let what would come come. Nothing could be any worse. He had reached the limit of his strength. If the storm ever ended, well, then he would think about it…

At this moment Dick slid back the hatch. Neither of them could believe their eyes. Neither could think of anything to say. It was funny when they looked back on it and, indeed whenever they had discussed it, it was always with roars of laughter. So near is comedy to tragedy. 'Hullo, Dick!' Tom had said, and Dick had echoed, 'Hullo, Tom.' For all the world as if they had met on a street corner. Even the bathos of 'Mr Livingstone, I presume?' was no deeper than this.

Still there was no wind. The unbelievable chaos of the universe continued. But, though the *Dolphin* was torn and flung hither and thither like a cork, by some miracle she escaped the raging mountains of water. Everything on deck had been carried away, dinghy, boom, mainsail, part of the rail; all this was gone. She was swept clean from end to end. And yet, there above them was the blue sky and the sun! And not a breath of wind!

A few minutes later the hurricane engulfed them again. Again the sea and sky mingled in flying water. But even this was safer than the heart of the maelstrom. Besides, the boys were more confident. They had weathered one half of it, they would weather the other. They were on their way out and the thought that there must be an end to it gave them unnatural strength. Another interminable twenty-four hours dragged by. But the glass was rising, and on the evening of the next day wind and sea began to moderate. Soon there was nothing but a breeze and a dying swell. The battered *Dolphin* rocked on it, her mast still proud, erect. Weather-scarred but triumphant she was there! She was floating! She had won! Below decks, her crew were stretched out like dead men. They did not wake for forty-eight hours.

It was at Tongatabu, the main port of the Friendly Isles that they learned the news. Britain had declared war on Germany. Even in that remote corner of the Pacific the ripples of the great event had begun to set things in motion. Men of military age who had settled in the islands began to think about packing up and getting back to New Zealand to 'do their bit'. Strange bonds of loyalty and patriotism, so little spoken of, so deeply felt, began to pull at their minds and consciences. The scanty war news, received daily over the radio, was the only topic of conversation, and the *Dolphin*, when she sailed a month later, had a volunteer crew of six, who were eager to work their passage back to civilisation.

The Trades had set in again. So leaving the lovely coral islands, the white beaches and the palms, they set sail down the Biha passage, and conned the *Dolphin* out into deep water. Four days later they dropped anchor at Suva.

There, after wiring back to New Zealand, the boys decided to lay up the *Dolphin* 'for the duration'. They carried out some necessary repairs, gave the hull a coat of grey paint, stored their gear and booked their passages back to Auckland.

Ben Bridgeman sat in his little office overlooking the Waitemata. It was above the store, and from the window you could see the harbour. It used to be full of life and movement; liners, merchantmen, yachts and row boats were always to be seen moving up and down the channel. But now, at the end of 1941, things were very much quieter. The yacht moorings were almost deserted. The young men were all gone or going overseas. Troopships had replaced liners, and these, with the freighters, were almost the only commerce to be seen in the roadstead. There was something urgent and business-like about their sudden appearances and stealthy departures. The old ease and spaciousness of the life had gone. Only the beautiful climate remained, and even this seemed somehow useless, like a light burning in an empty room.

Ben had aged considerably. After the sudden death of his wife many years before, he had devoted himself to Dick. Now the news of his son's death made everything seem futile and useless. He was like a man who has saved up all his life to retire in modest comfort, and when he is on the point of doing so, loses his fortune overnight. He carried on, of course, and put the best face on things he could; but in truth he had no further interest in life and nothing to look forward to.

Now he sat down at his desk, covered with piles of papers and orders, old files, samples, receipts, ledgers, a miscellaneous collection of months, dusty and brittle with sunshine. He lit his pipe and looked out of the window, glanced across at the half model of the *Dolphin* which hung on the wall opposite, and pulled a bulky letter out of his pocket. He took it out of its envelope, unfolded it and placed it on the desk before him. Then he searched for his spectacle-case, slowly put on his glasses, picked up the letter and began to read it again...

My dear Uncle Ben (it ran), *I should have written to you before this, but I have not done so, partly because we have been having a pretty busy time of it and partly because I was waiting to hear if Bob Scott had any further details about Dick that might be of interest to you. Now I have finished my first 'tour of Ops', as we call it, which means that I am resting, more or less, and engaged in less strenuous work, and so have some leisure to collect my thoughts. I have also heard from Bob. He can't tell me much more than I wrote you in my first letter, but he says that Dick was a tower of strength in the Flight and that it has never been the same since he was lost. Flights are very intimate little bodies of men, you know, and the loss of one man often puts the whole crowd out of gear.*

I can't exactly explain how; but I can well understand that his loss would be deeply felt... This sounds awfully stilted and official, like a letter of condolence from the CO. I can't express myself well on paper – or any other way for that matter.

Dick and I went through things together which bound us as closely as any two men can ever be. He was always pretending to be in a panic, but in fact he was brave as a lion only he hid it under comical or facetious remarks. I remember in the very worst part of that hurricane, when we were absolutely all in, he suddenly shouted to me, 'I vote we anchor, Tom, and have dinner ashore!' It may not sound very humorous when you read this, but at that time the wind was blowing about sixty miles an hour, the nearest land was four hundred miles away and the ocean was about five miles deep!

It was things like this that endeared him to me, and to all he met. When we managed to make Tongatabu after the storm, he made friends with everyone. The natives adored him and it was he who managed to wheedle some sails out of a trading schooner without which we should never have been able to make the passage to Suva. 'Be a good girl till we come back,' was his last remark to the Dolphin when we had laid her up. It hit us both pretty hard to have to leave the ship and somehow that remark exactly expressed what we both felt. We were pretty proud of her, you know. You get to love a ship when you have been through tight places with her and she hasn't let you down.

Uncle Ben, Dick won't come back to the Dolphin or to you or me – the only three people he cared about – and I expect you feel pretty low, as I often do when I think of him, and wonder whether his death, and the death of thousands of others, is really worth while. He has sacrificed his life and for all I know I may have to sacrifice mine. We talked about this once or twice (when we were a little tight; it isn't the sort of thing you talk about when you're sober) and I know what he felt, what we both felt. Perhaps if I tell you it will help.

In the last war, as far as I can make out, millions of young chaps, like me and Dick, fought for England and the ideals that England stands for. Thousands of them died and their deaths didn't do any good to the children they left behind. The children are now having to do the same thing over again. I think the boys see much more clearly what they are fighting about than their elders. When you get into the 'front line', wherever it is, everything gets awfully simple. I've always had a sort of passion to know where I am and where I'm going, as you know. You grow up rather quickly when you've done a few raids. The excitement soon wears off and then, if you want to keep going, you have to have a good reason to go on – or I do. Some of them seem to get along without it, but the best ones, though they don't say much, seem to have thought it out.

What it comes to is this. The English way of life is fairly tolerant and broadminded. Of course we've had lapses and made mistakes; but all the same the British Commonwealth of Nations stands for something that the world needs to preserve. It's a sort of genius for letting people run their own show. You can't do that unless you're friendly towards other people who don't run things the way you would. When we do have to interfere, as we did with Germany in this war and the last, I think we do it because we know the world can't be run dishonestly. Everything becomes impossible if nations lie and bully and cheat. So what we're really fighting for is to preserve a way of life. The trappings change with the times, but I don't think the spirit has altered much. Of course people say that England's a back number, that she's inefficient and all the rest of it. I think the Battle of Britain proved that she isn't – and lots of other things about England besides – but even if she is inefficient I don't mind much, because it seems to me that too much efficiency gets in the way of happiness. The papers over here are full of plans for this and that – they'll soon be rationing the air we breathe! – and I daresay some planning will help things; but the essence of democracy is to think and act for yourself. I hope England will never stifle that. I don't think she will, I don't think she can.

I suppose I've known the most complete freedom a man can ever know. I feel pretty strongly about freedom generally because I think it's the only way men can develop their own abilities and learn how to live. That hurricane in the Dolphin taught me more about life and about myself than I could have learned from twenty years study of theories. No society can be perfect, but the best is the one in which the common man has the greatest liberty of thought and action. I believe the English conception tops the lot. In fact I believe that we are easily the most civilised race on earth. That is why England is worth fighting for and, if necessary, dying for.

Dick felt the same, I know, though he wouldn't have been as long-winded as I am in saying so. He thought it was worthwhile, and so do I. It is worthwhile. So you may be quite sure that his death has not been useless, either to himself or to the country. He wasn't just a sheep doing what he was told. He believed in the way of life that he died for. And, just in case, Uncle Ben, so do I.

But if I had my way, after the war, I'd split things up. I wouldn't amalgamate. The little countries are the happiest. They're the best fun and offer the best scope for the individual. What a splendid place the Dominion is! And think of the other little countries, Norway, Denmark and Holland. A little ship is better than a big one, because you really sail her yourself, you're part of her, and if she's well-built she'll weather anything. I've proved it, so I know. Those of us who come *back won't want much – just a safe and reasonably decent world. Shall we get it? I see signs of the old power blocs emerging again. If we once start to make teams and pick sides when this war is over, we shall have another one on our hands within a generation. So stand out for self-determination and, as Wilkie puts it, one world.*

Well, this is too long a letter. Salute Rangitoto for me. Is old Ned still about? Did you tell him how we came through the storm? Take care of yourself. Your affectionate and devoted

Tom.

Every man carries in his heart an invisible allegiance to the days gone by. Like a mooring buoy on a rising tide, he breasts the surface of the present, lifting the link of the past which anchors him to the depth out of which he came. Tom was what he was because of what he had done. His ability to live wholly in the present was not, as it sometimes is, the mark of an inconsequent shallow nature; it was possible for him only because every action grew logically and inevitably from the one before. So, while a fleeting smile went over his face at the chord of memory struck by the Skipper's phrase 'Where are we now?', it quickly faded and he concentrated once more on his computer and his chart plotting P for Pathfinder across the night-shrouded sea below.

'Captain to rear-gunner. How are you getting on down there? Are we all right behind?' It was Thornly calling up Nobby Bligh. He made a point of doing it every now and then, partly so that he shouldn't feel lonely, partly to make sure he was awake. Of course Nobby was first class: but Thornly considered the safety of the crew was the Captain's concern and always made a point of checking up.

'Nicely thank you, sir. Few shooting Stars. Otherwise the same old basin full of glow-worms.'

'Okay, Nobby. Give me a call if you see anything.'

'I will, sir.'

Nobby switched off his mike, continued his sky search and went back to his thoughts.

NOBBY BLIGH

THEY WERE, AS USUAL, of Sally. Nobby had long since found he could do it with one part of his brain, while the other saw to searching the sky, up across down across, peering out into the blackness. On moonless, overcast nights the strain was greatest. More particularly when there were night fighters about, when you saw them for a second against the roving beam of a searchlight, and knew they might be coming up, invisible under your tail, then you hadn't a thought for anything outside the job. The safety of the crew depended on you and your thumb covered the firing button, peering, waiting. But usually that was only for a time, while you were over the target or near it. There were long hours when the chances of being surprised were much less. Then part of Nobby's brain went back to Sally.

The tail-gunner in a bomber gets a wonderful view. He can't see where he's going, but he knows where he's been. He is perched on the very lip of a gigantic precipice, two or three miles high, with nothing above or below him. Yet, strangely, dread of height is absent because he is in no way connected to the earth. Nobby had no head for height. He would never have dreamed of standing, say, on the parapet of a London building to look down on the street beneath. He would have felt connected to the ground by the walls below, and got that horrible constriction between the legs, a stabbing contracting pain, that is the sure sign of vertigo. He had it sometimes: when he tested his guns on NFT and saw the stream of empties falling. The little cartridge cases plunging down, down, down into those miles of emptiness, connected him with the earth. He felt himself falling with them. It was horrible. He had to look away quickly, look up and out to the horizon, and then the feeling disappeared. He was free again, suspended, divorced from the world below.

He liked this snug little isolated eyrie of his turret. He didn't feel cut off from the others, out of touch with them, although he hadn't the physical contact that the others had. They could all see each other, move about, change places and sometimes rest. He was alone. It suited him. The Huns, now, were no good unless they hung together. That was why their aircraft were designed to crowd the crew close, all under the eye of their captain; a sort of flying gestapo. The British despised that, and as a result, reaped an unrivalled field of fire. One gun behind the tail could cover more sky than two in the body. There were no blindspots.

Of course the tail-gunner had to have guts. He had to take the whole weight of a stern attack with no protection. But British tail-gunners asked nothing better. Nobby, for instance, had only one complaint: there weren't enough Huns.

Technically perhaps he was not a cockney, since London would have to be very still (and the wind in the right direction) to carry the sound of Bow Bells to the slums of Lisson Grove; but in every other way he was typical. Cheerful, perky, friendly, good-humoured, with a tongue for repartee and, beneath the surface, an aggressive self-confident determination, he came right out of the heart of the people. He wasn't a theorist, he didn't understand much about politics or economics; but he understood well enough when his father's little bakery was demolished by a direct hit and the old man was crushed under the ruins. That was clear enough, as clear as his answer at the reception centre when he reported to volunteer. 'What do you want to do for the country, me lad?' said the official he interviewed, rather patronisingly. 'To get behind a gun,' said Nobby, 'and the quicker the better.'

It was the obliteration of that simple little place that finally decided Nobby. He'd been getting hot under the collar ever since the spring when the Hun went into Norway; but the bombing of London really roused him. If the sods thought this sort of thing would lower British morale, they never made a greater mistake. Millions of pounds' worth of damage might have been done, thousands of non-combatants might have been killed: but the London Blitz did as much to raise England's morale as the Battle of Britain. It made them fighting mad. It was in devastated London that the seeds of victory were planted, and the sight of the mutilated city did all that was necessary to nourish their growth.

Nobby's little home was like a million others. But it was his. For as long as he could remember he had lived there. His father had moved in when he married twenty-five years before. When he'd starting baking on his own, he'd built the oven onto the back of the house. Nobby had awakened every morning of his childhood to the wonderful smell of fresh baked loaves. As a child he'd helped, while he was still too small to see over the table, to mix the flour and add the yeast. He could remember them in the bakery helping Dad, kneading the beautiful white dough in great earthenware basins. Mum in a print dress, her strong arms bare to the shoulder and all floury, kneading and kneading; the warmth of the oven when the doors slid back; the clatter of the baking tins; the long stick to push them in; the way Dad used to go to sleep while the baking was done and how he seemed to know just when to wake up; the excitement of opening the oven and fishing out the loaves, crisp, hot and brown; the whoop of delight he gave when Mum, for a treat, baked him his own little loaf in the shape of a mouse with currants for eyes: all this was as much part of his life as Sally. He'd grown up with it, as he'd grown up with her. Both were twined deep into his roots.

And now a bomb had knocked the little place flat. It was old, of course. Maybe it was practically a slum, maybe it was condemned to be knocked down anyway. That was different. Nobby wouldn't forget how he saw the place that morning, when a neighbour came in and told him it was gone. A pile of bricks and rubble, twisted laths, strips of wallpaper, and the little pushcart they'd had for fifteen years, lying on its side in the gutter with a wheel blown off. He'd helped to clear the place himself, worked in a frenzy all that morning, hoping that the old man might have escaped by some miracle. But he hadn't. They'd found him there, close to the oven, where he'd been baking away as usual, crushed and broken and quite dead. He'd carried on, right up to the end, doing his regular unspectacular job, and died at his post, as you might say. It was the truth.

Nobby didn't like to remember how he sat there in the gutter with the tears streaming down his cheeks. He was mourning then for his old Dad, and didn't know there was anyone else looking on.

It hadn't lasted long. An AFS lad had come up and slapped him on the back and given him a swig at his flask. Nobby had pulled himself together and got up to carry on. He would always carry on, you could bet on that. He'd only broken down once before in his life, and then, luckily there had been nobody to see.

The neighbours had been kind. Nobby was popular. They'd all known him for a good many years, doing the rounds with the little pushcart, bringing their morning loaves, always cheerful, with his quick tongue and a ready laugh. Now he was grown up, in work for himself, and Sally, who was as much a neighbour as he was, was his wife. So they rallied round and said they would look after the 'arrangements'. By which they meant the funeral. Nobby thanked them quietly. 'I got to see Mum,' he explained. 'I got to go down and break it to Mum.'

'What a blessing you got her away!' said one.

'Yes,' said Nobby.

'How's she finding it down there, Nobby?'

'Oh, all right; she's doing all right.'

'It's a mercy she's got Sally with her. How's Sally keeping?'

'Oh, she's fine,' said Nobby, 'Sally's fine.'

It was far from the truth; but it was Sally really that had decided his mother to evacuate. Both Nobby and his Dad had been worrying at the women for some time. The blitz was pretty bad. Dad wanted Mum out of the way; but she wouldn't leave him, until that bomb dropped close to Nobby's place and Sally got a mild case of shock. It wouldn't have mattered, if she'd not been so weak; but, after it, Nobby insisted she should go, and Dad put his foot down too: Mum had better go with her.

Mrs Smith was kind, really, taking them in. The little farm in a fold of the hills down near Marlow was a favourite place for campers. Mrs Smith was the farmer's wife. She had known Nobby for quite a time. His cycling club always pitched in her wood. So she'd taken them into her spare room in the old tumbledown cottage. It wasn't much of a place; but it was safe, and the country was good for Sally.

Sitting in the corner of a crowded third-class carriage, Nobby had plenty of time to think. The train had started late. It stopped at every station. People got in and out. They were all very talkative and friendly. The blitz had broken down their usual reserve. They were all in this together and discussed interminably their particular private disasters, the bombs that had ruined their homes, killed their friends and dear ones, and fatally disrupted their lives. But Nobby was too close to his grief that morning to join in. He stared out of the window hearing nothing of what went on around him. He was thinking of Mum. How was he going to tell her? What could he say? What could anyone say?

He wasn't often at a loss; but all the usual cheerfulness with which he faced difficulties – the armour of defence that he had built up to face Sally with, for instance – deserted him in this extremity. While there was life there was hope. There was something he could do about it. But a chance bomb had ended all hope for Mum, and nothing he could do or say would make it different. Nobby was no philosopher; but he understood, by his own hard experience, how lonely people are in the crises of life, how in the last resort there is nobody but oneself. The Valley of the Shadow is narrow: men and women walk that path alone.

That little family circle, Dad and Mum, Sally and him, it was smashed now, irrevocably smashed. It had meant a lot, it had bonds of inner strength that made you feel safe. Take Sally, now; Nobby felt he would never have been able to face that, but for Dad and Mum. Sally, poor darling Sally...

He brooded over her. There was hardly a time when he didn't remember her, but the first clear picture was of one morning when she came in for a loaf. She was hardly higher than the counter, and Nobby, running in from the sitting-room when the bell clanged, could hardly see over it himself. So these two stared at each other. Nobby saw a pale thin face, with strawcoloured hair brushed tightly down from a parting in the middle and hanging in two tight plaits that covered the ears. Two dingy white ribbons held the plaits. The eyes were pale and blue, and looked at you so straight, with such a trusting and yet forlorn expression.

'Hullo,' said Nobby. But Sally didn't answer. She was far too shy.

She just stared at him.

'What can I do for you, Miss?' Nobby was staring at her just as frankly, and imitating his Dad's manner with customers. She dropped her eyes and fiddled with a torn handkerchief from which she extracted a few coppers. These she pushed on to the counter with a small grubby hand.

'Want a loaf,' she whispered.

Nobby felt very grown up, serving in the shop. He showed off as he took the loaf, slipped it into a bag, twirled it round to close the end and shoved it across the counter.

'Tuppence 'apenny,' he announced, as he took the coppers. ''Ere's an 'apenny change.' And he pushed it over to her.

She took it, tucked the loaf under her arm, stared at Nobby again, started to say something, then thought better of it and turned to go out. Nobby just stood there.

'My name's Nobby,' he announced, as she reached the door. 'What's yours?'

She stopped, looked round and then down at the floor.

'Sally.'

'Sally what?' said Nobby. 'A'int you got no other name?'

'Course I 'ave.' Sally grew bolder. 'Everybody's got two names, silly. My name's Sally Mince. My Dad's got the cycle shop on the corner. We've got three new bicycles and I'm allowed to shine them.' She stopped, quite breathless. It was the first long speech she had ever made in her life.

'Oh,' said Nobby, trying not to be impressed, for he'd spent a long time with his nose to the window of the cycle shop, looking at the beautiful shiny wheels and handlebars, glittering like jewels. 'We've got a handcart and when I'm grown up I'm going to push it round and do all the 'liveries. And' – as an afterthought – 'I've got three names. Norman 'Erbert Bligh. But you can call me Nobby if you like.'

'Got to go 'ome now,' said Sally and whisked out of the door.

That was how it had started. From then on Nobby could only think of his childhood and youth as scenes in which Sally had figured as companion and, perhaps more often, admirer and audience. Every day they walked home together from the Board School round by the Power Station, Nobby sturdy and cocky, Sally frail and emaciated, as if she never had enough to eat. Nobby set himself up as her protector, and woe betide anyone who tried to bully or tease her. Nobby wouldn't forget how he'd come on Ned Slater, a boy five years older than he, pushing her into a corner near the sweet shop and viciously pulling at her plaits. Sally wasn't offering any resistance. She was holding her hands to her head to save her hair and shrieking 'Nobby! Nobby!' in her thin voice. Nobby had launched himself on the bully like a thunderbolt. He had seen red. He saw red now whenever he thought of it. Ned Slater had retired with a black eye and a very sore jaw, and although Nobby's nose was bleeding freely and his knuckles were barked and his shirt torn, it was a victory, a decisive victory. Neither Ned nor anyone else bothered Sally from then on.

Dad and Mum smiled indulgently at this childish infatuation. There was something touching about it. It didn't seem to go with the rest of Nobby's effervescent temperament.

'Might be grown up, the way they carry on,' said Mum.

'There's no 'arm in it that I can see,' Dad re-joined. 'She's a nice kiddie.'

'I think I'll have a word with Mrs Mince all the same,' Mum went on. 'See what she makes of it.'

So the two gossips got together and talked it over. They came to the same conclusion.

'If they're 'appy together, leave 'em alone I say. There's little enough 'appiness about,' was Mrs Mince's final word.

In fact the children's affection for each other brought their parents together. Mr and Mrs Bligh took to dropping in on Mr and Mrs Mince of an evening. They took their Bank Holiday trips together, and even went to Margate one year to spend their annual holiday. Sally and Nobby built sand castles, paddled and had donkey rides. It was the first time either of them had seen the sea and even Sally's pale face was touched with a glow of colour and her hair with a sheen of life.

These scenes and a thousand others ran through Nobby's mind as the train crawled out into the country. Remembering how Sally had looked there, down by the seaside, he wished he could have seen into the future then. If she had stayed longer, if she had got fatter and stronger, perhaps it would have given her the strength in after years to have thrown it off... perhaps she would never have fallen a victim to it... He remembered how well she looked then. It was the first time he consciously knew she was beautiful. Beautiful to him. To the rest of the world she was nothing more than a pale gangling girl, with a curious wistful and forlorn expression in her eyes.

Then there had been the accident. Sally had been knocked down by a butcher's van and taken to hospital with a compound fracture of the leg. For weeks she had had to lie flat on her back with her leg in plaster, lying there, pale and white and still, while the bones mended. The nurses took quite a fancy to her. She was so good and patient. They teased her good-naturedly about her 'boyfriend' Nobby; but they stopped when they saw that she took it quite literally. Nobby was her boyfriend. He was her only friend. When he came to see her, with his pathetic little presents of an orange, some sweets or a penny bunch of violets, they noticed how her eyes glowed and a spot of colour burned in her cheeks. It didn't seem natural for two children to behave so... so, 'well, just as if they were in love,' as one of the sisters said. They were amazed and amused at Nobby's proprietory air, at the matter-of-fact enquiries he made about her health, the probable length of her convalescence, and the best treatment for her when she left hospital. The boy might have been grown up. The matron shook her head. She was full of pity for these slum children, who were adult at fourteen and had to accept all the responsibilities of life, the girls nursing the younger children, the boys going out to work, at an age when they should have been running wild in the country. But there it was. They were born and bred to it. They didn't know they had fortitude or patience or courage. It seemed natural to them.

It was after Sally came home that Nobby first joined Mr Mince in the bicycle shop. Dad didn't fancy letting him go on the rounds any longer as a baker's boy.

'Joe,' he said to his friend one evening, as the two had a pint together at the Four Feathers, 'Joe, it's no good bringing Nobby up to the bakery, is it now? The small tradesman don't get the custom he used to, what with all these co-operatives and combines and things. The business'll do to last me out, but it's no good to him. He ought to have a chance at something more progressive-like, more modern. He ought to be a mechanic, or something.'

Joe nodded and thought for a minute or two. 'How about him giving me a hand, Jim? I could do with a boy. You'd be surprised what a lot there is going on in the cycle trade these days, what with all these clubs and rambles and things. To tell you the truth Jim, I could do with some help. I'm getting on – and I'd give the boy a fair wage. He'd be learning and, you never know, it might lead to something.'

Jim Bligh nodded in his turn. 'I'll put it to him, Joe, and see what he says.'

Nobby took to the idea eagerly. He loved to mess about with a spanner and an oil-can, and soon became invaluable to Mr Mince. He quickly picked up the trade, learned to mend punctures and adjust brakes, knew the price of everything and where it was, remembered all the orders when the salesmen called, and didn't seem to mind what hours he worked. Within a couple of years he was the mainstay of the shop. Trade had doubled, and Nobby was all the time urging his boss to move out of his poky little shop and get some decent premises in the Edgware Road. But the older man, though he saw the sense in it, lacked capital and initiative. He was frightened to take the plunge.

When he talked it over with Jim Bligh, the little baker spoke his mind. 'We're getting old, Joe; that's what's the matter with us. I feel the same when the missus starts trying to talk me into getting in help and enlarging the bakery. I won't do it and I reckon I'm right. But this cycle trade's different. It's a coming thing, it's mechanical. 'Course Nobby's talked to me about it...' Jim paused and sucked at his pipe. 'I've got a couple of hundred put away, Joe. Enough to pay rent for the new place for a year or two. With what you can put into it, that ought to give you time to get on your feet. So here's what I'll do: I'll put that money in your business, Joe, if you'll take young Nobby in as a partner on equal terms, share and share alike. I reckon Nobby's got a head on his shoulders. He's young but he's going places, as they say, and I reckon you'll make more with half the business than you made out of the whole lot up till now. What do you say?'

Nobby had taken a ticket to High Wycombe, but when the train stopped at Loudwater, he decided to get out and walk over the hills to the farm. It was still winter, but the year was turning towards the spring. The catkins had let down their yellow tails. The wind came in cold from the north-west, but in the sunken lanes, it was sheltered and warm in the sun. Nobby trudged up through the beechwoods, past the cottages where the first snowdrops were pushing through, and out past the cherry orchards along the saddle of the hills. It was a four-mile walk. It would give him time to think up what to say to Mum, and what to say to Sally. It wouldn't do to upset her either... But somehow his mind refused to face the problem, kept on veering away, back into the past when they'd all been together...

'Mince and Bligh. Everything for your Bike.' That was the sign they'd put up, and Nobby remembered how proud he was at seeing his name in twelve-inch letters over the shop window. The place was old and squalid when they took it, but a coat of paint had done wonders. There was a shop window, then a small room with the new bikes in it, and the workshop for repairs at the back. At one side of the 'showroom', as they proudly called it, was a counter with shelves behind it going right up to the ceiling. Here was their 'stock', and Mr Mince was alarmed at the amount Nobby put out filling those shelves. But the boy insisted: 'You got to have everything, Mr Mince. You got to stock it.' He printed out two streamers and pasted them inside the window. 'You can GET IT at Mince and Bligh,' said one, and the other, 'Mince and Bligh STOCK it'.

Nobody that owned a bike could pass that window. It was like Aladdin's cave. Mudguards, rear lights, chains, repair outfits, inner tubes, brake levers, bells, saddles, pumps, handlebars, eye shields, all these and many other accessories jostled each other for place in the window and hung in festoons from the ceiling. Every article was clearly priced in bold black figures on slips of yellow cardboard, and surmounting the whole was the very latest racing machine, with a pale blue frame, yellow rims and red tyres. There were always half a dozen people gaping at that window, and Nobby reckoned that one out of every six opened the door and came in.

The shop made money from the word go; but the work was terrific. Mr Mince wilted under it. 'I know we're making money, son; but there's too much goin' on for me. That dratted doorbell keeps on ringing and ringing. By seven at night it fair gives me the willies, straight it does.' Nobby laughed. The bustle of the Edgware Road suited him. It was the poor man's Bond Street. Crowds wandered up and down before the brightly lit shops until all hours. Every night Nobby stayed late, printing out price cards, ordering stock, clearing off repairs. Usually Sally stayed to help him. She had quite a good head for figures and sat there, quietly casting up from the paper slip in the cashbox, checking the takings, counting the silver and copper into heaps, and putting them in bags to go off to the bank next morning.

Nobby found the whole thing an adventure. He lived and worked for the shop. From six in the morning till after midnight most nights, he was on the job, and Sally, although she had never really got strong again after her accident, helped him. She never complained and Nobby was too absorbed to notice how tired she was. Mr Mince took to going home at seven, but Nobby would eat a sandwich and Sally would brew him some tea over the gas ring and he'd work on till all hours.

The shop hadn't been open long before Nobby struck up acquaintance with some of the boys of the local cycle club, and agreed to go along with them one weekend for an outing. They seemed a decent crowd, and besides, he saw that if he could get the club's trade it would be quite valuable. So they set off, one Saturday afternoon, twenty strong. They made good time out on to Western Avenue, down through Uxbridge and Denham, and came at last to their camping ground in the wood near Smith's farm.

Nobby could see the wood now, as he reached the top of the hill. It was four years ago, the first time he had seen it, and he remembered how they'd all arrived, hot and tired, stripped to the waist and sluiced themselves with buckets of water from the well. There were a few girls in the party, and while they went off to the farm to get milk and eggs, the boys got out their kit and began to set up camp. Some of the couples had tents just big enough for two, others had sleeping bags and these they pitched round a natural hollow in the beechwoods. It was a little crater about ten feet deep and thirty feet across. At the bottom there were irons for the fire. They soon got this going, while some fetched water from the well, and others unpacked the food and started to cook the evening meal.

As the sun went down and night fell, they all clustered round the fire. Twisted shadows danced on the trunks of the beeches. Smoke rose into the canopy of leaves overhead. It was the first time Nobby had done anything like this, and he took a great fancy to it. It was all free-and-easy and friendly. One of the boys had quite a nice voice. Nobby had brought his mouthorgan, and they all joined in the choruses of the songs they knew. At last, with a good deal of cheerful banter at the couples in the tents, they settled down for the night.

'Feel like joining the club, Nobby?' said Charlie, the secretary, who had pitched his bag next to Nobby.

'You betcha life, Charlie. It's a bit of all right, this is. You can count me in – and Sally too.'

'Who's Sally?' asked a voice from the darkness.

'She's – she's a friend of mine,' answered Nobby. He almost said 'girlfriend', but that might have been open to misinterpretation. He wanted it understood that Sally was 'on the level'.

'Bring her along next weekend. The more the merrier.'

Nobby had passed the rise and now he could see over the brow down into the valley below. It was a small fold in the hills, with a meadow each side of the lane, and behind the meadow, upsloping beechwoods, dark and still. At the corner where two lanes met, stood the farm with its thatched roof. One fine barn stood beside it. Other outhouses, with corrugated iron roofs, were ranged round the midden with cow-byres and pigsties and, on one side, a plot of vegetable garden. The smoke curled up from the chimney through the branches of an oak that stood on a rise behind the house. As Nobby looked down on this secret corner of England, he could not reconcile it with the fury of the London Blitz. It did not seem possible that the two kinds of life, one so peaceful, the other so full of terror, could be going on at the same time within thirty miles of each other.

The door of the farm opened, and Sally came out. She called to Prince, the brown collie, and the two set out for some other cottages just visible down in the wood. Nobby could hear her voice quite clearly, drifting uphill with the wind, as she talked to the dog. He watched her till she rounded the corner and was hidden by the hedges.

It looked very different, now in winter, from the leafy shadowy place of the summertime, with its patches of loosestrife and campion; its hawthorn, its tangles of honeysuckle, blackberry and dog-rose. Very different from the day when Nobby and Sally got married and came down for their honeymoon.

It was Sally fainting in the shop, that night when they'd been working late, that suddenly woke Nobby up. He was so scared and helpless with her lying there on the floor and nobody within call, and hadn't the slightest idea what to do. At first he thought she was dead and knelt over her, trying to lift her and calling her, 'Sally! Sally!' She didn't answer but he heard her breathing with a sense of wonderful relief, put his coat under her head and went quickly for a cup of water. By the time he was back, she had come to, and was staring at him with those pale steadfast eyes.

'Sally! Are you all right? Here, drink this.' And he managed to raise her head and get her to sip some water.

'What happened, Nobby?' she whispered.

'You – you just dropped off to sleep for a moment.' Nobby was smiling at her reassuringly.

'I was sitting there and suddenly it all went dark and I don't remember anything till I saw you with the cup. I'm all right now. I must be a bit tired, I think.'

He helped her to her feet, and she stood, hanging on to him, with all her weight.

'Sally, me love,' said Nobby, 'you fair gave me a turn, you did. Now come on! Bed for you.' He sat her down while he turned out the lights, and putting an arm round her waist, almost carried her home.

In the narrow hallway, he called her mother and, managing to get in a wink, told her that Sally was feeling a bit tired and ought to go straight to bed. So Mrs Mince, who was quick on the uptake, had hurried her upstairs. When she came down she turned on Nobby.

'You ought to be ashamed of yourself, Nobby Bligh, keeping the girl there in the shop working till all hours. You know she's always been delicate. You'll be the death of her. Downright selfish, that's what you are, like all men, and I hope this'll be a lesson to you.' But Nobby looked so shamefaced and upset, she relented and asked what had happened. Nobby told her. Mrs Mince thought a moment, then chuckled.

'I was just the same meself, till Mr Mince came along.'

Nobby looked at her, not understanding. The puzzled expression on his face set her off laughing outright.

'Cheer up, Nobby, my lad. It's nothing to worry about. Girls go like that when they grow up and want a bit of loving.' And she laughed again, seeing Nobby blushing to the roots of his hair. 'She wants a husband, Sally does. Is that plain enough for you, Nobby?' But Nobby only stood there, twisting his hat, looking at the floor, like a schoolboy. Mrs Mince clapped him on the shoulder and laughed again. 'Go along with you, Nobby. Don't act the innocent with me. Why don't you pop the question? I'm sure Dad and I wouldn't have no objection.'

Nobby went home, quite dazed. He lay awake most of the night, thinking. Next morning, bringing his little gift of narcissus and grapes, he found her there, lying in bed, looking so pale and wonderful and sat down on the bed beside her, stroking her hair; but he felt shy and strange beside her in a way he had never felt before.

'Sally,' and he took her hand that lay there beside his on the counterpane. 'What would you say to us getting' spliced?'

For what seemed an age there was no answer. 'You see,' he went on, nervously, 'I reckon I must be in love with you, Sal, though I didn't properly realise it till last night... Will you have me, Sally?' She squeezed his hand.

'There must be lots of girls who'd make you a better wife than I could.'

'Don't talk silly. You know there's nobody for me but you.'

'I'm not good enough for you, Nobby. I'm not, really. But I do – love you, Nobby, with all my heart,' and she laid her cheek against his arm. For a moment they held each other, and it was for ever.

Then Nobby couldn't contain himself. He jumped up. 'Now, Mrs Bligh, name the day! What do you say to this morning? No? Then tomorrow, next week, next Saturday? Come on, don't be shy!'

'Oh, Nobby, you are a tease, really. I dunno when. I'll have to get a dress and a hat and... things.' Her eyes were shining bright and the colour mounting to her cheek transfigured her there for Nobby, so that, ever afterwards, when the vision of her face rose to his mind, he saw her so, pale and glowing, like an angel.

The back room of the Four Feathers was crowded for the wedding breakfast. It seemed the whole place knew Nobby and Sally and wished them well. There had been a whip-round to give them a real slap-up do, with champagne and chicken and trifles and ices and a wedding cake, with some nice port to top it all off and set the speeches going. To Nobby and Sally, sitting there at the head of the table, trying hard to pretend they were enjoying themselves (and failing dismally), it seemed as if it would never end. All the speeches, getting more alcoholic and sentimental as the port circulated, were well worn variants on the theme 'may all your troubles be little ones'. Each was an excuse for another glass of port, and by four o'clock the whole party was nicely squiffy and had begun singing songs and laughing hysterically and, in fact, enjoying itself in the traditional manner. At last, amid showers of confetti and rice and old shoes, Nobby and Sally managed to get away.

Both had fallen in love with their weekends camping down in the woods. Mondays always came too soon. When they were talking over their honeymoon, it seemed natural to decide to camp for a fortnight, right in the woods at Smith's farm. Dad and Mum, dreaming of Brighton or Margate, couldn't understand how they could prefer 'living out in the woods like savages' to a 'nice double bed and h. and c. laid on'. But there it was. After all, as Mum remarked, it was their funeral.

But, of course the Club was delighted. Charlie the secretary, who had taken a great fancy to Nobby, suggested they got married on a Saturday so that all the gang could ride down and settle them in. 'Oh, we won't hang around and spoil the fun, Nobby, my lad. But we sort of feel you're one of us and we'd like to give you a send-off.'

So it was agreed that the gang should go down early and that Nobby and Sally should follow by car. Charlie and his girlfriend, Daisy, would look after everything. They'd all have supper together and then they'd go. Sally and Nobby were looking forward to it. The gang were pals of their own age. The wedding breakfast had been parents, relations, duty; the evening would be friends and fun.

When the car drew up at the rickety old gate of the field and they got out with their bags, there was no one in sight.

'Funny,' said Nobby. 'Wonder if they're having a lark with us?' He picked up the suitcases and they walked up over the slope towards the hollow which was hidden from the road. It was high summer, the day was hot, and as they walked through the tall grass and thistles, Nobby was swearing under his breath.

'Blimey, Sally, I believe the whole lot's done a bunk and left us in the cart with no tent or food or anything. I'll be even with young Charlie for this.'

Then suddenly they heard Charlie's voice sing out, 'Hullo, Nobby! Hullo, Sally!' and he came running out of the wood with some of the others.

'What cheer, the newlyweds! Here, give us your bags, chum. We're just about ready for you.'

When they reached the shade of the trees, Nobby and Sally saw, standing on the lip of the hollow and facing out through the trees to the meadow, a tiny green caravan.

'Gawd's truth, Charlie, what in heaven's name's that?'

'It's a wedding present from the gang. You see, it might turn out wet, or anything. So when young Daisy hit on the idea of a caravan, we had a whip round, hired it and had it towed down. It was some job getting up that slope into the wood, believe me.'

Sally and Nobby stood staring at the caravan, not knowing what to say. They'd often planned that 'someday', when Nobby had made a lot of money, they'd have one. And now, suddenly, here it was, parked in their favourite spot, theirs for a whole fortnight.

'Oh, Charlie, it's wonderful! Really, it's wonderful. But you shouldn't have. Really, you shouldn't.' It was Sally's formula for anything that she wanted very much and made her very happy. Nobby was no less delighted though he expressed it differently.

'It's like the Indian rope trick, that's what it is, Charlie. Fancy you thinking of a thing like this!'

'Come on, Sal,' said Daisy, 'let's show you where everything is.' And she led the way, while all the rest, shaking hands with Sally and Nobby, wishing them luck and clustering round, followed behind.

There wasn't room for all of them inside, but those that couldn't get in poked their heads through the windows and kept on pointing out things:

'There's a sink under that lid.'

'And the stove's there, next to it.'

'Paraffin's in the cupboard underneath.'

'What price that for a double bed, Nobby?'

'All the tinned stuff's under the seats, Sally, and there's a frying pan and a saucepan under here,' and Daisy opened still another cupboard.

Sally and Nobby looked round this little home with amazement. 'You'd never think you could get so much in, would you, Sal?' said Daisy. Yet when all the cupboards were shut, it looked so neat, with the foxgloves and daisies in a tumbler on the table, and a bright check cloth and all the varnished wood.

'It's bloody marvellous, that's what it is,' was Nobby's comment. Sally could only nod at all the things Daisy showed her. She couldn't find words. She was too happy.

At last, when everything had been seen and explained, they all came out again. Nobby was last. He stood on the step. 'Folks,' he said, 'Sally and I won't ever be able to thank you. We didn't know what a lot of good friends we had; but I reckon we know now, and no error – Don't we, Sal?' And Sally, her eyes moist with happiness, echoed, 'It's ever so good of you. I don't know what to say; but you shouldn't have, really you shouldn't.'

It was a beautiful evening. Clouds sailed in the sky. Pigeons flew in swoops over the woods. Tree shadows lengthened along the meadow grass. The cows drifted home for milking. Butterflies fluttered among the thistle heads. Wind shudders ran over the standing corn. And soon the moon would rise.

The girls were busy preparing a picnic feast, while the boys brought kindling for the fire, buckets of water, a case of beer, and bottles of milk from the farm. The party broke up into groups, sitting about on the grass, lolling away the time till supper should be ready. It was wonderful to be out in the country after the rush of town. Nobby set everybody off laughing, imitating the speeches at the wedding breakfast, exaggerating all the silly things people had said and done. It seemed much funnier now than when it had been going on, thought Sally: but people had been kind, really kind. And she and Nobby were married, actually married. It didn't feel different, and yet it was different... She lay back in the grass and looked up at the sky... 'All my life,' she thought. 'All my life.'

It was dark before supper was over, everything washed up and cleared away, and all of them, gay and laughing, clustered round Nobby and Sally on the grass. 'Give us a speech, Nobby. Come on, Nobby. On your feet, Nobby. Speech. Speech.' It was too insistent a chorus to refuse. So Nobby, awkward and protesting, scrambled to his feet.

'Ladies and Gents, I'm not much of a hand at this 'ere speechy-fying and this is the second today. So I'll keep it short and sweet. I've had two wedding breakfasts – the first was dinner and the second supper. I've had too much to eat, too much to drink and I don't know how to put one word after another. But one thing I do know and that is how many good friends we've both got. May you all be as happy as me and Sally. And now that's enough of me, so thanks again and God bless you all.'

Then there were songs, sentimental songs, comic songs, old songs sung in chorus, and even one that Charlie had made up especially for the occasion:

Nobby Bligh, I see a sparkle in your eye.
Nobby Bligh, and I don't have to ask you why.
Nobby Bligh, because I know you're riding high.
Now that sweet young Sally's your wife.

Sally Bligh, you're just as pretty as a rose.
Sally Bligh, the reason everybody knows.
Sally Bligh, now mind you lead him by the nose.
So God bless you both all your life.

And then, abruptly, the party broke up. They remembered that this was Sally and Nobby's wedding night, and that they had to get back to town, that thirty miles would take a bit of covering and that they'd meant to leave an hour before. So soon, bikes were got out, lamps were lit, and the Club gathered in the lane. Sally and Nobby stood leaning over the gate to see them off. Then with a chorus of Goodnights and Good Luck and See you soons, they all slid away into the gloom.

Nobby and Sally turned and walked back through the moonlight. They walked slowly, waist in waist, and their two shadows made but one shadow on the grass. They passed the sleeping cows, skirted the bracken, and turned into the shadow of the wood.

Nobby reached the farm, opened the parlour door and found his Mother, sitting by the fire.

'Why, Nobby! Whatever brings you down here today?' She jumped up. 'You must be cold. 'Ere, come in to the fire. Mrs Smith's out in the barn and Sally's gone down to the cottage with Prince. They'll both be back in a minute.'

'Give us a kiss, Mum.'

'Getting affectionate in your old age, are you?' She started to tease him, but something in his eyes made her stop and she put out her arms and took his head in her hands and kissed him. Nobby put his arms round her. He could tell her better when he was holding her, when he could get his face in her shoulder and not have to look into her eyes. So he hugged her tight.

'Why, whatever's the matter with you, Nobby?' Nobby didn't answer for a moment. The words wouldn't come.

'It's... it's Dad, Mum. He's... gone.'

'Nobby!' It was an astonished whisper that died out into silence. She disengaged herself from him, backed away, felt for the chair and sat down.

'When?'

'Last night – or rather this morning, early. The house caught it. Knocked flat, it was. I got round as quick as I could when they told me. But it weren't no good, Mum. We was digging all night and we got him out at last, but...'

'Nobby.' She stopped him, with a gesture. Then, as if to excuse herself, she went on nervously: 'I never could stand the chamber of 'orrors. You can tell me the rest some other time.'

She sat there, quite still, looking into the fire, and Nobby stood and looked at her. It was some time before either of them spoke.

'I can't believe it, Nobby.'

'No more can I, Mum.'

She was silent again, sitting there, calm and dry-eyed, but lost, utterly lost...

'Oh, Mum!' The last few hours had been a nightmare to Nobby. He was overwrought, and suddenly felt weak in the knees and slumped down by her chair and clutched at her hand. A sob came out of him, a convulsion of grief.

'Nobby! None of that!' Her voice was suddenly sharp and commanding. It pulled Nobby up short. 'We mustn't let go. If once we let go...' She stopped and squeezed his hand, quietly, reassuringly. Nobby pulled himself together.

'Sorry, Mum; but I...'

'Whatever 'ave you done to your hands?' she changed the subject. They were plentifully patched with plaster. The dressing station had stuck it on.

'I got 'em a bit grazed workin' on all that rubble. It's nothing.'

'Was it bad, last night?'

'Pretty bad. Not so bad as some.'

They were both silent again. Then Nobby spoke the thought that had been forming in his mind all day: 'I got to join up, Mum. I got to get at those buggers. I'm not going to stand for it no more.'

His mother nodded. And then she actually smiled, growing, for a moment, wise in her loss. 'Yes... yes... That's the way it goes. They kill Dad, so you want to kill them, and when you've killed some of them, they kill you, and so it goes on and on and on...' Her voice rose, strained with grief. 'Won't you men never 'ave no sense... after all the trouble you've been to us? You stay at home, young Nobby. Two wrongs don't make a right. You stay at home.'

Mum had been wonderfully brave, Nobby thought, as he sat in the train going back to town next morning. Damn sight braver than he'd been, breaking down like that. You would never have known that anything had happened, the way they'd kept it all from Sally. It was Mum's idea. It would never do to upset her, Mum had said, and she could make some excuse to get up to town for the funeral. Nobby had nodded, marvelling at his mother's selflessness. He did want everything kept from Sally that might weaken her. She was keeping up pretty well.

But dear old Ma Mince (or Ma Mite, as Nobby called her on account of her being so small) had made a mistake, saying that marriage would put Sally right. It was wonderful being together, really together as man and wife, but after six months Sally wasn't any better. She was all right and then suddenly he'd get those dizzy fits, fits of weakness, like after 'flu. It got Nobby worried and he insisted on taking her to a proper doctor at a hospital.

He was a little surprised when they said they must keep her under observation for a few days; but she came back, better for the rest, and when Nobby was sent for by the hospital he was quite cheerful. A nurse ushered him in to the doctor's office.

'Hullo, doctor,' he said. 'You seem to have done the little lady some good. She came home feeling fine.'

The doctor smiled. 'Sit down, Mr Bligh.' He offered him a chair next to his desk. 'Just a moment.' He spent a second finding a paper among others in his tray. 'Ah, yes. Here it is.' He looked through it thoughtfully, then turned to Nobby.

'Mr Bligh, I'm afraid I've bad news for you. I've made a very thorough examination of your wife. I've had our best people on it and taken three separate blood tests. She's always been delicate, hasn't she?'

'Well, yes; but nothing out of the way.' Nobby's face was bewildered and scared.

'And she's been getting a bit weaker all the time?'

'Well, she's up and down. But she isn't right, that's certain.'

'Mm. Well, I must be frank with you, Mr Bligh. Your wife has a very rare and serious disease, known as leucemia. Her blood is gradually getting thinner and thinner. I expect you know what anaemia is? Well, this is a sort of anaemia; but it doesn't respond to the treatment. In fact,' – and the doctor paused and looked at Nobby gravely – 'it doesn't respond to any known treatment.'

'You mean it's incurable?' Nobby was dazed.

'At the moment, yes. You see it is so rare, we have practically no experience of it. Ultimately of course science will find a remedy. But at the moment...' He put the paper aside and looked at Nobby again, 'we have to confess we are powerless.'

'But, Doctor, she's not as bad as that. She's a bit weak, I know; but I can't believe it's that serious.'

'It is, Mr Bligh. You must take my word for it. I shouldn't be talking to you like this, unless I had made the most exhaustive tests...'

'But what's going to happen to her, will she go off suddenly, or...?'

'Oh, no. Nothing sudden will happen to her. She will gradually get weaker and weaker. It may take a year, two years, even more... The course of the disease varies. She will never know she is really ill. She will just feel weak and probably hardly notice herself that she is getting weaker. She'll never be in any pain. She'll just slip away as if she was falling asleep.'

Then, in the face of this impassive damnable destiny, Nobby exploded: 'I suppose you think that's some consolation.'

The doctor looked at him, surprised. 'Believe me, Mr Bligh, it is. A great consolation to her – and to you. I have some experience of serious diseases. The end is often very far from pleasant.'

'Pleasant! 'Course it's not pleasant. No end's pleasant, is it?' Nobby had got to his feet, refusing to accept this ghastly ultimatum, this defeat, this disaster. 'I don't believe you. D'you hear? I don't believe you. Why, Sally's all right. She only wants rest and nursing and p'raps a bit of a rest in the country, or...' he tailed off, trying to grasp the enormity of the thing.

'Believe me or not as you please, Mr Bligh. You don't suggest that I would deliberately mislead you, I hope?'

'I dunno... No, I spose you're doing the best you know; but...'

'There is only one man in Europe who may know more about this than we do. I would suggest you went to him and got a second opinion... Only it isn't easy.'

'I'm going to get a second opinion, don't you fret. I'm going to get it double quick. Why isn't it easy?'

'Because Dr Shroeder – the specialist I refer to – practices in a little Swiss village called Adelboden. It would be somewhat expensive to take your wife there. But, of course, if you care to visit him, I'll give you all the help I can, a letter of introduction, and so on... I know him well.'

Nobby sat down again and passed his hand over his forehead. Then he raised his head.

'I'm sorry, doctor. I didn't mean to burst out like... like a bloody lunatic. But we must get her better, Doc. We got to cure her. Where did you say this bloke hangs out?'

Of course it had been a great adventure for both of them. The neighbours thought they were crazy. 'What! Switzerland! Never 'eard of such a thing! Whatever for?' Only Mum and Dad knew the real reason. Sally, to whom Nobby hadn't said a word of his visit to the hospital, thought her husband quite mad; but, at the same time, she had always wanted to travel. The Movies had done it.

Those Travelogues in colour '... and so we say farewell to beautiful Madeira,' or beautiful anywhere else, for by the time Fitzpatrick and Technicolour had finished with them, they were all equally 'beautiful', all equally slimed over with hot rancid colour. But still they were romantic... with the music and all...

Nobby pretended it was just an idea. 'Things look pretty bloody, Sal. There'll be a war, as like as not. I wouldn't mind 'aving a look at all them mountains and chalets and cows and things. Let's go on the bust. Just for a week. What d'you say? Maybe we won't ever get another chance.'

It was funny actually being in France, eating in a restaurant car, drinking your soup out of a cup, and that funny food, and paying in strange money; funny listening to the waiters and porters jabbering away in their outlandish lingo, funny sleeping in a train and horrible the way the inspectors and customs officials just opened the door and came in any time of night. 'It's not right, Nobby, is it? Why, I might be undressin' or anything.' Nobby laughed. 'No good taking any notice of them ruddy foreigners, Sal. They're all balmy.'

In the morning the train was running through pastoral country, with rich green meadows and orchards. The sun was shining, the air was clean and pure and in the distance were mountains.

'Coo, look at them mountains, Sal! This is a bit of all right, ain't it?'

Sally nodded and both of them gazed out of the window. 'It's just like the pictures,' she said.

The signals worked the other way round and there were little gongs at the stations that rang out very clear when the train was due to move on. They were mounting now, up through narrow gorges and tunnels, between dark pinewoods, and the villages had funny wooden houses with big listening eaves and stones on the roofs. The mountain air was sweet and fresh. Everything was so neat and clean. 'Looks for all the world as if they'd scrubbed it, don't it, Nobby?'

At last they got to their station. Nobby lifted Sally down, fetched the suitcases, and gave everything to the hotel porter who came up, touching his cap and speaking quite good English. They packed into a motor-bus and started climbing still higher up into the mountains.

At last they arrived at the village. That evening, after supper, they sat on the veranda of the little Pension Edelweiss, looking out over the deep valley with mountains all round and snow on their peaks. In the distance they could hear the cow-bells. As night fell, all over the valley, little points of light beamed out from the windows of chalets and farms. Everything was very clear and still. There was something, Sally couldn't exactly say what, that made it all quaint and fairylike.

'Isn't it wonderful, Nobby. I can't believe it. I can't believe it's real.'

The journey had tired Sally dreadfully. Nobby made her lie down for a rest after lunch. As soon as he had tucked her up in their little pinewood room (smelling of resin and so clean), he went down to the office and enquired where Dr Shroeder's house was. The manager came to the door with him and pointed out a white stuccoed villa, not far away, standing on the slope above the village street. Several long wooden huts with big glass windows facing south stood behind it. The manager explained that the doctor had a clinic in his grounds. He spoke of him with great respect. 'Dr Schroeder is one of the foremost physicians in Europe. It is international, his reputation.'

Nobby thanked him and walked off to the villa, found the iron gate with the little enamel plaque beside it, 'Clinic Shroeder', and rang the front-door bell. A pleasant-faced woman answered it. Nobby asked for the doctor, and the woman replied in curious singsong voice, 'You want to speak with the doctor Shroeder? Come in, please.' Nobby was conducted to a waiting room, handed the woman a letter from the London Hospital and sat down to wait. Soon the doctor appeared.

He was a stoutish middle-aged man, with black hair, a black pointed beard and strong glasses. He wore a long white coat and had very supple delicate hands. His rather forbidding appearance was softened by an expression of great intelligence and geniality. He welcomed Nobby warmly and took him through to his consulting room, a bare room with a polished oilcloth floor, instruments in white enamelled cabinets, an electric heater, white walls and a glass-topped desk. Everything was spotless. The desk stood in the bay of a big window overlooking the valley.

The doctor seated Nobby opposite him and took up the letter which he had left open on his desk. 'It is a great pleasure to welcome a patient of my old colleague, Dr Richards. For two years we studied together at Vienna. But that was many years ago. Just excuse me please while I read again what he says.' He adjusted his glasses and concentrated on the letter, reading slowly and carefully. Then he put it down. 'You have brought your wife with you, Mr Bligh?'

Nobby explained she was resting at the Pension and the doctor nodded. 'Quite right. Quite right. After the long journey, she will be tired.' Something thorough and capable about the doctor's manner gave Nobby great confidence and hope.

'Doctor,' he said, 'I haven't said nothing to Sally – that's my wife – about what Dr Richards says she's got. It 'ud be sinful to frighten her when she mayn't have anything serious. So, whatever you think when you examine her, you're not to let on, see? She thinks she's just come out for a holiday. All I've told her is that she's got a touch of anaemia and is a bit run down. I haven't broke it to her that she's to see you. I'm going to suggest it offhand like, saying you're a specialist in anaemia and now we're here, why not see you. I don't believe it's that serious; but if it is, you can tell me, but take good care you don't tell her. She's to know nothin'. Nothin', you understand.'

The doctor beamed at Nobby's earnestness. 'Herr Bligh, I think you have a very poor opinion of the medical profession. Naturally I should say nothing to upset your wife. Have no anxiety. Now, bring her to me whenever you can and we will see what must be done.'

But when Nobby broached the subject, Sally wouldn't hear of it. It was bad enough in London, she said; but she was scared stiff of foreigners, especially doctors. 'You never know what they mightn't do to you.' She couldn't make out why Nobby was so set on it. She even cried, and tired herself so she had to stay in bed. Nobby was desperate. He went to see the doctor again. 'I fully understand.' He nodded his head, wisely. 'I will come in to see her this afternoon.'

He won Sally's confidence at once. He was so simple and fatherly with her. She found herself agreeing to do just what he wanted, without hardly knowing why. Nobby stayed with her during the examination, she wouldn't leave go of his hand; but the doctor's cheerfulness, the way he teased and rallied her, made her feel better. 'Now you are not to worry over such a little thing. You will stay here with your husband in this good air and soon you will be wanting to jump over the mountains like our chamois. Come and see me before you go.'

Nobby was walking alone up a narrow path that climbed over the meadows on the fringe of the woods above. It was night. The sky was glittering with stars. He had put Sally to bed early and told her he was just going down for a drink; but in reality he felt he could not stand it another minute. He had to get out, away from everybody, and think it out. He had been in to see Dr Shroeder that afternoon and heard his diagnosis. It was exactly the same as the one given him in London.

If Sally had come to see him some years ago, the Doctor explained, before the disease had taken hold, something might have been done. But now it was too late. Of course he could operate, but it was very doubtful if the operation would do any good and it might accelerate things... He did not advise it... No, taking tonics and keeping as quiet as possible would lengthen the time she would live, and that was the best, the only thing to do...

'Herr Bligh, I expect that you think we doctors grow indifferent to personal suffering, but I assure you that last night when I had the results of the blood tests, I could not sleep. It is a terrible thing to know you are powerless to avert this premature death of a young and charming woman. But...' and he made a hopeless gesture with his hands '...There it is. All we can do is redouble our efforts, enlarge the field of research... I have devoted my life to this work. Something, too little, I have been able to contribute to our knowledge. But in your wife's case, alas, I am powerless.'

Nobby accepted it all in silence. He was quite numb. He got up to go, fumbled in his pocket for money and began to ask the fee. But the doctor would not hear of it. 'Please! I could not in such tragic circumstances accept anything from you. No, no. It is out of the question. Please!' He went with Nobby to the door and shook hands, very warmly. 'As a man now, not as a doctor, let me advise you to take good care of yourself. In some respects this will be harder for you than for her. Please accept my deep sympathy. Goodbye, Mr Bligh.'

Nobby reached the edge of the wood and sat down on a rock to look out over the valley. It was a magnificent panorama of mountain peaks, impassive and eternal. It dwarfed Nobby's grief into insignificance. Yet the very contrast of all this beauty and peace to his own impotence and distress overpowered him. He put his head in his hands, and let himself go. He did not give way easily and the sobs that now came from him seemed wrenched out of his very vitals. He rocked himself from side to side and shook in a convulsion of grief. But at last the hysteria passed and left him exhausted, but in some way calm and resigned. He wiped his eyes and looked out again to the mountains, and now, somehow, they were different. He could draw strength from their strength and composure from their calm. He must face whatever came, as they did. That was his task from now on: to behave exactly as if nothing had happened, to strengthen and succour Sally, right up to the very moment of death; and then to carry on without her as best he could...

He had done the task he had set himself. He had sworn his mother and father to secrecy, and carried on as his usual cheerful self. Sally knew nothing. He wouldn't let her work in the shop in the evenings, but she came in during the day to help. Then the war came, and, with the blitz, she had gone to the farm. But she didn't seem any worse, Nobby thought. Of course she was weak, but Mum said she didn't seem much weaker. The course of the disease was so slow that it was almost imperceptible, and often Nobby thought that the doctors must both have been mistaken and that there was nothing wrong with her at all... But, in any case, he had done his part. Now Dad had gone, and nobody knew but himself and Mum. He couldn't be with Sally now she was in the country, and the war might go on for a long time. He had felt for some time that he was not doing enough... The bombing of his home and the death of his father decided him.

At that time there was a dearth of Air Gunners, and particularly of rear-gunners. Nobby was asked if he would volunteer for the job.

He had never been in the air; but when they told him that he would have a couple of machine guns and a chance to get to grips with the Luftwaffe that had wrecked his home, he jumped at it. The training, if somewhat slow, was thorough, and by the time Nobby arrived at OTU to join up with the crew he would go on Ops with, there was nothing about his 'trade', as the RAF laconically phrased it, that he did not know. He had gone through all his tests, his gunnery tests, his air firing tests, his night vision tests, and had passed 'average'. But, as it often happens, a man's qualities on the job do not show up in training, and when at last he was posted to an Operational Unit and really got down to work, he soon began to be much more than 'average'. It wasn't anything special to start with, just a feeling that he could be trusted to keep cool and have his eyes open. But then on two successive raids he fought off fighters, saw one go down out of control and the other in flames, and in both cases displayed such skill and determination that he began to earn himself quite a reputation. It was not only what he did, but the man's whole character; his cheerful, perky humour, his willingness and keenness, his evident 'guts'. He became one of the personalities of the Squadron. The whole station called him 'Nobby'. And then his career nearly came to an end.

Some aircraft go on sortie after sortie over enemy territory without incident. They don't see any Huns, they miss the searchlights, they never collect any flak. Others, from the word go, get into the middle of it and never come home without some adventure. Nobby's aircraft always seemed to be marked down by the Hun. The very night after he had fought off the Me. 110 and seen it go down in flames, his aircraft went on a show to the Ruhr. They got 'coned' over the target, badly shot up and, as they were limping home, were attacked by two Ju. 88s. Nobby got both of them, one after another. It was beautiful shooting. Both went down in flames, and if the captain of the aircraft hadn't been urgently preoccupied with other things, Nobby might have got the congratulations he deserved. But the second pilot had been badly wounded in the shoulder, the wireless operator had collected a flesh wound, and the port engine had packed up. The aircraft, unable to make the coast, sent out an

SOS and its position, and ditched. They all managed to get into the dinghy, pulled in the wounded men, and after a few hours were picked up by a trawler. It was out on a three weeks trip and was forced to maintain radio silence. After a week a destroyer passed. The trawler signalled her. She stopped and took the aircrew off. But the destroyer was out on escort duty. She too maintained wireless silence, and eventually put into Gibraltar six weeks later. 'Blimey,' said Nobby, 'who'd 'a thought we was goin' on a pleasure cruise like this when we left the station that night?' At last the crew got a troopship home. Nobby and the rest of the crew were, of course, posted as missing.

The telegram giving the bad news to the next of kin arrived one day after lunch. Sally was taking her usual rest, Mrs Bligh was sitting with Mrs Smith gossiping over the fire. When she read the telegram, Mrs Bligh broke down. It was a year since she had lost her husband and the passage of time had only increased her loneliness. She had nobody to turn to. The last remaining link with the old life was Nobby, her only child. Keeping up appearances, pretending that Sally was only just a bit seedy, ('but you'll get over it, dear, when the spring comes and the weather warms up a bit'), was a constant strain and having nobody to confide in made it worse. And now Nobby, her only reason for going on at all, had been taken from her. It was too much. Life had never been easy, but it had always been worthwhile because of those she loved. Now two had been taken and the third lay asleep upstairs – and she was not going to be left...

So Mrs Bligh stared at the telegram and the tears started to run down her cheeks.

'Why, whatever's the matter, Mrs Bligh?'

Mrs Smith, seeing her tears, knew it must be bad news. It upset her. The two women were good friends. Mrs Smith had come to enjoy having someone of her own age to talk to. Besides, she admired Mrs Bligh's courage. She'd lost her husband and her home, and everything. That wasn't much fun when you were getting on...

'Whatever's the matter, my dear?'

Mrs Bligh couldn't answer. Instead she silently passed over the telegram. The other woman took it and read it slowly.

'Well, don't take on so!' she said. 'It only says he's missing. He'll turn up, as the saying is. Don't you fret yourself.'

Mrs Bligh shook her head and the flood of sorrow, once unloosed, ran out in a paroxysm of sobbing. All the pent-up emotion so long contained came out of her, the long empty days, the long sleepless nights... Life was a wilderness, a bleak desert under a leaden sky, and there was nothing to hope for any more...

Mrs Smith came and put her arm round the suffering woman's shoulders. 'There, there!' She kept on saying. 'There, there! Don't take on so. It'll be all right. He'll turn up. I know he'll turn up.'

But she could offer no more comfort, and turned to practical things. 'I'll make you a nice cup of tea, dear, that's what I'll do. You'll feel better after a cup of tea.' And she busied herself with teapot and cups and took the singing kettle from the hob.

The sound of the sobbing awakened Sally. She always slept lightly, and often during her afternoon rest she spent the time in a sort of doze, half waking and half asleep. It was a curious feeling, as if she was floating away and had no body, nothing to connect her to life. Sometimes it was quite an effort to get back, but she always made the effort, for Sally, in her quiet way, had plenty of courage and would never let herself believe that she wouldn't be better soon. If only this stupid weakness wouldn't get between her and health. But she'd get over that. Nobby said she would. There was nothing wrong with her. And when the warmer weather came...

She listened to the sobbing, vaguely thinking it must be some dream she was dreaming. The sound came clearly up from the room below. There was only a floor over the rafters and sometimes, when her room was dark, she could see chinks of light coming through from downstairs. Now she heard the clink of cups and spoons, and the voices of Mum and Mrs Smith. It all seemed to come from a long way away.

'Here now, drink up your tea,' Mrs Smith was saying. 'It'll do you good, as the saying is.'

There was a pause. 'And after all,' the voice went on, 'you've still got Sally, haven't you?'

'No,' came Mum's answer, and her sobbing began afresh. 'No,

we shan't have poor Sal with us much longer...'

'Why, Mrs Bligh, whatever do you mean?'

So it was that Sally, trying not to listen, but hearing everything so clearly, learned her fate. For once Mrs Bligh started, she confided everything. What the hospital had said and that man in Switzerland, how Sally was never to be told; but now she must tell somebody, must share it with somebody... She went on talking for a long time. Sally heard it all; but it didn't make any difference. She didn't really believe it. Nobby had told her she would get better. Nobby was always right. She was getting better. When at last she got up and came down to tea, she found both women cheerful and composed. She was sure she must have dreamed it all. It couldn't be true.

When Nobby walked in a couple of months later, Mrs Bligh fainted. He was so glad to be back, the idea of writing or wiring first didn't occur to him. He didn't realise what it had meant to all of them. Mum tried to keep it from Sally for a week or two, in case, as Mrs Smith insisted, he should turn up. But when his letters stopped, they had to tell her. She didn't say much. But it lowered her dreadfully. The truth was that now that Nobby was gone, Sally didn't care what happened to her any more. She still didn't believe what she had overheard that afternoon; but now it might just as well be true. She had no interest in living. When Mum rallied her, as she had done before, she didn't respond. She didn't laugh or talk at all. She just went through the days like an automaton.

But on Nobby's return she nearly died of joy. She collapsed and was carried to bed. She didn't cry. The tears just welled out of her eyes. She couldn't stop. It went on for two whole days and all Nobby's tenderness and care had no effect.

But then she grew better at once. It really did seem as if Nobby's vitality entered into her, as if she lived from his strength, as if he had the power (for which he often prayed) to keep her alive because he loved her so.

He was given a month's leave, and during all that time Sally steadily got better, or seemed to, and some of the old happiness came back to Mum too. The farm was cosy in winter. Something about the work itself and the sturdy men who laboured was full of life in itself. The earth was a great healer. Just to be near it gave strength...

When Nobby left everything was different. Spring was on the way. The talk was all of sowing, of coming crops, of lambs, of piglets, of chicks... By the time he came on leave again, in a couple of months' time, the fruit would be in blossom...

He was posted to the Pathfinder Squadron and reported for duty. When Hugh Thornly interviewed him on arrival, he took an immediate liking to the little man. He knew he was up for his DFM. He knew he was a crack rear-gunner. His own had gone sick, so he offered to take Nobby into his crew. Nobby accepted gratefully. It was the highest honour his Commanding Officer could pay him.

The work went on as usual. It was fairly slack in the winter. The bombers were weatherbound three nights out of five. Nobby wrote to Sally every day, settled down in the Mess, got to know his crew, did a few shows and felt on top of the world. It was three years now since the doctors had given Sally her sentence and she was still alive. Indeed, as far as he could see, she was hardly any different from that day they arrived in Adelboden. He had no idea that anybody had told her anything. Mum had only hinted that she had been upset when he was posted missing. She did not tell him she had confided in Mrs Smith, and it never occurred to her that Sally had overheard that conversation.

As soon as Nobby left Sally suddenly weakened. It was as if she needed his presence to keep her alive and, deprived of it, she wilted. She wrote to him regularly and her simple letters were as cheerful as ever; but it was a great strain. Sometimes writing to Nobby took all her strength for the day. She stayed more and more in bed, and only on the fine warm days ventured out for a short walk after lunch.

She thought again, after Nobby had left, of that conversation she had overheard. Now, as she felt herself getting weaker, it seemed that it might be true, after all. But, if it was, it only made her love her husband more. How could he have carried the whole burden for all these years, and never said a word or changed a scrap from the cheery jolly boy she had always known? She was so proud of him, but it made her feel small and worthless herself, not to share it with him. She had always shared everything with him. If he could be brave, so could she. If he could face death every time he went out on a raid and carry this as well, could she not help by telling him that she knew, that she was not dismayed, that love made everything else unreal? It was the least she could do. Soon she might be too weak to do it properly...

So one day she took pen and paper and walked slowly out across the field to the wood, the wood where they had spent their honeymoon. She sat down on the edge of the hollow where the little green caravan had stood. The sun was warm. Thrushes and blackbirds were calling in the hedgerows, and Sally sent out her soul to her husband in her big unformed handwriting. Sometimes she stopped to look out over the meadow and think, but then her pen hurried on over the cheap paper, as if Time were falling headlong from her feet into the abyss.

'Nobby, dear,' (the letter read), *'it is sunny and warm today. I hope it is raining where you are, then I know you are safe. I feel quite well. I am sitting on the bank where the caravan was. Do you remember the gang? I wonder where they are now. Do you hear from them sometimes? It is lovely here. The birds are singing. I love you Nobby, you know that. I know you love me too. You are so brave and tender and always so kind and good to me, I feel I must tell you that I know about myself. Don't worry about me, dearest. I am not sad. I never could be unless you stopped loving me. You have made all my life happy. I can never remember a day when you weren't near me and my only fear is that you may not be with me when the time comes. I am angry with you for not telling me sooner. I know you did it for me. But you have too much to think about without having to pretend about me. I have only one wish – for you to come home and hold my hand at the end. But perhaps you will not be able to, so I must make up my mind to being alone. It won't hurt much, will it? If I had your arms around me, it would be easy, like falling asleep with you. I would like it*

to be like that. Please come back to me if you can. I should not say it, but I think perhaps you must be quick to catch me. Oh, my dearest and dearest husband if this must be so, I will come and live in your heart for ever. Please come soon to your Sally.'

It was a couple of hours after all aircraft were airborne that the van drove into camp with the evening mail. The driver carried the sacks to the Orderly Room where the clerks sorted them. Then they were distributed to the various Messes. The Mess Orderlies took the letters and put them in the racks. Into Nobby's rack, where he could pick it up when he next came in, was a fat letter addressed to 564392, F-Sgt HN Bligh, DFM, and in the corner was written: Sender, Sally Bligh.

'Navigator to Captain,' Cookson was calling up, 'I think we should alter course now, sir, to one six zero.'

'One six zero. Okay. Altering now.' Thornly put down the right wing and the aircraft swung southward. He watched the numbers in the gyro compass come past the lubber line and steadied down on one six zero. 'On course,' he called back to Cookson.

Cookson noted the change of course and the time in his log.

'We should make our landfall in about half an hour, sir.'

'Right. Captain to Front-Gunner. Let me know when you pick anything up.'

'Okay, sir,' came back from Sam.

'Watch out for flakships.'

'You betcha.'

Thornly motioned to Peter to undo the thermos. He always liked a cup of coffee before going in. They were getting near that five or ten minutes of glorious hell known as making a bombing run. Thornly felt the prospect bracing him as he knew it braced all the crew. You could feel it in the way they answered on the intercomm; they were on their toes.

Thornly held his course and the aircraft drove on under the stars.

HUGH THORNLY

BEFORE WAR BROKE out Hugh Thornly would have classed himself as an idealist, a pacifist and, in a sense, a defeatist. The disgraceful handling of his country's affairs through two decades had made him despair of it. The hopeless ineptitude of the government, the opportunism, the hypocrisy, the brazen incompetence on every side drove him to the point of view that if this was what England had become, she deserved the fate that plainly awaited her. There were thousands like him, thousands proud of their birth right, proud of their country's past, proud of the fine qualities they knew existed in English men and women. It was not true that the country was moribund and effete. There was plenty of talent, initiative and enterprise everywhere; but its voice could not be heard, it could not get through the damnable miasma of official complacence and *laissez faire*. The true patriots – for this is what they were – lived through moods of violent frustration and as violent despair. If there were defeatists in England when war broke out, the English government had bred them.

Now, in the third year of the war, things had changed so much that Thornly could hardly focus the way he had felt in those disastrous years. He smiled to think of himself, the erstwhile pacifist, now the leader of the bomber offensive. Yet this complete change of heart was a thing that had happened to tens of thousands of people. He was only an instance of it. It had been frightfully important to him, the only really important thing that had happened in all his life. His personal affairs were happy and humdrum. He loved Helen, his wife, and she loved him. That was so axiomatic that he almost took it for granted. But this conversion was an adventure, a social and spiritual metamorphosis, a rebirth. It had been tremendously exciting to find himself, to see the way, to have a duty and a purpose. His stature had been doubled by it: it had made a man of him.

Originally he had been perfectly tailored to take up his position in what used to be known as the 'ruling classes'. Winchester and

Balliol, Church of England, family well established in the City with branches in the Church and Law and, on his wife's side, in the Army and the Foreign Office, comfortable private means, an assured position in his father's firm, good clubs, a fair aptitude for outdoor sports, well mannered, pleasant looking, at home in any society... these were his credentials. He might have been expected to go in for politics and finish on the Treasury Bench.

But although he could be pigeon-holed in this way as a typical 'boiled shirt' Englishman, the facts gave no indication of his character. In a country where the Prime Minister may be a painter, the Governor of the Bank of England a violinist, and high-ranking officers poets, archaeologists and students of oriental languages, a man's background can hardly be expected to give much idea of his personality. Of course you will be sure to find certain traits: humour, tolerance and patience and, if you look deeper, the Englishman's less obvious but equally common characteristics, natural optimism, incurable romanticism and ingrained idealism. Indeed it is these bizarre contrasts that make him incalculable to the foreigner. Modest, yet absurdly conceited, friendly yet unapproachable, likeable yet ridiculous, gentle yet incalculably courageous, easy-going yet suddenly pugnacious: a riddle made less pleasant by an insufferable superiority which, however detestable, cannot be entirely ignored.

Thornly stood out from his orthodox background by reason of an avid curiosity and appetite for social, economic and political questions. At the University he read English History, with particular reference to the Nineteenth Century and the Industrial Revolution. He chose to specialise in this subject because he was by nature a reformer. He felt that only by understanding the past could men hope to master the future. But, as is so often the case with study, one thing leads on to another. The River of Knowledge is fed by many tributary streams, each leading to fascinating unknown regions, each beckoning and demanding exploration. Thornly soon found himself pursuing a hundred clues, knocking at a thousand doors. The study of the structure of society was fascinating. There was no end to it. Yet it must be grasped, must be mapped in the mind, if the ideals and hopes of humanity were to be crystallised into constitutions and laws.

As a young man at the University, he never forgot the peroration of his Professor of History who, in those ominous days of the thirties, concluded his final lecture by a consideration of war.

'Gentlemen,' he had said, as far as Thornly could remember it, 'our examination of the crises in the history of mankind has shown us how often the aim is lost in the result, how often men are led away by the ignorance and folly of their leaders, how political expediency betrays the masses, how greed and revenge breed war after war, how popular liberties have been increasingly curtailed, how taxation has bled nations white. Every war is for Liberty, every war is for Freedom, every war is for Right, Justice, Truth and Honour and – every war is the last.

'These are sombre truths. It is not surprising therefore if we look to the future with some misgiving. Human nature does not suddenly change, yet I believe that it is slowly changing. In other words it is hope which, beyond reason, sustains us. For, as you will observe, the matter grows steadily more serious. In the past wars have been local and professional. But today it is clear they will demand the service of the entire adult population of both sexes in every country which is party to the conflict – and that is likely to be the whole world. Such a state of affairs is bound to disrupt the entire structure of society and shake our civilisation to its foundations.

'Man, gentlemen, is a conservative animal. He loves his own chains and will die sooner than submit to be shackled by those of another. But he cannot fight in chains. In order to strike the first blow, he is obliged to kick them off. When the fight is over, the old chains – that all the fight was about – seem rusty and useless. He no longer wants to return to them. In fact he cannot. That is why war is so useless.

'It is my great privilege to address you on these matters. Among you are some who will, no doubt, in the future, have to face the reality of problems about which I speak only in theory. Some of you will have the burden and distinction of helping to steer the world through the difficult times that, I am afraid, lie ahead. Therefore I should like to leave a final thought with you, the crux, as I see it, of the whole matter, the final lesson of History. It is this. In moments of crisis, man, who is for ever boasting of his reason, invariably throws it to the winds. He becomes the slave of his passions and this entangles him in the most ridiculous paradoxes. He will make gigantic sacrifices to kill, and next to none to live. He renounces freedom in an attempt to gain it. He will discipline himself for death but not for life. In other words, altho' he will plan for the future industrially and scientifically, he will not use his reason to do so politically. He does not understand the art of government. Government, gentlemen, is the only thing that can put order into chaos, the only thing that can canalise and control the titanic forces of human progress. Only wise government can promote the basic security of mankind. This is the lesson of History: we have got to learn how to govern.'

That lecture decided the course of Thornly's life. It fired his imagination and gave him an ambition. He would master the subject of government. Then, by every means in his power, he would bring the failure of past governments to the notice of his fellow men, indicate the reforms that were necessary and set out to carry them into effect. It would entail considerable work to digest it all; but what of that? In youth life seems endless. He planned it out: five years for study, five years to digest the lessons he had learned and postulate the necessary reforms. The rest of his life to lecture, to speak, to write, to form a body of opinion, a party and, by middle age, if all went well – and it would, it must go well – a government. It was a somewhat ambitious programme, but it was selfless. It was planned to help the world, not to help himself, for Thornly did not see himself as a Leader. His function would be to expose the wrongs and the mistakes. Then the public would find its own leader to right them. Impracticable? but at least it was a plan. Idealistic? but who shall dream of Utopia, if not the young?

Projects planned with skill and foresight can and do often come to nothing when launched on the treacherous waters of politics and sucked into the whirlpools of national egotisms. They emerge as wrecks, mere rafts and lifebuoys, bearing the old ship's name, but in effect no more than the flotsam and jetsam of compromise

– and the old game of grab goes on as fiercely as ever. Versailles was an excellent example of it. Political considerations and national differences swamped the great hope that lay in the League of Nations and scuttled the prophets who, on economic grounds, had foretold the disasters which would follow on Reparations. Yes, plans were one thing, getting them agreed another and carrying them out yet a third. Only a resolute, organised and articulate body of public opinion could do it. That body must be formed, must be awakened to its duties and responsibilities, must be injected with fire and enthusiasm for the world that lay within its grasp, for the moulding of its own destiny. So Thornly mused and dreamed. The scope of the task he had set himself did not appall him. On the contrary, it inspired him, as a climber is inspired by the mountain peak before him.

'You haven't got a hope,' said young Don Freeman, when Thornly had unfolded his great plan. Don was a close friend. The two had been up at Oxford together. He was brilliant and cynical. Hugh admired his quick incisive mind, though he deplored his lack of public spirit. Don, in his turn, admired Hugh's grasp of generalities and laughed at his idealism. As is often the case with opposites, the two got on well. Privately Hugh always hoped to make a convert of Don: but nothing came of it. 'You haven't got a hope, Hugh. Government isn't fashionable.'

'Fashionable!' Hugh snorted in disgust. 'Don't be so trivial, Don.'

'I'm not. Fashions aren't trivial. They're one of the great mysteries of life. How do they arrive and why? Why did the Greeks have such a rage for the arts of citizenship and public life? That was about the only time the art of government was really in the fashion. But it died out. Why? Nobody can explain why. Then came the fashion of spreading the new religion, Christianity. Then that wore off. after that came a whole string of other fashions, Exploration, the Renaissance, Colonisation, and so on. Now the fashion is Science.'

'But these things are not fashions: passions would be nearer the mark.'

'Possibly. But historically we can regard them as fashions.

Whatever you call them, the point is they attracted the best brains of their time. All those whose talents and interests didn't happen to lie in that direction felt out of it. Men get an enormous kick from having the eyes of the world on them. Look at the scientist today! Everything he does and says is received as if it were a revelation. He is the world's high priest. Compare the way people feel about Science to, say, Religion. What is it? Something you switch off on the radio. Or Art? Something 'highbrow' you don't understand, and vaguely resent. But once, don't forget, the world hung on the preacher's lips. Once, the crowd watched breathless every movement of the painter's brush. What is it Andrea del Sarto says? "My hand kept plying by those hearts." Now all that's out of fashion.'

'Then we've got to make it "fashionable".'

'Ah, yes, if you can do that, it's another matter. But there'll have to be a clean sweep first – as in Russia. She's a perfect example of what I mean. After the Revolution the place was knocked flat. It's been completely reorganised, from the bottom up. Educated, industrialised, administered on brand new lines, with new codes, new laws, new morals, new philosophies – a vast territory, one-sixth of the whole earth, all reborn and very much alive and kicking, in the space of twenty years! That's quite impossible unless government, as such, has become a fashion, or a passion if you prefer, of the whole people. But it can't be done unless everything has been knocked flat.'

'It looks very much as if it's going to be.'

'Well, there's your chance – if people have got any life left in them.'

As Thornly began to get to grips with his problem, he felt the need to get it into perspective. It was all very well to know about the past, but to use it to understand the present and plan the future, you had to condense it into generalities, into trends. You had to get a sense of the way things had moved and the speed at which they had moved. After a lot of thought, he decided that communication was the key to it.

For centuries information, orders, instructions were carried as letters and messages by hand or by horse overland and sailed in long arduous voyages overseas. All forms of communication were slow and uncertain. So, altho' loosely knit Empires had existed, countries tended to split up into petty dukedoms and principalities, each independent, self-reliant and self-supporting. These little worlds were largely ignorant of what went on outside their own borders. They were self-contained and self-sufficient. But with the coming of better roads and vehicles communications began to improve. Printing came. Knowledge and news began to travel more widely and more freely. Gradually – and it is important to note that it was gradually – walled cities began to merge into states and states into nations. They grew in size and coherence as it was found possible to administer them effectively from a single capital. But these changes were gradual enough to enable people to widen their allegiances, first from their feudal lords to state princes and then from princes to monarchs. Today it seems impossible that Wales and Scotland were independent states often at war with England. Yet once the Welshman's allegiance to Wales and the Scotsman to Scotland was every bit as strong and exclusive as national allegiances are today.

Of course that was making it too simple. There were other factors, natural frontiers, religious bigotry, the banding together of states against a common enemy, the influence of language, and so on. But broadly speaking the stabilisation of states of any size depended on their communications. Once the Nineteenth Century arrived with its steamships and railways, communications became simple and cheap and far quicker. Rigid national blocs emerged with jealously guarded frontiers. Trains and ships made possible the wholesale movement of goods. Exports and imports grew in importance and the involved modern picture took shape.

So the tendency was from simple to complex, from small to big. It had gathered momentum at first slowly, then with a rush. Now it was practically out of control. Why? Because it was out of step, because the technical staff had bolted with the management. Government had failed to keep up with Science. It all came back to that. And the situation had burst on the world in the twinkling of an eye, in under two hundred years. What was that in comparison with the thousands of years of civilisations that had gone before? It was nothing. The modern world had literally exploded over men's heads. Small wonder if they were bewildered and made mistakes. The thing had happened too quickly.

But, nevertheless, there it was. Communications had telescoped space and time. The Antipodes could be reached in a few days, the Atlantic crossed in a few hours. From now on frontiers could have only an arbitrary significance. The planet was a unit.

'It's just like a conjuring trick,' said Hugh to Helen. They had met at the London School of Economics and were dining together. Hugh, young and enthusiastic, full of his picture of the world, was pouring it all out to her. And she was listening, putting in a word here and there, listening with that quiet absorbed expression, gravely watching him, carried away out of herself, as a woman can be, by the vigour and enthusiasm of a man.

'I'm afraid I adore conjurors,' she laughed.

'So do I! Ever since my favourite uncle made a halfpenny disappear up his sleeve and produced it from behind my ear! And really, you see, that's exactly what Science is doing all the time. At a pinch most of us would class Oliver Lodge with Maskelyne and Devant, and throw in the astrologers for good measure! After all, they do things that are completely beyond us. And when their "tricks" are things like the radio, the telephone or the aeroplane, we just sit and gape, hypnotised… But, there's the devil in it, all the same.'

'Why?'

'Because science is completely a-moral. You see the scientist always excuses himself by saying that his business is the pursuit of knowledge, and the use to which it is put is nothing to do with him. So people get hold of his ideas and apply them, usually for gain. One development leads to another, each seems sort of – hydra-headed and divides into a thousand others. Each seems to support and inform the next and the whole horde rushes madly forward, shouting with excitement. The public is swept off its feet. They catch the infection and join in the hubbub. It's a sort of… of oafish delirium, as if, poor people, they had suddenly been turned loose among the treasures of Aladdin's cave and told to take anything they wanted.'

'But, all the same, it's wonderful, Hugh.'

'No doubt about that, and damnable too.'

'But surely, Hugh, take medical science. You wouldn't say the advances there were evil, would you?'

'No. Of course, it isn't all bad. If it were the problem would be fairly simple. Medicine is one of the few branches of applied Science that has an aim in view. But most of it has no definite aim, beyond profit. Of course there are selling points, labour saving, time saving, raising the "standard of living," and so on. But raising the standard of living lowers the standard of life. You see what happens. When business can be stepped up – as it can by rapid communication – it soon becomes quite a different thing. Companies become corporations, corporations trusts. Huge networks for buying and selling come into existence. Their interests are worldwide. Their outlook is essentially international. Side by side with this come all the other international influences – radio hook-ups, the cinema, cheap printing, television. There's no aim in all this. It's just a spontaneous outcropping of human activity. But look at the mess it's landing us in! It's the old business of God and Mammon, trying to have your cake and eat it, trying to reap the harvest of international intercourse and retain the old pride and prejudice of patriotism. Our reason and our self-interest are making us internationalists; but our emotions remain isolationist. It's like giving a young man a latchkey and saying you'll thrash him if he isn't in bed by nine.'

'But governments must see that, Hugh. It's so obvious.'

'They don't – or won't. Or else they're so bewildered they can't. But it is obvious, as you say. It's precisely as if the men of Kent, while enjoying the privileges of the Southern Railway, the Green Line, the Grid and the BBC, were suddenly to announce that the Surrey County Council was corrupt, effete and wholly irresponsible, the Surrey Police were a lot of bastards and the population of Surrey generally stank to high heaven. Surrey would declare as one man that honour would not be satisfied until they had entirely exterminated the people of Kent. The county border would be manned, passports examined, customs barriers set up, mobilisation ordered. There would be "incidents". Essex would offer to arbitrate. Sussex would declare she was in danger of encirclement...'

They were both laughing. 'You see,' said Hugh, 'it's so irrational and preposterous we can't take it seriously. But it's really precisely the same thing – county emotions living side by side with inter-county facilities and communications. But at this level, thank God, co-operation and interdependence have become second nature to us. We have learned to confine rivalry to the football ground and the cricket pitch where it is harmless and enjoyable enough to those who like the games.'

Helen was looking at him with such a sad, hopeless expression. 'Oh, Hugh, if people could only look at it all as sanely and humorously as you do. If only nations could.'

'They will. They must. We've got to make them.'

But Helen shook her head. Hugh seemed wonderful to her, setting out with his little enthusiastic sling against the embattled world. His spirits were infectious: she was glowing with admiration. 'It's David and Goliath,' she said.

'And who won that fight?' he came back. 'We can't have wars, Helen. We can't afford to. They're useless. They settle nothing permanently. Each one breeds the next. We've got to break the vicious circle. Got to.'

In those troubled years before the war, its spectre seemed to pervade every conversation. As the tarantula mesmerises the bird on a branch far out of its reach, till the poor creature falls to the ground in fright, so the world seemed hypnotised by the prospect of war, almost to desire it, to long to fall before the Juggernaut. To forget the impending disaster, most people plunged into a frenzy of irresponsible pleasure seeking. The tarantula was there, but if they didn't look at it, perhaps it would go away. Only a few tried to stem the tide, proposing utterly impracticable remedies, appeasements, soporifics. Like bees before swarming time, the whole population rushed hither and thither in frenzied excitement. The great moment was approaching, but it had not come.

'When d'you think it will be?' asked Don one day when he and Hugh were lunching together at the Gargoyle.

'Never, I hope,' Hugh answered. 'Surely the world can't be so mad.'

'The world isn't a bit mad, old boy. It's perfectly sane and sensible. It dislikes the idea of war, of course; but it realises that it's the only way out of the impasse. The world wants war – that's why it's always saying how horrible it will be. You're a very poor psychologist.'

'Nonsense, Don. War settles nothing and you know it.'

'It'll settle a hell of a lot this time – and it needs to. I don't think you've any idea of the mess the world is in. Everyone in the know is looking forward to it.'

'I daresay they are – if there's any profit to be made out of it.'

Don laughed sardonically. 'Not the old bogey of the armament rings! Don't bring up that one! Really you're very gullible in some ways, Hugh.'

'Well, why do we sell arms abroad anyway? If that's not stirring up trouble, what is?'

Don waved him aside. 'We may be selling a bit here and there. But our armament output is so minute all we could sell wouldn't keep a revolution going in Paraguay. The trouble doesn't lie there. I shall have to educate you.'

'Go ahead!' said Hugh. 'That's the only reason I put up with you.'

'Very well then.' Don lit a cigarette. 'The world's highly industrialised today, isn't it?' Hugh nodded. 'And the biggest prizes in the industrial race go to the biggest countries, because they have the man-power, the resources, the raw materials and the markets. Agreed?' Hugh nodded again. 'The smaller countries lag behind and have to be satisfied with a lower standard of living, because of the lack of man-power, raw materials and so on. Their small home industries are threatened with annihilation by the imports from the big chaps. So what do they do?'

'Put up tariff walls.'

'Correct, my dear Watson, they put up tariffs. Soon every country starts copying them, for they are all, on a larger or smaller scale, making the same sort of goods and jockeying for position to sell them abroad. But this doesn't suit the big countries. They need to sell in the small ones for, collectively, they represent quite a big market.

So, on condition they let certain goods pass, the big chaps agree to lend the little 'uns the money to pay for them with!'

'And the scheme works very well,' Hugh put in.

'No, it doesn't. It has worked here and there in certain special cases. But, by and large, countries can't live by taking in one another's washing. That's why, as you've noticed, the tariff walls are growing higher and higher. But that's only the beginning of the trouble. Ever heard of the Gold Standard?'

'Never!' Hugh smiled at the banter. 'What is it?'

'A convenient medium for world exchange. The coins have now disappeared and paper notes have taken their place. You'll be paying for my lunch with one.'

'Thanks.'

'A bit of paper. Obviously quite valueless.'

'But convenient.'

'Yes, convenient and useful as long as their issue is, as we say, "linked" to the gold reserve of the country. But when the country has no more reserve, what then? She can still go on printing notes. As long as they don't go outside the country, they can be given value within it. So a country may be bankrupt internationally and still maintain a prosperous domestic economy. Provided, of course, that the financial tariff walls are quite impregnable – otherwise the whole thing would collapse. All money would be found to be worthless – which is pretty well what it is. Today almost every country, except America, is off the gold standard, a polite way of saying that they are all bankrupt.'

'So what?'

'So a fantastic and insoluble muddle. All the channels of trade dammed up. Huge loans floated by the countries that can afford it in an attempt to ease the situation. Small countries repudiating their debts, defaulting on their interest payments. All the debtor countries growing steadily more irresponsible – morally as well as financially bankrupt. The thing is now so hopelessly involved, so immensely complicated, that no solution is possible. The only thing is to raze it all to the ground and start again. That can't be done without a thumping big war, my boy. The sooner the better, and the bigger the better.'

'And what do you suppose England is going to fight with?'

'Ah, there you have me! I was simply considering the problem financially and economically. Whether England fights or doesn't, whether she loses or wins, doesn't matter from that point of view. Everything will start from scratch after it's over. What England ought to do about defending her own interests is quite another matter. When you stand me another lunch, I'll give you the answer to that one.'

It was an explosion, the Industrial Revolution, that was the thing to keep in mind. We were still running round in circles trying to straighten up the mess. It was a sudden and unaccountable flare-up in mechanical ingenuity. The 'machine' would make the craftsman's labour lighter, shorten his hours, increase the amount he could do and so raise his earning capacity. That was the way they argued when they had the idea and lit the fuse. It seemed the millennium. Most men can do with more money and a strain of laziness runs right through the human race. So the idea caught on like wildfire. Everything appeared to be solved: the long arduous years of apprenticeship were unnecessary, the need for skilled tradesmen disappeared: the machine provided the skill and all that was required was the 'labour'. So although at first the old crafts continued, the majority soon ceased working for themselves and were hired by those who sponsored the machines. They were without ownership, therefore without pride and soon without interest in the things they created. That was the beginning of the trouble.

'A thing I can never understand,' said Helen, when Hugh was trying to get it clear in his own mind by talking it all out with her, 'is how the craftsmen managed to make enough of everything. All those fine pieces of furniture at the Victoria and Albert, for instance, they must have taken years to make. How was there enough to go round?'

'There wasn't. All that was the privilege of the very few. Lords and Ladies were rare. A great gulf divided riches from poverty. It was a luxury trade. The squalor and poverty of the masses seems unbelievable nowadays – a rough table, a few stools, bowls to eat from, straw to sleep on, that was how the poor lived. But the machine soon began to change all that. It made articles available to the poor, and, in their wages, gave them the money to pay for them. Of course the first "machine-made" articles were inferior to the hand-made things, and the craftsmen scoffed at their rivals; but very soon the boot was on the other foot. Today, we tend to look on the "Arts and Crafts" as something quaint and outmoded.'

'Ye Oldey Worldey,' nodded Helen.

'Yes, that's the idea. Old maiden ladies. Plaits and lavender and a diet of nuts. One of the first things the explosion did was to shoot the aristocracy out of the saddle. You see, the men who owned the machines soon began to grow rich and influential. A new class grew up living either directly or indirectly on industry. It became a bitter rivalry – as you can see in plays like Galsworthy's *Skin Game* – a rivalry that hasn't died out even today when the influence of the aristocracy, as such, is almost nil and the House of Lords has become an organ of doubtful value, like an appendix. But, of course, though the landed gentry tried to ignore the businessmen, the Exchequer couldn't afford to. They were beginning to make the country tremendously rich. Englishmen looked out over their vast Empire. The thing seemed to have no end: endless sources of raw materials, endless markets, endless rivers of wealth.

'Just like the legend of Midas.'

'Exactly, and with just as awkward an ending. The manpower to run all the machines came from the peasants, who drifted into the ugly squalid sprawling towns, thinking to better themselves by "making money". Living and working conditions became such a scandal that, ultimately Parliament had to intervene. There were riots and strikes. The labour movement was born. Now, as you know, although there is a good deal of talk of co-operative management, things have been reversed. It is labour that really controls the managements. The tail is wagging the dog.'

'But, Hugh, if all this took place in England, what happened abroad? That's surely part of the problem?'

'Yes, of course. It was more or less the same in all the so-called "civilised" countries. England was in the lead, but the rest were hot on her heels and went through exactly the same phases. Russia, coming last of all, telescoped the whole of the Nineteenth Century into twenty years and boldly made their national symbol that of the Workers – the Hammer and Sickle. But the point to remember is that the astonishing scientific discoveries don't stand alone. While they are advancing at ever increasing speed on an international front, at the same time, the whole pyramid of society has been stood on its apex. Power has passed from the few to the many, from the "classes" to the masses.'

'But, Hugh, isn't it extraordinary, if it's been such an explosion, as you call it, that it's all happened with so little fuss?'

'Well, the Great War was quite a fuss in its way! England is dependent on raw materials brought from overseas to keep her industries going, and equally dependent on export trade for her markets. That was what the last war was about, and the one that's brewing is really based, fundamentally, on markets. When a country ceases to be self-supporting, the whole population faces ruin if they can't import and export. Those aren't the reasons Hitler gives, or the reasons we give, but that's what it amounts to.'

'Then oughtn't the raw materials and the markets to be guaranteed to all countries somehow or other?'

'Of course. They must be. One of the essentials of stability is a fair sharing of raw materials and some sort of zoning of markets; but try and persuade our politicians of that. They just won't face these things. You see, when all this started, it was just a game of grab. It didn't appear so because the amount to be grabbed seemed without limit. It was everybody for himself or what is more politely called "individual enterprise". True a few cranky half-baked philosophers, like Karl Marx, saw where it was all leading and warned people, but who took any notice of that when gold was pouring in? When entire generations have been brought up on the principles of private enterprise, individual effort and the stimulus of competition, you can't expect them to agree to put the whole thing into reverse. It takes something more than persuasion to do that.'

'Hugh, there's another thing I've never understood. If one machine can do the work of ten men, what happens to the other nine?'

Hugh laughed. 'That's an old chestnut! The official answer is: "We shall produce ten times as much and so everybody will be fully employed".'

'But it isn't true.'

'Of course not. Probably when the question was first asked, it was. Machines weren't so wonderful then and there were lots of things of common use that everybody wanted. But as the markets got used up, there wasn't the same need for production, and meanwhile the machine was getting more and more ingenious. It would do the work of a hundred or a thousand men. That is why export markets are so important, why it becomes a matter of life and death to create new markets, like teaching the Chinese to cultivate a taste for tobacco or to use paraffin. Today, without question, machines are producing more than enough for human needs, with fewer and fewer men. You've only to look at the unemployment figures. Two million in England, six in America. My God, Helen, it makes me see red. If you want any proof of the scandalous inability of governments to govern, think of those wretched millions, whom their countries don't want, doomed to exist on a grudging dole, who have no place in the life on the community. They're a cancer on the body of society. And the terrible thing is that they never will get work until there's a war. Their only chance of life lies in a plan for the wholesale destruction of their fellow men. It's the most shameful paradox in history.'

It was when she felt the fire rising in him that Helen knew she loved Hugh. It was then she worshipped him because he was noble in purpose and selfless in ideal. But she took particular pains to hide it, because she knew he did not really think of her as a woman. Personal things and personal relations were somehow too small for him. If she intruded trivialities on him the plane of their friendship would be lowered. It might even be lost. And she so loved to hear him talk.

'All the same, I don't see how you can have any progress without competition,' she prodded him. 'Nobody will work, nobody will make an effort unless they are going to get something out of it.'

'Nonsense! Limits must be set to it. It must be controlled. What would you think of the schoolboy who wanted to win a scholarship and started by bribing the examiner to find out the questions beforehand, took a crib to the examination, doped the other candidates, arranged for the papers of his rivals to be "mislaid", and so got the prize? You'd say he was a crook. But that's exactly the sort of sharp practice competition leads to. It's the sort of thing that's praised as smart business. That's what happens when competition gets acute. But when it gets worse still, what do you find? Rings, trusts and combines. Deadly rivals meeting and agreeing to maintain their prices.'

'But that's co-operation. That's what you want.'

'It might be if the price was fixed by a disinterested party. But nowadays these rings are monopolies and a law to themselves. They hoard or destroy their goods sooner than reduce the prices. They conspire to keep things off the market. It's the economies of scarcity, not of plenty. Look at the diamond market – a totally fictitious price is maintained. Or take Brazilian coffee, which was burned sooner than allow the price to fall, or the millions of bushels of Canadian wheat that went rotten in the fields. It always comes back to the same thing, Helen. If you want a fair deal, if you want an honest world, if you want some degree of security and decent life, you must control and co-operate. In other words you must govern. We must stop this game of grab. It's the end of the world, the disintegration of society, it's anarchy if we don't. And it's staring us straight in the face.'

'The trouble about you, Hugh,' said Don Freeman when they met, as they always did, to argue, 'is that you think government is the solution to the problem. It isn't.'

'Then what is?'

'Education.'

'Naturally part of the business of good government is to see there is good education.'

'Which came first: the chicken or the egg?' laughed Don.

'Biologically no doubt the egg; but – '

'Obviously,' said Don, as if that settled the matter. 'All education ought to be in the hands of the Church.'

'Of *the what*?' Hugh was incredulous.

'The most successful empire the world has ever seen and the one that lasted the longest was the Holy Roman Empire. One of the reasons it lasted is because the children were brought up by the Church.'

'I never heard such nonsense!'

'Not a bit of it! Argue it out from first principles. What are you after, fundamentally? From the way you talk, it sounds to me like the universal brotherhood of man.'

'Well, I shouldn't phrase it quite like that; but without question, international agreement is a necessity for any durable and prosperous society.'

'That's only a pompous way of saying the same thing! Now listen to me. There's no such thing as impartial education. The teacher is bound to colour what he teaches. He is bound to bring up his charges in a way of life of which he approves and to encourage them to live by standards he considers good, isn't he?'

'I suppose so; but I don't see that it matters provided you have the right curriculum.'

'Doesn't matter! Really, Hugh! If the teacher owes his first allegiance to God, who is not interested in patriotism, the children will have a universal outlook. That will be the colouring behind all they are taught. If the teacher is a layman – that is a nationalist – the children will be brought up as patriots. You can't escape it. Unfortunately at the time the Church guided the young, the desirability of teaching everybody was not understood. That didn't come till much later, when the power of the Church had waned and the division between the spiritual and temporal powers had become acute. There had always been some division, of course; but up till your precious Nineteenth Century, men, however worldly, had always paid some lip-service to heaven. Excommunication meant something. When the spiritual control was gone, there was nothing to stop the rush towards the things that could be realised *now*. Hope of heaven might comfort a man on his deathbed, but a gas-fire would comfort him all his life. That was the idea. Now though there are some Catholic schools, the only education permitted to the Church is "Sunday School" – and you know what that's worth. The whole thing's retrogressive. The only body with a world outlook and a world influence is the Catholic Church. If you want to increase the number of people who think that way, put them in the hands of the people who stand above nationality.'

'Does making a man a good Christian necessarily make him a good citizen?' Hugh was reluctantly impressed.

'Obviously. But not necessarily a good patriot, mind. That's the point. Now come back to the chicken and the egg. Your average teacher is an average layman – if he held any eccentric views he wouldn't get the chance to teach. Therefore he teaches his children to grow up loving and honouring their country, to read history from the national point of view and to look for the red on the map. In other words, to grow up in the steps of their elders. The school is the microcosm of the State. But, the trouble is that nowadays there's a whole lot of other subjects the teacher has to teach. You can roughly lump these together and call them "science". They have nothing to do with nationalism. They are universal in outlook and application. So the child is inevitably brought up with a mixture of the two ideas. The conflict between nationalism and internationalism is the problem of the elders, and the children are brought up with it. What is it DH Lawrence says? "The elders have eaten the bitter fruit of knowledge and the children's teeth are set on edge." We are muddled so they are muddled. It's a perfect way to achieve universal unrest – and have we got it!'

'We have. I agree. But it isn't due to education.'

'My dear Hugh, look at the children, look at the youth of today! Almost universally frustrated. They've no sense of direction, for they haven't been given any lead. No lead, because there isn't any leader. No hope, because they see the almighty mess their parents have made of things and no way out to a better. On the one hand patriotism, which means militarism, regimentation and war and leads to division. On the other, scientific development and world-wide enterprise which leads to co-operation. What are they to believe? So-called modern schools stress the international future of the world and then turn the young hopefuls out into the world full to bursting-point with national egotisms! It's ludicrous! Farcical! And tragic. So I repeat, is it the egg or the chicken? Clearly the egg, the education. You must break into the vicious circle somewhere, and that's the place to break in. Teach the children right, and they'll grow up right.'

'But the children can't grow up right till the adults are right. If half the energy expended on Fascism had been expended on Internationalism, the world might already be quite a safe place to live in. We've got to get the adult world right first.'

Don suddenly dropped his arrogant, dogmatic manner and said earnestly: 'Hugh, I only argue to shake you up. But what I said to you the other day at lunch is true. Wherever you turn, the situation is quite insoluble. You won't get those who rule the world today to revise their ideas on finance, education, government or anything else, until everything they've lived by and regarded as axiomatic has been completely swept away. Then, after the flood, you may stand a chance of doing something, if you can get in quick enough, before they rush back to their old bolt holes. There's a psychological moment for starting a new world. It's just after peace has been signed. If you miss it, the whole cycle will start again. We've got to have a war, my boy. It's profoundly and mysteriously true, all that about death and resurrection, about throwing away your life in order to gain it, about rising over the bodies of our dead selves! It isn't just allegory; it's hard fact. The world must die before it can be born again.'

'Hugh, I've just been reading a new book. It's fascinating. I think it would interest you.'

Helen was sitting by the fire in Hugh's flat in Albany. The two were having a drink before going out to dinner.

'What's it about?' Hugh handed her a glass.

'About animals.'

'Animals! Why should that interest me?'

'Because they seem to get in the same sort of jams that we do.'

'Who's the book by?'

'A man called Sanderson. He's been investigating the sorts of animals you find in different parts of a tropical forest. According to the type of forest, the humidity, the amount of sun, type of vegetation and so on, he found he could predict the sort of animals you would find in it. They varied with the local climate, as you might say. When he got smart at it, he found he could do it the other way round: show him the animal – or snake or insect or what have you – and he could give a pretty good guess at the sort of forest you would find it in.'

'Very interesting. So what?'

'Well, it wasn't only the type, it was the distribution, the number that a given patch of forest would support. There seemed to be a sort of population level, fairly constant; but – and this is part I thought might be up your street – if any external force came along and changed the character of the forest, it entirely upset the population levels. If you cut down the trees, or cleared out the undergrowth or drained the swamp or cultivated the land, the whole balance was disturbed. Some creatures died out or migrated, some increased a thousand-fold, some were unaffected. After a while a new set of levels was established matching the new conditions.'

'Again I say, so what?'

'Do you remember when we were talking the other day about the evils of scientific progress and I said it wasn't all bad and that some things were good, such as medical science...'

'Yes, because it is directed to a known goal. You see...'

'Wait a minute. I've been thinking about it, and now I'm not so sure it is good. I believe doctors are doing just what men do when they clear the forest – interfering with the natural levels of life...'

'You mean, decreasing our natural powers of resistance and so on?'

'No, just introducing hygiene and sanitation. The huge increases in world population are due to that. Far more than to medicine or surgery.'

'But now the birth rate is falling.'

'Because the new level, under the new conditions, has been reached.'

Hugh was sitting smiling at her tolerantly. 'Helen, I admire you immensely, you're charming, intelligent, and beautifully educated;

but again I say, so what?'

'Don't laugh, Hugh. I've been reading it up in the *Enc. Britt.* The population increases are frightening. Three hundred per cent in England in a century, and more than twice that in Russia and the States. At first there seems no harm in it. The Empire's nice and big and there are plenty of places to go to. Russia's enormous, and so on. But what's going to happen in overcrowded places like India, China and Japan, where the populations are huge already? It will, you know. It's on its way. What's going to happen if India, say, doubles her population in a century? It will give her four hundred million more people. Where are they going to go to? They've got no Empire. The countries all around are already packed. It's just the same in Japan. She's already crowded to overflowing. I can't see the end of things like this. Wars don't settle anything. They may kill off the odd million or two, just like famines do in China; but that hardly touches the fringe of the problem.'

Hugh put his head in his hands. 'You know, Helen, there are times when I despair of the whole thing. I started out thinking it was all within the power of man to put right, if he went the right way about it, and I began to study the way. But the deeper you get in, the more vast and insoluble the problems seem to become.'

Helen laughed and patted his arm. 'You should give it up, dear, raise a family and cultivate your garden.'

Hugh looked up quickly. 'I ask nothing better. But where can I do it? Where can I do it in the whole world today and be sure the children won't be gassed and the garden ravaged?'

'Everybody has to take chances. You can never be certain of anything. You must just go ahead and trust.'

'In what?'

Helen hesitated. 'I don't know… In God, in the purpose of Life, perhaps. We can't reason out and foresee everything. I don't know… I feel we ought to seize the minute. Nowadays everybody's waiting and putting things off because they're afraid it's the end of the world. But it isn't. Or if it is, it must be the beginning of a new one. I'm for going ahead and meeting things as they come.'

Hugh looked up at her suddenly, as if he was seeing something

231

glorious for the first time and couldn't believe his eyes.

'What is Democracy, comrades? I'll tell you. It ain't representative government. It ain't the greatest good for the greatest number. It ain't any of them things those ruddy windbags down at Westminster say it is. Democracy's just the committee system. Ever served on a committee? No? Well, I 'ave. What did it amount to? Talk, talk, talk – and no action, comrades. Action! That's what we've got to have today, and if the gasbags won't give it us, what are we goin' to do about it? I'll tell you, comrades. We're goin' to chuck 'em aht!'

It was Hyde Park on a Sunday morning before lunch. An idle crowd was milling round before the line of rostrums, listening to the open-air orators, most of them fanatics exercising their oldest English liberty – to grumble. Hyde Park was a safety valve: a sign, really, of the healthy strength of the country. Nobody made any attempt to interfere with these men who were often seditious, often scandalous in their comment on the State and those responsible for running it. The Police stood by in the background, just in case any real trouble were to develop, but it was rare for them to have to interfere. Hugh, walking past, stopped to listen to a middle-aged shabby creature with a grey mop of disordered hair, glasses perched on a thin nose and the remains of powerful strength in his frame. 'What would you think,' he ranted on, throwing his voice out to the fringes of the crowd, trying to catch the passers-by with a phrase, with a gesture, with the very vehemence of his tirade – 'What would you think of a ship run on the committee system? Tacking this way and that, always changing course to meet every new wind, missing the tides, drifting with the currents. You'd say, "Where's the Captain?", wouldn't you? And that's what I say. Where's the Captain? And I tell you there ain't no captain. And another thing, comrades. They tell you that all this poppycock that goes on down at Westminster is done in our interests, in the interests of you and me. What's our greatest interest in the world today? To stop this war we can all see coming. And what are they doing about it, comrades? Nothing but talk! We've got to have action. We've got to chuck 'em aht. Look at Germany! Look at Italy! They've got captains aboard their ships!

And fine ships they are too. They're going places, comrades, and why? Because they know where they're going. Do we know where we're going? I say we don't. I say we're drifting. We've got to have action, comrades. Action...'

Hugh walked on down towards Hyde Park Corner, deep in thought. Wherever you went you found this same dissatisfaction with our manner of government. Among the intellectuals, the businessmen, the public at large, everywhere. It all came down to one thing: Fear – and no hope. But Hope casts out fear, so it was really hope the world wanted. Hugh's thoughts went back to the Professor's peroration three years ago. 'It is hope which beyond reason sustains us.' But how could you give hope to a world which, on every side, was rotten with doubt? It was so far gone it couldn't even make up its mind to prepare against the rising tide of war. True a big rearmament programme had been announced. But Hugh knew the inside talk in the clubs and in the City; it was eyewash, a thing that had to be done, but it was undertaken with no sense of urgency. It was hopeless to catch up with the start that Germany and Italy had got. Hopeless! There it was again. And yet Hugh couldn't help thinking: If only the young blood could get at it! If only all those with courage and determination could be given a free hand! A lot could be done. And in the very doing of it, would come the hope of its success. Action bred hope and inaction doubt. The old tub-thumper was right, it was Action we needed.

'It isn't a question of hope or fear.' Don was laying down the law as usual, in his trenchant arrogant way. 'You will not go into these things deeply enough, Hugh. The real difficulty is far more subtle: it's irresponsibility. Why are we collectively more restless, neurotic, introspective and dyspeptic than any other generation has ever been?'

'Probably because we have more money.'

'But everything costs more. That shouldn't affect things. We also have votes, all of us, but we're not governed any better than we were; probably worse. The "masses" are supposed to be "free", that is free to obey the orders of their trade union leaders, with the risk of going on the dole if they don't. All these modern "opportunities" to have more leisure and variety in life which are supposed to make us better off, have precisely the opposite effect. The cumulative effect is not to give us more freedom, but less. In our work we are part of a complex machine; and when we leave off, wherever we turn, whatever we want to do, we are hedged in by everlasting directions, forms to fill up, and regulations to comply with. A thousand "Don'ts" or "Musts" shout at us from posters, sky signs and indicators. We are cautioned, directed, exhorted at every turn. The press and the radio tell us what to think, the cinema what to feel. We are beset, from waking to sleeping, with the million tentacles of the great octopus compulsion.'

'And the result is we're hopeless,' Hugh insisted.

'No, the result is boredom, then anger and revolt, and finally a feeling of irresponsibility. There comes a time when we don't care what happens to the damnable mechanical world, and set out to use it as best we can for our own ends. In other words we've no sense of belonging to the community. We're irresponsible.'

'I agree that this machine-minding that passes for work is the devil. It leaves men utterly exhausted. The old satisfaction of putting your life into your work has quite gone. Life begins now when work is over.'

'But does it?' queried Don. 'I don't think we do live, in the old sense, or if we do it's at second-hand. We've forgotten how to amuse ourselves. We get all our amusements ready-made. The radio, the cinema, football, the dogs – and we pay for them! Fancy paying for pleasure! And what pleasure! Shallow, meaningless, un-recreative, they're worth nobody's money. And the whole vast vapid array, with the world gaping at it, goes round and round, endlessly repeating itself like – like the flushing of some gigantic w.c.'

'You're a machine wrecker, in fact?'

Don was emphatic. 'I am.'

'But we can't go back, Don! We're faced with the thing. It's here. We've got to learn to control it. We've got to learn how to govern it.'

'The only way is to get rid of it altogether.'

'You can't get rid of it. You can't put the clock back – and you know it. The only way to solve the problem of mechanisation is to drive ahead with it so fast that the whole of the world's necessary work, its chores, so to speak, can be knocked off in a few hours a day, say four hours. Then all the bleat about the deadening effects of mechanisation will disappear. For the first time the world will have real leisure. Imagine having twelve waking hours of leisure every day of your life! What an immense boon that will be to mankind!'

'Boon! What on earth do you suppose the world's going to do with that leisure? The few hours they have almost drives them crazy – and no wonder, when you consider their recreations. I tell you the Devil finds work for idle hands to do. All this leisure will simply speed up anarchy. It's fatal.'

'It's a challenge of course.' Hugh's tone was buoyant, confident. 'Its effects will be further reaching than any revolution. It will, in fact, be the Great Revolution of mankind. Then we shall really have to educate. Life must be made so varied and fascinating that men and women, living constructive and integrated lives for the first time, begin to appreciate what Liberty and Freedom really mean.'

'Oh, Hugh, I wish you'd keep your feet on the ground. You're always looking a thousand years ahead.'

'A thousand years! Why? There's nothing to stop the world getting its chores organised on these lines within a century. It's all within our grasp. It can all be done.'

Don shook his head sadly. Then he looked at Hugh and smiled.

'Hurry up and get the war started.'

'Don! That's your fixation.'

'Why won't you face it? War has its assets, very great assets too. One of the greatest is that it speeds up all methods of production and gives a tremendous fillip to invention and technology. If you want to get the world's work down to four hours a day, you need a good war to teach the world how.'

'Don't be so cynical, Don. Once people see the goal...'

'They won't, my boy, they won't. The public sees nothing until it's stuffed right under their silly noses and then they sniff at it.'

It would not be true to say that Hugh grew more disillusioned as time went on. Still, during those crowded years of youthful idealism and buoyant hope for mankind, his opinions had undergone a change.

He had started off, like most young men, as an idealist, full of sweeping generalities and lofty hopes. Everywhere he found men in high positions who ascribed to his ideals, who, in conversation and public utterance, looked forward to the same things as he did. But when it came to translating these fervours into fact, to acting upon their convictions, Hugh found it was quite a different matter. What they said in their after-dinner speeches, and what they did in their offices next day, were directly contradictory. Each man, Hugh discovered, with a sense of surprise, was not one individual, but two or three or four, and all these parts of the man lived in apparent amity behind his smile, though the beliefs of each part might be directly contradictory. When taxed with the discrepancy the answer would be a bland: 'Of course I'm an idealist; but you have to take the world as it is.' Hugh was shocked. The power in the world was deeply entrenched in the hedgehog of tradition, law, money and middle-age. You could not charm them out of it, like the Pied Piper. You could not smoke them out. You could not drive them out. You could only blow them out.

Don had seen this. He had carried the argument through to its conclusion; but most young men who thought and argued about the problem did not take it that far. They stopped short when they found they could do nothing, and lapsed into defeatism. They had a deep-seated conviction, fully borne out by facts, that until people got together to tackle world problems instead of shutting their eyes to them, until the whole bundle of vested interests and petty profits was scrapped and replaced by a living dynamic purpose, there was no hope. Defeatists were not people who wanted to do nothing and let things slide; they were people who wanted to do a very great deal. They did not want things to go wrong, but they held it a logical certainty that, unless a miracle happened nothing could stop them going wrong. They were often intelligent and progressive with positive ideals and purposes, like Hugh. Yet they were trapped and powerless. Things in those tragic hopeless years before 1939 went from bad to worse. Nothing could be done.

Hugh certainly saw that Democracy, as constituted in England before the war, didn't work. It was another case of the ideal and the real being quite contradictory. Democracy talked interminably, as the Hyde Park orator had pointed out; but the talk resulted in no action and was therefore wind. It argued and squabbled and washed the country's dirty linen in public and only succeeded in making itself and the country ridiculous in the eyes of the world. And while it argued, the danger grew ever more ominous. Systems must be judged by their results. If things could deteriorate so decisively in two decades, there must be something seriously wrong with the system.

What was true of democratic government was also true of the democratic way of life. It magnified each little ego. Scientific developments had magnified them still more. No longer need the man in the street join the crowd to listen to speeches of public men, no longer need he visit picture galleries or concerts, no longer need he go to parks, fairs or theatres All this was brought to him at home by the radio, television, the press and rotogravure. He was therefore in the community but not of it. He 'belonged'; but he prided himself that, as a democrat, he was 'different'. In this he was pandered to in a thousand ways by press publicity, and politician. He had, he was told, originality, personality and individuality. Even though he was a mere pea in a sieve, he never dreamed of thinking of himself in this way. He was important, he was someone apart from the rest – and therefore against the rest. Factories turned out millions of identical cars, radios and reach-me-downs; but such was the eternal gullibility of the man in the street, that he believed, as the advertisements told him, that his were 'different'!

Such a fantastic egoism could only occur in a democracy where personal initiative and private gain were not only countenanced but encouraged. It was part of the English way of life, part of the democratic tradition. So men excused their selfishness, even when it was clear to all that liberty had become licence and freedom folly.

Yet there was so much good in Democracy that no man who had lived under it would swap it for any other system. It was this really that made Hugh a pacifist. This was the reason why he could not, like Don, face up to the idea of war. He saw we could only compete with dictatorships by becoming more efficient, more regimented, more dictatorially ruled than they. In the name of freedom we should be obliged to renounce all freedom. It was a fundamental question: Shall Man belong to the State, or shall the State be the servant of the citizen? If we went to war, we should all belong to the State, win or lose. The old freedoms would never come back. It was a terrible dilemma.

Hugh could not look clearly enough into the future to see the advantages that men might gain by becoming more fully knit into society, nor could he fathom the truism of a few years later, that no liberty, freedom or peace could ever be secured until people developed a sense of responsibility to the community.

But on that grey cheerless London day when the news of Munich came through, and he heard the hooters blowing and the news on broadcast, though there was a momentary sense of relief, Hugh came subconsciously to two conclusions. The first was that war was inevitable and necessary, the second that he had better offer his services to the country. He rang up Don and the two men met at the Café Royal for dinner.

'Don,' said Hugh, 'when we came down from college, I thought I should convert you; but it's no good. You win.'

'Why,' laughed Don, 'wonders will never cease! Let's have a drink!'

'I've been a fool. I ought to have seen it before.'

'On the contrary you've been a wise man. Good men grow: only a fool never changes his mind.'

'I don't renounce my ideals, Don. I only say they can never be realised till we've got Hitler and all he stands for out of the way.'

'Hitler's only a symbol, don't forget. Situations like this don't arise just because dictators set their armies in motion. They're the result of profound maladjustments in social and economic conditions. Hitler's just a convenient villain to saddle it all on to. We made the Treaty of Versailles, remember. It was a bloody awful document, and it's no good our trying to escape the responsibility of being one of the first causes of the present chaos.'

'All right. We made a mistake – with the best intentions. Now it's landed us in a mess, a hell of a mess. Very well then, we must get out of it.'

'Your logic is irrefutable, my dear Hugh,' smiled Don in his quiet sardonic way. 'Have you joined the armed forces yet?'

'No, but I'm going down to the Air Ministry tomorrow. I've got an A licence. I hope they'll have me in the Auxiliary Air Force.'

'A fine keen young chap like you, Hugh! They'll jump at you!'

'I'll break your bloody neck if you don't shut up. What are you joining?'

'I? I've been in the Secret Service for years.'

So Hugh had reasoned himself through to a conversion, had faced the issue which so many were soon to face, and found, as they were later to find, that, once the decision was taken, everything was enormously simplified. He would go to war, as so many hundreds of thousands had done before him, in order to end war, because war cut the gordian knot, because when all had been said it was better to die with honour than go on living in dishonour. It was true that war settled nothing permanently, that the seeds of the next war rose from the blood of the last, yet in the choice of the two ways of life, the democratic way, with all its shortcomings, was so immeasurably nobler in ideal – and in past record – that it was worth trying to preserve. From it the world could go forward; from the brutality and persecution of the other regimes, it could only go back. Therefore, whatever the problems on the long road ahead, this had to be settled first.

Besides, Hugh sensed a deep stirring in the conscience of mankind. At the end of the struggle which lay ahead, he believed things would not slide back as they had done in 1918. Perhaps it was only an ardent hope, but it was based on the resurgent spirit of man, duped too long and fobbed off too often.

All this and much more Hugh discussed with Helen down at Squirrels. He had caught the night train for Falmouth the day after he had been accepted for the RAF. She met him at the station and motored him out to the old house. It stood at the head of a small valley looking down over a broad estuary to the sea. Here Sir

Reginald, her father, a retired General, lived out his declining years, pottering in the garden of a place which had been in his family for over a century. His sons were grown up. They had gone into the Army and the Navy and the Foreign Office. Only Helen, his youngest child, remained. The old man, now widowed for fifteen years, knew that he would be a good deal alone from now on. It didn't worry him. He had his beloved rhododendrons and azaleas, about which he kept up an erudite correspondence with various experts all over the world. It was quite enough to keep him going and last him out.

Helen had fallen in love with Hugh at first sight. She could give plenty of reasons for it, that he was young and brilliant, an enthusiast, a thinker, a type of which the world stood greatly in need; but truthfully, though it was all these things, it was more because of his boyishness that she found him irresistible. She wanted to mother him, to live for him, and bear him sons.

'I've been a damned fool, Helen,' he said, as they sat on the rocks and looked down over the water. 'I've been going about with my head in the clouds, full of fine ideas and long words, as if my private recipe for the millennium was infallible. But now I've realised – first things first. The new world must grow out of the ashes of this one, but those of us who are still reasonably young must start now to get our own lives established on a solid basis that will stand all the shocks of change, and lead through to the world beyond. We are the link between the two, and we shall have a lot to lose and learn and go through before we can start again. I've been a fool because I've lived all the time in generalities and abstract ideas. It's only half a life really – so, will you marry me, Helen?'

Helen almost laughed at him. What a proposal! It was so like Hugh, always expounding himself, explaining his motives, his impulses, trying to reason about things which were beyond the anatomy of thought. He was transparently honest and hopelessly, oh so hopelessly, young. He would always be like that, to her at least, always the exuberant and adorable child... But he was going on:

'You see, my sweet, things have always been too complicated and involved for me to realise properly how much you were part of my life and my growing up. But now everything's awfully simple. I'm out of the fog, and I see it quite clearly. Forgive me for not having seen it before. It was that night, after I'd talked to Don and got it out of myself, that I suddenly knew I had to see you, to tell you, because if you didn't think I had made the right choice, I shouldn't be sure myself.'

Helen was silent for a little, staring before her.

'I think it's a terrible prospect and a fearful indictment of mankind; but, after all, I'm a General's daughter, and I suppose the old fighting stock dies hard. So – yes. I think you're right, Hugh.'

Hugh took her hand and looked at her. 'Helen, there's another thing – it's stupid to talk about it – I may be killed. If you don't think it's worth starting up something that mightn't lead anywhere, so to speak, I shall quite...'

'Oh, Hugh, Hugh, don't talk such nonsense. As if any woman who loved a man thinks of that sort of thing! Why, you silly, if I knew you were to be killed tomorrow, I'd marry you tonight – if you wanted me to.'

Pamela was born at Squirrels in the spring of 1940. Hugh was with his Squadron in France, and Helen had returned to her father's house to have her first child. It had been a hard winter, but now the spring had come and the Cornish lanes were full of violets and periwinkles. Squirrels was at its best, and the old General grew quite sprightly, forgot his rheumatism and spoiled his daughter and his grandchild, so proud he was of them both and of his beloved garden. 'Never was such a spring! Never!' he kept on saying and Helen, lying in the sun on a day-bed on the lawn, overlooking the valley, smiled after him as he hurried here and there seeing the gardeners and arranging for the bedding-out of his seedlings. No, there never was such a spring, in spite of the war, in spite of everything, because Hugh was her husband and she had borne him his child.

It hadn't been an easy time for him. He had known that they couldn't be together as they might have been in peace, but he chafed at the separation, more especially because the war hung fire. He wrote to her long and often, letters that were full of life and vigour, letters that were so much part of him that she could almost hear him speaking as she read them. In fact, when she felt more than usually lonely or depressed (loving him so and never having him near except in snatches, never having him there over her shoulder, in the next room, to throw a question at and to hear his voice, his answer, in the odd moments that make the communion of marriage, as bubbles on a river show the movement of still water) she would take up his letters again, hear him speaking as she read them, and sometimes, if she was alone, answer him and talk to him aloud.

Yes, it had been a bad time for him. Once he had taken the decision he threw himself into his job as earnestly and thoroughly as he had pursued the riddles of social evolution. Once the war had been declared, he had always said, we should see a great change in England. Everybody would get down to it, as he had been getting down to it, and all the laziness and defeatism would disappear. It was when this didn't happen that he began to get anxious again.

'You see the terrible subtlety of the Industrial Revolution now, I hope! It puts immense power at our disposal and at the same time dopes us so that we are too lazy to use it. We are letting things slide still, even when we know that power is being ruthlessly massed for our own destruction. By whom? By a man whose appetite has not been satiated with these superficial sweets that science has given us to suck, by a man who knows how to utilise every weapon in the modern armoury. We had better look out. If we don't get down to it soon, it will be too late. Lots of people think it's too late already...'

And again: 'Flew almost a thousand miles last night, through filthy weather, engines cutting out through icing up, controls freezing, mostly through cloud. Hadn't the dimmest idea where we were most of the time. Saved, as usual, by my king-pin navigator. And when we got to the target, what did we drop? Bombs? Incendiaries? No, my sweet, we dropped leaflets! Leaflets. You can imagine what the boys think...'

'Did you see the trees after the frost? Here it rained and the rain froze as it fell. The telegraph wires and the grass and the trees were all encased in ice, sometimes almost an inch thick. It's a thing I never saw before. There's a chestnut tree outside the mess, and when the wind began to blow, the whole thing, encased in crystal, began to ring like a chandelier. Many trees lost branches through the weight of the ice when the wind got up...'

That was so typical of Hugh, the sudden swing from exasperation to delight. Helen, as she read the letter, remembered how on his last leave before Pam was born, they had been for a walk. Hugh had been grousing and railing against the inefficiency everywhere, the way nobody seemed to grasp the gravity of the emergency. Then suddenly he had seen a cluster of wild violets in the hedge and dived for them and brought them out to her. That was why she loved him... because of a little thing like that, because he was so sensitive, so simple, so young...

When she saw he was worried she would deliberately provoke him to write long letters, because she knew that in so doing he would work off his frustrations. 'Are you still quite sure that war is a good thing? Are you sure it's the way out?' She had written. And his answer was so realistic, so splendid, she thought that, if anything happened to him, she would have to publish these letters of his, his testimony to the time. 'War is never a way out,' he wrote, 'but it is a way through. What is the story of the past? It is one long and shameful record of religious and military persecution, oppression, conquest, rapine, poverty and disease. Only here and there is it leavened by glimpses of nobility and generosity in Thoughts and in Art – and these steadfast fingers pointing a way to a wider and richer way of life have been consistently mutilated and destroyed by every despot since time began. Men have never been richer for war. They have always been poorer materially and spiritually. Where mankind has gained lasting good and made spiritual progress – the only kind of progress that matters – it has always been in spite of and not because of war. Still, we have one on our hands now, quite different in character from any other that was ever waged. I only hope we make the best of it. War accelerates the rate of change. Reforms are so long overdue on every side that anything which will accelerate them is of inestimable value. It would take centuries of peaceful evolution to effect the changes that this war will bring about before it is over. That is one good reason why we should welcome it and fight it obstinately to its conclusion. This is a war of principle, not of loot. People talk about us being one of the "have" nations, but the Empire, which America is so fond of attacking, is really independent of us. The Dominions are self-governing and needn't have joined us in the struggle if they hadn't wanted to. I suppose our actual colonial dependencies (if you except India) are less than those of France or Holland. Certainly not much more. We have nothing to gain except the preservation of the nobler purpose. We shall be a debtor nation before peace is signed. That is why I say that war is a way through. It is not a way out, unless we know how to use the victory, unless we can cut into this vicious circle of war and peace and so order the progress of society, that these great boils of human frustration do not burst in the filthy pus of war. Can we do it? I believe we can. In fact I know we can, if we are prepared to co-operate instead of compete, if we realise that the planet is a unit, and can get our petty patriotisms into focus as part of the world pattern. We can do all this. Whether we shall make up our minds to, is another matter... But there is a great stirring in men's hearts today. I believe in the world to come.'

With the great offensives of 1940 the tone of his letters had changed. The fall of Norway, Holland, Belgium and France had taken the world's breath away. The RAF were busy and Hugh was in the thick of it. Gone was all the smug talk of peace aims of which the papers had been full before the issue was joined. It was the eleventh hour, one of the great crises in the world's history, and England, when she stood alone, rose to it, buoyant and resilient in the face of disaster after disaster. Hugh's letters were rapid notes, but they were incurably confident. 'We're all right now. Don't worry. Churchill will save England and civilisation with it. As much as one man may, he may claim to have shaped the course of history.' The country was at last aroused, at long last getting down to work; all the frustration and defeatism had disappeared. Hugh was happy. 'We're getting on with it now. We're all right. Don't worry. We shall come through.'

Then he had been seriously wounded, and brought his aircraft home with half a wing shot away and one motor dead. After a long spell in hospital, he had come down to Squirrels to convalesce.

He was very much older, Helen thought, and somehow simpler, easier, bigger than he had been. He didn't talk about the war. Only occasionally could old Sir Reginald draw him out. The old man felt his age acutely. He was out of it and immensely grateful for any scraps of adventure that he could hear at second-hand.

'Glad you're all right, my boy. Glad you're getting better. Didn't think much of you, if you want to know, when you married Helen. Too much talk, too many ideas. Got to do things in life, not talk about them. I wish I was younger. Won't have me in the Home Guard now, you know. But if there's an invasion, they'll want me all right. I've still got my rifle and I can use it too.'

Hugh laughed admiringly. There was a lot of fire left in the old man, a lot of steadfast courage. Helen had it too, and young Pamela would have it, you could see that. She was as imperious and wilful as any young lady of one and a half could be. Hugh was immensely proud. There was something un-ostentatious about the English blood, something immensely tenacious, a great spirit that went on down through the centuries from father to son. Helen would bear him a son one day... He reached for her hand as she sat beside him reading, and kissed it.

'But the country's all right now, isn't it, my boy? Wonderful how it's pulled itself together. Great country. Always comes up to the mark in emergency.'

'Yes. We left it a bit late this time though.'

The old man laughed. 'We did, we did – and we aren't through yet. But Churchill's sound. Churchill's saved the country.'

'Yes,' Hugh rejoined, 'he has. And we're supporting his dictatorship today, in a way that would have seemed intolerable in, say, 1938. We're as much regimented and taxed as the enemy – more, in fact.'

'That's war, my boy. It'll all go back when peace comes.'

'I hope not! I'm not fighting to put back the clock. I don't want to see all the old pieces set up on the old chessboard of Europe for another and bloodier game. There's a grand feeling in the country today. The State is really starting to look after the interests of the man in the street. This loyalty to the people is beginning to earn their loyalty in return. There wasn't much of that before the war.'

'How much of it was self-preservation?' Helen put in.

'A lot. Everybody behaves well in an emergency: the difficulty is to get them to do so when there is no emergency. That's why the problems of peace are going to be greater than those of war. But still, now we have seen what can be done when life has a common interest and purpose, when people do put the general good before their personal ends, I don't think we shall ever go back.'

Sir Reginald sighed and shook his head. 'I heard just the same sort of talk during the last war. But it all came to nothing. You can't change human nature, my boy.'

'Oh, I think you can. I think it has changed – and is always changing. If you can't, it's a poor look-out for mankind. It would mean we'd reached the limit of our development, that we weren't intelligent and adaptable enough to advance further. I don't believe we have. I think we all see that the old national methods of governing the world don't work. After all it isn't very complicated; all we have to learn is that individual enterprise, that is a "free for all", always ends in a scrap – and that's pretty obvious now, God knows. No one has the right to beggar his neighbour. No one must be forced to eat dirt because he has no money. Everyone must have private means – that's all social security is. It can all be done, easily, provided the world works – and doesn't blow its wealth away in high explosive every twenty-five years. There's more than enough for us all. There's nothing to be afraid of. We must get rid of fear. Once we do that, all the other freedoms that Roosevelt talks about, follow. To get rid of it, we must have geographic and economic stability. Until we have a single standard of living throughout the world, we must zone exports so that the East can't undersell the West, nor the West out-produce the East. We need central authorities for money and food and justice and power. The basic necessities of life must be internationally controlled.

'I think everybody's beginning to see these things. But it's needed a world war to open our eyes. We have to thank Hitler for that. So even he, in a backhanded way, has been of some use. The trouble before the war was that we had no united aim. Now we have. We can all see what needs to be done – though, of course, we're sure to make some mistakes in attempting to do it. Still, I do believe that we stand on the threshold of a splendid future. It's all within our grasp. It's all before us, like the Promised Land. We've done our forty years in the wilderness. We've only got ourselves to blame if we backslide and throw it all away; but I don't believe we shall. I believe...'

So, sitting there, looking down the valley to the sea, his eyes fixed not on the scene before him, but on his inner vision of the world to come, Hugh gave form and substance to the things for which he fought. Sir Reginald couldn't follow it all. It didn't really interest him. His life was over and his world to come was hidden. But Helen listened, praying not so much for the world as for her husband. For he was her world and her future his. She desired that his dream might come to fulfilment, of course; but she desired more that he should live, should endure to inherit his part in it. And yet... and yet... soon he would have to go back...

'Navigator to Captain. I think I'll come forward now, sir.'

'Righto, Cooky. Where are we?'

'About a couple of minutes ahead of our ETA. The coast should be coming up pretty soon and I'll get a pinpoint.'

'Okay.'

Cookson collected his target map and papers, unplugged his intercomm and pushed the end into his boot, uncoupled his oxygen supply and got up from his seat.

Peter Morelli had left his seat by the Captain and moved aft to let Cookson get by. Cookson squeezed past him with a smile, clambered over the seat, pausing to look at the Captain, who grinned at him; then let himself down through the hatchway into the nose and lay down flat on his stomach in the bomb-aimer's position, plugged in his intercomm and his oxygen.

'Navigator to Captain. I'm just doing a check, sir.'

'Okay, Cooky. Let me know when you're all set.'

Cookson busied himself with the bomb sight and started testing the selector switches...

THE SOLAR SYSTEM drives through interstellar spaces at fantastic speed, yet planets keep to their appointed places, swinging upon their orbits, unmindful of the great velocity of which they form a part. The earth is our familiar; meadow, coppice and cloud. We do not hear its whirling music as it runs about the sun, nor the low hum of the great top as it spins. These movements have been calculated, tabulated, and we know them to be so, but in our lives we quite ignore them, seeking the everlasting amid ceaseless change, extolling stillness, permanence and peace, when every winking star shouts that the Universe is out on incandescent wing and the containing infinite itself perhaps is sliding like a dream into some deeper Mystery.

So while the bombers roared on miles above the earth, like gnats in the cathedral of the night, those who went with them had no sense of speed. As morning turns to midday, as clouds roll up the sky, so slowly and majestically the earth slid by beneath them. They observed it all, aloof, apart, snug in their little ordered worlds.

There were hundreds of those worlds aloft, climbing steadily and slowly up the shoulders of the night, each with its complement of men, each dedicated to a single task, each trained and disciplined, each nothing but a name and number while the job was on, yet each one a Life! A life, precious to some, or one, for little things, the way the hair grew or a tone of voice or tender hands or body's strength, precious because of memories; mothers, of travail and the long hard years bringing them up to this; wives, of their husbands, clasped and torn apart, dearer than life and gone; lovers, of promises, the future in a kiss, the hope, the dream stretched out to; brothers and friends, of sport and work and the old coat of friendship: precious and separate, more than the jobs they gave their skill to, more than the messengers of death, more than their country's sons. More than all that, these sparks of the Eternal Fire, these men with dreams and hopes and plans of things to come, each with his past, the sheaf of personality, the soul.

And, from this past, night after night, from bench and fireside, from the watched cradle and the sleepless bed, a gossamer of thought crept starwards, seeking the absent men. Each thread like a young tendril, thrusting its way surely to its goal and holding there with infinite elasticity, tugging so gently and persistently: Come home, my love, come home.

But the men, as they approached the whirlpool of the target, cut the cord of memory, sucked into the vortex of the present. Then they became automata, embodied wills of a rehearsed technique. They were most gloriously alive, but in another world, a world which none but they could know. It was a tense and throbbing place, outwardly calm, clothed in laconic phrases; a place in which the clock went wrong and seconds stretched to hours; a place packed with the formless shape of danger; a mint of courage where 'Can I?' became 'I must', and 'Shall I?' froze into 'I will'. Yet, none the less, it was a fearful corridor, shaped like a question mark, whose bottom dot was some dim runway in the English shires.

Now, as they neared the target and the tension grew, Sam leaned forward on his guns, looking intently at the earth below, a map of misty water. He wriggled his toes in his thick flying boots to keep them warm. He had forgotten the sun on the snow and the spoor of the moose in the thickets. He was looking for golden pinpoints in the gloom beneath, flashes which meant shells were on their way, screaming up towards them, shells it would be better to avoid. Behind him Cookson did the same, staring through the bomb sight at the earth, waiting for the coast to loom up through the murk, so that he could pinpoint their position and decide their course. He had forgotten the great whale asleep in luminous water and the peril of the storm. As he waited he rechecked his selector gear, noted height, temperature and airspeed, and then fell back to peering, peering, peering at the sea below.

It was harder for Peter, for he had nothing to do. When he tried to think, after a show, what his sensations were as they went in, he found his mind had been a blank. It was a state of animal awareness, keyed up, nerves at stretch, ready for instant action, and yet, while he waited, utterly still. Sometimes during those few seconds when the aircraft was held straight on the bombing run, those endless seconds that dragged on and the guns were bound to get you, sometimes then, to distract himself, he tried to think of Estha, tried to think of the moonlit lake, tried to hold the image of beauty in his heart; but he could not do it for long. It dissolved into flak bursts, into the creeping tentacles of searchlights, into the figures on dials and moving pointers. In the emergency Then could not stand against Now. Now always won.

For Benjy, it was hardest of all. At his seat in the belly of the aircraft, he had no idea what was going on. The little window through which he might have looked, had been blacked out so that he could use a light to keep his log or take down messages. He too had nothing to do. Sometimes he thought that since he could not see when hell was breaking loose outside, it made it easier. Like a man undergoing an operation with a local anaesthetic, he guessed it might be pretty bad, but never knew how bad. He heard the flak bursts when they were near and the rattle of the shrapnel on the hull. He listened to the short ejaculated phrases on the intercomm. He saw a glint of light through the forward perspex when they were coned. He swayed as the aircraft weaved. Sometimes, when it was not too bad, he thought of Ruth, thought of their time together in Venice, thought of their parting in the London Blitz. When it got worse he concentrated on his Shakespeare, forcing himself to read. When it was bloody awful, like that night over Essen, he just gripped the edge of his table and held on. You lived through things somehow. If you didn't count too much on it, you might get through; that was the way he looked at it. Sometimes before a raid, he had a premonition that he wouldn't come back, but it had so often been wrong that now, if he was not indifferent to his fate, he was inured to it.

Now, with the book under his hand, he thought to himself: Here it comes again. Wish I had something to do. And he stared at the floor, mechanically followed the curves of the geodetics as they wound round the body, followed a pipe which ran along the roof and disappeared into the darkness behind him. The engines kept up their steady droning. A little eddy of dust danced on one of the floorboards. A curious sense of unreality came to Benjy. The things around him were so familiar, so solid, so permanent, so still. Yet one well-placed shell could blow the lot to hell. In that event you couldn't imagine what might happen. Any more than you could visualise the idea of a comet running into the earth. No good thinking what you would do about it. Waste of time.

Nobby, very wide awake, was doing his eternal sky search, down across, up across. Good night for fighters, he thought. No moon, but plenty of stars. Difficult to spot them when they came up from below, and they almost always did come up from below, pulling the nose up and raking the whole underbody with their guns. Bastards. You had to see them first. A good burst would usually scare them off and then you could give them the slip before they settled down and found you again. Sometimes they'd follow for miles just out of range and never attack at all. It was a tricky business. If you fired too early you gave your own position away. If you left it too late, the Hun might get his burst in first and that was apt to be unpleasant. Lot of cloud coming up from the west. Must be a warm front. Probably raining over England. Journey home won't be much fun for the Captain, flying on instruments for bloody hours. Raining in England, raining on the farm, raining just above Sally's head, running down the thatch into the gutter, down into the green tub. 'Hullo, Sal. I'm here. Just going to make the run in. See you soon, Sal! Here we go!' Gosh, it was black over there. One thing about it, fighters wouldn't follow them into that. And just nice time to get the load down before the target was obscured. Nice timing. He stroked the firing button with his thumb...

'Flakship on the port bow, sir.' It was Sam's voice, sharp, alert. He was watching the tiny black cigar intently.

'Firing?' Thornly came back.

'Not yet, sir.'

'Keep your eyes open.'

'You bet, sir.'

'Navigator to Captain. I can make out the coast now, sir.' Cookson spoke slowly and deliberately. He was wonderfully cool and steady. The hotter things got, the quieter and more imperturbable he became. Actually he had seen the flakship before Sam, noted that it hadn't opened up, seen the coast beyond, and was just making certain of his landfall before calling up the Captain. There was no hurry. When things had to be done quickly, he could do them quickly; when there was time, he took it. Slow but sure.

'Good! Got a pinpoint yet?'

'Yes. Just off the river mouth, sir. Will you alter course twenty degrees to port, sir?'

'Altering now.'

The aircraft swung off eastwards. Though a man's voice could not have been heard above the roar of the engines, it seemed to the crew that they were waiting now in tense and absolute silence. Flak and searchlights might open up at any moment. But a minute passed, two minutes and there wasn't a sign. The whole place seemed asleep. Not a light showed.

'Any flashes, Sam?' It was the Captain's voice.

'Nothing, sir.'

'Nobby?'

'Not a sausage, sir.'

'Damn funny.'

Somehow this ominous quietness was more trying to the nerves than a good barrage.

'Spect they think we're going on to Rostock,' Nobby observed.

'Alter course thirty degrees to starboard, sir,' came from Tom.

'Okay.'

The aircraft swung southwards again. She had crossed the coast and soon would turn south-west and make her run up over the Deutsche Werke, the great shipyards that lay in the heart of the town. Tom was staring at the ground. He had memorised all the details on the map, the shapes of the woods, the positions of the lakes, the pattern of the railways. They would just make it nicely.

'Start the glide, sir.'

Thornly throttled back. The roar died to a low drumming. Everything seemed even more silent than before. He trimmed the aircraft and the Wellington slid earthwards. Still not a sign came from the earth that their presence near the target was observed.

'Alter course to two six five,' came from Tom.

'Two six five,' Thornly repeated, and the aircraft swung steadily to starboard and steadied down again.

'Bomb doors open.' There was a slight shudder as the belly of the aircraft opened to disgorge its load.

'Bomb doors open,' Thornly repeated when the indicator showed. 'Still no flashes?'

'Nothing, sir,' came alike an echo from Nobby and Sam.

'Might be a practice run,' laughed Thornly cheerfully. But he didn't like it. They were up to something. No, he didn't like it. He remembered one Observer telling him how his Captain, making a run in on Boulogne, had been met with this same ominous silence. It gave him such jitters that he turned tail without ever attacking at all! 'Bad show,' Thornly had thought to himself at the time; but now he could understand. There was something intimidating about it. He had a sudden violent cramp in the pit of his stomach. 'Frightened!' He said to himself. Of course he was frightened. Everybody was. Fear was the sand in the cement of courage. He'd been frightened before. They all had. So what?

'Left! Left!' came from Tom. He was settling the aircraft on to course, bringing the shipyards into position so that they would slide down between the sighting wires till the red dot was reached. Then he would press the tit.

Thornly swung the aircraft slightly left. He concentrated on the gyro. The fit had passed.

'Steady.'

He held her straight: he held the ring dead steady against the lubber line.

'Right!' came from Tom.

Thornly swung back again.

'Steady! Stand by. Bomb doors open?'

It was a check. Thornly glanced down. 'Bomb doors open.'

'Here we go!'

Thornly held the course and speed. The aircraft glided on. Everyone waited, breathless, for the 'Bombs gone!'

The seconds ticked. One, two, three... A blinding light impaled the aircraft with a silver spear. It was a master beam and it had opened dead on. A second later thirty others opened and swung on to it. They were caught in the apex of this pyramid of light. They were coned.

The cockpit was lit up like day. Their night-adapted eyes were utterly dazzled. The instruments were blotted out. Thornly jerked a curtain across the perspex, almost closed his eyes and managed somehow to see the gyro compass and to hold it steady.

'Batteries opened up,' came from Sam, hurriedly.

'Left! Left!' came Tom's voice, quiet and steady. 'Right!' There was an interminable pause. One... two... three... four... five... Interminable seconds, during which they knew the shells were screaming up.

Tom pressed the tit. 'Bombs gone!' he said.

Thornly banged the throttles open, kicked on left rudder, pulled the stick right back before Peter and Benjy were dead. He was stunned and his right thigh was shattered and the starboard engine was on fire and the aircraft, with one engine roaring, flicked into a spin and dropped down out of the lights.

Sam was fighting to get out of his turret. Tom, flung sideways by the blast and crump of the near miss which had turned their little ordered world into a spinning death trap picked himself up and fought against the terrific centrifugal force, to get back up to the Captain. He had been hit over the target before. It was no fun. But every second he expected to hear the engines throttled back and to come out of the spin. Then they would have time to sort things out.

But it didn't happen. The aircraft plunged on like a whirling torch, straight for the earth. Tom managed to struggle up through the hatch, under the second pilot's feet, twist himself round and close the throttles. Just then Thornly came to. A piece of flying shrapnel, glancing off a window frame, had struck his temple. For a moment he looked dazed and helpless; but when he saw Tom struggling to wind back the tail trimmer, he realised what had happened and began to ease the aircraft out of her dive. In those few seconds she had dropped ten thousand feet and her flaming engine made her a perfect target for the light flak. It was then Tom saw Peter's limp legs dangling. He must be seriously wounded. Somehow he managed to half lift, half drag him off his seat and pass him through to Sam. Sam was all prepared to jump; but Tom shouted at him, pointing to the bomb-aimer's mattress. Sam nodded and took charge. Tom climbed through up to the second pilot's seat. There was no time to lose.

Thornly could keep the aircraft gliding but he still seemed dazed. Tom cut off the starboard engine's petrol supply, feathered the prop and then operated the fire extinguisher. The flames leapt, coughed once or twice and then miraculously, went out. Tom glanced at the altimeter. They were down to three thousand. He plugged in his intercomm.

'Port engine, sir. I'll trim the rudder bias.'

Thornly seemed to understand. He nodded and his hand went to the throttle, while Tom spun the rudder bias handle. The engine came to life and in a moment the aircraft was flying on an even keel, under control.

'Can you hold her, sir?'

Thornly didn't answer at once. Then, weakly: 'Take the weight of my left foot, will you? Right leg's hit... Brandy.'

Tom got out the flask and handed it over, keeping his foot on the rudder. Thornly got his mask off, took a gulp of brandy, handed back the flask. 'Any casualties?'

Then Sam came through on the intercomm. 'Mr Morelli's bought it, sir.' His voice sounded strained, anxious. 'There's no pulse, sir. His head's an awful mess. Neck's broken.'

'You all right?'

'Yes, sir. I'm fine.'

'Same here, sir!' Nobby piped up from the tail. 'Got bloody giddy going round like that, though. Is everything under control, sir?'

Tom answered: 'The Captain's hit in the leg. But we're okay. Navigator to Wireless Operator, you okay?' There was no answer. 'Lukin! are you okay?' No answer again. 'Nobby nip forward and see what's happened to Mr Lukin. I can't leave the Captain.'

'Okay, sir.'

Tom heard the click of his microphone going off. He turned back to the Captain. 'You all right, sir?'

'Can't use my right leg,' Thornly answered. 'Take all the weight off the rudder while I shift myself a bit.'

Tom took the controls and as he did so glanced down at the compass. They were heading south. 'That's better,' he heard Thornly say. 'I can hold her now. Okay, Cooky, let me have her.'

Tom let go of the controls. 'Better get on a course for the coast, sir. Three six zero.'

'Right. Just have a look round, will you?' Tom nodded and unplugged. He climbed over the back of the seat. The starboard side of the fuselage was peppered with holes. A big rent gaped just by the second pilot's head. The stuff that killed Morelli must have come through that one. There was another big one just aft of it and the bank of wireless sets opposite looked pretty well knocked about. Nobby was kneeling over a prostrate figure stretched on the floor. Tom tapped him on the shoulder. Nobby looked round and shook his head. Tom lifted the right hand of the fallen man and put his fingers on the pulse. There was no sign of life. He let the hand fall back. Nobby got the sidcot open. There was a big tear on the chest. There was a tear on the tunic as well and when he got this cleared back, the shirt beneath was sodden with blood. The shell fragment had gone in over the heart. Nobby closed shirt, tunic and sidcot, looked up and shook his head. 'Gone for a Burton,' he said.

Tom plugged in his intercomm. 'Poor Lukin's gone, sir. Big piece of shrapnel right over the heart. Damn bad luck.'

'Is Nobby okay?' came Thornly's voice.

'Yes, sir. He's just going back to his turret.' He signed to Nobby, who nodded and disappeared into the darkness of the after fuselage.

'Cooky,' came the Captain's voice again, after a pause. 'We ought to get rid of all the surplus weight we can.' He paused. 'I think we might put the rest of our bomb load down on the target. No sense in wasting it.'

Cookson grinned behind his mask. The Captain was terrific.

'Okay, sir. I'll come forward.'

It was going to be warm, running right over the centre of Kiel at that height... Cookson regained the second pilot's seat and sat for a moment by the Captain, looking out. There was no mistaking where the target lay. Other bombers were beginning to come in. Three cones of searchlights were concentrated high above their heads. The darkness was full of gun flashes and the slow rising curve of tracer, golden balls swinging up into the night, as if attached to each other by invisible strings. A fire was beginning to get going south of the town. Cookson looked at it carefully. Dummy fire? He pointed it out to the Captain. The target proper was north of it. He could see the line made by the stick of incendiaries they had dropped. Right across the target. Now, if they could drop another with a good cut on the first, that would give the boys their aiming point, that would complete their job.

'Don't think I can do much weaving with this leg,' Thornly was saying. 'Probably safest to come right down on the deck and put our Nav. Lights on. They'll take us for one of their own blokes in trouble.'

Cookson grinned again. He liked low level work. You felt you were going places. It was safer too, he believed.

'Okay, sir. I won't use the sight. I'll use the front turret. Sam can press the tit on a word from me. Hear that, Sam?'

'Sure. Okay by me. If you set the selector gear, that is.'

'Quite sure you're all right, sir?' Cookson couldn't gauge how badly the Captain was hit.

'Me? I'm fine and dandy!'

Cookson knew it couldn't be true; but he unplugged, let himself down through the hatch, to find Sam crouching by Morelli. He had lifted him to one side and covered his face. Tom checked the selector panel, held up the tit for Sam, nodding at him. It was like an electric bell-push on a length of flex. Sam took it, and Tom squeezed past him and up into the front turret. He settled himself and plugged in.

'Okay, sir, I'm all set. Alter course ten degree to port, sir.'

Thornly closed the throttle back and the Wellington started to glide, turning to the right. In their concentration on the coming attack, the Huns were not on the look-out for anything coming up from the south especially right down on the deck. Ever since they had been hit and fallen out of the cone, the flak had left them alone. Now, as they glided towards the shipyards, Thornly could see the target before him. He was watching the altimeter. When they got down to 500 feet, he opened up the engine and switched on his navigation lights. The Wellington moved fast, still losing height, till she was just skimming the roof-tops. Not a shot was fired at her. Now it was harder for Thornly to see.

'Left! Left,' came from Tom. 'Steady, sir. Stand by, Sam.'

As they came in a big bomb burst on the port bow, a second to starboard, and a shower of incendiaries glittered like a flowerbed of stars off the port beam. Flares were floating down. It was getting quite a party. The Wellington rocked in the detonations of the bombs. The place was lit up clear as day.

'Let go, Sam,' came Tom's voice. Sam pressed the tit and the falling canisters of incendiaries streamed out in a line behind them. In the rear turret, Nobby could see them. He saw the white flash as they burst and the sputter of smoky white flame as the phosphorus began its dreadful work. 'Lovely! Lovely,' he shouted on the intercomm. 'We've pranged it properly this time.'

As the Wellington shot away across the water, he fired a long burst into the wharves for luck. Bombs were beginning to come down fast. Behind them the town gouted flying debris, fire and smoke. The attack was developing nicely.

The Wellington, still low on the deck, swerved away into the safety of the darkness. Thornly switched off the nav. lights again and began to climb as best he could on his one engine.

Well, that was that. The next problem was getting home. He felt his leg tentatively, gently. It was beginning to ache and throb. He had no use in it. The bone must be shattered. He could feel a warm wet patch trickling back towards the seat of his pants. Must be losing some blood. He took his decision.

'Look, chaps. I'm hit in the leg. I'm losing blood and I don't know if we can get enough height to make the run home. If the other engine packs up, we shall be sunk – literally. So it's a one-way ticket. Bale out. Now's the time. Get cracking. Before we reach the coast.'

There was a moment's pause. The boys couldn't believe it. Bale out! Not much.

'Guess I'll stick around and take a chance with you, sir,' came from Sam.

'Bale out, sir!' Nobby was outraged. 'Why, I might break me ankle, landing. No bloody fear!'

But Thornly knew there was no time to lose; he stiffened his voice. 'Come on. Get cracking. It's an order.'

'Very good, sir,' same from Sam reluctantly. Below in the bomb-aimer's compartment, he slowly clipped on his parachute. 'Shall I go first?' Thornly heard him say to Tom, and Tom replied, 'Yes. My brollie's up behind. I'll have to nip up and get it.' There was a pause. Sam opened the escape hatch. He hesitated.

'Well – good luck, sir. I sure hate to leave you like this.'

'Happy landings! See you soon. Cheerioh!' Thornly kept his voice matter-of-fact.

'Cheerioh, sir!'

There was a pause. Then Tom's head appeared from beneath. He climbed up into the second pilot's seat next to Thornly.

'Have you gone yet, Nobby?' Thornly was saying.

'Just off, sir. Cheerioh, sir. Good luck!'

'Good luck!'

Tom plugged in his intercomm. 'You're badly hit, sir. I'm not going to leave you,' he said.

The Wellington limped across the coast, got through the shore batteries with no more than a few holes in the port wing and, once out to sea, turned westwards and set course for base. The port engine was holding up well. Revs steady, temperature and oil pressure good, plenty of boost. The suction line to the Blind Flying panel had gone, but the airspeed was working. Compass and airspeed, enough fuel and a good engine would get them home all right. Men had often got back with less. So Tom was thinking, as he carefully noted time and course and calculated their ETA at base. Two and a half hours ought to do it. The only thing that worried him was the weather. It was clamping down. They couldn't fly through it without instruments. They'd have to stay below cloud base. He noted their height: almost three thousand feet. Not bad to scrape up that on one engine. Pity to throw any of it away. The sea would be getting up with this wind. That reminded him. 'Wonder if they got the dinghy?' he thought. He shone his torch out on to the starboard nacelle. It was pretty well chewed up. The top had opened up and had been bent over. Five or six feet of the trailing edge were torn away. If the dinghy hadn't been thrown out, it certainly wouldn't release. Well, they'd have to make the coast, that was all... The Transmitter was gone. Receivers might be okay; but they could navigate home. He didn't need fixes...

But he was worried about the Captain. Couldn't do anything for him, couldn't shift him. Didn't like the dead tone of his voice. Wasn't like him. Must be pretty bad... Pigeons! Wonder if they were still there. He went aft and found them safe in their container. He brought them forward and put them just aft of his seat, so he could reach them – just in case they did have to ditch. No good sending them off at night. Have to wait till morning. Lucky they had flotation gear... Tom got up and fetched the food. He gave the captain coffee and took some himself. He munched a sandwich. The Captain wouldn't eat. He didn't say a word. Funny. Unlike him. Must be bad... The Wellington droned on and on...

A long steady vibrato of machine gun fire brought him out of his reflections with a start. Guns! Their own guns! How...

'Got you, you bastard!' It was Nobby's voice. There was a pause. 'Rear-gunner to Captain. Sorry to be here, sir – but one Ju. 88 down in flames, sir.'

'Good show, Nobby.' Thornly's voice sounded tired. 'Damn fine show. Decent of you to stick, Nobby.'

'Couldn't desert the ship, sir,' came Nobby's perky irrepressible voice. 'I knew something like this might happen, sir.'

'Had he been following us long?' asked Tom.

'No, sir. It was a quarter beam shot, sir. He came right up. Not sure he even saw us, sir. Couldn't have been fifty yards away. His port engine blew up when I got him, sir. He spun straight in.'

'What's that make your score?'

'Five, sir, including this one.'

'You'll be getting a bar to your gong.'

Nobby laughed. 'Not much, sir. Have to chalk up a few more yet. I'm pretty well out of ammo, sir. I think I'd better nip out for a couple of belts and reload. Will that be okay, sir?'

'Okay, Nobby,' came from Thornly. 'Let's know when you're back.'

Nobby backed out of the turret and came up the belly of the aircraft to the racks where the spare ammunition was stored. He lifted a couple of the heavy belts out of their boxes, and carrying them in his arms turned to go back to the turret.

The second enemy night fighter attacked from below. He had seen the long burst that had destroyed his friend, and came in behind in a shallow dive, overtaking the Wellington rapidly. Two hundred feet beneath he pulled up sharply and pressed his firing button. The murderous jets of fire raked the fuselage from end to end. He saw the Wellington lurch and nose down, saw an explosion towards the tail and a shower of sparks, then he was over the vertical and fell away to the left expecting a burst from the rear turret. None came. He claimed the enemy as destroyed, and returned to base.

That deadly traverse at point-blank range had, besides putting a few more hundred holes through the Wellington, smashed the front turret, holed the oil tank, shattered Thornly's left ankle, cut the elevators, smashed the intercomm and hit the belt of ammunition that Nobby was carrying. The little man never knew that he was dead. The explosion of the ammunition, besides killing him, tore a four-foot hole in the side of the fuselage.

The aircraft swerved sharply when Thornly's ankle was hit; but Tom, at his side, corrected at once. When he heard the explosion and felt the aircraft drop, he instinctively eased back the elevators. They were free in his hand. He looked at the Captain and saw him draw the stick in towards him, saw his head drop forward over it, leaning on it, gripping it to fight the pain that shot up from his foot. But still the Wellington flew on. For a moment Tom could not understand why they didn't dive vertically into the sea. He thought it was a sort of miracle or perhaps one of those split seconds that seem to last for ever. When the normal sense of time came back, they would be diving. But the seconds passed. The engine continued to give full power. Yet the elevators were back in his stomach. Something must be holding them. Then he remembered the trimming tabs. They had held! Well, that was miracle enough. He had a moment of intense and wonderful relief. They would still make it. If that fighter didn't do another attack... What a wonderful kite it was! They would make it yet!

He flipped over his microphone switch and spoke to the Captain. There was no answer. He called Nobby. No answer there either. The intercomm was dead. He let go the stick and touched the Captain's arm. He saw him raise his head and speak into his mike. He touched him again. Thornly looked at him, then pointed to his mike and shook his head, then to his foot and put his thumb down. Tom nodded and pointed to himself: he would fly the aircraft. He moved the free elevators and smiled at the Captain, and pointed to the trimming control and smiled again and put both thumbs up. Thornly nodded and held out his hand. Tom realised he wanted the flask and handed it over. The Captain took a long gulp and handed it back. Then he seemed to revive, laid his arm on Tom's affectionately, smiled, folded his arms and sat back. 'I'm out,' the gesture said. 'It's up to you now.'

Tom maintained a slight pressure on his left foot to keep them on course, touched the trimming wheel very lightly and turned it back a fraction. The speed fell off. That was about right. They had only lost five hundred feet. The cold wind buffeted him through the hole on the perspex at his side; but he didn't notice it. It was very dark; but he could just make out the line of the horizon. He glanced at the compass. They were on course. It was all right. They would make it all right. He glanced at his watch. In about an hour. Not long. Once they got to the coast, he would do a belly landing on the first airfield he saw. He would get her down somehow on the tabs. Fly her in, cut the engine, switch off, petrol off, wind the tabs back and chance it. That was the way...

Thornly sat looking out, trying to think of things to distract his mind from the waves of pain that were rising over him. Sometimes they engulfed him for a moment, and he closed his eyes and felt as if he were falling; but he fought his way back up out of it. He thought of Helen; thought of little Pam, blowing bubbles and clutching at the shiny buttons on his tunic and gurgling with delight. He thought of how they would get him out of the seat and take him away and there would be a bed and clean sheets and he would sleep, sleep. It would be good to sleep... Not to be in pain for a bit. He seemed to be sitting in blood... Must have lost a lot of blood. He looked at the rev counter and the oil pressure. It still held. Wonderful engines! Wonderful aircraft to take such a beating and still be flying. He would help Tom with the touchdown, save the last of his strength for that. It would be a bit of a jolt; but he was well strapped in. Wonderful chap, Tom. Steady as a rock. Nobody like him. And Nobby. Wonder if he's all right back there? There was certainly a bit of an explosion. Must have been the ammo. Damn his leg. Damn it. Damn it. Damn it. He closed his eyes... Helen, sitting there at his side and Squirrels and the view over the secret valley to the sea and the bluebells under the apple blossom... bluebells under the apple blossom...

Under the port engine a thin trickle of black oil seeped back over the cowling. The hole in the oil tank wasn't big. A man could have plugged it with his finger; but the oil was leaking away, running down, creeping back along the cowling in a little crinkly river, wisping off into the night. Oil, precious oil, running away, wisping off, falling in droplets on to the angry sea. Only one hole among so many hundred. A pity it was there...

The cloud base had come down to a thousand; but Tom was still coaxing her along. The hour was up. They should sight the coast any moment. What a mercy he hadn't been hit! There was a rip in his sidcot; nothing more. He peered ahead, looking for his landfall. Then he stared – and shouted! Look! Look! It was a searchlight beam, standing erect like a white pillar, ending in a creamy disc on the cloud. That meant land, That meant England! That meant home! It looked pretty good to him. Even Dick's face looking down through the hatchway in the heart of the hurricane hadn't looked better. He smiled with relief and headed for the light. It had been pretty rough; but if you held on you came through. He shook the Captain's arm. His head had fallen forward on his chest; he was asleep. But he roused up, saw the light when Tom pointed, smiled and closed his eyes again.

Tom felt on top of his form. That light was better than a whole bottle of brandy. He didn't feel tired. He wasn't tired. The run out and the attack and all the night's work seemed to have happened ages ago. That was something belonging to another life. Getting down was the only important thing now. They were coming up on the light. Couldn't be more than five miles away. Good oh, chaps! Here we come!

He glanced down at the instruments. His gaze froze. There was no oil pressure. His eyes flicked over to the temperature. The pointer was hard over, well beyond the red line. His heart missed a beat. He listened to the engine. The note had changed. It was deeper, rougher. He watched the Rev Counter needle. It was moving; up and down, up and down, wavering... He put his heart out into the engine, his whole being concentrated on willing it to run. Keep up, keep up, keep up, he commanded. Keep going for the Captain! Only a mile more! The last mile! Keep going! I shall be all right if we have to ditch, but the Captain... The engine seized, ground itself to a standstill. The nose dropped.

Well... Even now he could do something. Keep her straight, trim, ditch her well. She'd float. He'd send off a pigeon when day broke. He'd get the Captain out on to the wing, lift him... The thoughts raced through his mind as the aircraft sank steadily towards the black water...

There are plenty of gongs for the men who come home. Gongs and ribbons and slaps on the back. And every one deserved. But what of the men who were out of luck, the lost men who fought against odds, hoped against hope; the men whose story is never told, who just didn't make it, who 'failed to return'? Who sings their praises, writes their epitaph?

The sudden stoppage of the engine roused Thornly from his stupor. Both legs broken, fainting from loss of blood... Engine off? They must be coming in. Tom would need him now... He opened his eyes and sat up. But when he saw no twinkling runway, but only darkness before him, he knew. Engine packed up. They weren't going to make it. Well... there it was. He looked at Tom fondly. The man sat there, one hand on the tail trimmer, utterly composed. Splendid chap! Summoning his last strength, he touched his arm, leaned over towards him and shouted: 'This is it, Tom. Save yourself!'

Tom switched on the headlight, saw the sea below, an angry sea with short white crests. Now... He wound the tabs back slowly, the nose came up. He braced his feet against the panel before him. There would be a bounce before she settled. Here it came...

The Wellington hit the crest of the sea. There was a heavy crack as the tail broke off and sank. Her nose dropped. She lurched into the next crest. The water rushed in.

The upper escape hatch was jammed. The axe was gone. Tom struggled with the knob. No good. He tried to move the Captain; but there was too much water. He was under water. He was drowning. No good. No good. Then he remembered the hole in the side, managed to pull himself through it and came to the surface, gasping. He inflated his Mae West, clambered up on the wing. She was floating: but the waves broke over her...

THE TELEGRAM FLUTTERED in the old man's hand. He came out of the house and walked across the lawn. He walked slowly and heavily as if the piece of paper that he carried weighed him down. He stared at the ground before him, but he did not see the dew dimples and the daisies in the old turf, nor the spring in blossom, nor the cloudless sky. He did not see anything, nor think anything. Automatically he made for his favourite seat under the great tulip tree and sat down.

He had been up all night. Minnie had knocked on his door about two. 'If you please, sir, Miss Helen thinks the doctor should come now.' He had not been asleep. He didn't sleep much at night. He soon bundled into his old dressing-gown and went down to the phone. He sent Minnie to wake the nurse, to cut some sandwiches and make a thermos of hot coffee. When he came, the doctor went straight upstairs.

Sir Reginald poked up the embers of the fire, put on some logs, pulled his chair up to it and prepared to wait. He took up the *Times* crossword to pass the time, but he couldn't concentrate and found himself listening to the muffled movements of feet on the carpeted landing above. When the logs burst into flame he sat and looked at them, lit his pipe, and went on waiting.

He had been born in that room above and Helen had been born there and now she was bearing her child there. There was something satisfying about that. Life went on. Things repeated themselves. Old houses had a sort of patina of the life that had been lived in them. They reflected the spirits of the past. Why, twenty-five years ago, he had sat just as he was sitting now, in the very same chair waiting for Helen to be born. He was younger then, but he worried and waited, waited and listened, trying to deduce something from each step, each movement, hoping, praying, longing for it to be over. The night watches were long; but the sentries must keep awake... must keep awake... He dozed off in the warmth of the fire.

He awoke with a start. The morning light shone through the chinks in the blackout curtains. The fire was a bed of grey ash and the nurse was standing over him.

'Now wake up, Sir Reginald, and have a cup of tea. You should be in bed, you know. No sense in losing a night's sleep when…'

But the old man was on his feet. 'Is it over, nurse? How is she?'

Nurse patted his arm in that patronising professionally cheerful way he found so maddening. 'Now, don't worry. It isn't over yet. But she's doing very nicely. There's nothing to worry about. Now, come along, drink this up and eat something. You must take care of yourself, you know. We can't have you on our hands, as well as Mrs Thornly.' The loud blatant voice seemed to shock the quietness of the room. Sir Reginald took the tray and put it down. Then he said, very concisely and calmly: 'I should be glad if you would ask the doctor to let me know when it's all over.'

'Of course, Sir Reginald. That's the first thing he'll do.'

'And please be good enough to invite him to stay to breakfast, if he cares to.'

'I'll tell him; but I expect he'll want to get home. He's got to be down at the hospital by ten. Well, I must go. Now, don't *worry*.'

Nurse hurried out, her starched apron rustling. Sir Reginald went to the window and pulled back the big curtains.

The first rays of the sun were slanting across the lawn. The light had the lucid sanctity of morning. At the foot of a big pine just across the path, two squirrels were playing tag. They scampered up the tree trunk, down again, round and round the grass in circles, uttering little frenzied cries. Then they stopped as if petrified, their tails twitching, eyeing each other. Then they were off again. Sir Reginald opened the window latch. Instantly they froze, perched on their hind legs, their muzzles working. Then with a bound and a stream of anxious chattering, they whisked up the tree trunk and disappeared…

It was nine o'clock when the telegram arrived. It was addressed to Helen; but Sir Reginald took it from the silver salver on which Minnie brought it in, and opened it. He read it and stared at it for a long time.

'Will there be any answer, sir?' asked Minnie.

But Sir Reginald had already turned away. 'What? No. No answer.' He looked at the paper again; but he couldn't read it, couldn't force his mind to follow the sequence of words... 'deeply regret to inform you... your husband... killed in action...' He couldn't take it in.

Without thinking he opened the window and stepped out. The house was oppressive. He wanted space to breathe, to think. He wanted time and solitude to face it, to realise it... He would have to tell Helen. But when? Not yet... Not for some time yet... How long could he put it off?

Now, sitting on the old garden seat, he suddenly felt very tired, very old. He leant forward, elbow on knee, resting his forehead in his hand. He must think, he told himself; but the thoughts didn't come... There was nothing to think... It was final.

The morning was still and the sun warm. Behind the house it shone down into a walled garden, shone on the peaches and grapefruit in the glasshouses, on the cordons of nectarines and fans of cherries against the walls. It drew the odour up out of the clumps of lilies of the valley and coaxed the bronze peony shoots out of the mould. The earth seemed to exhale the very essence of spring. The old house with its broad low windows basked and smiled in the golden light. It smiled at the grove of camelia trees, heavy with white blossom, at the great clumps of scarlet rhododendrons, as high as houses, shouting their eastern lineage, the uplands of Himalaya, the fastnesses of Yunnan, here in this puritan country of thatch and whitewash. Wherever the eye rested, all down the length of the dell there was colour. In artful clearings azaleas were splashed in crimsons and pinks, curious rhubarbs rose on thorny stems, clumps of bamboo, noble palms. So damp and warm and sunbathed was the place that all the trees had heavy hanging beards. Grey venerable trunks held aloft a maiden-hair of beech against the dome of a blue sky. And where the dell dropped lower to the village at its mouth, an old forgotten orchard stood. The bearded apple trees clouded with blossom seemed floating on a lake of bluebells...

This was England. England, that was also city and slum, moorland and fen, downland and shire, was always in the minds of its sons, a garden. A garden which reached out to distant lands and brought back the emblems of their soil, and bringing them, brought something more profound. Something hard to define, but very real, a love of beauty and of simple things, of nature's ways, of peace and leisure and the twilight hours, of age and dignity and privacy, of goodness, jollity and peace. And this would stand, whatever went, as it had stood down through the stormy centuries, born to endure, sung by its poets, guarded by brave hearts...

Sir Reginald looked up. He had heard the window latch and turned to see the doctor striding genially across the lawn.

'Good news, general,' he called, as the old man came towards him. 'A son!'

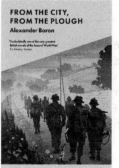

ISBN 9781912423071
£8.99

'Alexander Baron's *From the City, From the Plough* is undoubtedly one of the very greatest British novels of the Second World War and provides the most honest and authentic account of front line life for an infantryman in North West Europe.'

ANTONY BEEVOR

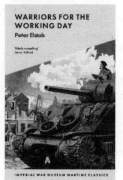

ISBN 9781912423163
£8.99

'Few other novels of the war describe the grinding claustrophobia, violence and lethal danger of being in a tank crew with the stark vividness of Peter Elstob... a forgotten classic that deserves to be read and read.'

JAMES HOLLAND

ISBN 9781912423095
£8.99

'Takes you straight back to Blitzed London... boasts everything a great whodunit should have, and more.'

ANDREW ROBERTS

ISBN 9781912423156
£8.99

'When a man has been a soldier and seen action, he writes of war with true understanding, and with authority. When that man writes with with, elegance and imagination, as Fred Majdalany does in *Patrol*, he produces a military masterpiece.'

ALLAN MALLINSON

ISBN 9781912423088
£8.99

'A tremendous rediscovery of a brilliant novel. Extremely well-written, its effects are both sophisticated and visceral. Remarkable.'

WILLIAM BOYD

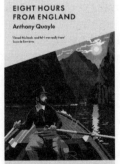

ISBN 9781912423101
£8.99

'Much more than a novel'

RODERICK BAILEY

'I loved this book, and felt I was really there'

LOUIS de BERNIÈRES

'One of the greatest adventure stories of the Second World War'

ANDREW ROBERTS

ISBN 9781912423385
£8.99

'Brilliant... a quietly confident masterwork'

WILLIAM BOYD

'One of the best books to come out of the Second World War'

JOSHUA LEVINE

ISBN 9781912423279
£8.99

'A hidden masterpiece, crackling with authenticity'

PATRICK BISHOP

'Supposedly fiction, but these pages live — and so, for a brief inspiring hour, do the young men who lived in them.'

FREDERICK FORSYTH

ISBN 9781912423262
£8.99

'Witty, warm and hugely endearing... a lovely novel'

AJ PEARCE

'Evokes the highs and lows, joys and agonies of being a Land Girl'

JULIE SUMMERS